ADVANCE PRAISE I
NEWARK MINUTEN

D0969790

"A roller coaster ride of revenge and avenge. Inglorious Bastards, Peaky Blinders, and Titanic all rolled into one."

–Kevin Joseph, producer, Fulwell 73 Productions

"An almost unbelievable true tale of the 1930s. Imagining Nazi swastikas draped across George Washington's portrait feels like a sinister made-for-movie dystopian story."

–Susan Turley, documentary film producer and executive producer, XRM Media

"*Newark Minutemen* is a fascinating account about America's lost history. The unholy alliance of the mob and FBI prevented the story from being printed until now. An untold family story that was meant to be told."

–Steve Katz, senior vice president, CBS Corp.

"The unlikely love affair in *Newark Minutemen* carries the epic conflict of Romeo and Juliet, West Side Story and the Titanic's Jack and Rose."

–Leo Pearlman, managing partner and producer, Fulwell 73

"*Newark Minutemen* tells the inspiring story of how an unlikely group of Jewish boxers helped wake up Depression-era Americans to Nazis on our doorstep. It is the book for anyone interested in understanding how complacency can be our worst enemy and how the Newark Minutemen were a heroic example of how to fight back."

–Ethan Tuttle, Congressional intern and University of Maryland student

"Leslie K. Barry's narrative brings to life in vivid detail a lost era of heroes who give voice to victims even as authorities turn a blind eye."

–Stacy Friedman, rabbi, Congregation Rodef Sholom

"A rare perspective of 1930s American defending their own soil."

–**Lt. David Hall**, United States Navy

"*Newark Minutemen* is a timeless tale of the vigilance, intelligence, and surveillance necessary to thwart vulnerabilities against our country."

–**Robin Abrams**, former director Investigative
Services, Entertainment Security Company

"*Newark Minutemen* is a fascinating story made even more potent by the author's personal connection. A must read!"

–**Rabbi Stacia Deutsch**, *New York Times* bestselling author

"A dramatic tale of the brave *Newark Minutemen* who with muscular patriotism stopped the American-Nazi's from wiping their feet on the soul of America."

–**William S. Hochman**, short story writer and Newark
resident from 1935–1942 who vividly remembers the
dangers posed by the German American Bund

"A striking and poignant tale of an oft-neglected part of U.S. history, including the rise of the pro-Nazi movement that gathered 20,000 supporters in Madison Square Garden in 1939 and recruited children to attend Nazi summer camps in New York. An important reminder of the dangers of anti-Semitism and white Nationalism that are still prevalent in our country today."

–**Samantha Parent Walravens**, award-winning
journalist and *New York Times* acclaimed author

"The history of the Nazis' rise to power in the U.S. should be part of every high school curriculum. Why do we not learn about this in school? Recognizing the vulnerability of our democracy will inspire my generation to pay attention to what's happening in the world, to become more involved, and to not take our freedoms from granted."

–**Satchel Kaplan**, high school student

Newark Minutemen

NEWARK MINUTEMEN

A True 1930's Legend About
One Man's Mission to
Save a Nation's Soul
Without Losing His Own

A NOVEL

LESLIE K. BARRY

Inspired by Esther Kaplan and Bruce Levine

NEW YORK

LONDON • NASHVILLE • MELBOURNE • VANCOUVER

NEWARK MINUTEMEN A NOVEL

A True 1930's Legend About One Man's Mission to Save a Nation's Soul Without Losing His Own

© 2021 Leslie K. Barry

All rights reserved. No portion of this book may be reproduced, stored in a retrieval system, or transmitted in any form or by any means—electronic, mechanical, photocopy, recording, scanning, or other—except for brief quotations in critical reviews or articles, without the prior written permission of the publisher.

Published in New York, New York, by Morgan James Publishing. Morgan James is a trademark of Morgan James, LLC. www.MorganJamesPublishing.com

Publisher's Note: This novel is a work of fiction. Names, characters, places, and incidents are either products of the author's imagination or used fictitiously. All characters are fictional, and any similarity to people living or dead is purely coincidental.

ISBN 9781631950728 paperback
ISBN 9781631950735 eBook
Library of Congress Control Number: 2020904486

Cover photo citation:
German American Bund parade in New York City on East 86th St./ World-Telegram photo. New York, 1937. Photograph. https://www.loc.gov/item/96520973/.

All scripture references are taken from the New Century Version.

Cover Design by:
Katrina Johanson

Interior Design by:
Chris Treccani
www.3dogcreative.net

Morgan James is a proud partner of Habitat for Humanity Peninsula and Greater Williamsburg. Partners in building since 2006.

Get involved today! Visit
MorganJamesPublishing.com/giving-back

In between the world wars, during the Great Depression, American democracy is being threatened by a shadow Hitler-Nazi party in America, complete with a self-proclaimed American Hitler and a 1939 Nuremberg-like rally at Madison Square Garden.

Inspired by a true American legend, *Newark Minutemen* follows a Jewish boxer trained by the mafia and FBI fights the rising American-Nazi party. During his undercover mission to rid the country of the American Führer, he falls in love with the enemy's daughter.

Dedicated to
my mother, Esther Levine Kaplan

IN SPECIAL RECOGNITION OF
THE NEWARK MINUTEMEN

*King David had his massive army with three powerful
leaders and his thirty mighty men. His best men were said
that one man is equal to a thousand.*
–2 Samuel 23:8–39, 1 Chronicles 12:14

Between 1910 and 1940, boxing was the most popular sport in America. Jewish boxers dominated the sport with 20,000 registered fighters and twenty-six world championships. During the 1930s in Newark, NJ, these boxers were recruited by Mob King Longie Zwillman and trained by champion fighter Nat Arno to help the FBI fight a Hitler-shadow party of Nazis taking over America.

PREFACE

All my life, my mom and her family told us stories about growing up in Newark, NJ through the Depression and War years. We indulged them so many times that the images felt familiar yet foreign at the same time. But it wasn't until her ninetieth birthday reunion, that the stories became vivid, especially one in particular.

At the party, I gulped as she told the story about her older brother Harry, a prize-fighting boxer. I had long read the newspaper article and seen the picture of my uncle winning the Golden Glove at Madison Square Garden in 1936. But the questions she answered that night about him beating up Nazis who were taking over America during the Depression caught me off guard. The family exchanged tales about the secret militia he belonged to, which had been set up between the FBI and the Jewish mob to stop the rise of fascism. She called my Uncle Harry a Newark Minuteman and said all the boxers were Minutemen fighting under the Jewish Mob Boss Longie Zwillman. For the first time, I really listened. Hitler's party in America? During the Depression? Before World War II? My first reaction was the story could not have been true. We had never learned about this in school.

I was determined to understand. I spent hours and hours asking her to describe her life during this time—her brothers, the house, where they bought food, how they took out the trash, how they talked to relatives overseas. I transported myself back to the Great Depression, well before

World War II, to understand who, what and why. My mom remembered everything, some things like it was yesterday, and others took clearing the cobwebs. She laughed, she cried, and she sighed through the months we spent unpacking the story. She talked about her brothers running numbers for Longie in his hideout behind the candy store, how Longie was adored like a Robin Hood, and how she wrote up the power of attorney for his trial. She explained that during the Depression, the mob took care of the neighborhood when the government couldn't. I started to unpuzzle the role of the mob, their relationship with the FBI, and the unorthodox systems of rules and power propping up America during this teetering decade.

Reconnecting her big family brought forward a whole new life for my mom. They were part of a generation that gave up everything to come to America. She was part of a family that was connected to horrors, escaped concentration camps, and worked for the Underground. They were survivors and fighters. So it made perfect sense that the family was also a part of saving America from the same threats. Around the same time, I reconnected with my oldest cousin, Bruce Levine, who is very close to my mom. He became fascinated with the family stories and started researching with me. He found videos about President's Day in 1939 at Madison Square Garden when the Nazi leader, Führer Fritz Kuhn, filled the Garden with his Nazi uniformed soldiers and twenty-five thousand supporters. Kuhn called out to take over the country and *Make America Great*. American-Nazis marched and saluted Heil Hitler while 200,000 protested outside. It was then we put the pieces together. My uncle was part of the FBI-mob militia that went out and infiltrated the rising Party that was being ignored by others.

We visited my mom's family. We corroborated her story. Her four brothers worked with Longie Zwillman. One cousin, Pauline Levine, lived next door to the Mob's hideout, which was behind the candy shop. Pauline's father Irving was Longie Zwillman's barber. She told me how Longie helped relatives and others escape from Europe. We also learned about the Nazi youth camps set up across America to train and indoctrinate

German youth and worse. My mom went to Weequahic High School, along with many of the Jews from the area. My cousin, Bruce, went there as well and reached out on their alumnae site to gather stories about the Newark Minutemen. We received many anecdotes.

The story pulled me into a time in our country that has been forgotten. This is NOT another WWII Nazi story, nor a dystopian story where Hitler wins. This is a real-life, forgotten, fictionalized American story about waking up to the enemy sitting on our doorstep. Wherever possible, I have included factual information based on historical first-hand sources, including FBI and Senate hearing documents, interviews, testimonies, archives, diaries, timelines, newsreels, radio announcements, and news articles. However, because of the death of so many characters by the time the story was captured, the overshadowing of the horrors of the second World War and the secretive nature between the mob and the FBI, I have constructed scenes and dialogue where missing pieces arise or where it makes sense to combine characters. I have compressed events to best work for a novel and have dramatized events that were abridged accounts. But much of *Newark Minutemen* is true.

Führer Fritz Kuhn was the American Führer, the self-professed American Hitler. He managed and unified tens of thousands of American-Nazi Bund members into hundreds of cells and managed twenty-five Nazi youth camps across the U.S. These camps indoctrinated youth with Nazi ideology, culture, and military training. Kuhn's six-company corporation generated millions. He exploited U.S. resources like the NRA and National Guard to equip his army with guns and training. The FBI tracked millions of dollars in leading banks to Germany, which proved ties between the American Bund and German Nazis. Many of the Nazi Americans became leaders for the German Nazis. Many Germans tied to Camp Siegfried were later tried and found guilty for espionage. Newark Minutemen went to war.

The protagonist, Yael, embodies John C. Metcalfe, *Chicago Times* undercover reporter who became a Nazi Stormtrooper to uncover the threat of Nazism in America, testified for the Senate hearings and FBI, and consulted on *Confessions of a Nazi Spy* movie. I had the pleasure of speaking with his son and reading John's undercover diaries. The heroine, Krista, embodies Helen Vooros, who testified for the Senate hearings and FBI that she was raped in American Hitler Youth camps. In America, Jews were bullied, even hung with swastikas carved into their chests.

The story of *Newark Minutemen* is a real-life story that is relevant today—racism that embraces dehumanizing language (such as immigrants infesting our country, politicians called animals), normalizes militant Neo-Nazis, and ignores rumors about ISIS cells buried in our soil. Fascism is on the rise globally, and our ground is fertile for its rise. The warning signals include the blurring between real and fake news, the dangers of surveillance, resistance to cede power after losing elections, offering nationalism as a solution to inequality and poverty, and the simmering xenophobia. *Newark Minutemen* is a message about fighting the greatest threat to freedom of all—complacency.

NEWARKMINUTEMEN.COM provides information, the speeches from 1939 President's Day, full FBI documents, confiscated videos, photos, diaries, links, and more.

PROLOGUE

February 20, 1939

YAEL:
Madison Square Garden. New York, USA

If we fail today, we might as well throw in the towel.

My ears hammer against the roarin' crowd. We must stop the rallying call for a Nazi Party in America. The last thing we need in the middle of the Depression is a fascist party here to support the one the Nazis are building in Germany. Everyone's still nursin' their wounds from the Great War.

I catch the cold iron bar—the one I spent all night sawin' off with my hacksaw—on the first bounce. But the clank it makes between *Sieg Heil* chants signals our death warrant. My heart freezes as I scan forty-thousand blinkin' eyes around the arena. I wonder which ones have read through my fake salute? Blood thrusts through my veins like water loadin' in a fire hose. I almost vomit. Dangit! I'm my own worst enemy.

The pumpin' in my body mounts like a geyser ready to blow. Right here and now, maybe I should grab my fellow fighters and exit the Germandom defiling the Garden. Yes. Madison Square Garden. New York City, USA. The last time I was here I was sixteen and my best pal, Harry

Levine, knocked out another heavyweight to win the 1936 Golden Glove. Now, just three years later, the Bund's American Führer, Fritz Kuhn, is celebrating *Der Tag*—The Day—on Washington's birthday in the most iconic American arena we have.

Another cheer goes up and shakes the ceiling rafters. The heat from heiling bodies curdles my stomach as if I'd swallowed gasoline. I fume when I think about how Kuhn is bastardizing our American symbol into a red, white and blue Nuremberg Rally on our sacred President's Day, February 20, 1939. Today, the stainin' of an American symbol, tomorrow our country could be consumed by a brewin' dictatorship if Hitler marches on Europe. The disgust rears saliva in the back of my throat. I hack out the salty vile.

Even if I'm not as stupid as I am brave, my options are limited. Blockin' the aisles, seven hundred brown-shirted, swastika wielding, high-booted Hitler replicas are poundin' their boots against the coliseum floor to the beat of the drum corps. Many of them are not much older than me. Addin' insult to injury, the mockin' color guards wave their swastika flags side by side with American ones. I clamp myself to the floor. Let's face it. At this point, I have one choice. Pray no one kills me.

Beads of sweat simmer on my brow. Any false hopes of escape are dashed as a glint bounces off the brass knuckles of my worst nightmare, Axel Von du Croy. The light licks my good wool suit. Well, my only suit. Behind the uniformed soldier, his fixer, Frank Schenk, pokes another Gestapo-type stormtrooper and grabs a third. He leads a squad through the masses toward us, disrupting unified party cheers of *Free America. Free America. Free America.*

But we, they call us the Newark Minutemen, are trained boxers. We won't be knocked out without a fight. Our members are scattered throughout The Garden. To the left are Maxie and Al Fisher, Nat Arno, and Abie Pain. Nearby are Puddy Hinkes, Harry Levine, and his cousin Benny. And then there's me, Yael Newman. The eight of us muscle against the press of fanatics, forcin' our way through the crowd. We wedge between Hitler disciples and chafe against Nazi regalia. The evil glares tell me we're not makin' friends. We clamber over seats, step on black boots and duck under Hitler salutes. We're searchin' for the other members of our militia to gain a foothold that will help disrupt this ominous occasion. I'm countin' on the rest of our scattered troops to slide their hidden iron bars down their sleeves into their fists. As I dodge a swastika-banded arm, my own bar falls again. But this time, I catch it breathlessly before it sets off alarms. Harry and I hurry toward the swarmin' center aisle.

An amplified German accent booms. "Fellow Americans. American Patriots. I do not come before you tonight as a stranger. You will have heard of me through the Jewish-controlled press as a creature with horns, a cloven hoof, and a long tail." I glance up at the stage. Below the towering portrait of George Washington, the Hitler uniformed Bund leader, Führer Fritz Julius Kuhn, leans into the microphone at the podium.

The hard-faced, square-jawed Führer pronounces what he calls a unified Germandom in America. "We Gentiles are fighting for an Aryan-ruled United States, insulated from dirty blacks, Japanese, Chinese, vermin Jews, dishonest Arabs, homosexuals, Catholics, and even useless cripples and alcoholics." This shadow-Hitler party is putting democracy up for negotiation. There's no doubt. I'll bet my right arm that the Nazis are gonna start another world war.

Around me, the shoulder-belt wearin' audience raises Hitler salutes to the six-foot, two-hundred plus pound bully. They're cheering a man who is dehumanizing people. Peerin' into the crowd, I cringe at the notion that so many good German-Americans who could be my own neighbors have bought into the Nazi stance. Sure they have inherited the high cheeked look. But it's more. They have assumed that stiff carriage, that humorless expression. That mind that screams discipline and punctuality, rules and obedience. A heart that freezes everything they touch, like a tongue that freezes on an icy flagpole.

Kuhn commands his Aryan audience to demand that the government be returned to the American people. "We, the German-American Nazi

Bund, will protect America against Jewish Communism parasites,"
he says. My teeth clench. He's a master at twisting thoughts. "We will
protect our glorious republic and defend our Constitution from the slimy
conspirators and … *WE WILL MAKE AMERICA GREAT.*"

Führer Kuhn stuns me with his words. From the next aisle, the
commander of our Newark Minutemen, prizefighter Nat Arno, waves at
me to keep movin'. But my distraction is costly. In the time it takes me to
blink, khaki arms trimmed with a black spider woven on a red armband
lock around me. They drag me toward the exit to the tune of a female
voice singin' the American anthem. *"Oh, say can you see, by the dawn's early
light, What so proudly we hailed at the twilight's last gleaming—"*

CHAPTER 1

Put on The Gloves

February 20, 1933

YAEL:
Yael's Apt. Hawthorne Avenue. Newark, NJ

It's dark, but the light seeps through my closed eyes.

"Farshiltn!" my mother swears.

One eye peeks at Mama across the room. She picks up a worn leather bag in the kitchen near the scratched enamel gas stove. She zips the bag closed and tip-toes toward me.

My small bed creaks when she sits down. She runs her fingers through my hair. "Good morning my 'golden kherd farshlofn kop," she says the ending in Yiddish. Translated, that means blond-haired sleepy head. I stir under the scratchy blanket but pretend I'm not really awake. My Ma, Esther, whispers, "Your katzisher-kop of a father forgot this."

I open my eyes.

She holds up the leather bag.

1

I can't help myself. I giggle.

She puts her finger to her mouth to shush me so I won't wake my two older brothers. Our beds are close, packed into the converted living room we share as our bedroom in the third story apartment above the candy shop. Ma and Pop sleep in the only bedroom. Ma used to curse at us in Yiddish when we jumped on her bed, tellin' us to never forget we were born in there and to not knock the portrait of our Russian grandfather off the wall. Then we'd make her laugh. But she's not laughing now. "I need you to take this to Papa at the docks," she whispers. "He's working for Mr. Zwillman. It's his food and clothes." She sets it next to the bed.

"How many days will he be gone this time?" I ask.

Mama holds up five fingers and plants a kiss on my head. My brothers would never let her do that, but I'm gonna let her until I turn thirteen in a few months. "Dress warmly," she says. She plonks Pop's worn boots and socks next to the bed and hands me some change. "Geyn, geyn," she says. "Take the trolley so you won't be late for school." She returns to the kitchen and her chores.

I swing my legs off the bed and press the change into the pocket of the pants I wore to bed. My feet scuffle against the cold floor until I pull on the scratchy socks and slide into the oversized boots. Our drafty apartment warns me about the unfriendly morning I must face, so I sneak my brother Dov's sweater off his bed. I tug it over my head and come face to face with boxer Benny Leonard. Not the real life Benny Leonard. But the photo of my icon on the cover of *Muscle Builder* magazine that's taped on the wall above my bed. My father says Leonard is a more important Jew than Albert Einstein since more people know who he is. Pop's promised to take me to a match. I'm gonna be a boxer just like Leonard. He attacks like a machine gun. Perfect aim. Rapid fire. And he believes he's gonna win. I slip on a coat and gloves and grab the leather bag. As I open the door, Mama pulls down a wool newsboy cap over my ears and pushes a cream cheese sandwich into my empty hand.

YAEL:
Third Ward and Newark Bay Docks. Newark, NJ

On the trolley toward the docks, I clutch the suitcase between my legs so it won't bounce. The window is frosty, but I can see Prince Street of the Third Ward where we used to live. Carts begin to line the curbs next to the shops. Pop says in this part of town they still don't have hot water upstairs in the apartments like we do.

We pass the live poultry market where I often shop with Mama to buy chicken for Friday dinners. When we're at the market, Ma sticks her hand in the cage and picks the chicken with the most fat on the bottom. The butcher chops it's head off and plucks the feathers. My oldest brother, Marty, can't stand all the blood splattered in the sawdust, but it doesn't bother me.

The trolley clacks past dry goods stores, soda fountain shops, movie houses, bakeries, breweries, and synagogues. We stop for passengers. As bodies pack the trolley, the accents of Russians, Irish, Germans, and Italians collide. I can't help but breathe in the hodgepodge of baked bread mixed with freshly gutted fish. Last week, I picked out a fish at the market. My ma smelled the gills and made me throw it back into the tank. Mama drives the butcher crazy. She embarrasses me when she makes him clean out the meat grinder every time. Still, he admires her.

I draw a triangle on the frosty window with the finger that sticks out of my glove and wipe away the film inside the shape. Through the cleared glass, I spot men waitin' in the soup lines. Their knees judder against their baggy clothes like a car engine without enough fuel. Jobs are rare these days. My father and uncles are lucky. They're bootleggers for Longie Zwillman. Pop calls Longie the King of the Jewish mob. Pop makes good money at the docks where runner boats drop booze. That's illegal. The cops don't bother him, though, because Longie takes care of everyone. With my finger, I add an upside-down triangle to make a star.

Just as I arrive at the foggy Newark bay docks, an old war truck swerves

3

around me. "This ain't a place for a kid!" the gunman hangin' off the side yells at me. The curlin' fog reminds me of ghosts clawin' for my throat. Through it, it's hard to spot any ship riggin'. I can only see the tips of bouncin' bows. I balance myself along a braided boat line that guides me down the dock toward Pop's runner boat at the end of the pier. I swing the suitcase to pitch me forward. As I near the boat, the mist shifts just enough for me to see my tall father. Next to him another man scratches the red stubble across his face. They're securing ropes over the side of their boat.

When Pop opens a thermos and fills two cups, I'm close enough to sniff the roasted coffee, but he still doesn't know I'm here. The opportunity is too good to pass. I smile to myself and spring into the boat, landin' with a bang. Pop and the man swing around with guns aimed at my head. I dodge the flyin' coffee just in time.

"Drek!" Pop curses. "Yael Newman! You know better than that." He and his mate tuck the guns back under their shirts into their waistbands. Red-faced, he won't look at me.

With my heart in my throat, I try to break the ice. "You forgot your clothes bag, Pop. I brought it for ya." I hold his scuffed suitcase high like a trophy. My brother's sweater swings across my knees.

After an awkward moment, Pop pulls the bag, along with me, into his arms for a hug. "Danks my son. I would have frozen and starved. Then what good would I be to Mr. Zwillman?" He slides the suitcase and pumps my cap over my eyes and back up again. The crow's feet that bloom into a dozen crinkles around his eyes when he smiles warm me. When my father smiles, nothing in the world can hurt me.

"Joseph," Pop's friend says. "Longie Zwillman wouldn't abandon you. He's as loyal as any Jewish mob boss can be."

"Longie takes care of his own," my pop says. "Yael, this is my pal, Ruby." He nods toward his partner.

Ruby extends his hand toward me, shakes it, and will not let go. "Oy vey," Ruby says in his heavy Yiddish accent. "Your father's right. You are very strong. I can see why you want to be a boxer."

Suddenly, we hear heavy boots clomp against the wooden dock. Through the haunting fog, we see three men dressed like German soldiers appear and disappear. They remind me of that Grim Reaper flick with the creeper who has black holes for eyes. Their military coats sway in the wind. Adolph Hitler's new German party haunts everyone now, even in America.

"Quick, Yael, hide," Pop whispers, nudgin' me. "Get under the bow."

I scramble inside the shelter and close the canvas cover from inside. I hear Pop and Ruby's coffee cups rattle inside the crate.

Peerin' through a rip in the canvas, I see my hat floatin' on the deck. With a pinch in my chest, I hear the men's boots scrape to a stop.

"Gut morning, Kamerads," the soldier says in a heavy German accent.

"May we help you?" my father asks. He lifts his flat, tweed cap, runs his hands through his wavy copper hair, and replaces the hat.

"How considerate," the soldier cajoles. "I like a man with hospitality." He squeezes the peak of his military cap.

The canvas slit is just big enough for me to see him and his tall, sinewy partner jump down into the boat. Their high black boots splash the water. With a hitch in my throat, I bend my eyes toward the dock and view the knees of a brawny third soldier.

"That's a Yiddish accent I hear, yah?" the leader in the boat says. He trudges toward me. Before I know what hits me, a cold splash spurts through the opening and thwacks my eye. I bite my fist. He's so close that any tweet will give me away. "My doctor in Berlin was Jewish," he adds. "But our new German Chancellor, Führer Hitler, scared him out of town." Through blurry vision, I see him whip a full-faced grin to the soldier on the dock.

The taller soldier behind him roams around. He checks under seats and opens crates. The black swastika on his blood-red armband plugs a lump in my throat. He rubs his sharp chin and points to the ledge of the boat. "It's okay for me to sit here, sir?" His wry, amused voice solicits my father's permission. As the soldier sits on the ledge without waitin' for an answer, Pop rubs the stubble on his square jaw. The man spreads his legs. "I hope you will excuse our intrusion." He apologizes in that fake polite way.

At the front of the boat, the leader hops up on the bow above my hidin' place. His loud landin' jolts me. "So, meine Freunde," he says. "Please, have a seat. Relax on your nice boat." He unbuttons his overcoat and the flaps slap against the canvas. Even from where I crouch under the cover, the mud on his boots reeks of rotten eggs.

Pop and Ruby follow orders and sit across from the other intruder on the boat ledge. This soldier also unbuttons his dark coat to reveal his military Sam Browne belt, supported by a narrow strap passin' diagonally over his right shoulder. He reaches with his long arms, removes the thermos from the crate, and pours himself coffee. "Nothing like a hot cup of coffee," he says. He wipes germs off the cup with his sleeve. "Grateful for your hospitality." His eyes close as the muddy liquid passes between his lips. "Let me ask you," he inhales and only then does he open his eyes. "As Americans, do you believe in democracy?"

Without a word, Pop clenches and opens his fists.

"Democracy gives you free choice, yes?" the soldier says with a condescending edge.

I hear Pop ignore him with all his might. After livin' under the boots of Russia, my father knows the importance of bein' able to say what's on your mind. My throat clogs, fightin' a scream that wants to shatter this transparent intruder into dust.

"My Kamerads and I believe in free choice, too. Don't we?" the soldier says. He flips his head toward each of his men. "So, we are going to give you free choice today. You can choose. Hmh? You can freely surprise us with the treasures hidden on your boat. Or, we can tear you and the boat limb from limb." He spreads his arms and smirks. "You choose."

A cold sweat runs down my spine. They're threatening my pop. I see his jowls bulge. He won't let these terrorists win.

"You've made a mistake," Ruby says. "There's nothing we can do for you."

A thin metal pipe dangles in my line of sight. It's so close, my breath fogs it's skin. The man sittin' above me rubs it. My heart pops. Does he know I'm down here? I watch the steel Luger pistol roll between his hands. Then, with one swift movement, I hear him bang the grip of the barrel on the wooden bow above my head twice, flip it over, and clack the muzzle against the plank. My chest pounds. I hold my breath, imagining a bullet exiting through the gun, splintering the wood and burying itself into my skull.

Pop springs.

The soldier on the ledge of the boat aims his weapon at him.

Ruby whips out his gun and aims it at the leader above me.

The third partner on the dock aims his gun down at Ruby. "Halt!" he shouts.

The man from the ledge of the boat jumps up, seizes the gun from Ruby, and shoves him back into his seat. He pats Pop's waist, finds his pistol, and disarms him.

Pop raises his hands and steps back.

The black boot in front of me kicks my gray cap and it slides across the slick deck. "Hmm," he murmurs. "Do you think the stowaway can help us? He spreads his leathered legs. "Come join us, my boy!"

My brain reels for what seems like forever. I try to convince myself I'm hidden and safe. Maybe this soldier isn't really talkin' to me. Could be that ignoring the order is my best choice. On the other hand, if I explode through the tarp, I can surprise attack and push these evil men into the freezin' water. The starburst from the risin' sun beams through the canvas hole. It blinds me. I lose control of my own free will. In that moment, I push the canvas aside, crawl between the man's legs, and search my father's steel eyes. Papa flicks his eyebrows, signaling me to calm. I stiffen my trembling legs.

The officer rotates me with the tip of his gun. The medals on his chest rattle. "You could pass for a German lad with your blond hair and blue eyes," he says as he runs the barrel through my hair. "A shame you have the dirty blood of a Jew." He props his other leather-gloved hand on his silver swastika belt buckle.

The strappin' soldier standin' on the dock spreads his legs. The wood thumps below his heel. "You know who we are boy?"

My eyes roll up at him. "You are Americans in the German Nazi party. Like Hitler is in Germany," I say as steadily as I can.

"Well said." The man's stiff iron grin stamps his cruel manner down on me. "And you know what American-Nazis are going to do for this great country?"

"Build an Aryan movement under the swastika," I answer.

The three Nazis laugh. One almost chokes. "Your father has been filling your blond head," the leader next to me says. "So, mein junger Freund. What does this mean?" He stomps his foot and water splashes up my wool pants. The freezin' wet doesn't cool my searin' body.

"We true Americans are going to take our country back," he continues and leans in close. As he speaks, his face muscles move his wiry eyebrows. "We're going to clean up America. Because our country has gotten all mixed up with all these different colored Jews, Niggers, Catholics, the unclean gays. They have muddied our pure white blood."

"When we mix blood, kid, we lose common morals," his cohort from the boat ledge adds. "And civilization falls. That's the last thing any of us would want to happen to America. Don't you agree?"

The Nazi from the wharf extends his skin-tight gloved hand to me. "Get up here, boy!" he orders.

Pop nods to me. "Do as they say."

The German soldier from the boat ledge yanks me by the collar. My throat gags and gasps at the same time. My fingers claw at his hands and my legs pedal against his hips. He shoves me toward the Nazi on the wharf and lifts himself up on the dock. The soldier on the dock locks his arm around my neck, but not before I fill my lungs.

"Chop nicht—take it easy!" my father says.

The leader from the bow waves his luger. "Why don't you show us what you know we want. Maybe we can make a deal?"

The gun cocks and my pop finds himself starin' down the iron barrel. He stands. "Of course. My choice," Pop says as he raises his hands. He wags his head at Ruby. They wrap their chapped hands around the spiky ropes hangin' over the side of the boat. They pull up a long, steel torpedo. Pop unscrews the warhead and extracts canisters of booze hidden inside.

The leader reaches in his pocket and removes a small metal box. He plucks a rolled-up cigarette from it and pinches it between his lips. He strikes a match against the side of the box and lights the cigarette. "Ingenious!" he says as he bares his teeth. "The bombs are rigged with air so they can float." He inhales and then holds the cigarette between his two right fingers. "See, now we can be Freunde," he says to my father. He blows the smoke and stabs it with his right hand. "Heil Hitler!" He waits for Pop and Ruby to return the salute. They refuse. He grins and neighs like a horse.

The American-Nazi leader rubs his leather-covered palms together. He throws Pop's worn suitcase onto the dock at my feet. He springs from the boat onto the wharf and joins me. "Shnell!" the leader barks at Pop and Ruby. "Get the merchandise out and into the truck at the end of the dock."

Then he orders his soldiers. "We don't have all morning. Get these vermin working." The soldiers aim their guns at my father and Ruby and watch them labor.

The leader sits down on the edge of the dock next to me. "Junge! Open the suitcase," he says as if he's celebrating his birthday. "Show me the goodies you brought us."

I click the latches and hand him my mother's homemade food from the bag. His cigarette flips off his fingertips and sails into the gnashin' water below. He chomps into the thick bread that sandwiches my mother's lamb from Friday night. Crumbs flip everywhere. He pats the dock. "Relax with me, Junge," he says.

Burnin' with outrage, I raise my chin and watch Pop and Ruby unload the bottles.

"I said sit!" he shouts. My insides curdle like milk with lemon as the foreign beast chews my family's food like a horse. But I do as he commands.

His chewin' pricks my nerves like barbwire, but not as bad as the German tune he hums. I distract myself by watchin' Pop lift crates. His powerful chest loads with air each time he hoists. His strong back stretches his jacket when he lifts.

When Pop and Ruby finish, they stand on the dock between the two other soldiers.

The Nazi leader pushes himself up and kicks my thigh. I have never been so close to raw evil before, glimpsing its underbelly, reading it's pockmarks and bulgin' red veins. The Nazi extends his hand. He tries to overpower me.

"We had a deal," Pop's monotone voice warns.

A stillness wafts. I scramble up on my own.

Pop grits his jaw and narrows his eyes.

The Nazi's breath scalds my neck for what seems like minutes.

"Abhauen!" the commander yells at me to scram. Maybe manmade evil has a soft spot? I'm not sure, but I hesitate. If I flee, my fear will give it power.

My father breaks the stalemate. "Yael, leave." The sound of my name flutters against my cheek like a moth. "Geyn. My malach."

I step backwards, heal-first, down the dock, alternating my eyes between the raiders and the footprints my wet shoes stamp against the wood. I strain to hear the voices, but the splashin' water against the pylons muffles them. My father vanishes and reappears through the smoky fog. I hear the Nazis command Pop and Ruby to strip off their shirts and put their hands behind their backs.

In a moment when the fog clears, father's chalky torso appears. His arm blurs and he slinks a knife from underneath his belt. He swings it. The fog hinders my view. But the sounds tell the story. I hear the knife clack against the dock. My throat moans.

The haze thins. The soldiers' licorice-colored coats waft through the mist. Pop and Ruby struggle. The Nazis bind the prisoners' pink arms behind their backs. I watch, horrified as one of the crow-like men slips a muddy rope-loop around each of the bare necks.

The commander scoops up the knife from the dock and points it at my father's face. "You dropped your knife," he jeers. A loud, low fog horn in the harbor bellows. "Hold him still," I hear him say. The officer twists the blade into my father's chest. He carves a swastika. The whale-like drone of the foghorn swallows Pop's groan.

My heart rants at the men. *Stop! How could you?* My thoughts race in circles like a marble loopin' down a pipe. Then my heart rants at me. *Act!* My desperation double-crosses me. My boots nail to the wharf. My feet won't move.

The two other Nazis push Pop and Ruby off the pier. The early sun paints the sea under them a yellow green. I grasp one last look from my pop's valiant eyes as he falls. My heart rips like a cotton bedsheet torn for rags. There is a snap. My father and Ruby swing from the pylons. Their ankles quiver. Then their heavy shoes dangle toward the waves. Their bodies bounce against the post, knock into each other and revolve like two stones on strings.

The American-Nazi waves his Heil Hitler salute at me. Now that I've grasped evil, its shadow stands toe to toe with me. I have nowhere to hide. That only leaves me one choice—to fight for my life.

KRISTA:
Bookstore. Hawthorne Avenue. Newark, NJ

Papa shakes me so hard that the hair braid I'm sucking on flicks out of my mouth. When he bellows bloodcurdling threats into my hearing ear, my heart wishes I could erase the upside-down triangle off the damp bookshop window. I drew it so I could see inside through the dark. I promise him I'll never toy with the Jude symbol again, that yellow Star of David I saw in Papa's German newspaper. There was a photo of a Jewish shop window near our old home in Berlin. The idea came to me when my older sister, Heidi, stamped her face against the frosty window. The cold made her cheek turn red and hid the bruise under her eye. My father rubs the symbol so hard with his bare palm that it seems like he's trying to erase my reflection, too. Shivering, I wipe the rain off my face and watch it spring off the glassy sidewalk like it's afraid of breaking the bricks.

I know I must not cry or Papa will get madder. He's already angry at the rain for ruining his new uniform. He's so proud to be an officer in America for the National Socialist Party under our new leader, Adolph Hitler. He calls his group the Friends of New Germany. Yesterday, he said, "Be grateful that I'm helping the new Führer take back what's ours." Heidi told me we are lucky and Papa and the Nazis around the world will finally be treated with respect. She said we might even raise an army even though Germany's not allowed.

My father pounds on the bookstore door. "Aufmachen!" he hollers. "I know you're in there. Open up!" I know my father expects obedience, so I don't flinch when he dents the wood door panel with his fist. But I don't like how he treats people, and I guess my face shows it because Heidi blocks his view. I glance at her. Since my mother died giving birth to me, Heidi's the only mother I've ever known. I'm torn between thanking her for saving me from a knuckling and wishing I could stand up to Papa on my own. I see Heidi zip up her jacket to her neck and I copy her.

There is movement inside the shop. The light waltzes and spills across shelves and boxes and tables of books. A willowy figure appears and bends his wire-rimmed glasses until they hold behind his ears. His alarmed eyes peer through the window at Heidi and me. He scuttles to the door of his store and unlocks it.

Before the man can speak, Papa forces open the unlatched door. My father shoves the thin man into a pile of books stacked on the floor. The books collapse like the burning Reichstag Building that Führer Hitler blamed on the Communists. Heidi and I crouch down, hiding under Papa's shadow as the musty smell of the shop pinches my nose.

The shaken man on the floor adjusts his glasses. "Günther?" his low voice cracks. How does he know our father? He even calls him by his first name, like an old friend.

My father grabs the top book from a pile on a table. "*A Farewell to Arms*," he reads. "Ach! Hemingway. Insolent writer! He insults our Kamerad in Italy, Benito Mussolini." Last year, when I read this book about the Great War in school, Papa complained the story betrays our German soldiers, making them feel their fight in the Great War was a waste of time. My teacher said the book is just about learning to expect the unexpected. He told us the book's not about war, but about love, and that feelings just happen to people who connect. I'm close enough to my father to smell a sour belch. Abruptly, Papa rears his arm back like a catapult. I jerk sideways to avoid getting struck. He hurls the book at the shopkeeper's head, who isn't as lucky.

The man rolls, his chin curls against his chest. His elbows hoist him off the ground and he stands on his knees. I imagine he once stood like a statue. His strong cheekbones push against his weathered face as if they'd fought against windy rain for too long. He palms his head. Red ooze paints his light hair. When he sees his blood-smeared hand, his eyes dart from my father to me. His olive eyes graze my green ones. "How did you find me?" he asks Papa.

"Töchter!" Papa orders my sister and I. "Empty the boxes. Put the filth of the treacherous authors on the floor where it belongs." He picks up another book. "*The Metamorphosis* by Kafka," he reads. "Actually, the man in this story who turns into a beetle is a wonderful metaphor of the Jew, don't you think, mein Freund?" He chucks the book at his enemy, who ducks just in time.

I instinctively step to help the man, but Heidi grabs me before my father sees. She's right, as always. This man must have done something very bad.

"Papa, can I keep this book?" Heidi holds up *Westen nichts Neues*. "My friend is thirteen, too, and she read *All Quiet on the Western Front* last

13

summer." She nudges me with her eyes to grab a book of my own.

"If Heidi gets one, I want this one, Papa." I hold *Emil und die Detektive* close to my nose and sniff the green apple smell of new ink. Back in Berlin, I used to read this adventure to my imaginary mother up in heaven, about a hero who rallied the city to catch the bank robbers. For a moment, the memory transforms me into a warrior leading the charge.

Papa marches toward us and whips Heidi's book from her hand. He backhands me across my arm with it. "This book is dirt written by that unpatriotic author, Remarque," he exclaims. "He dares to present Germans as cowards afraid of war!" He wings the book at a bookshelf and reams of paper cascade to the floor. *The Three Penny Opera, Helen Keller, Albert Einstein, Sigmund Freud, Bambi.* "The German man will throw these books aside, so his character can live!" Papa cries.

I squeeze my book. When I'm sure no one is looking, I stuff it into the pocket of my jacket. The man kneeling on the floor sees me. I exchange furtive glances with him. His face is unfamiliar. But somehow, I know him. Maybe he was at the school gathering on Sunday for Führer Kuhn's *Eintopf,* the one-pot sauerkraut and beans dinner that helps us save money for important donations to the Party. Or maybe I met him the night we all dressed up and went to the New York Philharmonic to hear Hanz Pfitzer because Papa wanted us to experience respectable music that's everything American jazz isn't. Plus, he told us, listening to the Party's music would bring us all together under one roof—Gleichshaltung. I remember Heidi and I wore matching new dresses and Papa wore his white bow tie and long tails. He reminds me of a penguin in that suit, but I don't dare tell him. After all, he's my father.

Papa scolds the man on the floor. "We no longer tolerate vulgar words that criticize German soldiers." Then he turns to Heidi and me. "Let's recite Reich Minister of Propaganda, Joseph Goebbels' command for burning books. Mein Freund here has been away from Berlin for a long time now. Not sure if he knows it."

We chant the mantra we've heard many times before. "From this

wreckage the new times will arise from the flame that burns in our hearts."
Papa has told us that burning blasphemous books gives us hope, especially
in America.

"Heidi! Krista!' he yells. "Gehen! Meet me at home. Schnell!"

Something bad is going to happen. I can feel it in my bones. "What
are you going to do, Papa?" I look down at the stranger and my heart
shivers with his. His caked hair sticks to his cracked glasses. His heaving
chest stings my heart.

Heidi yanks me out the front door and hustles me down the slick
sidewalk. Moments later, a bellowing roar scorches our ears and nostrils.
I turn and see my father preaching to the burning shop. What happened?
He tips his bottle of bootleg whiskey to his lips. Then hot orange flames
glint in his eyes. As the fire cremates the bookstore, I strain to understand
his muffled words above the crackling rumble. My hearing isn't good
enough to hear. He flicks a roasting cigarette into the heap.

CHAPTER 2

Shadow Boxing

1938

YAEL:
YMHA Boxing Gym. 652 High St. Newark, NJ

I bounce out of the corner of the boxin' ring and throw my body weight behind my right-cross into Harry's cleft chin. He barely flinches. I draw my hand back and left-jab my towering best friend twice in the ribs. Nothing. We shuffle in the center ring of the Y, preparing our bodies for what lies ahead. He extends his long arm and clips my cheek with a crisp left punch. I hear a click in my neck and the room tilts. My body stumbles to catch up with my head. I recover and then hook my right into Harry's long torso above the Star of David emblem on his boxin' shorts.

In the noisy gym of the YMHA in the Third Ward of Newark, the ding of the practice bell signals us back to our corners. The splinters of the wooden stool prick my thighs. I close my eyes and cover my throbbin' face with a water-soaked towel. For a kid like me, boxin' for Longie Zwillman is my only option for work. But it suits me. I hear jump-ropes whip the floor, gloves thud against stiff pads, and fists snap speed bags with the racket of a typewriter. The clamor fires adrenaline through my drained body. The rank sweat and smoke-filled air fuels my determination.

I spend most days at the Y. For me and my community, our world revolves around life here and lets us escape the despair of the Depression. On any given day, five thousand members pass in and out of the million-dollar, three-story Georgian building on High Street. Through the arched doors, across the marble floor, and past the reception counter enter boxers, swimmers, bowlers, and every type of ball player and performer. Below the vaulted ceiling, in front of the double glass-paneled library doors, the massive lobby sizzles with Yiddish cursin' mothers, old men playin' chess, kids chasin' around couches, teens flirtin' at the soda bar, and babies cryin'. The building houses everything from a swimming pool to a woodworking shop, bowling alley in the basement, theater stage and of course, the boxin' gym. But there's more here than meets the eye.

I whiff the musk cologne that skids across the dense air before I hear the click of the Oxford shoes against the wooden gym floor. The scent forces my swollen eyes to flip open. I swipe the soggy towel off my face. No matter how exhausted y'are, when Longie Zwillman shows up, ya jump to attention. Mobster Abner Longie Zwillman is the godfather of Newark, New Jersey. At thirty-four, he's the youngest boss the Jewish Mafia's ever had. And he's the most revered, especially by me. When Nazis murdered my pop five years ago, back in '33, and Mama died from the news, Longie took guardianship over my brothers and me. After all, my father had been one of his most loyal workers. Pop wore that same cologne.

Longie stops in front of an oak table and flops his large briefcase on it. Prize-fightin' boxer Nat Arno swags at his side, a cigar dangling from his mouth. Longie scans the room, tallying his army of boxers, thirty men building their bodies, three more in one ring, two more in another, and Harry and me in the center. Thirty-seven in total.

The boxin' arena is the heart of Longie Zwillman's covert operation.

Just after the whole thing went down with Pop's murder, the FBI knocked on Longie's door. That's when Longie's mobsters and the FBI formed an unholy alliance to plug Hitler from seedin' his budding Nazi army in America. Longie's prize-fightin' boxers have become America's secret weapon against the threat of the German American-Nazi Bund. They call us *The Newark Minutemen*.

Nat Arno, the thirty-two-year-old commander of Longie's underground Minutemen militia, crosses his massive arms and signals me, Harry, and the rest of his lieutenants, including the cocksure Maxie and Al Fisher, the tough Benny Levine, brash Puddy Hinkes, and concrete-jawed Abie Bain. Eight leaders in all. We respond and fall in beside him.

Other boxers join around us, their husky breath announcing their presence, their muscles flecked with blood and skin glossed with sweat. The younger ones sprint like golden retrievers called for dinner and hunker close to their idols. The veterans mark their space with solid stances, rollin' their shoulders and crackin' their knuckles.

While the militia gathers, Longie turns to the swayin' Puddy Hinkes. "Hey, ya get the dough to Mayor Ellenstein?" Longie tosses his fedora on the table and his wavy, dark hair glistens.

"Aye, Aye, Mr. Zwillman," the waggish Hinkes says. Like a regimented soldier, he salutes Longie. Puddy's a regular. When he's not punchin' middleweights out, he's cheerin' for his buddies.

Bodies chafe around me. The burn of static electricity rubbin' against the thick air singes my nose.

"What codes have you picked up in the Bund's newspaper?" I hear Longie ask Harry. Longie removes his jacket. He dresses it over the arms of a young man in a baggy suit.

Harry tugs a white t-shirt down over his dark, thick hair and slides it onto his glistening body. "There's rumblings about a shortwave radio show from Germany tomorrow," Harry says to Longie. "I'll listen in and report back, Boss." In addition to Yiddish, Harry grew up hearin' German around the house and can read stuff between the lines. Before Germany's march on Austria even happened, he found the announcement in the American Bund newspaper. He even showed Longie a photo of Jews washin' the streets with toothbrushes. Harry pulls out an apple from his gym bag and crunches his teeth into its skin.

Longie nods as he catches his own reflection in the mirror behind the speed bag. He straightens his tie. He's not called the Gatsby of Gangsters for nothing.

"Abie! Did you pay protection dough to the cops this week?" Nat Arno yaps in a tough New Jersey accent, as if he's askin' if a sucker punch is kosher.

"Roger that, Nat." The raspy voice of Abie Bain rises above the racket. Ten years ago, Abie stepped into the ring. He was too young to even shave. He made his name when he challenged "Slapsie Maxie" Rosenbloom for the Championship at Madison Square Garden. Now, he's a feared fighter for the cause, and I'm proud to call him my brother.

"Fellas! Everyone here?" Nat shouts out in his gravelly voice. He claps Abie's titan shoulders and other boxers tense to attention. Back in the day, Longie boxed too. He gets respect. I know he's got mine. He's the only man who could even have come close to fillin' my father's shoes.

Longie spreads his arms. "I'm lucky to be surrounded by the best soldier militia Newark, and America for that matter, can muster." Longie's not just givin' us a cock and bull story. He means it. Hails and cheers rock the gym.

Nat tosses his suit jacket on a chair and rolls up his sleeves. At five-foot-six inches, he commands like a giant. "Here's what we got, boys. Our cops tell us the German-American Nazi Bund is meetin' downtown tonight at City Hall Tavern. And none other than their leader, Führer Fritz Kuhn will be there."

The room booms as we all digest this staggering news. Some of the glistening bodies flex their muscles. Others cover their skin with shields of clothes, readying themselves.

"The American Hitler?" The eyes of lightweight sensation Maxie

Fisher pop open. Maxie and his older brother Al started their boxin'
careers beatin' off thugs tryin' to steal their family groceries. Now they not
only box, but they also serve Longie.

"I'm shinin' my spiked shoes." Al Fisher shuffles his foot. Given his
ninety-eight percent win record, he's not someone you wanna fool with.

"That's a skull I wanna crack." Puddy knocks his own head with his
hand. "Ouch!" he exclaims, bringin' on laughs from the boys. Thank
goodness for Puddy's flippancy. He keeps us sane.

"They think they own the place," I say. It's bloodcurdling how Kuhn
marches his Hitler boys right through towns from New York to San Fran,"
I say. It makes my blood curdle. In contrast, I try to imagine American
soldiers struttin' through Berlin. They'd be dragged into a back alley and
walloped like butcher meat.

"Kuhn's soldiers move like a bunch of geese swinging their legs straight
in the air," Abie says. "It's ludicrous." He turns his whole body toward me.
The muscles in his neck bulge so much he can't just twist his head.

Maxie swings his leg up to mimic the kick. "It's called the Stechschritt."

"Don't underestimate it," Harry says. Heads nod around the room
and voices grunt agreement. I know what my buddy's gettin' at. My pop
told my brothers and me that the goosestep marchin' on their old villages
meant you would be crushed if you stepped out of line. And not just by
boys in uniform. Supermen.

Nat snorts. "The goosestep is right out of a Dr. Seuss cartoon."

But it's much more, I realize. It makes men stop thinkin'. I picture the
lineup of zombies. The unit obeys like a human missile. I cross my arms.

"There's no doubt that Kuhn's building an army in America for Hitler
with Gestapo Troopers to boot," Longie says. "There's a lot of good
Germans in America, but he's reeling in any of them who are on the
fence."

"These bums are hitting below the belt," Benny says. "This Nazi crap
is banned now." Benny spins the most feared fist in the business into the
palm of his hand. He's a one round knockout guy.

"Nazis here in America don't give a rat's ass, Benny," Nat growls. He shakes his fist. "That Jew-hatin, Negro-muggin', homophobic Kuhn wants to bust up anyone who doesn't walk or talk Aryan. Do you think I fall into that group?" He rubs his many-time broken nose and gets some laughs.

My sure-footed friend, Harry, raises his voice above the chatter. "So what do ya need, Boss?" The room settles like boilin' kettle water that's been turned down. Harry's the type of guy who leads, then follows.

Longie scans the room and speaks slowly. "Tonight, we need the skilled fists of the Newark Minutemen for a commando attack against an American-Nazi rally." He walks around the front of the table and leans back against it. "Only yesterday, FBI Chief Hoover told me that their Bund is stockpiling weapons." Surprised grunts rise from the crowd.

"KA-POW!" Al Fisher punches the air.

"We got one job that Longie pays us for," Nat says. "Stop Hitler's Nazis from takin' over America."

The boxers cheer.

When I punch my fist into my hand, it sounds off like a gunshot through the racket. Overseas, Hitler's rampin' for another Great War, and at the same time, he's settin' up shop right here in our backyard. If Hitler controls America, he'll be able to roll a red carpet across France into the United Kingdom. My neck hairs bristle. I watch my frustration pass to the others like a flu spreadin' through a grammar school.

"The bums are everywhere," Puddy says. He's rockin' from side to side, like he's duckin' the fire in his belly.

Nat rests his elbow on Al's shoulder and side-eyes Maxie. "Ya ready to stop chasin' skirts and get blood on your knuckles, Maxie-boy?"

Maxie chuckles low in his throat. "What ya think boys?" His eyes hop from boxer to boxer. "Let's just send the rumor we'll be there, and those Nazis will scatter, right Puddy?"

"The saps will doggie paddle back to Germanland," Puddy spouts back.

The rallying cheers drown out even the sound of my own heartbeat.

21

"The American Nazi Bund marches to their leader, Führer Fritz Kuhn," I yell. "If we take him down, we take down the American Nazis." And I'll swallow my words if I'm wrong.

"Hear, hear!" the cheer goes up. I scan the clamoring room. The veins in Abie's thick neck pulsate. The ones in Benny's clenched jaws flush his face. If I wasn't standin' face to face with these boxers, I'd swear they were wild horses rearin' to break through a rodeo gate.

My own heart is kickin' too. "Führer Kuhn triggers street fights," I say. "He trains with guns, he indoctrinates German-American youth. He's not playin' by the rules."

Longie pulls some pamphlets off his briefcase. He moves into the center of the crowd, lighting life into the force of men. "The Bund's been floodin' the country with propaganda," he says. "Until now, Kuhn's been beating around the bush, but now he's getting down to business." He hands out the papers to the boys. "Fresh off the presses from Germany, his campaigns call for cleansing the entire world of Jews, Bolsheviks, homosexuals, blacks, Eastern Europeans, beggars, and whores or anyone who doesn't look or think like a German Aryan. This whole thing's spreading like a virus."

The boxers scan the blasphemous words in the paper. A pregnant pause fills the room. Even I have to stop and remind myself that a Jules Verne time machine hasn't shot me back to some medieval war.

Nat breaks the shock with some of his own seismic blast. "So who's up for a battle?" he yells.

"We'll be there, Longie!" the obedient boxers thunder. Their chime of voices sails through the voluminous room, rebounds against the high ceiling and crashes back down against their chiseled shoulders. But like the ancient mounts indulging the storms beatin' against them, they persevere. I never get tired of watchin' these men and their buoyancy. There's endless stories behind each scar on their bodies. They're unafraid to weather the storm for others, no matter the price. It's because they know they're part of many generations, livin' and past.

Longie returns to the table and clicks open the briefcase. He pats the bricks of cash inside. "Pay the boys, Puddy." Longie lobs one over to him.

Puddy riffles through the package of fresh dough that flings over a sniff of sweetness at me. The only smell I like better is new cars. He brags, "A little better pay than the twenty-five cents minimum." He counts out the allotments and distributes the cash to each boxer.

"Yael!" Arno calls and throws me a pack of hundreds. "Recruit forty more to the militia. We need firepower."

I pocket the dough and smile at the guys. "Hey, I got twenty thousand boxers chompin' at the bit to join the Newark Minutemen and clobber Hitler Nazis."

"You're my kemfer," Longie whispers to me privately. I'm touched that he considers me a fighter who goes beyond the call of duty. He gives me a rousin' pat on the back. "I can always count on you just like I could your pop, Joseph." Hearin' the name of Pop clogs a golf ball in my throat. I breathe faster and hold my breath at the same time. Because if I don't, I'm gonna' sob like a baby.

"Ya know I have one goal, Boss," I say. "Some call it *vengeance*." I flip my palms up. "Some call it *justice*. Either way, I'll deliver what's due." Longie witnesses the glassiness over my eyes but won't let his gaze retreat. He reminds me that he harbors my soul.

Thankfully, Nat Arno barks orders. "Tell our guys to break legs and arms. We promised the G-men no heads, unless they miss, of course." He puffs his cigar fast and fierce and turns the air sweet like apples with his smoke. "Marinate them bastards."

Longie cautions Harry to keep us outta the news. "Make sure the reporters' palms are greased," he says. "The last thing I want is fingers pointing."

Harry nods. His muscles stretch his t-shirt so tight, they rupture the seam.

"I'll stash cable wire and lead pipes in bushes," Abie informs, ever efficient.

Al Fisher holds up his fists. "Here's all the lead pipes I need."

"Don't get that pretty face messed up, Al," Nat says, jabbin' back. "Ya think ya lazy brother Maxie can help knock out those sons-of-sailors?"

Two lead pipes slip from Maxie's jacket sleeves into his hands. "KAY-O!" Maxie shouts his signature slang for knockout, and we bump shoulders.

There are some who say it's impossible to stop what's already comin'. Yet, not too long ago there was a ship they said was impossible to sink. It was called the Titanic. The hard lesson I learned from that was never underestimate impossible. If anyone can stop it, we can.

KRISTA:
Krista's Apt. Nye Avenue. Newark, NJ

The bedroom Heidi and I share is right next to the foyer of our small Nye Avenue apartment in the Second Ward of Newark. It's not hard to hear my father curse out there when my bedroom door is open.

"Gott verdammt!" he yells. We are going to be late for Führer Kuhn's American Nazi Bund rally!"

It's also easy to see everything he's doing through my bedroom mirror. As I braid my hair, creating the German-born look Papa will be proud of, I watch his reflection brush lint off the national emblem above his right breast pocket. He evens his white-braided collar tabs on his uniform and pulls down his gray-green wool tunic. Now that we've moved next to the Bund's Newark office around the corner from our old Hawthorne Avenue apartment, I can't remember a time when Papa isn't wearing his Nazi uniform from Germany. I have to admit—years ago, when we lived in Germany, my heart filled as I ran alongside my marching father. I remember the smell of his new leather jackboots and singing the songs. But now, it's kind of embarrassing when I'm with my American friends. Heidi says to be proud of his station in life and his patriotism. After all, he believes a lot of our cities are full of criminals and no longer the real

America. He's sworn an oath to right the wrong.

My father sucks in his large belly and pushes his belt through the buckle with the godly inscription *Gott mins uns*. He pulls the leather tight to slip the prong through the last hole in the belt. He's exactly what his reflection shows, an obedient follower of people who think they're the superior race doing good for the world. Good thing no one can see the real me. My ideas are so different.

"Schnell!" He yells in our native language.

Outside my bedroom door, my stepmother, Wilhelmina, trots to my father's side, fumbles with his overcoat and closes his popped button.

"Aufhoren!" he yells. "Quit bothering me." He slaps her hand away. "Where are Heidi and Krista?"

In our cramped room, Heidi leans her back toward me so I can zip up her black cinched-waist silk dress. She likes the trendy hourglass shape to offset her tall, lean body. She leans over my shoulder and primps her plaited blonde hair in the mirror. Her eyes gleam in horror.

"What's wrong?" I cringe and close my eyes, nervous that my dreaded fear, a spider, is crawling somewhere on me.

Heidi reaches under my arm and unhooks the little safety pin that holds the black thread of the store price tag. She wags it in front of my face. "What would you do without me, little sister?" She leaves our room and struts to our father's arm. "We are ready, my Vater," she says.

As usual, Papa compliments her. "You look beautiful, my tochter. I can't believe my little girl is already eighteen." He steps back and admires her. Then, not surprisingly, he fires a command through my door. "Krista! Hup hup!" He'll probably remind me that a seventeen-year-old young lady should be more prompt. It's not his anger that's the worst. I get it. Since my mother died giving birth to me, Heidi fills his void while I'm just a constant reminder of his pain. It's his random fury and iron grip that make me, and everyone else for that matter, quiver. Plus, I'm not sure he likes it when I question his Nazi views. It's not that I don't think he's smart. I do. I just give my honest opinions. But he says I'm arrogant to think I know better than the brilliant minds who lead us.

I saunter into the entrance hall in my red Elizabeth Hawes knock-off dress from the latest Wrigley chewing gum ad. I don't care about style like Heidi does. I just like that the red dress puts a little sparkle into my drab life. "I'm ready."

Three sharp knocks clacking on the front door gives my father an excuse to dodge doting on me. "Krista and Heidi. Your boyfriends are finally here!" he complains and opens the door to our house. He receives Heil Hitler salutes from our two uniformed escorts. "Axel and Frank," he says. "We must hurry if we are to keep our standing with the American Hitler. Like all good Germans, Führer Kuhn expects reliability."

Papa has always expected the punctuality of the German rail in his home. He says the rail was created in the image of the German people. They both perform, keep order, and complete their tasks. Without punctuality, there would be no discipline he says, and vice versa.

CHAPTER 3

In Your Corner

YAEL:
Across from City Hall. Union City, NJ

"Watch out! Incoming!" Harry spreads his arms to shield me from missiles that shoot past our bodies on the third-floor open patio. More bombs zoom past us, whistle to the ground below, and explode in a melee of scorchin' yellow flares on the sidewalk in front of the demonstrators. Smoke smudges the lights shinin' from Union City Hall across the street. Hundreds of people scream and scatter like chickens with their heads cut off. Usually, I let fear blow by me, but my legs are shakin'. That took me off guard.

I point up. "Holy Moly!" I say to Harry over the ear-splittin' noise below. "Someone's launchin' bricks from that rooftop."

On the street below, a raucous crowd is amassing to demonstrate the rally of American Nazi Bund leader, Führer Fritz Kuhn. They wave signs with messages like *Stop Fascist Terror, Keep America Free*. We hear their chants of "Deport Fritz Kuhn! Nazis Want War." The crowd is bigger than I imagined it would be.

Harry and I drape ourselves over the iron patio rail of Dr. William Kalb's apartment to inspect the damage below. A bit older than Longie, Dr. Kalb is the left to Longie's right. They both fight Hitler's risin' party here more than anyone I know. But while Longie uses the Minutemen and good old-fashioned knuckles and iron bars to knock out Nazis in America, the Doc works boycotts to stop sales of anything from Bayer aspirin to German cameras to Woolworths' malt shakes. Dr. Kalb tells us if we can stop the sale of German goods in American stores like Sears, Montgomery Ward, FAO Schwartz, and Abercrombie & Fitch, we can strangle money flowin' to build up German tanks and subs.

Taken by surprise, I jump when someone slaps my back. A puff of dust clouds from my jacket. "Sorry we're late, boys," Longie says over the clamor below.

I swing around to find both Longie and Dr. Kalb.

"Had to sneak up the back way around that crowd out there," Longie says. He's in his fine fashion that puts movie stars to shame. That suit's gotta cost at least twice my $75 threads.

Dr. Kalb's a little more conservative with his dark gray relaxed fit and six-button vest. I shout to him over the noise. "Nat and the rest of the gang thank you for lettin' us base camp from your place." I shake his chiseled hand. "Scopin' the scene from up here gives us an edge to plan our attack." I point across the street to a door. "Look up on top of the building. There's a roof entrance into the Hall. And down there, near the basement steps, a window."

"Also, crashing through those side windows will give us the element of surprise," Harry says.

"I like it," Dr. Kalb says, wrinkling his forehead. "You Newark Minutemen got tactics, unlike the thugs-for-hire in New York. They just pummel the bad guys until they don't move anymore."

"Who wouldn't want our prize-fighting boxers as their militia?" Longie says. "We got more boys winning in the ring than anyone in the world."

Dr. Kalb unbuttons his suit jacket and reads his pocket watch.

"The secret is the juice running through these boys' veins," he says in his forthright tone. "They're kids like I was, who cut their teeth fighting Russian Cossacks. As a boy, I watched mothers hacked to death with machetes and baby brothers splatted against the wall." The contrast of the blood and guts he's describing against his clean-shaven, compassionate reputation is dizzying. "We're the fierce kids who battled with guns, knives, and bombs. Became a prime militia." I know these stories from my father, but to hear them again fills my ire like an empty gas tank.

"We're also the battle-hardened survivors of the Great War who reclaimed Palestine from the Turks," Longie says. Our leaders are describing the boxers and their sons who are the Newark Minutemen. I swell with pride whenever Longie compares us to King David's mighty warriors. The timin' is lucky that Longie's got an army of boxers he can pivot into a band of soldiers for the FBI.

Suddenly, there's more commotion from below. We all look down. I holler over the racket, the whistling wind makin' it even harder to sound out the words. "There's gotta be five hundred American Nazis marchin' through the main doors of City Hall."

The scene below has turned into chaos. Crowds of people flow down the avenue, squeezed together, restricted from their free movements, but pushin' like a beast without a brain. My eyes blink against a gust as I watch a group of wild men flip over a car. It lands with a metallic screech that burns my ears.

"Look! Hundreds of Kuhn's soldiers are attacking the people." Harry's arm points toward the entrance where a horde of stormtroopers fan out into the crowd swingin' pipes and bars.

The protestors swing back with their bars, chairs, belts, and anything else not tied down. From my view, it's hard to distinguish the actions through the chaos because there's so many things happening at once. Arms and legs rotate like cranks on butter churns, bodies crumble to the ground like flakes off toast, and glass from car windows sprays through the air like icy snowflakes in a storm.

From four directions, firecrackers shoot ear-splittin' pops. The wind coils so hard, we can smell the gunpowder from three stories up. Harry and I read each other's minds. In sync, we grab our baseball bats. "We're going down, Boss," I say. We hop over the side railing and scale the outside of the brick building.

At street level, we struggle to find an empty space of concrete to plant our feet. We are swept up with the protestors. They charge with battle cries toward City Hall. To our left, crowbars smash windows. To our right, hatchets slash tires. Bund members are torn from their cars and beaten. Harry and I snake through the press of people. We hit a police fortress that stops us cold.

A thuddin' noise grabs my attention and I turn. The cops are whackin' protestors with billy clubs. A steely-eyed giant of a copper flings a body at me, warnin' me to stay back. I almost take his dare when out of the blue, Puddy grabs my arm and waves Harry over. Puddy steers us toward Nat who is up on the hood of a car. Abie swings a trashcan cover next to Nat's head. Golf balls clatter against it like a machine gun. Maxie, Al and Benny surround our commander. They bat back bodies like they're thwackin' cow carcasses.

"Divide into four units of eight," Nat shouts. I can barely hear him. "Flank the police echelon. Team leaders stay mobile, don't get boxed in." He swings his fist in a circle signaling units to infiltrate. "Bring down their Gestapo, those stormtroopers." He points at the Nazi soldiers. The arms and clubs of the Newark Minutemen blur as they fight the SS throng.

Through the City Hall war zone, Harry and I duck under flyin' fists to unite with our commander. "Nat!" I yell and knock on my head. I point at the roof and basement.

Nat leans toward Abie and Maxie and aims his fist at the roof. His hat soars off his head. The two Minutemen head to infiltrate the building through the air ducts. With a shake of his hand, Nat deploys Al and Benny toward the basement opening. Hopefully there's a good path down there that leads up to the main hall.

Sirens scream and red lights stop us in our tracks. A police escort pulls up to the entrance. Other cops block demonstrators. Harry and I squeeze through the barricade. In front of us, six American Nazis exit a car and march within feet of us.

Harry elbows me and cocks his head to one side. "Why does that Nazi wear his iron cross medal from the Great War?" Regalia drips from the beefy man's uniform. The fortyish-lookin' leader must be a high-rankin' officer.

"I guess no one told him the Germans lost that one twenty years ago?" I snicker.

A jiggly woman shuffles beside him. I assume it's his wife. Behind the couple, two Nazi wanna-be soldiers escort two young women who can't be more than eighteen years old. The taller boy in front struts with his blonde partner.

"Harry," I say. "That girl's red dress and black sweater goes so nicely against the Swastika flag." The blonde hooks her green eyes into mine. I can't help but stare back. Hard to say whether she's attacking me, consuming me, or grabbin' a lifeline. The other guy brings up the rear with his pigtailed partner.

Like a dang whale knockin' a ship, two stormtroopers clock me in the back. Off balance, I fling around and hurl a punch. The Trooper ducks and pops me in the jaw. I go flyin' into the inner circle and crash right into the looker with the red dress who then dominoes into her Nazi boyfriend. The guy rights his gal, grabs my shoulders, and rams me into the street. My head hits the concrete, firing a spike of pain below my eyes.

"Axel!" she yells at him.

I shake myself. Blood pools in my mouth.

The girl offers her hand.

Her hand?

This is awkward. But I take it. She clutches me in her soft grasp.

The Nazi boyfriend isn't happy. He rips the girl away. "Krista! Don't touch that!" Then he hauls her up the steps and through the doors.

31

My palm is warm. I search for the red dress. It's gone.

Harry slaps my empty hand and hauls me up by the collar. "Forget her, Yael," he says. "She might be hot, but she's from yenemsvelt, a different world."

My ears ring with the weight of his words or the bang from the concrete. I can't tell.

FRITZ KUHN:
Private Tavern Room. City Hall. Union City, NJ

My elite eight stormtroopers escort six special American Nazi Bund guests into the private tavern room attached to the Union City Hall coliseum for the reception before the rally tonight. Our secret police, modeled after Hitler's Schutzstaffel SS Guard, rob my breath. But I breathe anyway. Because Adolph will be proud of me when he learns that this evening, over five hundred German-American Nazi Bund members will fill the room of City Hall to hear me speak in one of the stronghold cities of our people.

The anteroom is packed. My guests of honor weave past my beer-guzzling divisional Führers, the foam slipping down the frosty sides of their steins. But my night is cramped. Thousands of misguided protesters clamber outside, demonstrating tonight's message of *True Americanism*. They can't see the threat to everything we hold dear. I even have to strain to absorb the violin playing one of my favorite Wagner pieces. Through the large window, I survey the police as they hold the hooligans back. Apparently, freedom to meet means nothing to that mob. Soon, even the naysayers will understand that the intention of the German-American Nazi Bund remains loyal to the ideas of George Washington. Pride ripples down my spine as the sight of my fighting stormtroopers outside brings memories of my own service on the Great War battlefield. It's a shame it took so long for others to appreciate me, but now they eat up my values.

Just now, my special guests entered the room. Here's my most trusted

Kamerad, Günther Brecht. I haven't seen him in a while. He's been back and forth to Germany on a high-level mission. He snakes through the top brass as he escorts his replacement wife, Wilhelmina—a bit too many strudels on her hips for my taste—and family to our rally. Tonight, we will ready thousands of followers for Hitler's inevitable takeover of America. My smile hides behind my lips.

And behold! Günther's golden daughter, Krista. She sways around guests, guided by the arm of her young escort, offering her hand as her father introduces her. Her presence is beyond her years. She reminds me of my own daughter back in Chicago with my wife and son. I miss them, but I have a responsibility bigger than myself. Plus, the freedom's not so bad and the fringe benefits are galvanizing. Now, my smile double crosses me.

Krista is a key to our strategy. She doesn't even know yet, but the crisp uniformed arm she grasps belongs to her own arranged match, Axel Von du Croy. He is the son of one of Hitler's high command in Berlin. She might be a tad young, but Axel's maturity is well beyond his nineteen years. He can handle her. He's certainly mature enough to stand beside his father in the Fatherland. When Axel heads to Berlin with Krista, their union will bridge the American-German Bund to Nazi headquarters. My mind jitters just thinking how this will strengthen ties. On the other side of the coin, Günther has warned me that Krista's an unpredictable one, always questioning the hierarchy of races and challenging her role as a Nazi woman. Even tonight, I eye with a shudder of distaste. That American red dress needs to go. It's rebellious! All the more reason to ingrain the wild youth living in America with ideals of the homeland. Günther must stay vigilant.

Two steps behind, Krista's older sister Heidi, a classic beauty, sets her purse on a table and urges her escort to fetch a drink. Must be her boyfriend, Frank Schenk. Günther has described him to me, and we've discussed Heidi's role with Herr Schenk. I have higher hopes for her. An obedient one like her could be useful.

As Günther approaches, I seize the command expected of a German Führer. "Herr Günther Brecht. Dear blood brother from Hitler's Beer

Hall Putsch."

Günther, adorned in his decorated Nazi uniform, clicks his heels and tosses a Heil Hitler salute. "1923!" His jowls joggle.

As I flip a salute back, my Iron Cross medal from the Great War swings from my buttonhole. I steady it. My fingers warm when I think of the foresight Emperor Wilhelm II had back in 1914 when he stole the ancient Teutonic knight's design for bravery. There's an immortality beaming from it.

Günther's own medals rise when he puffs out his chest. "We almost brought 'em down. That double-crossing Weimar Republic. Barely escaped the bloody fate of the sixteen."

"At least our sacrifice was not in vain," I say. "We planted the seeds of Austottung of the Jews mit Stumptf und Stiel."

Günther chuckles. "Ja! Extermination of the under-races from root to branch."

We exchange a hefty handshake and clap each other on the back. "In Germany marches us!" I say. Then together, we approach Bund Secretary James Wheeler-Hill. Günther's family tags behind like his own mini-brigade. I envy that man. He has it all.

"James. Good to see you again," Günther says as he and my secretary slap each other's shoulder. "Your national youth camps are well-oiled revenue machines."

I stretch my arm toward James. "Secretary Wheeler-Hill. May I introduce Günther's exquisite wife, Wilhelmina, and their ripe Fräuleins, Heidi and Krista."

Krista's nostrils flare, and I get a first-hand glimpse of that rebelliousness. That's okay. She's got that caramel and salty layering to her that can be magical. Once I have a moment with her, I will wrap her around my finger. She will be the inspiration for all American Nazi girls.

The Secretary gleams into the girls' eyes as he grasps a hand from each. "Führer Hitler believes our most important weapon for Nazism in America is our youth." His voice doesn't match his strapping body. His iron jaw lets out a sound as sweet as a Kristy Kreme doughnut. "A pleasure," he says. Our nickname for the thirty-five-year-old is Little Napoleon because he often rests his hand inside his jacket.

Heidi feeds the man's ego with a beaming smile while Krista delivers a poker-face to the guy old enough to be her father. I blush just thinking about how she'll soon understand her female responsibilities.

"Führer Kuhn," Günther interrupts. "I believe you also know the Von du Croys from Germany. May I present their son, Axel Von du Croy."

Krista's escort, Axel, steps forward. Up close, the boy in his starched uniform is as debonair as I imagined. His stiff neck and haughty eyes knock aside his peers. He doesn't even need to try. The soldier clicks his heels.

My chest hums. Much nicer to receive this respect than the belligerence in my early days here. I knew in my bones that I had what it took. But I had to let the people running the show swallow their own tails. They laughed at me at first. Ach! If I'd been in their shoes, maybe I would have, too. After all, I spoke English like a boar and had just two coins to rattle in my pocket. My own father's to blame for the biggest snub, though. I still want to bury him alive for turning me to the Polizei just because I took a few coats from his friend's factory. Even my mother didn't forgive him for shipping me to Mexico to avoid jail. The greatest tragedy though, Adolph wouldn't talk to me for years.

But payback is sweet. When the founding leaders were punished and shipped back to Germany, I emerged like a snake with a shiny new skin. I delivered the organization in America that would have taken Germany years. My heart pounds each time I recall the applause.

Axel's body remains stiff, waiting for my cue. "A pleasure, Herr Von Du Croy," I say. "A tragedy what the Jew Communists did to your family's lands after the Great War. However, I hear your rightful property may be recovered." If only my son could be as impressive as this boy. All he does when I telephone is complain about money and his mother. My greatest fear is that he may be a homosexual.

"Ya! As soon as the papers go through, Krista and I will marry and take our place," Axel answers. Over his shoulder, his gray eyes give Krista an appraising glance. The alliance brokered between the Von du Croys and Brechts will advance my power and breed an American-German dynasty.

Heidi bounces on her toes and squeals. "Krista! You're getting married!"

Krista starts coughing. Her hand covers her throat to settle the fit.

Without even looking at Krista, Axel reaches back and swats her back. "Vater wants me to take my place against the enemies who committed the *Dolchstosslegende* and—"

"Stabbed us in the back during the Great War," I finish his sentence.

"Exactly! He says our destiny will save the world from diabolical Bolshevism." Axel is a soldier with clarity and purpose.

"Marriage! Good news, Axel." Frank slaps his back. "The best man is always the last to know." He forces a grin.

"This time the wife is the last to know," Krista mutters under the clattering of the room. But I hear her. As Wilhelmina squeezes her elbow, Krista beams a blistering glare at Axel. That defiance again.

I sigh. A smart girl would know this is her shining moment. Krista could learn a thing or two from her step-mother about the female's role in the Reich. She will soon accept that a German man leads his woman as well as his country. She's young, yet. And she's bright. By tomorrow she will appreciate this gift.

"BundesFührer Kuhn," Günther bellows over the noise. "One night soon, we shall celebrate. Tonight, we are here for you and our future." He flashes a smile. His teeth have yellowed over his five years in America.

I spread my black leather jackboots. "I believe in a real democracy and America doesn't have one right now," I say. "Tonight, we speak of Freeing Amerika." The energy in the room buzzes between my fingertips. The crowd jerks and paces like caged tigers on caffeine, anticipating my promises. The stroking inside me is so much more than pride. It's dignity.

Führer Frederick Vandenberg appears. He's the leader of Camp Siegfried, my showcase camp and the Kron juwel of the multi-million dollar German Bund corporation. He peeks over his thick round glasses.

His words spill over his thin lips. "The only thing Amerikan freedom brings to this country is shacks and soup lines. Millions are out of work. Roosevelt's New Deal only creates jobs like apple sellers and shoe shiners."

"Kamerads!" I extend my arm. "Please welcome Frederick Vandenberg, Camp Siegfried's brilliant Führer. And a friend of liberty." Frederick's receding hairline makes him look older than his actual years. His perennial red cheeks reveal his drinking habits. But his ruthless work ethic makes him as efficient as the German railway. As the group salutes him, I smile and nod at Vandenberg's patriotic red, white and blue swastika on his lapel. "Führer Vandenberg's right," I say. "Democracy won't revive Amerika."

"This country is a broken down skeleton!" Vandenberg says. The body of the apple cheeked forty-something twitches with each word he speaks. He faces Axel and Frank. "Boys! Are you ready to help re-nourish this decaying country!" he says.

"Aryans will stop the degeneration," Axel says, nodding.

"I look forward to contributing at Camp with you this summer, mein Führer," Frank chimes.

Out of the corner of my eye, I catch a smirk from Krista when Frank speaks. She's obviously not impressed with Heidi's choice in partners either. Smart girl. I do like her.

Behind Vandenberg is his director of youth, the debonair, Theodore Dinkelacker. I wave him over. "Also, may I introduce the Youth Director for Camp Siegfried, Theodore Dinkelacker."

Without a hair out of place, the man bows to his colleagues and then to Günther's daughters. Heidi blushes. Caught between deference and jealousy, Frank puffs his cheeks.

I am anxious to connect everyone. I point to another officer. "Look who's here from Andover, New Jersey. Camp Nordland Führer, Hermann Schwartzman." His tight belt around his thick middle shows his wife's been feeding him well. "He's the most decorated German veteran in America. Naturally, he's my choice for training our stormtroopers."

Schwartzman's garrison hat slips as he tips his hairless head to greet us.

I encourage discussion between my guests. But my priority is to rally around the ein kommender Politiker, the up-and-coming German Nazi, Axel Von du Croy. Axel will have the ears of important people in Berlin. "If you need anything, I have a direct line to our Führer Hitler," I say. "Germany depends on me to unify our racial brothers." Axel concentrates on my every word. "We are producing everything we need right here in Amerika. Our presses print anti-Roosevelt, anti-Semitic news. Our tailor makes uniforms in Queens."

"Sounds less risky than smuggling them in on German ships," Axel says.

"You are astute. Please, come by my New York office on 85th. Or better yet, the office on Nye Avenue in Newark." If I can engage Axel in the day to day, my connection will be that much stronger. I can smell der Kaffee.

"Danke, mein Führer." Axel stiffens his neck.

"Fritz, how often will our girls see you at Camp Siegfried this summer?" Günther asks. He puts his arm around Heidi.

"I'll be up in Long Island a lot setting examples for our youth. In fact, you will all join me for the Camp Siegfried reception in a few weeks before the Götterdämmerung Assembly." I hook my thumbs in my Sam Browne belt.

"You will visit, Herr Brecht," Vandenberg says. "Our camp mimics our sacred homeland with much nostalgia."

"And plus, the knockwurst is the best in the country." James says, rubbing his stout stomach.

The group bellows.

"Axel's favorite celebration at Camp Siegfried is Götterdämmerung," Krista says, stone-faced. "Burning the old world for the new."

"The celebration revitalizes us each year, Fräulein Brecht," I say. It's great to see my youth appreciate traditions.

"Do you agree with the myth, mein Führer?" Krista asks. "That war is the path to renewal." She taps her foot, impatient for my answer. Her rebellious twinkle celebrates our mission.

"Your reflection shows your dedication and reveals the answer," I answer. Her charisma is enchanting.

The panic-stricken Chief of Police Jenkins storms into the tavern. He stops short and his eyes scan our swastikas and Hitler uniforms. He's impressed. Then he addresses the business at hand with me. "Mr. Kuhn. There are thousands of protestors invading the building. You need to leave or else the police can't be responsible for your safety."

"Leave?" I cry. "Those Commies should leave this country. They are terrorists. I will not leave for five thousand of them." I pound my fist against a cocktail table so hard that an empty glass teeters, rolls, and shatters against the floor.

"We don't have to leave!" James says. "We have freedom of speech rights."

The chief of police reminds us that after the last American Bund riot when our members sang "Our greatest Joy Comes when Jewish blood flows through the streets," laws changed. The words made the courts decide that Freedom of Speech did not apply to corporations. The discrimination toward us Germans irks me.

Dinkelacker yanks Axel and Frank. The three of them leave to investigate.

"We've got all these convoluted laws that convict us of hate if we say anything against race or religion," I say to James. These laws have shaken the core of democracy.

"It's ridiculous. The Great War laws still haunt us," James says. "Germans are being convicted for so-called disloyal comments. This is an un-American attack against our liberties!"

"This is happening in Newark, Union City, North Bergen, and West New York," Günther pines. "It's now illegal to wear our Nazi uniforms, give the Heil salute, or display our dear swastika." He wags his head in disgust. "Ein Unglück kommt selten allein." In other words, when it rains it pours.

With a clattering of boots, Axel and Frank rush back into the Hall.

"Mein Führer," Axel rasps. "There are ten thousand protesters yelling, 'Kill Kuhn.'"

"The Newark Minutemen thugs are moving in," Frank adds. A ring of perspiration wets his garrison hat.

My blood boils and I unholster my gun. "You mean those flipping boxers that gangster Longie Zwillman calls his FBI militia? He can lick my arsch!"

The doors fling open and attackers swarm the room.

YAEL:
Private Tavern Room. City Hall. Union City, NJ

Our swingin' bats shatter the City Hall Tavern windows like a cascading ocean wave. The crash seizes my heart faster than a gunshot blast. The guests of Kuhn, who had just a moment ago been juicin' up for a rousing night, now squeeze their eyes to block the shards and slivers of glass sprayin' them like cactus spine.

Harry, Puddy, and I barge through the openings under cover of the rainin' glass. We strike a wall of stormtroopers who fight back with just as much vigor. Nat and the rest of the Minutemen pour in and ambush like seasoned lions—focused, fierce, bloodthirsty. The good news for us— Führer Fritz Kuhn won't have his Bund rally anytime tonight.

As Al creaks open a floor trapdoor, a stormtrooper raises his belt buckle to whack him. Behind the trooper, Nat points to the Nazi's back and wallops him with his bat. The trooper flies faster than a Babe Ruth baseball sheddin' its canvas. The loser twirls in front of me and I deliver a left-handed knockout punch.

As the heads of Al and Benny emerge from below ground, they sing "Peek-a-boo." Their arms wrap around high black boots. Troopers topple, crunching glass against the floor.

Our pal Puddy is toe to toe with Trooper Frank. Three more Troopers join the sparring. Harry and I come to the rescue. The Nazis hear us before they see us and scramble like pigs bein' rounded up for slaughter. Puddy winds up and knocks Frank out. We didn't even have to get our hands dirty on that one.

Out of the corner of my eye, I catch something comin' at me. Just in time, I duck out of the way of Trooper Axel's lead-lined rubber hose. On the backswing, it wraps around my bat. I pull tight, and hurl him into a fightin' scrum. Around me, the grunts and smacks make me wince. I glance up and raise a fist to signal the boys above. The distraction gets the better of me because the next thing I know, a jolt of pain rips though my ribs. The taste of iron swishes in my mouth, and I drop to my knees. My muscles ripple in anticipation of another blow when I hear the chime, "Doy-resn." Abie soars down and flattens the crow-body broodin' over me. I hear bones crunch. Next to me, Maxie lands on uniformed shoulders and rides the soldier like a swashbuckler. Abie throws a punch to the swayin' Nazi's breadbasket and Maxie slides down just before the guy splinters a wooden table to pieces.

The heavy-duty German officer from earlier hunkers behind Kuhn's guards. He covers his head with one arm and maneuvers his stout wife around the twisted limbs on the floor. From a heap of bloodied torsos, Heidi grabs the shoulder belt of her shaky boyfriend Frank and hanks him up. She huddles them both behind the guards to safety.

The other daughter, Krista, hangs in the crux of rowdy bedlam. In a flash, my eye spots a blurry object rocketing toward her red dress. I spiral through the air and bat it away. A brick. It would've bruised her badly. Steps away, her boyfriend ducks out under the diverted weapon. From the ground, I growl at the girl. "Get out of here before we hurt you." My mouth tastes like a spoonful of pennies.

Her Nazi boy's face is flushed. His eyes blaze red, and in a mad scramble to rescue her, Axel shoves aside Troopers and dodges Minutemen. He grips her. She writhes like a cat. He drags her body to the escape route. He turns and scowls at me like a rabid wolf.

LONGIE ZWILLMAN:
Club Miami. Clinton Avenue. Newark, NJ

Right before midnight, I raise a glass through the dark, hazy air at my Club Miami in the red light district of Clinton Avenue. "We plugged this one before the Nazis rallied, men." I congratulate over two hundred Minutemen on a successful battle at City Hall. "Everyone, eat! Drink!" My club might not clamor the tropical vacation of its namesake, but the "bucket of blood," as it's known, welcomes my clientele to be themselves. The overcrowded room rumbles as the Minutemen cheer their victory. They pound their bruised fists against the leather-backed booths.

From the stage, brassy notes and quick drum-taps spray from the swing band and the crowd begins to sway. In front of the bandstand, Benny, Yael, Harry, and Abie raise their drinks to me. Our elbows rub as we clink the glasses.

"KAY-O!" Maxie shouts from a few feet away. He lobs an ice pack to Abie over the head of a food server who is balancing two trays. "The numbskulls kept getting in the way of my fists." He snatches deviled eggs off of each tray.

"Congrats on a record knockout night, Maxie," I say with a wink.

He raises the eggs and licks out the mustardy yellow cream just as Al and Puddy appear from opposite directions.

Al fake-punches Puddy's chafed chin. "KA-POW! They got ya good, pal," he says to Puddy.

Nat barrels over to Puddy and swings his arm around his shoulders. "Let me take a look at that," Nat says. He calls over one of the cigarette gals. "Lillian! Come here, doll. Puddy needs ya to kiss his boo-boo."

Puddy shoves Nat away. On cue, Lil sets down her tray and cuddles Puddy's chin in one hand. She leads him through the reveling pack of Minutemen into the kitchen with the other.

Nat nicks a drink off Lil's tray. "How come the biggest losers get the girls?" With a weighty arm, he corrals his "eight" and me to sit down at a white linen-covered table. He waves over the white-tux waiters carrying bowls of food. Before we know it, the table is covered with choices. Maxie and Abie splat mashed potatoes onto their plates. Benny smothers his greens with A1 sauce. Yael carves his double helping of rare steak. Al streams golden whiskey over his glass of ice and then Harry's. Then, as if someone turns down Louis Armstrong trumpeting on a radio, the voices fade. Only the music of silverware scratching against plates can be heard as the men chow down.

After dinner, the boys barely rub their full stomachs before they scramble to find cigars and girls. Yael and I are left eating dessert alone.

"How's that cheesecake?" I ask.

Yael's mouth is so full he can't answer. I smile at my boy who has grown into the man who holds the strength for many.

My arm rests around his sturdy shoulders. "How's the family?"

Yael wipes his mouth with the red cloth napkin. "Everyone's good, Boss. I haven't had a chance to tell ya. My brother, Dov, had his boy two days ago. He wants you at the bris. He's namin' him Abner, after you."

"Mazel Tov," I laugh." This gives me a thrill, it really does. When Yael was barely thirteen, he and his two older brothers clung to me after the death of their parents. At barely thirty, I'd had a lot of responsibility, but nothing like this. I taught them the important stuff. They learned from me how family radiates into the community. And from the community, we fix the world. "Hah. Abner. No one even knows that's my real name anymore," I chuckle. Yael grins.

I ask about his Austrian cousins. "Did Uncle Irving's cousins get our visas? Are they out of Vienna or not?" These days a piece of paper with a stamp on it is the difference between life and death.

"They're safe in Newark now," Yael assures me. His expression grows serious. He hits me with the question he's asked a thousand times. "Nat said you have a lead on Pop's killer?"

After five years, it's a relief to deliver a decent tip to Yael. "Mayor Ellenstein came through for us. We got our target landing on the 46th

Street Pier two weeks ago. A Hamburg-American Line vessel." My heart warms when Yael's face lights up. "But there's more. He lives right under our noses here in Newark." I cup my hand around my mouth and call across the room. "Nat, ya got the mug shots for Yael?"

Nat grabs a drink off Lil's abandoned serving tray with one hand and clutches his briefcase with the other. He approaches the table. "Right here, Boss." The tablecloth creases up when he places the briefcase in front of me. He flips it open and hands Yael an envelope. "The photos are dark and blurry, nothing like your quality. But they should do the job."

"Newark Minutemen always get their foes," I tell Yael. "By the way, I need you and Harry to chauffeur tomorrow. Good?" I often offer extra work to the boys. My family won't dare wear the shameful idleness and humiliation of the Depression.

Yael handles the envelope like it's an ancient treasure. He peeks inside just as Harry approaches. He slips it inside his suit pocket. "What time should we pick ya up in the Pierce Arrow, Boss?" he asks me and then turns to Harry. "Boss needs us to work tomorrow night."

"Seven sharp," I answer. "We got big guns. New York bosses Meyer Lansky and Willie Moretti." It's always an interesting night when the Jewish and Italian mob socialize together." Then I sweeten the pie. "If ya do a good job, I got an old Ford auto that fell into my lap. You two can share some wheels."

Yael and Harry grant me big bonus smiles. Since the death of Yael's parents, he understands I'm protecting him, making him feel secure to take risks or just be himself.

Then we're interrupted. But I'm okay with it because a beautiful woman I've never met before puts her arms around me. Another sits on Yael's lap, a third on Harry's. Harry wraps his long arms around the dame. Yael drinks and lets his new girl run her fingers through his golden wavy hair. I call it a night with the gal who's rubbing my shoulders. "Good night, boys."

As I step away, I hear Yael. "Okay enough, babe. I'm busy," he says. I turn back. He prods the dame away.

"That's not the Yael Newman I know. Wishin' you had that Nazi girl in your pants instead?" Harry says.

"Dry up!" Yael stands and snatches Harry's girl right from his arms. Harry rears up. He pushes his chair back against the tray, sending dirty plates crashing to the floor. Yael drops the gal's arm and leaves, alone. I put my hand on Harry's arm to stop him.

My bouncer, "Jumpin' Jack" Gleason who doubles as a comic some nights, springs to my side. "Need help, Boss?"

"Nah, it's just Yael letting off some steam." Yael isn't usually a firestorm of fury. That dame Harry teased him about must be shooting him with a lethal concoction of lust and guilt.

CHAPTER 4

The Heavyweights

YAEL:
Hawthorne Avenue. Newark, NJ

I drive Longie's sleek Pierce Arrow up to the curb in front of Abraham Block's candy store. Heads turn. I watch Harry's cleft chin tilt and his eyes check the windows above the store. His father, Isaac, waves. That's where Harry lives.

Harry and I hop out to serve our boss. Before opening the door for Longie and New York Mob King Meyer Lansky, I brush lint off the arms of my wool suit. These new broad shoulders hang just right for us boxers. When Longie gets out, he holds his fedora and crouches his head to fit his tallness through the door. Behind him, Lansky's five-and half-foot body sportin' a striped double-breasted suit slips out. The men's suits luster against the Hawthorne Avenue evening crowd wearing their ruffian slacks and ill-fitted skirts. I have to admit, gangsters do set the fashion bar.

I hang Longie's overcoat over one arm and elbow Harry with the other. There's trouble buddin' on the corner. A gang of teens lean against the shop window, chuggin' Hamm's beer and smokin.' Candy stores are found on every corner, but there's more to them than meets the eye. Sure, if you peek inside the shop, the shelves are lined with grape gumballs and nickel Milky Ways, Baby Ruth's, and Reeses. You can innocently quench your thirst with a Cherry Coke or malted. And you can buy everything from ballpoint pens to comic books to toothpaste. But behind the candy store is a hidden world. Block's Candy is the front for Longie's illicit operation. It's the only hope for countless unemployed to put bread on the table.

A few feet across from the gang, a teenage boy riffles through a deck of cards and fans them for the audience to see. He dares his mark to choose one, replace it in the deck, and shuffle. From my angle, the con is as plain as the nose on my face. Bettors throw down money on the sidewalk, vexing when coins roll into the cracks. The game begins. Of course, the young dealer guesses the card. He scoops up the winnings off the ground.

"Hey!" a voice in the crowd shouts. "He saw our cards in the window." Before you can say, "shark," the kid dodges his victims and slips sideways between two mothers strollin' babies. Then he ducks under a sheet of glass carried by four men and shuffles past three girls singin' "To Me You're Beautiful." All the while, my knee pops to this swing version of the hit "Bei Mir Bist Du Schön" from the old country, and Harry and I howl. The three Andrew sisters singin' on our corner are gonna make it big.

Feet away, the notorious New Jersey Mob Boss, Guarino "Willie" Moretti of the rulin' Genovese crime family, exits the barbershop of Harry's cousin Irving. His big Italian personality matches his bulk. Willie's a nice guy whose belly brags the love for his mama's cookin'.

"Appreciate the haircut, Irving," he says. He peels off bills from his wad of dough. "I'll bring by my up and comer, Frankie Sinatra. Ya gotta hear him swoon. Willie's got an ear for talent. He's helping another kid, Dino Crocetti, and a funny young boy over in Irvington who calls himself Jerry Lewis."

Willie rests his hat over his freshly slicked hair. The crowd on the sidewalk parts as he approaches Longie and Lansky. "Miei amici! Meyer Lansky, the Jewish Godfather," Willie says. "Been awhile."

A couple years before my father was rubbed out, I overhead Longie tellin' Pop that Meyer Lansky was doin' a deal with Willie Moretti and his boss, Lucky Luciano. They wanted no more fightin' between the Italian mafiosa dagos and the Jewish gangster yids. These matchmakers rounded up their families. Lansky's were some sharp frickin' businessmen. His best buddy was Bugsy Siegel. And there was Louis Lepke Buchalter, Harry Big Greenie Greenberg, and all the rest of 'em.

Over the honkin' cars, Lansky shakes Willie's hand. "I'm impressed that an Italian's keeping peace in New Jersey," he says. "The Corporation sends their praises." The oath of loyalty runs deep between these so-called brothers.

Willie waves his free hand toward the street. "Here comes Nat Arno!"

Without lookin', Nat crosses through heavy traffic. Three cars honk. Tires squeal and I close my eyes. Nat pounds a man's car hood. A cigar wags from his mouth as he steps onto the curb and exchanges handshakes with Lansky and Willie. I admire his nerve.

"I hear ya got New York under your thumb and FBI arranged the whole shebang," Willie says to Lansky. "Judge Perlman and Mayor LaGuardia offered ya a deal?" Willie plugs a cigar into his mouth. Nat leans in with a lighter, just far enough away for Willie to rotate it like he's roastin' a marshmallow. Their cigar smoke puffs into a single cloud.

"Took the good judge's hit list but turned down the cash," Lansky explains. "He promised to look the other way. Our guys are like kids in a candy store ready to bust loose." He drops his cigar on the sidewalk and twists the glowin' embers out with his shoe. "We're signed up to rub out New York Nazis so they get the message we're not just gonna accept insults."

"Well, nice to have a free pass on screwin' up Hitler-goose-steppers marchin' down Park Avenue with their bony arms in the air," Nat says.

"We're fightin' back," Lansky says. "But our volunteers in the Big Apple can be rough around the edges." In New York, Lansky recruited thugs. Let's just say it got out of hand and the newspapers had a field day.

"What can I tell ya?"

Longie takes his overcoat from me and layers it over his own arm. "Nat's got the Newark system down," Longie says over the noise around us. He turns to a woman bouncin' her cranky baby and shakes the baby's hand. The baby stops cryin' and its mama smiles.

Meyer Lansky nods. "Gatsby of Gangsters, Longie Zwillman and commander Nat Arno, turnin' our Jewish boxers into a trained militia of Nazi-busters. Ain't that something! The Newark Minutemen."

Longie digs inside his trouser pocket and rattles coins. He tosses nickels and dimes on the sidewalk to a bunch of street kids. They scramble and scoop up the bouncin' silver and run into the candy store.

"Geez, Longie," Lansky jokes. "If ya gonna give your dough away to every bum in Newark, give me a chance to win it first. Let's get inside and play some cards and show those Italians what the Jews got." Lansky leans down and picks up a shiny Jefferson nickel next to Longie's polished shoe. He flips it in the air.

Longie intercepts the coin and puts his hand on Lansky's shoulder. In front of them, the gang of men push each other into the candy store. They're headin' to the action in the back. I note the roll call of the toughest of the Third Ward and Hawthorne Avenue. It's Longie, Lansky, Moretti, and of course Nat Arno, Abie, Puddy, Benny, Maxie, and Al, to name a few.

At the entrance to the shop, Longie holds the door open for two pigtailed dames escapin' the pandemonium. He catches me starin' at the blonde girls and gives me a curious look.

I hate to admit he's got a spider sense with me. My heart is hammering. "Harry!" I say. "Those are the dames from the American Nazi riot." The memory of the girl's soft hand intoxicates me. My face sizzles with guilt. How can I let anyone from the enemy camp captivate me? The blonde pigtails, the sexy red dress and her rebellious gesture, givin' me a helpin' hand, right there in front of her people. The dang paradox of it all. Krista, yeah, that's her name. I dip into the car for the bottle of whiskey waitin' on

49

the seat. "We got ourselves some victims for tonight," I rumble to Harry. I blow across the bottle top and a loud whistle sounds. Then, tippin' my head back, I chug.

Harry grabs the bottle from me. "You're right. They were with Fritz Kuhn. You're playing with fire. Why don't ya rein in that charm tonight, buddy. You know it's gonna be your downfall." Harry ingests a long pull of whiskey.

I notice that Krista has replaced her red dress with a sporty blue thingamajig that fits her body just right. Does she want me to watch her sway her hips? 'Cause her eyes are eatin' me up. "Gosh," I whisper to Harry. "They're inspecting us up and down. Maybe we're the victims?" Like a matchstick struck next to a gas leak, my guilty lust sparks my ire.

"We gonna go through another night of this?" Harry asks before he guzzles another slug of the golden liquid.

"Ya know how Nazis just naturally gnaw away at my humanity," I say. "Revenge is my only satisfaction." I whip the bottle from Harry and call to the girls. "How about a ride, dolls?" Then I whisper to him. "I haven't had action for three whole days."

The older of the two girls rolls her eyes. "No, thank you."

Krista pulls her close. "Heidi, that's the guy who saved me the other night at the rally." She eyes the sleek vehicle we're leanin' against. "Plus, we've never been in a movie star car like that before."

"Son of a gun," Harry says and winks at me. "Ya' cornered another girl on the ropes."

Heidi frowns at Krista. "That's because German Lutherans don't hang out with Jewish gangsters, Krista. And if you marry Axel, like Father has arranged, you might ride in something like this in Berlin."

Krista seems even more eager now. "Come on, Heidi, please let's go!" She pulls the older sister toward the car. "I'm not Axel's prisoner yet." She simpers.

I point to myself and curl my lip in a half smile. "How can you say no to *this*?" I say to the girls. I tilt my hat toward my left ear and swing my bangs over my right eye.

Heidi does a major eye roll. "Fine. I'm only doing this because it's one of our last nights before summer camp." As they near, she gleers at me. "Geez. I can't believe I'm agreeing to a ride with Jewish gangsters."

Harry and I steer the girls into the backseat of Longie's car and toss our blazers and hats into the trunk.

YAEL:
Longie's Car. Hawthorne Avenue. Newark, NJ

I climb behind the wheel of Longie's car. Harry sits shotgun.

"As far as gangsters go, we're just hired help," Harry says to Heidi. "Longie Zwillman hires us boxers as his bodyguards."

"Uh hunh, like I believe you." Heidi chides.

I turn and see Krista strokin' the buttery seat leather and my pants tighten.

"This car is swanky," she says. "By the way, who is Longie Zwillman?" She scoots forward, peerin' at us from over the back seats.

I turn on the ignition. "Who's Longie?" I respond as I hand Krista the bottle. "He's only *the* Jewish Mob Boss of Newark. You just saw him hold court." I shift the car into drive. "Nothing happens without Longie's stamp of approval. And he takes care of all of us." I press on the gas pedal and dart through the busy Friday night traffic.

"Don't you dare, Krista!" Heidi snaps and grabs for the bottle. Krista dodges her. "You can't touch his germs. You know what he is."

"Names will never hurt me," I say with a smile. I swerve and the girls grab the seats. "Does she always ruin your fun, doll?" I tease.

"No one ruins my fun, especially not my stuffy sister." Krista swigs the liquor. "You're both boxers?" she asks. She offers the bottle to Heidi, who snubs her. "Didn't we see you fighting outside City Hall the other night?" Krista passes the bottle forward to Harry, who accepts.

"We do damage, gloves on or off," I brag. "This is Harry *Dropper*

51

Vines Levine. Madison Square Garden Golden Glove Champ of '36. I'm Yael *Slinger* Newman." I reach back and shake hands with Krista. I swear, electricity races to all parts of me from that hand of hers.

Heidi stares out the window. "Where are we going?" she asks.

"To the edge." I press the gas pedal and the car speeds down the city streets of Newark. I tempt danger because danger keeps me vigilant. Just like boxin'. Reminds me to keep fists up, punches swift, and instincts guarded.

"I'm up for that," Krista says. She leans closer and the wind rushin' through the windows blows her two braids back. "I'm Krista Brecht. And this is my uptight older sister, Heidi." I love the way she says her own name.

Heidi huffs. We laugh and Heidi huffs again.

Harry turns on the radio, and we hear the announcer say, "and now from Frank Dailey's Meadowbrook in the heart of Cedar Grove comes the African tune, 'The Lion Sleeps Tonight.'" Through the speakers, the song blasts, and I sway. "Cedar Grove has an amazing beach," I say. "We're goin' right now!" I floor the accelerator and drive onto the turnpike.

Heidi rolls up the window and pats her bangs down. "Let's get it over with so we can get home where we belong."

"Sounds fun to me," Krista says. "Hey, Harry. Why do they call you Dropper Vines?"

"Got lots of knock outs, ya know," Harry explains. His rigid knuckles wrap around the bottle of whiskey as he returns it to Krista.

"Be honest, buddy," I say. "You fake your name cause your mama would *drop you* for boxin'." I lift my hands off the wheel as I drive. "Did she give you milk and honey before you went out to play tonight?"

Harry doesn't react. He's hard to push over the edge. He maintains this dignity that makes me think he can even stop the wind from blowin'. I have to admit. He's saved my back more than once. We've been friends all our lives and when my folks died, he became family. On the other hand, Harry says I rustle thunderclouds. What the heck does that even mean?

I check Krista through the rearview. "So, what's this summer camp you gals are goin' to?" I ask with a hard blink of my eyes. "Drink up, babe."

"We're attending Camp Siegfried," Heidi says. She leans over and checks herself in the mirror. "It's a German Bund Camp in Long Island. I'll be on staff training our youth."

"A camp with tents and campfires and that marshmallow and chocolate thingamajig?" I ask her.

Heidi snickers. "It's called s'mores. Camp Siegfried is where we learn obligations as American citizens. And also practice our German customs."

"Sounds stressful," Harry says. His deadpan response makes Heidi frown.

"Heidi just wants to go because her boyfriend Frank is going," Krista says and slurps more liquor. Dimples pierce her cheeks.

"Horsefeathers!" Heidi retorts. "I'm preparing for my future. As Führer Kuhn says, camp is where we learn to carry German ideals into America." She wags her finger at Krista. "And remember, your boyfriend, Axel, is going, too."

"I told my father, I'm almost an adult and have no interest playing volleyball and singing German songs all summer," Krista grumbles. "But he says it's our duty. So, we have to go." Her cheeks flush, and she smiles. "And I have to admit. I can't wait to see my five best friends."

YAEL:
Waterfront. Cedar Groves, NJ

The car bumps along the road. I pull up next to the undeveloped waterfront at Cedar Groves. Mission accomplished. Krista's drunk. "C'mon babe. To the water. And grab the bottle." Unlike the madness of Newark, without a lot of honkin' horns in the background, I can actually hear the car radio music as we walk toward the shore.

"Harry, flip the headlights on, will ya?" I yell over my shoulder. Our shoes squeak against the sand. The beam sheds light.

I see Harry open Heidi's door, but she stays glued in the car. From the foamy water's edge, I can hear Heidi goading him. "I can't believe I'm stuck with a Jewish mobster," she says. "My father swears your whole race is criminals. Have you ever killed anyone?"

My ears burn tryin' to hear.

After a dramatic pause, he glances at Heidi. "That's a family secret," he says. He looks over at me. "Yael can be dark, though."

Krista raises her eyebrows. My arms wrap around her, and I bury my head in her neck. She giggles.

Heidi gets out of the car and stretches her neck until she has her eye on us. "What do you mean, dark?" she asks Harry, starin' straight at me.

I give Heidi a show and sway Krista, hummin' the tunes from the radio, warmin' us both up. "My dark quality isn't a color roamin' around inside me," I say to Krista. "It's more of an alchemy that changes color when you shake me up." I curl my lip. "So you shouldn't trifle with me."

"Trifle like this?" She socks my chest with both fists like I'm a speed bag.

I lift her up. "Like revenge shakin' up avenge creates justice."

Krista kicks my legs with her feet, but they slow to a paddle and her arms wrap around my neck.

"Yael's done things that would flip your wig," I hear Harry say. "Our world right now is weak. Yael keeps order. He worships eye for an eye." And then Harry goes for Heidi's jugular. "I hear the Bund has secrets, too. Like oaths to Hitler."

"None of the kind," Heidi answers. "We salute the nation's flag as proud Americans of the White Race."

I'm about to make a big move on Krista when Heidi's silhouette stamps a shape against a burgundy sky. Her right arm extends up with her palm down.

"Is she raisin' a Hitler salute to Harry?" I mumble against Krista's neck. Krista's eyes are closed, takin' me all in.

"That's an American salute?" Harry asks Heidi.

Heidi's image tells me Harry needs me, but my hands gain a mind of their own and glide up Krista's shirt.

"It will be!" Heidi pronounces.

The answer jolts me and makes me suck Krista's skin pretty hard. She jerks away and slaps me. "How dare you!" She dashes toward the car.

The burn on my cheek warms me up as I glide behind her. "Whacha so sore about?" At the car, I shrug my shoulders at Harry.

Heidi flips her wig when she sees Krista's torn neck. "What happened?" Heidi screeches as she rushes into the car. "Take us home now! You're a vampire!"

"What? A vampire?" I bare my teeth and hiss. "I kinda like that. Your little sis was sendin' strong signals. Just tryin' to roll with the punches." Harry and I get into the car.

"At camp, our father says we will meet people like *us*, our equals," Heidi growls. "Not a bunch of … *your* type."

"Blood suckin' vermin?" I finish her thought with a deep, crackly voice.

"Actually, Father wants us Nazified," Krista mumbles. It's clear she's liquored four sheets to the wind.

KRISTA:
Longie's Car. Hawthorne Avenue. Newark, NJ

My head flops onto Heidi's shoulder when Yael whips the car around Clinton Place corner past the dark Hawthorne Avenue three-story apartments. It's so dark because no one can afford to waste electricity in our neighborhood.

My stomach fizzes. I close my eyes. I feel the car slow. "Hey Al, Benny, Abie! Makin' trouble?" Yael yells out the window. I open one eye and see Yael's friends smoking cigars in front of the one and only lit place on the block—the candy store.

As the car rolls, knuckles bang against the metal roof, and I jolt like someone just brought a hammer down on an anvil.

Yael calls over to the others. "Hey, Maxie. Where's Puddy?"

Heidi pushes my head off her shoulder. "Drop us here. Papa will murder us if he catches us with Jews."

Yael pulls the car over. When we get out, the chatter of his rowdy friends pecks at my brain. But that doesn't compare to the silence that explodes in my one hearing eardrum when my boyfriend Axel and his friend Frank appear out of the blackness with their gang. Their uniforms howl action. Everyone freezes.

The calm before the storm doesn't last long. Like gray wolves joining forces, Yael's smaller pack surrounds our German boys. The tension crackles like static electricity from a sock. This town could ignite. I've had too much to drink, but I have to admit, our own boys with their military air might have an edge.

"What are you doing with Jews?" Frank says. He pushes me toward Axel.

"Frank, I swear, it was Krista's idea," Heidi tattles.

Yeah, so what if it was my idea. One thing's for sure. I'll never forget this night.

Axel pinches my chin and inspects my neck. "You are drunk, Krista!" At least he's screaming in my deaf ear, so I can't hear his rubbish, and I don't care if he thinks I'm not ladylike.

I want to tell him he's controlling like my father and he's got another thing coming if he thinks I'm gonna bow to him. But instead, I drawl. "Axel. You *snow* I don't *trink*." The world tips. Then my stomach gurgles and starts heaving all over Axel's uniform.

Axel shoves me into Heidi. "Scram, you drunken whore." He grabs Frank's handkerchief out of his pocket and swats slimy chunks off his uniform.

Heidi drags me from the fuse that's going to blow. From steps away, we watch it unfold like a handkerchief before a sneeze.

Axel squints his eyes at Yael. "Well, lookie here, Frank. If it isn't a Newark Minuteman from the rally the other night."

"You frickin' Nazis!" Yael shouts. Even stone drunk I can see his blood bulge the vein in his neck. Behind him, his men punch their fists into their hands and rock from side to side.

In an empty second, I catch Axel's eyes flick to Frank. Then, I hear the crack before I see it. Yael's chin vaults off Axel's fist.

The dark alchemy Yael was talking about ripples the six-pack under his wet shirt and detonates a chain reaction. As a thunderous sound like aluminum foil covering a Thanksgiving turkey shakes the sky above us, Yael lets loose a barrage of blows that should have knocked Axel, my future sovereign, from here to Weequahic High School.

But, Axel isn't one to stand down. He bends his elbows and blocks Yael's blows. Finding an opening, he clobbers Yael in the face. A part of me feels Yael deserves a few hits from Axel. After all, he shouldn't have run his hand up my blouse.

As if someone higher up is orchestrating this battle, the next clap of thunder signals war between the gangs. I gulp the storm's spicy-sweet down draft as the scene becomes a powder-keg rumble. Rain whips the bodies. The enemy camps don't just want to hurt each other. They want to obliterate each other.

FRITZ KUHN:
German Biergarten. Newark, NJ

"Four liters of beer!" I shout to the German-dressed waitress. Today is Sunday. One of the many days Germans drink. And the best place to drink on Sundays in Newark, New Jersey is the German Biergarten.

"This is what democracy is all about, mein Freunde," I tell Günther and the boys. Along with Axel and Frank, Günther sits with me at the freshly painted patio table. "Sharing tables, talking with our own, eating our food, drinking endless liters of beer." The chill of winter is gone and I feel the future among my many German compatriots. Most are uniformed like us. Others have turned into good ole' Americans hiding behind the American flag. They'll learn!

"This, my boys, is choice," Günther responds. He spreads his arms wide.

The wunderschöne waitress delivers our beer. She's beautiful, but it took her long enough. I lift my stein toward the others and then gulp the beer down before she has time to step away. Tasting the first sip of my favorite drink never gets old. "Another round!" I say to the Fräulein whose Bavarian skirt flips up from a breeze as she walks away.

Frank gulps his beer. "Heidi and Krista barely made it home alive the other night," he says, lifting his eyebrows like a gossiping teenage girl. Clearly, he's itching to pat himself on the back for facing Zwillman's gang. Maybe I should give him a break? Heck! I've been in his shoes before. After the failed coup attempt with Adolph, I remember trying to impress my father. In front of all his friends, he laughed. He said he was not surprised with the fiasco since I had always been a coward—the type of boy who threw snowballs with gloves on.

"What Frank means to report is that these were the same gangsters who wrecked the Bund rally the other night at City Hall," Axel says to cover for his Freund. "They're part of the Zwillman gang who are constantly causing trouble."

"You mean the catastrophe in Union City?" I bob my head. "Now this is interesting news," I say. "I hope the girls lambasted the schlagers for destroying City Hall."

"Yes!" Frank says. "Heidi told them off good. She said they should respect freedom of speech. But Krista's a different story, right Axel?"

Axel grits his teeth. "The scum got her drunk. I'd expect nothing less from these people. Krista knows what she did was wrong. And she's ready to pay back!" Normally the blacks of Axel's eyes are big with excitement. But right now the stony turquoise surrounds a beady black dot in the center. The spot hammers, like a serpent who's ready to pounce. And pounce we will.

The waitress rushes over with our beer so quickly that it splashes in my lap. "Es tut mir Leid, I'm so sorry," she blurts. Finally, she recognizes me. She bows her head. "Oh, forgive me, mein Führer. You are the Führer Kuhn." She shivers like a newborn calf and wipes my pants with her apron. I spread my legs to indulge her.

Her soft flushed cheeks are framed with blonde braids, and when I look into her eyes she knows I will forgive her. "No matter, Fräulein. That's what Biergartens are for." I slide my hand under her ruffled dirnl apron-dress and down her curvy hips. She smiles. "Bring us sandwiches and sauerkraut." I wink at Günther. We will not have to wait very long now.

"How come Zwillman is always one step ahead of us. How does he know so much about our plans?" Frank asks, slurping the rest of his beer.

Finally, a worthwhile question. "I'll tell you. Gangster Abner Longie Zwillman is a criminal. He hobbles knees and cracks knuckles until he gets information. His Murder Inc. runs America like an evil dictatorship. All the while, U.S. government dances for him like a puppet."

Günther chuckles low in his throat. "Three Jews and three Italians keep peace with machine guns and assassinations," he says. Günther's familiar with the Big Six crime syndicate that props up America—Zwillman, Bugsy Siegel, Meyer Lansky, Lucky Luciano, Joey Adonis and Frank Costello. No wonder the country is in shambles.

I clack my empty stein on the table. "Zwillman smuggled in half the country's illegal alcohol during the Prohibition from right here in the bay," I say. "In fact, they call Zwillman the Capone of New Jersey." Zwillman probably considers it a compliment. Can't blame him too much for that, though. After all, I swell with pride when they call me the American Hitler.

"While good Americans like us grow hungry, they bring in millions from gambling, prostitution, dirty money washed through clubs, and labor union rackets," Günther says.

"And the cops just let it slide?" asks Axel, astonishment in the rise of his voice.

"The rat coined the word *payoff* in Newark. He controls cops all the way up to the judges," Günther says. "He puts mayors and attorney generals in office.

"I get it. And now he's using his connections to disrupt our rallies and uncover our secrets," Axel says as he extends his lower jaw toward Frank.

A fascist government would never allow criminals to run a country. Yet in America, they bankroll them. "Is this democracy?" I ask, scanning everyone's eyes for an answer. I get nothing. "I want a plan to stop this slimy man's conspiracy to bring down America!" I yell.

My skin broils when I consider Zwillman's threat to this country. I want to cut the head off this dragon. The bastard is worshipped like some Robin Hood hero. But face it. He's a flachwichser, just a corrupt scumbag and destroyer of everything American! Then, like vinegar clearing filth from a pipe, the rush clears my mind. I have an idea to discuss later with Günther.

Thankfully, my blood pressure decreases as soon as I see our lovely waitress sprinting toward us with our feast! After lunch, she will get to escort me to the officers' toilette. Letting her entertain me will help give her a sense of duty that all our women crave. My eyes wash over her body like soap. I breathe in the spring air mixed with the cheesy smell of sauerkraut. The band in their lederhosen shorts and suspenders returns me to the Fatherland. I know this song will be stuck in my head now for days.

CHAPTER 5

The Challenger

KRISTA:
Newark Bund Headquarters. Nye Avenue. Newark, NJ

A spring breeze wisps the back of my neck when my father and stepmother rush into Führer Kuhn's Nye Avenue headquarters. But it doesn't relieve the stuffiness in the room.

Führer Kuhn flashes the whites of his eyes from behind his desk. Is that a cold vapor from his breath? He isn't pleased that my parents are late.

Next to me, Axel shoves his seat back from the front of the Führer's massive mahogany desk. He stands to greet my parents. I shadow Axel with a little less enthusiasm. From the couch across the room flanked by the crisp swastika flag and a faded American one, Frank and Heidi follow suit and rise.

"Ich entschuldige miche," my father apologizes to Führer Kuhn. He reverts to German when he's nervous.

"It's all my fault, Fritz," Wilhelmina says and clasps her hands. "To keep a man of your status waiting just because I could not find my glasses is unforgivable," she fawns. Papa scowls and prods her toward a chair near the couch that Frank and Heidi have claimed.

"Everyone sit! Let's get down to business!" the Führer commands.

Papa stays standing. The Führer blinks at him, signaling him to begin. My father crosses his arms. "Führer Kuhn has decided to silence Longie Zwillman's gang once and for all," he says. Sounds of approval hum through the room.

"Krista. I hear you have breached their inner circle," Führer Kuhn says. He rolls a pencil between his thumb and finger and stands. "Sounds like you have this young Minuteman in the palm of your hands, mein Liebling." He walks around the front of his desk and leans against it, just inches from me.

My jaw drops. Am I in a cesspool of gossip? What does this have to do with me? The hairs on my arms stand up. I glance at Heidi. Her eyes jab me like a wire coat hanger breaching a door lock. My throat tightens.

My father circles like a shark after blood. "From what we hear, you have made the rat hungry," my father says. "Now, you will tempt him across hot embers. His blisters will puss and fester. And when his flesh is raw, we will hang the carcasses of Yael and his Minutemen like hogs on a meat hook for butchering. Zwillman will know our power."

"What are you talking about?" I ask. They sound like wild animals and are taking this cat and fish business to a bloodthirsty level I'm not sure I'm up for.

"You will do whatever it takes," Axel says in the steely tone of a good soldier. He's a model Nazi with his tight, side-fade haircut. He has no agenda in patronizing Führer Kuhn other than his own extreme devotion to the cause. His obsession chafes me. And the sacrifice he's asking for sends shockwaves through me.

I open my mouth to protest. "What the—"

"No backtalk!" my father bellows. As always, my father expects me to follow orders and fall in line. Before today, I never really understood what Papa meant when he said that Führer Hitler is giving Germans their identity back after the Great War took it away. Now I glimpse his desperation.

"Halt die Klappe!" Führer Kuhn screams for everyone to quiet. He stiffens and points toward the door. "Everyone out! Except Krista. I want to speak with her alone."

Axel examines me like a bug under glass. Am I his to command? Or is he to be commanded? There's no question. He obeys and the others follow.

My wrists pulse. I've never felt so gagged in my life. As everyone clears the room, I gaze up from my seat at the giant portrait of Hitler behind Führer Kuhn's massive mahogany desk. It takes me off guard. When my eyes connect with his, they ease my fears.

"He inspires you to lead, doesn't he, Krista?" Führer Kuhn says. He twists to admire the image. "Look at his open arms." He points up at the image. "He's inviting all German blood around the globe to erase borders. I know this man. He wants harmony."

I realize that all Germans are going through the nightmare of today's oppression. Papa has told us that Germans aren't accepted as guests of this country. This irks me. I feel American as any of my friends born here. Führer Kuhn is saying that Hitler bonds us.

I maneuver behind the desk just inches from the oil painting. My braids bounce against my spine when I crook my neck up. I can almost hear that scratchy, fretful voice over the radio promising prosperity. Against my better judgment, I catch the fever of the appeal. "It's as if he's reading my innermost thoughts," I say. "How does he do it? How does Führer Hitler understand what we need?"

Like an unexpected serpent, Führer Kuhn is at my side. I flinch. Our eyes unite, and it feels like the beginning of a song we will sing together. I almost feel like this man will die for me.

"He is us." The Führer's voice drones. "He agrees with our pleas to raise Germany from the ashes. He agrees with our desire to eliminate our enemy." The pencil he's been stroking clacks against the floor. He reaches down to retrieve it.

In this moment, my mind blinks like the flash of a camera and breaks the spell. Is Führer Hitler shaping the truth? Or is his truth shaping me?

My thoughts jerk like a live wire. I reconcile everything I know. On one hand, Hitler promises to raise Germany from the ashes. My father has said that often enough. There are promises of good food for everyone, lights for homes, care for the sick. But Hitler asks for sacrifice. We must work where he tells us to, eat what he wants us to, use words he expects us to. And we must not do certain things. Like read certain books or have certain friends. If we don't do as he says, we are selfish. Maybe that's right for Germany, I'm not sure. He promises he will eliminate the enemy who caused the problems. But in the same breath, he vows to destroy them no matter what it takes. Are these our ideas? Or are they his?

"Hitler is a humble man who just wants to improve life for his fellow man," Führer Kuhn says. After all, he's put everyone to work and given everyone health care and schooling. That's more than Roosevelt's done." Führer Kuhn crosses his hands behind his back. "Now Krista, we can do the same thing here. We can stop the rich from getting richer. We can stop tax deals that burn holes in our pockets. You can join me near the top. You can be one of the founders of a new America, a nation who puts ourselves first."

This all sounds nice. But I know that words can be tricky. Apples are red, right? Not always. Apples can be green, too. He's making the answer seem so simple. With Führer Kuhn, there's more going on than meets the eye. Or maybe I'm just opening my eyes? The floor creaks as I step back. He's not just an ambassador of German culture. He wants to be Adolph Hitler in America. My chest rumbles.

LONGIE ZWILLMAN:
Barbershop. Hawthorne Avenue. Newark, NJ

Irving snaps a white sheet over me. I close my eyes and relax in the leather-upholstered chair to get a haircut and a shave at his barbershop on Hawthorne Avenue. The spring air blows through the propped open front door and wafts around the scent of cherry and butternut pipe smoke mixed with hair tonic. Yael should be joining me any second.

The other two oak chairs are occupied with men waiting for their turn. In other seats around the shop, men read the paper and drink coffee. Everyone's talking about something. I hear bits of news about the Yankees, a new type of pen they call a ballpoint, unemployment creepin' back up to nineteen percent, the new *Snow White* film that's made upwards of $8 million, Howard Hughes piloting around the world in record time, some secret Orson Welles project, and of course all the talk about Hitler building Germany.

As Irving wraps a hot towel around my face. I sink into my seat. "Hey, Irving. FBI Director Hoover thanks you for your horse yesterday." I tell the barber. "How did ya pick longshot Lawrin to win the race?"

"I didn't pick the horse," Irving replies. "I bet on that new jockey, Eddie Arcaro. He's gonna be a great." Irving massages my face with a lemony cream.

"I'm saving my dimes for Seabiscuit to beat War Admiral at Pimlico," I tell him.

Irving's always got an opinion. "I don't know, Longie," he says. "With his jockey Red hurt, I'm not betting Seabiscuit is making the Belmont and probably not Pimlico."

Irving wraps more hot towels and I'm floatin' on a cloud. I swear, I get more sleep here than in my own bed. "We've got a few months yet," I mumble.

"That boy's not gonna race again," he argues. "His chest is caved in from that horse falling on him." Irving removes the towels, and this time, he massages my face with cocoa butter. Smells like melted Hersheys. Then he works up the hot lather and scrapes my beard with a single sharp blade razor. "But if Red can get back in the saddle and boil Seabiscuit's juices outta the gate, he might take the win."

A man with a knife at my neck talking about cutthroat wins makes me feel alive. And it's at that moment, I hear a fiery conversation through the open door.

YAEL:
Outside Barbershop. Hawthorne Avenue. Newark, NJ

I stop on the sidewalk next to the red, white, and blue pole in front of Irving's Barbershop. I've been coming here ever since Pop overruled Mama and had my curls cut when I was three. I still remember when I asked my father why the pole was the same color as the American flag. I thought he was pullin' my leg at the time, but turns out his fable was true. He told me in the times of knights and armor, barbers were like doctors. The red color was for bloodletting; the white for bandages, bones, and teeth; the blue for blood in the veins. Pop's dream was to be a doctor.

Now all I see through the propped wood and glass door is men socializing while they get a shave and a haircut for thirty-five cents. I smile. It's a lifestyle. I see Longie spread out on his favorite leather chair in the back with a hot towel over his face. He's expecting me.

"You got messed up last night," an oddly familiar female voice rings out from behind me right before I enter.

I stop short. "Who the heck?" Turnin', I recognize my stalker, Krista, the blonde pigtailed Nazi. I'm suddenly a mess of conflicting emotions—angry, curious, and attracted. I squint my bruised eye. "Hah! I think we did your Hitler boyfriend up pretty good."

"You know you're a Jew," Krista says. She moves with flair, an expectation that both intrigues and annoys me.

"Sugar! Thought I tricked ya. Now I get why you fascists are tryin' to loop a rope around my neck." My banter triggers a traumatic memory from five years ago. *Men pull my father's body from the cold harbor, his body slaps the wharf, a rope is looped around his bloated neck. The fishy ammonia smell chews my lungs. Longie crouches down and examines Pop's body. He slips my father's watch off his wrist. "It stopped just after six, at 6:11," he says.* A gunshot pain shoots through my gut. The dang noose choked out Pop's last breath, put my mother in her dark grave, and punched out my light for years. This girl has no idea.

Krista reaches in her handbag for a stick of Wrigley's peppermint gum. She must see my stricken look. "Look," she says. "I just mean, that's why they were angry. We're not supposed to hang around your type." She offers me gum, the new secret, as the ad says, to stayin' young. I brush it and the superficiality of it away.

"Yeah, I've heard about your kind, too. You wanna rule the world and ship us bloodsucking rats back to Europe on leaky boats." I cut the air with my fist.

"Gosh. I'm sorry I upset you." Krista seems worried.

"Upset? Upset would mean I care. Du kanst nicht oif meinem fus pishen und mir sagen klass es regen ist."

"Hmm." Krista scrunches her forehead. "In German, that means 'Don't tell me it's raining?'"

"You're smart for a German Fraw-line. In Yiddish, it means don't pee on my foot and tell me it's rainin'." I snicker. "In other words, don't give me a bunch of hogwash."

"I didn't mean. Geez Louise." Krista's blue eyes implode. She darts off down the street like a kitten escaping a snarling dog."

I'm torn. On one hand this female distraction gets in my way. On the other, with a little eye contact, the business from last night could be rekindled. My broodin' eyes follow her every step. After all, she tracked me down today. She'll put out with one more dose of charm. Who cares if her father's a fascist? I jog down the block to her and tap on her shoulder. "Listen. I know I'm taboo."

"No." Krista spins around. "You don't get it. My family is German-American Nazi Bund. We aren't about branding people as taboo. We're victims who fight our enemies and then become American heroes."

"And hang us Jews from flagpoles under the swastika?" I can't help but mock her.

She shakes her head. "I don't need to explain this to you."

"Then why the heck are you standin' here? Don't you have books to burn?"

Krista slaps me. Without a look, she rushes away.

I smile and call after her. "This is beginning to become a habit." I backtrack to the barbershop and join Longie for a haircut.

KRISTA:
Fritz Kuhn's Car. Hawthorne Avenue. Newark, NJ

Through one hearing ear, I catch the muted screech before the fender knocks my hips. The car throws me on the hood and swings my handbag around my wrist. My chewing gum shoots down my throat and gags me. I cough it out into my hand.

Heidi stretches her head out the rear window. "Krista, what in tarnation are you doing?" she calls.

"What am I doing? Obviously, I was trying to get run over!" My mind is elsewhere. That dang Minuteman pulled the rug right out from under me. I don't care if I'm just using him for information. He's an idiot.

Through the windshield, Führer Kuhn and his driver gape at me. Then the Führer leans out his window. "Krista, dear," he says. "Thank goodness you are OK." He opens his door and helps me roll off the car. Well, at least he cares. He wraps his arm around my shoulders and supports me into the back seat next to Heidi before he returns to the front.

"Good timing, Krista!" he says as if this chance meet was planned. "We are meeting your father at the Nye Avenue office. Driver, Gehen!" The wind from his open window stings my scraped skin. He twists his neck and winks at Heidi. "Your sister has been working for me all day in the Manhattan office."

"Did you meet with that conniving Minuteman?" Heidi asks me and brushes off my dress. "We must all do our part."

I ignore her and rustle through my bag looking for nothing. The image of Yael's angular face, his athletic body and wide shoulders is etched in my mind, uninvited. Who the devil does he think he is?

"Krista answer me!" Heidi shouts.

My hand covers my good ear. "Oh sorry, I didn't hear you." My deafness is a convenient excuse.

"Tell us, my Fräulein," Führer Kuhn asks as he eyes me in the rearview mirror. "What news do you have?" He combs his eyebrows with his finger like my father does.

"He doesn't trust me," I say. A rift churns inside my hollow chest. As a Nazi German, there's a clash between who I really am on the inside and what I'm expected to prove on the outside.

"You failed!" Heidi's face twists into a scowl. "You can't even tempt a man."

"Heidi. I tried. What do you want from me?" I did try. A large part of me is an obedient soldier who craves support from my sister and my Führer.

"I'm trying to wake you," Heidi says. "When you were a baby, you wouldn't stop crying. Once, I covered your mouth. Right before you crumpled, I let you breathe. Again, I'm trying to wake you up." She cups my chin. "Because I love you."

"That's noble of you, Heidi." Führer Kuhn compliments her. Whose side is he on? "Krista, your sister is right. You have everything you need to trap this rat. Lure him in with your charm. Use it, my Fräulein. Let's keep those knees marching."

"Better yet, lil sis," Heidi whispers so Führer Kuhn can't hear. "Keep those knees spreading. For our Führer." She's ruthless.

None of this seems just, but everyone I trust is telling me it is. Maybe they're right.

LONGIE ZWILLMAN:
Yael's Apt. Hawthorne Avenue. Newark, NJ

When I enter Yael's third-floor apartment above Cohen's Deli, Baby Abner is asleep. But not for long. I pick him up. The baby's chubby legs kick and arms stretch out until I bundle him tight. His parents, Dov and

Linda, ignore me. They should. I'm family. After Yael's parents died, I paid rent for Yael and his two older brothers, Dov and Marty. Harry's mother, Lena, agreed to take care of them. Yael's oldest brother Marty and his wife Minnie live here, too. But last month, they visited Berlin. Bad decision. Now, we're trying to get 'em home.

Abner squawks, so I bounce him next to the open window in Dov's bedroom. A heaven-sent breeze sends his eyes fluttering and he forgets his problems. Down below is the Big Yard, the empty parking area behind the four-story apartments where the neighborhood congregates and dozens of kids play stickball and hopscotch. Abner gurgles at me, and I chat to my boy from the future generation. "The Big Yard isn't just any yard," I say. "Over there, see?" I raise him up. "In the Northeast quadrant, the Italians huddle. Across from them, on the west, the Irish Catholics scuffle. The Germans play ball on the southwest. Everyone has their special place." I couch the baby in my chest. "Along the southeast wall, that's where we hang out, the Jews." I smell his baby hair. "For us, there are no strangers. We all keep an eye on each other." Lil' Abner lets out a squeal that's pure joy, free of hurt. Let's keep it that way.

"Hey hey! There's Uncle Yael down there taking photos with that camera I got him."

YAEL:
Big Yard. Hawthorne Avenue. Newark, NJ

I lean against a wall in the *Big Yard* behind my apartment building and peer through the viewfinder of my new camera that Longie got me. I'm still learnin' how to use it. The focus is tricky, even with the rangefinder that merges the image together. *Click.* I snap a girl grabbin' a bouncin' rubber ball and scoopin' up six-prong jacks. I shift, aim, and focus the camera. *Click.* I shoot two kids kicking a dented can. When I take photos, it's like I'm crawlin' inside the box to another world—a place without sound or touch, only sight. I want to teach myself how to focus in and see beyond my eyes and capture moments before they disappear.

Uh oh. Did hades freeze over? Through the sighting, down the aiming point, across the yard, through a whippin' jump rope, I view the American Nazi girl, Krista. She's sittin' on a cement block, readin' a book. She sucks on the end of one of her flaxen braids. I groan. She's probably readin' some foul brainwashing propaganda. Hmm. The light will never hit her face like this again. I can't help myself. My finger pushes the shutter button. *Click.*

Across the yard, back through the whippin' rope, she glowers my way. Shoot, I'm caught red-handed. Some sixth sense must have warned her. She scans the playground, eyes dartin', suspicious for spies. Guilt forces me to slip the camera into my pocket. Krista gets up, brushes off her skirt, and weaves around the jumpers. Her body corners me.

I glance at a book in her hand. The edges are frayed. Did she drop it in a fire? I raise my fists to protect. "You're not comin' back for another round are ya?" For the first time, I'm close enough to read the title—*Emil und die Detektive.* That takes me off guard. She couldn't have chosen a more innocent story, one about a boy savin' his town.

Krista doesn't smile. "I'm not sorry I hit you." She slips the ragged book in her bag. "You deserved it. I was trying to explain our way. How the Bund believes we're saving America."

"Your way uses our flag to clean toilets and claims that's patriotic because you make 'em shine." I spit and the breeze almost blows it on some kids runnin' past.

Krista shutters. "You don't get it."

"What is there to get? C'mon," I say. "The Nazi Bund American patriotism thing, or whatever you call yourselves, brays like a fascist jack—."

"You only hear what you want. The truth depends on whose boots you walk in," Krista says. "And by the way, I walk in my own."

Time for a diversion. "Am I hearin' clues that maybe you don't care what others think? Or am I deaf?" I ask from behind my proverbial gloves.

Krista's playin' some form of Swastika poker, and heck, I'm pretty good at games.

"Careful, is that your sensitive side showing?" Krista asks.

She's playin' with fire. My burnin' eyes escape her glare and move to less explosive thoughts. Around us, the yard is alive. Everyone's movin' to their own beat. "When I was young, I loved spring in the Big Yard," I say to her. "It meant my ma wouldn't yell down at me from our apartment up there for not wearin' a jacket." I pick up a water hose meant for cleanin' the cement field and turn on the spigot. I let cold water gush between my lips. I offer the flowin' water to Krista. She opens her mouth and draws in a mouthful.

Krista scopes the yard. "My father brought us here, too. My sister and I shared one pair of roller skates." She shrugs. "I still come here to read. I guess I have a soft spot for the place."

We walk to the chalked hopscotch lines. "What's your pop's story?" I scoop up an oval stone. The smooth indentation carved from generations of runnin' water draws my finger and thumb like a magnet.

"After my mother died during my birth, my father joined Germany's Friekorps and bragged he beat the brains out of Marxist Jews with Hitler."

"At least you're authentic then," I say. "Made in Nazi, Germany."

She ignores me. "Back in the Fatherland, my father hid guns and a radio in our basement. Once, he caught me watching him send messages from behind some boxes. He grabbed me by the throat and shouted, 'Verräter-Spion!' It means traitor and spy. Then he fired his machine gun next to my ear." She raises a palm to that ear and rubs it, as if she can still feel the pain. "He pushed the muzzle against my head and told me never to spy on him again. I followed orders and was his good Nazi so he would love me."

I picture her eardrum vibrating against the clamor until it rips apart and dribbles blood, electrical impulses sprayin' her brain like shotgun pellets until her fragile body swallows the slivers. "That's one way to discipline," I say. I envision the shards inside her clankin' like ice cubes against glass. "I bet you didn't cry." I imagine her grittin' her teeth to make her father proud.

She stares at me. "He never could," she says. "Love me that is. I'm deaf in this ear." She shrugs. "Then we came to America when I was twelve."

"Why leave?" I ask. "The Nazis finally came to power. Wait. You said ya lost your mother?"

"Adolph Hitler ordered us to America. I never actually knew my mother. I never knew Hitler either but feels like I did."

"Your father blamed ya for your mother's death?"

"No." Krista pulls me in with her marble green eyes. They brim with clear emotion yet are inscrutable. "He didn't believe I was his real daughter."

"Hmm. Another man's child." With a one-two-one punch, I give her my story. "My pop died. You remember hopscotch? Murdered."

"What?" Krista does a double take.

"Do you remember hopscotch rules?" I ask.

"You said murdered. Your father."

"Yeah. Killed by one of yours. Hung by a rope for some booze." My eyes dart to avoid hers. She doesn't say anything. I guess I've finally shocked her into silence.

I hand her the smooth stone. "I'll get my revenge." I lean back against the wall, restin' the sole of my shoe against it. A big brick slides sideways and clunks to the ground. "Sugar!" I bend down and restore it best I can. "Let's see what ya got." My head nods toward the court of numbered squares.

Krista lobs the lucky stone into the first space and it lands without slidin'. She glares. She hops over the stone on one foot and continues through the course.

"So, why's your pop a Hitler-lover?" I ask

Krista returns toward me. "Hitler's our God, saving Germany," Krista says as she scoops up the stone. From her relaxed cheeks, I think she believes what she's sayin'.

73

"Yeah, he's a God as long as you have gold Aryan blood. Not brown rotten blood of the greedy Jews like me."

"It's what my father says, that Jewish parasite blood torments us, like fleas. So, we have to eliminate it." She lobs the stone to me. "Your turn."

My hand snatches it from the air. "Sounds efficient," I say. "Maybe just gas all the parasites at once, huh? Bring the world salvation with a seventh day to rest?"

Nearby, cheers snag our attention. A red-haired, freckled kid straddles a wiry one pinned against the ground. Red pummels his fists against the smaller boy's face. I plunge the stone into my pocket and dash toward the ruckus. "Hey! Hey!" I yell, yankin' the older boy off by his collar. When the victim scuffles up, dust coats my mouth.

"He started it," the older one says, fists clenched. "Just pushed me for no reason."

"He called my pop a dirty Jew," the cherry-faced younger boy shouts. He whips his arms at the older boy. I grab him. The kid has an inner toughness that makes his knobby body much nobler than it is. He jogs a buried memory inside me: *They called my father a mokey, a plague,* my *much younger self tells Longie. "I'm so angry. Will it go away?" Longie hands me boxin' gloves. "It's my job to protect you, kid. You're gonna learn to fight." But Longie doesn't make it easy, and he makes me fight Nat. Nat clobbers me. I get mad and complain to Longie. Longie just tells me that no one's gonna box me nice and neat in the ring.* Longie taught me to hold fear long enough to be brave.

I place my hands on this young kid's shoulders and walk him away from his tormentors. "Come down to the Y," I say. I'll teach ya how to box, turn ya into a mauler." The boy wipes his slimy face with the back of his dirty hand. "Tomorrow," I insist. "Right after school."

The boy's jaws bulge, and he suddenly seems older. He nods and runs off.

Why are you so dedicated to boxing?" Krista asks with a new curiosity, like a fish who discovers water when he loses his fins.

74

I swack the dust off my khakis. "It's money. A livin'. No school's gonna accept the kid of a Russian Jew. I push up my sleeve and flex. "Most important. Makes me ripped." I smirk.

Krista right crosses my weak side. "So, when do I get a lesson?"

"Come on down to the Y on High anytime. I'm at your service."

"I'm going to take you up on that," Krista dares. Her vow gives me a kick.

We walk toward a group of kids playin' stickball. Then, something seems to break in Krista. She stops and grabs my arm. Makes me face her. "I don't agree with him. My father. He's ignorant."

I swerve from her grip. "Hey, kid!" I call to the guy playin' stickball. "Let me borrow your bat." I flip the bat so it buzz-saws through the air. A bunch of kids stare, slack jawed.

Krista pursues me. "I don't hate people just because they're different from me," Krista persists. "Do you believe me?"

I point to the left wall. A boy pitches my way. I swing, make contact, and watch the ball soar out of the Big Yard. "Whatever you say." Dirt, unearthed from a sudden gust, scratches my eye. The pain reminds me not to let my guard down, no matter how innocuous the enemy seems.

CHAPTER 6

Fancy Footwork

KRISTA:
Krista's Apt. Nye Avenue. Newark, NJ

Heidi and I dust the posters of yellow-haired Germans hanging on the walls of our cramped second-floor apartment above the Nye Avenue bakery. Papa wings threats at us. "I vill koche das haar aus deinem körper!" He thunders the less than lovely phrase that means he'll boil the hair off our bodies if we spoil the dinner with Führer Kuhn. I tamp down my angst at him and bury the dread of my engagement celebration.

In a perverted way, Papa believes joining me with Axel will make me happy, even though we both know this is all about lining his own pockets. Sure, I have always dreamt about marrying someone who is strong and ambitious like Axel. But in my version, I get to choose. Who knows? Maybe Axel is fine. But I barely know him. Right now he's just a cardboard cut-out who hasn't even told me his favorite dessert or radio show.

Heidi straightens the picture of Adolph Hitler that hangs over our fireplace. It is flanked by an American flag on one side and Nazi flag on the other. Before she lets go of the frame, my father yells out with endearment. "Perfect, Schätzchen!" He makes her smile and that makes me happy, because I do love her.

I get a chance to catch my breath when Papa scurries to adjust the minute hand on the fireplace mantel clock to match his pocket watch. But only for a second, because he bangs the utensils down on the table and shouts. "My face should shine in the silverware!" Before I know it, the sun is setting. Führer Kuhn will be arriving any minute.

Once Führer Kuhn arrives, our house reels like a circus. Two uniformed stormtroopers guard our front door like German SS. At the head of the table, Führer Kuhn rests his elbows on the white embroidered tablecloth. Two other Troopers scurry back and forth bringing him papers, handing him messages, dabbing his sweaty brow, and replenishing his wine glass. I'm waiting for them to tie his shoes. The martial presence of the Reich-uniformed men and dressed up women cast a pall on our provincial Bavarian setting like a bizarre storm on a cloudless day. But the sweet scent of onion and bacon relieves me like a thunderstorm in July.

Führer Kuhn chats to my father across the formal set table. Papa's hefty body rests above his spot like the old Berlin Reich Chancellery. My father once told me that even Hitler didn't feel the boxy hunk of cement was suitable for a soap factory.

The Führer leans to his right and asks Axel a question. Even though I'm just on the other side of Axel, I can't really hear them and don't really care. I can't say the same for Heidi. Across from me, she leans over Frank. I drift away from the contrived pomp and circumstance and ignore the natter.

Wilhelmina appears with plates of steaming meat and potatoes. She places them on the table next to bowls of kraut and mash. Then she scuttles to the open seat between Papa and Heidi.

I clink my stainless-steel fork against the bone china plate. My one-sided deafness mutes the screech of metal against china, but the earsplitting sound makes everyone else cringe. Führer Kuhn inhales sharply.

"Careful Krista," my father says. "That's your grandmother's china from Germany." His sternness chills the air, and he knows it. He straightens. "Führer Kuhn, we're honored to host you in our home," he says. My father's gentle fawning of our honored guest is nauseating. But Führer Kuhn calms me with a wink. I guess being the Führer's golden ticket has some upside. I tap the china a little lighter.

Führer Kuhn raises his glass. "A toast to Axel and Krista, the blood of German youth."

"We are proud to call Axel, die Familie. He honors us!" Papa heaves his glass. "To Axel and Krista!"

Axel beams. Around the table, full glasses swing in the air. Axel's blond straight bangs wag across his face. His eyes stop on me. Uh oh. Is my dress unbuttoned? Heidi hisses and stares at my glass. It's still flat against the tablecloth. My throat tightens. I whisk my glass and lift it with the others. "I'm honored," I stammer.

The group toasts. "Prost! Heil Hitler!" We engage in the ritual of honor and goodwill. Rooted in concerns about poisoning, we clink the glasses and force the drinks to spill over into each other's cups in the traditional nod to trust.

"Axel. I hear it's official," Führer Kuhn says. "Your native lands are returned to your family, ya?"

"Yes, mein Führer," he says. "I received a telegram today from my father in Berlin." I watch Axel's Adam's apple bob up and down like a chunk of meat stuck in his throat.

Wilhelmina passes the plate of sausages to Heidi who in turn passes it to Frank. Frank holds the plate for Führer Kuhn so the Führer can fork his food. "Everything is perfect for you, Axel. Herzliche Glückwünsche!" Frank says in a tinny quality that reveals his envy.

"Danke. We will live nicely in Berlin," he says and tips his glass toward me without a glance. I don't think Frank's sarcasm breaches Axel's honor.

"You will be missed by your mother, though, ya?" Frank forks two sausages and passes the plate. He then continues protocol and holds the plates of cabbage and potatoes for Führer Kuhn.

Axel smiles. "My mother's on probation for helping people she shouldn't. She will house German spies. She won't have time to think about me." I can't tell if my stomach clenches more from his hubris or his selflessness. He acts so superior. Did he report his own mother? More and more, he draws a line between himself and anyone different. This attitude has its upsides. Axel says life in the Nazi party is comfortable. But it all seems so hypocritical. People can't be what they want. "In fact, she told me your kin from Germany will be stopping there for a few nights," Axel adds.

"Yes, this is my nephew," Papa says. I have never met him, but he's supposed to be a fine boy. Unfortunately, he will be busy training a few hours away so we may not see him until the end of summer."

"Axel, I have something for your mother," Führer Kuhn says. The guard hands the Führer a small paper book. "The code book for authenticating guests. We must be so careful these days." The Führer hands it to Axel who nods his thanks.

"I have a package for you too, mein Junge." My father hands Axel a brown paper wrapped gift.

Axel unwraps it. He holds up a copy of Hitler's *Mein Kampf*. His audience hums *oohs* and *aahs*. Hitler now requires ownership of our bible before a marriage is certified.

"Danke, Herr Brecht. I'm pleased to acquire your daughter and to be your liaison in Germany." Axel arcs my hair behind my ear. The whiff of his American Old Spice aftershave from his German neck makes me queasy. Axel's a nice enough guy and I like him even though he's a few years older. He's polite and sociable. But he's been dumped on me. I've been assigned a husband even before I finish high school. Worse, moving back to Berlin, away from everyone I know, is impossible to process. I can't imagine not being in America.

My father plugs his napkin into his shirt collar just under his double chin. "Hopefully, we will join Axel in the Homeland soon," Papa says. He hates his role in America. He craves the military life rising in Germany. He pines for the respect he would receive there as a high-level officer. While the Nazi army in America is on the rise, it's still as my father puts it, *in seine Stiefel passen,* or fitting into its boots.

Führer Kuhn signals permission to begin the meal. "Guten appetit!" He uses his fork in the left hand, as does Papa, without letting it travel to the right like Americans. "Günther, mein Freund, how did you steal the top-secret American Air Force bombsight prints from your factory?"

Wilhelmina gives Papa an adoring look. "Er ist unser Held." She pines him like a hero and slurps a soggy cabbage leaf at the same time.

Papa swallows the mélange of food he just stuffed into his mouth. "Ironic story," he says. "The master project was divided like a puzzle. No one person had the whole design. Each night, my job was to collect everyone's pieces for safe keeping. I simply used my handy-dandy micro-camera and taped together the master plan."

"The factory just cut everyone's pay in half," Wilhelmina says. "But my sweet Günther invested our ten-thousand-dollar reward from the Reich into a new Berlin home." This is the first I've heard of my father planting roots back in Germany. I thought we could barely afford our apartment here.

"And sneaking the plans out in an umbrella shows what a brilliant spymaster you are," Axel says. He jabs his fork at Papa like he's dotting a perfect row of *i*'s.

"We've also ordered our factory men to slow the armory assembly line production," my father says. "By the time the Americans make their bombs, German pilots will be hitting pickles in their barrels." He inhales the pungent vinegar of his own pickle, munches the green delicacy, and releases a belly laugh that would make a baby jealous.

"It's just the tip of des Eisbergs," Führer Kuhn brags. "Intel is flowing through all our pipelines. I must admit, our growing power sends voltage through my loins." He claps his thighs.

I snatch my napkin and cover a cough. Axel rubs my back. Heidi, like a dutiful sister, hands me another napkin. Enough is enough. The image of a sexed-up Führer Kuhn is revolting.

Perhaps this is even too much for my father, for Papa changes the subject. "Our peace-loving Führer Hitler is doing good things in Germany, ya?"

"Yes, Herr Brecht. Germany is thriving," Frank says. He carves his sausage into mini slices and chews each one.

"Wilhelmina!" Papa calls. "Ask the boys if they want more." He rubs his own belly and eyes the bowl of baked blood. "Pass the Gebackenes Blut."

"More anyone?" Wilhelmina holds up the dish of chunky potatoes in one hand and passes the crispy brown pig's blood to her husband with the other.

"Yes, more potatoes for us," Axel says. He takes the bowl and scoops some on his plate, then mine. Guess I might as well get used to him making all the decisions.

At least I feel I have a voice with Führer Kuhn. Tonight, I do not hold back. "Why do you think Hitler's Germany is good, mein Führer?" I ask. "Pass a hotdog, Frank."

"They are called Frankfurters!" My father scolds me. I can tell the way he juts is jaw to the side that he's not happy with my question.

Frank holds the plate of frankfurters across the table for me to fork. "Thanks for the frank, Frank." I smile at my unruliness.

Führer Kuhn folds his hands, rests them on the table, and leans forward. "As you know, meine Liebste, Hitler took back Germany from the crooked Commies and Jews," he says like he's telling me a bedtime story. "He put Germans back in the driver's seat. He cares deeply about all people and is helping us fight evil. Brick by brick, he's putting our home together again. But even stronger this time." Even though he's talking down to me, he's stealing the father figure role from Papa. From under the table, I hear the bouncing of my own father's knee.

"He gives us pride, mein Führer," Heidi comments before I can respond.

Her eyes watch me squash the mealy potatoes through my fork. She knows I'm not done. "But Hitler is arming for war with his great army and weapons," I say. Assaulting the vegetable's fleshy tenderness gives me courage.

"Quite the contrary, mein Liebste," Kuhn says. "Hitler is rearming for peace, not war." Words come out of his mouth, but they don't make sense. "He's giving Germans land to thrive," he adds.

"And Führer Kuhn is his right arm in America," my father says. Papa rests his heavy fists on the table. "He's uniting Hitlerism with the lands of America." He forces a moment of silence.

Heidi quashes the pause. "Just as you always say, Führer Kuhn," she rants in cheerleader style. "The German-American Nazi Bund will save America!" Geez Louise. I can't stand her apple-polishing. But that's not all she has to say. "And Axel will connect our youth with the Fatherland," she adds. How does Heidi know what Axel will do? She sees my mouth drop. A smile plays on her lips. She's so proud of herself. Even with my new life galloping out the door, she still holds the reins.

"It's true. I've been charged with uniting American and German youth," Axel says. His fists don't pound his chest right here at the table, but it sure seems like they do. It's getting harder to enjoy my dinner.

Führer Kuhn's hands are now crossed across his chest. He tilts back in his chair and examines the room like a chess player deciding on his next move. He uprights his chair. "Frank. Why not work for Axel in Berlin?" he says. "You can kill two flies with one swatter and fulfill your German military service."

A hunk of Frank's cabbage slides off his fork and into his lap. He scrubs his soggy pants with a napkin. "Work for Axel?" Frank mutters.

"Did you register yet, Herr Schenk?" the Führer asks." We've sent a million military forms to German-Americans and have only received 80,000 back."

"Of course, mein Führer," Frank answers. Bubbles of sweat appear on his forehead.

"Show your father you're going to do more than shine shoes on some corner like him," Axel says.

Frank clenches his jaw and hides his scowl, but I see it. I imagine him as one of those kids who thought he was a good boy if he stood back and didn't ruffle feathers, like not doing anything if he saw someone kick a dog. He's one of those self-centered people who go along out of fear.

"What if America drafts for war?" I ask. "Frank is an American citizen." I twirl my fork in my food. "Who would he fight for?" I already know the answer.

"America won't enter the war," Führer Kuhn says. He rubs his chest as if he's warming his heart. "Americans are committed to settling differences without firing guns. They surrender their principles instead. Plus, they know they can't win."

"Thank you, Uncle Sam." Franks salutes like an American soldier. When he gets an icy glare from Papa, his cheeks flare red.

"Naturally, our boys are Germans before Americans," Papa says. "They can't renounce German citizenship just because they were born on American soil. They must register for the German army."

"Never forget!" Axel cheers. "Germans first by blood. Deutschland uber Alles!" How does he say all the right things at all the right times?

Wilhelmina stabs her fork at each step-daughter. "Bear Kinder für das Vaterland." What? Does she believe I'm going to let the Reich force me to have five kids. What am I, a cow to breed calves? I'll decide how many children I'll have.

Führer Kuhn retrieves a thin cigar from his inner pocket and lights it. He walks to the bureau that displays our wireless radio. "To make believe there is no racial difference between us and non-Aryans is living a fairy-tale," Führer Kuhn explains. "If we mix races, an artificial human race will be running the planet before we know it." As if this were his own house, he lifts open the window. The breeze bends the flowers on the table. With the humidity, they will never stand back up.

"It's madness and blasphemy!" Papa pipes in. "We must take action or become a gray, raceless mess with no voice."

"As you say, mein Führer," Heidi says. "Visualize in your Kamerad, only the like-minded German clansman." She purses her thin lips. She milks his gigantic ego with words tailored just for him.

Führer Kuhn turns the knob on the two-way wireless. It crackles. He turns and smiles at Heidi.

I've had enough. "Excuse me, I'm not feeling well." I push back my chair, rush to the front door, and swing it open for air.

My father's eyes dilate, and I see him bite the inside of his cheek. "I apologize, my Führer, for this insubordination of my daughter," he says.

I blush but more out of anger than humiliation.

At the radio, Führer Kuhn dials past the static and zeroes in on a familiar scratchy German voice. "Deutschland uber alles," Führer Hitler's familiar chant rants. The cry for "Germany over everything" is the icing on the cake that crimps my stomach. I slip into the hallway, just out of sight.

I hear Führer's voice. "Günther. There's no need for alarm. Americanization threatens our youth." Guttural sounds from across the ocean seethe out of the box into our German-American home. "Ninety percent are embarrassed by their names," his voice rasps. "Camp Siegfried will straighten her out. Soon you'll be proud. More importantly, she will be proud."

KRISTA:
Outside. Krista's Apt. Nye Avenue. Newark, NJ

"Krista! That was rude and dangerous," Heidi hisses over me as I wretch in the bushes outside our apartment building.

I wipe my mouth with the back of my hand. "You're all cowards!" I say. These people, who call themselves family, disgust me. Their toxic hatred is born out of fear. I face my sister. "I need to be around people who aren't a bunch of copycats apologizing if they're different."

"And who might those somebodies be?" demands Heidi.

She knows exactly who I'm talking about. "Yael doesn't just accept limits. He tests them," I say.

"Yael?" Heidi's blood drains from her face. Maybe she didn't know who I was talking about. "The Jewish gangster? He's anything but noble. Are you a masochist? That sleazy Minuteman assaulted you."

"At least he doesn't order me to be someone I'm not," I argue. Every time I'm forced to fall into line around here, a part of me disappears.

"You're supposed to be spying on him, seducing him so we can topple their joke of an operation."

"Call me a traitor."

Heidi puts her hands on her hips. "What about Axel? " she asks. "He's rescuing us. We won't have to worry about money anymore. As an aristocrat, he brings the family prestige. And he thinks you're the perfect German woman."

I'm too ill and disgusted to fight back. My head rocks on my shoulders.

"Yes, Axel does adore you, Krista," Axel says, jolting me as he steps out of the shadows. I can't stand how he refers to himself in third person when he's exercising his control over me. "And what's this Axel overhears about assault? No one told me the scumbag tried to rape you."

"Because he didn't!" I insist. From two stories above, I hear the voice of a tight-lipped German grunting through the radio in our apartment.

"Then why did you scream?" Heidi asks.

"I slipped and he helped me." My excuse is weak. There's a slithering feeling in my spine. Is darkness looking for a host inside me?

Heidi shrugs at Axel. "I'm confused and hurt, Krista. I've always protected you. But you constantly make me come to you." Heidi leans close. "Nevertheless, you know I'll never abandon you," she says in a kinder voice but still with a huff.

"I know you wouldn't," I admit. For me, to disappoint Heidi is unbearable, even if it means giving up my own happiness. Just then, I hear a noise coming from the window unit above. My head tilts up. I catch the glint of the Führer's eye glaring down at me through the window. "I'm sorry, sister," I say, wrapping my arms around her. "I'm just a bit overwhelmed with all the excitement about Axel and me." It feels horrid to lie, but I'll let everyone chew on those little white ones.

"Danke, Heidi," Axel says. "Axel's got it from here." He grabs my hand and pulls me away like a dog on a leash.

YAEL:
Outside. Krista's Apt. Nye Avenue. Newark, NJ

Harry pounces toward my cranked and loaded arm. I duck away and launch pebbles up at Krista's dark apartment window. *Click. Clack.* They rebound and clank against the fire escape. I'm drunk as a skunk and can't aim. I scoop up some more dirt and stones. Wind up.

"Buddy. Be careful!" Harry begs. "You don't wanna wake up her old man."

"You're right. This is risky." My arm drops to my side.

Harry shouldn't have fallen for it. My arm fires ammunition and it rattles the glass.

A head pops out of the second-story window. "Who's there?" Krista whispers.

"Krista." I wave an arm over my head. "It's your gutter rat." I bounce on the balls of my feet and can't help from grinnin'.

"Yael? Oh, my stars!"

I cup my hands around my mouth. "I'm takin' you to a talkin' picture show," I shout. Krista intrigues the heck out of me. She's foreign, alien, German—forbidden fruit. On the one hand, she's everything I repel, oppose, must defeat, or at least use. But on the other hand, I wanna look under that steely car hood, so to speak. Gettin' her reaction to the newsreel about Germany will let me. My friends who've seen *March of Times: Inside*

Germany are shocked about Hitler's world and ties to Nazis in America.

"Do you know what time it is?" Krista calls down.

"My pop's old watch says 6:11, but it stopped." I put down my left wrist and raise my right. "Holy cow, Harry. I can't see the time on the watch Longie gave me."

"It's almost midnight, buddy." Harry's got my back as always.

"Geez Louise," Krista says. "Hold on." She disappears, and then reappears. She climbs through the window and down the fire escape. I can't help but admire her catlike agility, not to mention her sheer bravado for takin' this risk.

At the bottom, my hands grasp her waist and won't let go.

Harry gestures upward. There's a shadow behind the wavin' curtains in the open window. With Harry's two large hands, he urges Krista and I along.

YAEL:
Movie House. Hawthorne Avenue. Newark, NJ

On Hawthorne Avenue, we enter the movie house. I slap my leg. "Sugar! Too late."

The foreheads of Krista and Harry wrinkle.

"No popcorn tonight." My smile makes her smile. Through the almost empty theater, I lead the way down the steps into the plush red seats. Krista sits between Harry and me.

"Why all the urgency?" Krista asks.

"It's about your club," I say and put my arm around her. "The one Hitler set up here in America."

Krista stiffens, but before she can respond, the velvet drapes part and the screen flickers. The newsreel rolls to show beautiful Berlin cafes and parks and playgrounds filled with cheerful people. Krista's knees bounce. Her dimples indent her cheeks. I hope she doesn't expect this to be a happy ending.

Not soon enough, the tone changes. A slow, deep voiceover narrates. "Only those who get behind-the-scenes know that this outward cheerfulness is the creation of Adolph Hitler's most concentrated propaganda campaign the world has ever known. Propaganda Minister Goebbels turned sixty-five million people into a nation with one mind, one will, and one objective—expansion and the return of the million square miles which once comprised her African empire."

Harry points up at the part of the screen displaying yellow park benches labeled for Jews. "The deaths of Communists and hatred toward Jews are obvious," he whispers.

"Unless I'm dreaming, there's separate bathrooms at this movie house for men, women, and Negroes," Krista says. "Germany's not the only place with issues of race and religion." She isn't goin' to let our propaganda color her.

A headline flashes: *Headline: Nazis Assail Pope, Order Nuns to Trial.* Images of ruined churches and a nun behind bars follow.

"Geez. Not even God stands above Hitler," I say.

Not surprising, the next scenes show state-run newsstands and radio stations with government-controlled messages. A post office scene shows workers opening letters to ensure all communication glorifies the Nazis.

As the reel projects happy Germans workin' and farmin', I glance over at Krista. Her bright eyes smile at Hitler's thrivin' German economy. She's proud. Then the story intensifies. An ominous picture glorifies furnaces churnin' out artillery, tanks, and even U-boats.

"What bull," Harry hisses. "How do Germans think they pay to make those weapons? They're bankrupt. The money comes right out of food for their kids' stomachs."

Krista sighs, but it's hard to tell what she's thinkin'.

The view changes to apron-dressed housewives and men in suspendered pants whistling happy tunes as they set their tables for family dinner and read their newspapers after a work day. The voiceover says, "It's patriotic to make clothes last and save garbage to feed pigs. A half-pound of lard is the weekly quota. The farmer grows what he's told or loses his farm. Prices are kept high by the government to benefit him."

"Germans are so drenched in slogans ordering them to eat less beef and eggs, they have no clue they're bein' brainwashed," I whisper.

Krista fidgets in her seat, and I worry she might bolt, but the next part seems to seize her. Across the screen, Nazi youth march, build dams, bridges, and highways while girls farm, do housework, and rock babies. The voiceover says, "The German child is taught that he was born to die for the Fatherland. At fourteen, the Nazi boy receives rank in the German war machine. At eighteen, he must serve. The Nazi girl must serve in the girls' labor service and learn how to conserve food, which a nation preparing for war dare not waste. Most importantly, she learns how to care for the five babies the army expects her to bear."

For the first time since the film began, Krista leans toward me and speaks. "I was there with my father and sister for the Rally of Victory, the Nazi seizure of power. That was the first one after Führer Hitler took over."

I'm confused at first. But I zero in on the honeycomb of dots she's fixated on. There's hundreds of thousands of soldiers, tessellating across a boundless surface. Like a manicured cornfield of dense and limitless lines, the patterns etch a new regularity into this world. It's hypnotizing. Orange torchlit processions scorch the screen. Songs ring out. The massive black, red, and white flags with the Nazi swastika wash over the space like a new coat of paint.

"It was right before we left for America," she says, her breath brushin' my ear. "Nuremberg is the center of the Reich so it made sense to have it there." Is Krista in a trance? She rattles on. "Cute how the youth drummers are so eager. Look, that lucky guard is carrying the blood rag." The whites of her eyes shine in the dim light. "Do you know what that is?" She blinks with innocence and continues without waitin' for my answer. "The flag stained with the blood from Hitler's failed 1923 Beer Hall Putsch. My father was the one to retrieve it."

It's good that this theater is empty. No one hears my gulp. Krista's ties are even deeper than I imagined. I'm willin' to bet she supports the whole Nazi destiny thing. "Do you believe Aryans are a super race?" I ask.

Before she can answer, Harry shushes us. "Quiet! They're talking about Fritz Kuhn."

Cameos of Kuhn working in his office splash on the screen. He's whippin' his Hitler salutes right and left. The voiceover says, "In New York City, the loudest mouth piece in this Nazi propaganda drive is the national chairman of the Hitler-inspired German-American Nazi Bund. He is Fritz Kuhn, former German machine gunner, now a naturalized American citizen who claims to have enrolled 200,000 U.S. Germans under the swastika."

"To get footage of Kuhn, Longie and Lansky got the filmmakers to convince him this news was going to *Heil* the Bund," Harry says. He elbows me. "Good one, eh?"

"Welcome to Charlie Chaplin's world, Führer Kuhn." I snicker and ignore Krista's nails scratchin' the fabric of her seat. We listen.

The narrator continues. "Across the United States, Führer Kuhn has established twenty-five summer camps and drill grounds where Germans imitate Hitler's mighty military machine."

"Hey! Is that your youth camp, Krista?" I tease. Maybe she didn't hear me because she doesn't answer.

Harry nudges me. "Kuhn must be furious about this newsreel."

"Now we know why Hitler hates Hollywood's finest enough to assassinate them," I say. Longie had told me a story about his men goin' undercover to stop the filmmaker coup planned by American Nazis.

The film ends and Krista's eyes stare at the blank screen as if it's still filled with action. I hope something got through to her. After watchin' that news, anyone with a half a soul has to see the oily evil.

"What are you trying to prove?" Her fiery green eyes flash at me.

"I'm tryin' to show you that your controlled press and cannons-not-butter world is bad. It worships Mr. Aryan Superman."

"And your machine gun gangster world run by Mr. Godfather of corruption isn't?" she snaps.

"Hey! That was a low blow," Harry says.

"Look, Krista, Adolph Hitler wants you to believe he has all the answers. I want you to see that. That's all." I wish I had that popcorn as a peace offering. But there's more at stake than keepin' the peace, even with Krista. "Your supreme commander forces people into blind obedience," I say.

"Nazis get us to work against the enemy so we're not afraid," she says to me.

"Your dictator is a demigod who controls minds," I answer back.

Krista snaps. "Democracy is all talk. Fascism acts. Maybe our ideas can make the world better. Curb the flow of immigrants, give people real jobs, put food on the table."

My eyes shut. Then they open and linger over her raised brows. I take a breath to calm down. Blowin' my stack won't make me convince her. That's what her father does. "You can't go to that camp with all the people who want you to think like them, speak like them, and do like them," I say. Maybe if I appeal to her better angels. "Look, you're better than that."

"Thanks? I think," she says. "Don't judge me until you understand my world."

"But you judge me, my world," I say. "Worse. Your people want to be judge, jury, and executioner. You want the power to rid whoever you choose."

"You're both racist. You think I'm wrong because of the way I look and who I live with. I've heard you joking about my blonde pigtails and my German sayings. I'm not completely deaf. You're the ones who are going to start a war with your venomous thinking. Sure there are bad things about any group, but can't you see the good that our kind has done?" Krista wields logic like a swordsmith.

"Yeah, yeah, so some bellies are fed, some people feel bonded by the community, but..." I pause. "Your world also breaks people. Why can't you see?"

"Whether you like it or not, it's my world and we're here to stay." Krista sighs. "Anyway, I don't have a choice."

"What are you talkin' about?" I ask. "You can fight anything you want. A free man or woman answers to no one."

Krista points to herself. "Not when *this* woman has to surrender to the person she's going to marry."

"What?" My breath catches like a fish on a hook. She's gonna marry that creep, Axel. Conflicting emotions spar through me—anger, sadness, and a strange kind of possessiveness. Am I losin' it? All I know is that I've crossed some invisible line.

Krista stands. "Maybe I'm partly deaf. But you're blind." Krista brushes off her skirt. "Axel and I move to Berlin after summer. He's going to work for the Third Reich. The German Nazis. No matter what I believe, I've been ordered to assume my responsibilities."

My eyes blur. "I've made a horrible mistake," I say to Harry in the aisle. This is awkward. "Let's take Krista home."

Harry's never been afraid of my anger. But I imagine him watchin' the blue of my eyes turn glacial. His shiver tells me that even he feels the blast of frost that protects me from my past. Nothing he can say will thaw it.

Krista pushes me aside. "I can walk myself home," she says. She disappears past the red velvet theater chairs, through the black exit door.

KRISTA:
Krista's Apt. Nye Avenue. Newark, NJ

My bedroom window is now closed but not locked. I sneak back into my room after the wretched film with Yael. He's trying to brainwash me against my own people. In the darkness, I hear a creak. "Heidi?" I mutter.

From my raven-black room, snowy hands grab my neck. "You are supposed to spy on the Jew, not get knocked up in the middle of the night like your slut of a muter did with you," my father shrills.

My heart sprints.

The shadow of a rocky fist looms above me. I raise my elbow to shield my cheek. In the split second that it takes my eyes to adjust to the darkness, my face feels a smack and my body hurls onto Heidi's bed. I cringe, ready to collide with my sister. But I bounce against the empty mattress and land on the floor. Heidi's not in her bed. Of course not. She would have complained about the noise by now.

"If you disobey your Vater, what do you expect?" my father says. "I should have killed all of you when I caught the Jew bastard screwing your Mutter. Would have saved me a lot of problem. He was your Mutter's descent into—." Just then, the headlights of a passing car sweep across the room and smears his face. His normally slicked back hair twists up like horns. His chest heaves. "At least *she* paid for her sin. I strangled her after you slithered from the rotten inferno of her belly," he growls.

I wheeze. "What?" I clutch the chair next to the dressing mirror and pull myself up. "You killed my mother?" The whistling of cold air swirls inside my aching skull.

"Just like you helped me kill your Jew father five years ago at the bookstore fire." My father turns on the lamp. His frosty eyes ice me. He unrolls a book from his hand and shoves it in my face. "Where did you get this?" He holds up the tattered book from my past, *Emil und die Detektive*.

"The … the bookstore sells them for five cents," I stutter a lie. Through the iron smell of blood from my nose, a musty vanilla scent reaches me. This smell has endured ever since the night I snuck it from the shopkeeper. "The story happens in our hometown of Berlin."

"You imbecile! It takes place in Jew Berlin! I knew I could never sterilize your blood."

What is he talking about? I've glimpsed this monster in front of me before. But this time, he's fully out of his cage, bearing his claws. His polar blue eyes flicker inside a sea of red.

"I warned you to never touch the cursed book of a Jew." Papa's left thumb flicks his cigarette lighter and the flint ignites the paper. The orange fire licks the fragile cover, ripples through the crisp pages, and devours the book.

93

Visions of a long-ago night in a bookstore flood my mind, as horrid as if I'm seeing them for real. *My father stands in front of the burning building feeding the ravaging bonfire of the store with its own books. I hear his muffled words under the rumble. "You evil Jew bastard ..." Heidi covers my ears and huddles me home through the bitter night.*

Now here in my room, my father flings the burning *Emil* book out the apartment window onto the fire escape. As the flavor of smoke mingles with the memories, it singes my chest.

"That charred book should always remind you of your immoral legacy," Papa chides me through clamped teeth.

The crackling awakens more childhood memories. *Heidi drags me away from the fire. At home, at the wooden table in our dimly lit kitchen, Heidi takes my hands in hers to warm them. I squeeze my sobs. "I couldn't hear. What did Vater say in front of the burning shop?" I ask. Instead of answering, Heidi serves me tea. When we finish, she drops to her knees and clasps my hands again. "Our father was blessing us Germans, nothing more." I nod. The tears obey me, ossified in my eyes. But then I ask more. I can't help it. "He called me ein Mischling, mixed-breed. What does this mean?" Heidi explains to me. "He was blessing us. He said, 'To the dignity and purity of the German culture.'"* Now I know Heidi's lie.

"Shameless whore!" I return my focus to his angry voice. My surging emotions shoot lava-hot adrenaline to every nerve of my body. Like a gorilla on a rampage, my father charges at me. I flinch, spinning toward my mirror by the dresser. In its glass, my shocked face absorbs my father's backhand, and I watch myself bash against the bedpost, only half-hearing the thwack that sounds like wood chopped by an axe.

He waits, towering over me, crimson-faced and rasping.

He will get nothing from me. Not even the satisfaction of a whimper.

"Now you know the truth. Now you know your dirty secret, you half-Jew."

I'm a *Jew?* The words in my head seem like someone else's.

"Now you know the impurities I tried to cleanse from your life." His face is so close I feel his spittle as he yells. "Now you know my sacrifice for you." He pinches my cheeks between his thumbs and fingers. I won't cry out. I won't. "It's payback time," he rumbles. "Put your eyes back in your head. You will shovel dirt over this secret before your gut can eat you alive. You will marry Axel and obey his every order. The union brings survival for you and our family."

The room is laced and spinning. Where am I?

"Your alternative is a one-way ticket to das Mutterland. She will lock you in a prison for your filthy race crime." He puts a hand on each of my shoulders, shoving me onto my bed. For a second, I think he's going to rip my clothes off and attack me like he did Heidi that time before we came to America.

I wish I could scream, but I still can't find my voice.

CHAPTER 7

Duck and Cover

LONGIE ZWILLMAN:
Hotel Riviera. Clinton Avenue. Newark, NJ

Isaac's feet dangle a good six inches above the floor. Armed with our high-octane rot-gut from my private Prohibition collection, Harry's pop and I relax on bar stools in my Hotel Riviera office.

Isaac slides down and walks over to my built-in bookcase. He runs his fingers across the book bindings. "Many Americans have their heads in the sand while the Nazis build up their army in Europe," he says.

Every Tuesday afternoon, Isaac meets me here at the office. His ice cream white hair and thick mustache lends cred to his know-how, so I hired him to backfill my education. I had to quit school in eighth grade when my pop died. I figure a little post-school can't hurt. Gotta do something good with all my dough.

Without warning, my office door flies open. Standing in the doorway is my Minutemen commander, Nat Arno. "Boss," Nat says. "We found a friend of yours roaming the streets and kidnapped her for a visit." Nat takes no prisoners when it comes to etiquette.

On Nat's heels, Yael and Harry parade into my office and elevate the fanfare around the smartly-dressed fortyish woman behind them. To my pleasant surprise, the woman calls me by name. "Well, if it isn't Long-E Zwillman." A Parisian red beret tips sideways over the dark hair of none other than the charismatic Dorothy Thompson.

"Well, if it isn't the lovely lady, more famous than Eleanor Roosevelt, who dared to call Hitler an ordinary man." I grasp her puffed shoulder-sleeves and peck each of her high cheekbones. The statuesque woman propped up by her heels meets me eye to eye.

"My mistake as a newswoman for not recognizing Herr Hitler walks on water," she quips. She covers her heart with an open hand. "Word from Germany is I'll be rooming with New York Mayor LaGuardia in Hitler's concentration camp upon Adolph's arrival in America."

"As I believe you once said, Dorothy, a dictator isn't gonna tell you he's a dictator before you vote for him." I find her emotional energy to be beyond any man or woman I've ever met. My eyes follow her around the room.

"Longie, I'm flattered. You actually do read my news column." Her grand skirt waves as she sits down in one of the bar seats.

"Isaac, may I introduce you to Dorothy Thompson."

"Miss Thompson needs no introduction," Isaac says, tipping his head. "As they say, her reputation precedes her." He seems honored to meet the celebrated American writer and radio personality.

From behind the bar, Nat fills glasses for Yael and Harry to pass around. "Miss Thompson. What do you think about our own American Hitler running swastikas up our flagpoles?" Nat asks the famous commentator.

"Oh, you mean Führer Fritz Kuhn? Why he stands for everything American, doesn't he now?" she taunts. "All kidding aside, we must stand up against menaces like Mr. Kuhn and his mentor Mr. Hitler. Remember just a few years ago, Germans were fighting our Americans in the Great War."

"Dorothy, mark my word. One day soon, *Time* magazine is going to splash you on the cover." I gulp the thick caramel alcohol and swish it around my tongue.

"Flattery will get you everywhere, Longie. Now, serve me a drink and tell me, what did I interrupt?"

And then, when it rains it pours, because another character pops his hat-covered head into the doorway. "Did I hear mention of the luminary Fritz Kuhnazi?" radio personality Walter Winchell says. "I hear Longie's gang is wipin' the Newark streets up with his Swastinkas." He chuckles at his own wordplay.

I greet the mouthpiece for America with a hearty handshake. "Walter Winchell, good to see ya!" As he would say, if you don't listen to his Sunday night radio patter or read his gossip, you're six feet under, Mr. and Mrs. America.

"Thank you, Longie. It's good to be seen," Winchell recites his signature response. He hands his hat to Harry and accepts some booze from Yael. He shakes hands around the room and then kisses Miss Thompson's hand. "And good to see you, Miss Thompson."

"Isaac and I were saying that President Roosevelt is between a rock and hard place when it comes to helping Europe," I say.

Behind the bar, Nat gulps his drink and lights his cigar.

"But FDR is sittin' on his hands," Yael says. "He's lettin' Nazi spies worm their way into our gardens."

Harry hands Dorothy a drink. "Americans don't want to be involved in another war," Harry says. Then he picks up a full glass for himself and hands another to Yael.

"Cowards!" spurts out Nat.

"But Roosevelt's gotta respond," Yael chimes in. "Hitler's gonna march on Europe."

Winchell throws up his hands. "He'd better respond! He knows Hitler's bum-kisser Kuhn is paving the roads for an easy Nazi-landing over here."

"That hate-filled Kuhn strolls his army right down Fifth Avenue demanding first amendment freedom at the top of his lungs," Nat says.

"Don't underestimate FDR," I say. "He's working all the angles. How do you think the Newark Minutemen keep rising in power?"

"Meet ya in the funny papers, Boss." Nat eats up the compliment.

"Kuhn gives me Swatsi-cooties," Walter says, grinning at his own joke.

"Franklin's keeping the cover on a boiling pot," Dorothy says.

"To cap Nazi build-up in America, FDR uses an old war law," Isaac explains. "It makes it unlawful to give speeches that put national security at risk."

"Kuhn just lies and then says what he wants," Harry says.

"Americans believe in FDR right now," Dorothy says. "I do, too. He creates jobs. Look at his Chicago Outer Drive, San Fran's Golden Gate, all of the great golf courses, schools, airports, ski resorts."

"We've poured enough concrete for the Grand Coulee Dam to build a sidewalk around the globe," Isaac adds.

"And I'll pour us enough whiskey to flood the sidewalks down Bund Central," Nat says. "Drink 'er down."

"FDR's finally catching up to the Mob employment rates," I say with a smirk.

"Hitler's fake news is driving me crazy," Harry says in his low voice. "He's bragging he ended unemployment in Germany."

"Sure he did," Nat says. "He put everyone to work revving up his *Wehrmacht* War machine."

"How do we eliminate America's fear to fight fascism?" Yael asks.

"We'll get those Ratzis, don't worry," Walter Winchell says as he double fists whiskey shots.

"Only if we are not afraid, can we live." Dorothy says as she stands.

Winchell adds his classic gossip. "By the way, ya know Kuhn is *Adam and Eve-in it* with at least half a dozen dames."

Laughter clatters the glasses on the bar.

KRISTA:
Newark Bund Headquarters. Nye Avenue. Newark, NJ

The table in Führer Kuhn's office is scattered with newspapers and half-finished cups of coffee. I nudge between my father and Axel and set down the pan full of apple strudel. We've interrupted some sort of pow-wow with Secretary Wheeler-Hill and a priest. They sit around the table scratching notes, barely giving us notice.

"We didn't mean to intrude, Fritz," Papa says.

"Not at all!" Führer Kuhn says, standing to greet us. "You both know Father Coughlin. His voice is popular with our Bund. We are talking about a segment on his radio show that promotes fascism as the true Americanism."

Geez Louise! Father Coughlin is that radio star Papa makes us listen to. Papa agrees with him. He says FDR is in bed with the bankers. The men greet us with a bothered salute.

Führer Kuhn beams at me. His warmth elates me. He brushes my bruised cheek with the back of his hand. "Krista, I better not find out who did this to you, mein Schatz. You are too beautiful to be damaged in any way." He grimaces at my father.

Axel hops to my side. He wrinkles his forward as he examines my welt.

My eyes dare a flick at my father. I'm stunned. Führer Kuhn is taking my side, defending me, calling me his treasure. Ever since our private meeting, he seems to respect me. Maybe he does have compassion under that stiff uniform? Or when I least expect it, will he pull the rug out from under me? He uncovers the strudel. Across the table, he invites his guests to share the buttery whiff. Now we have their attention. Father Coughlin inhales.

"Krista, get plates and serve the men tea!" my father says. At least Papa's talking to me now. With my true identity hovering over my head, I can't make waves. I fetch the plates. I'm still in shock hosting this alien in my body—half an Aryan who I've known all my life and half a stranger who I'm trying to get to know. If I'm honest with myself, I'm a bit relieved. So much makes sense to me now. The one question that will always haunt me though, is whether the man who died in the bookstore loved my mother at my conception.

"We're here to update you on the Minutemen," Papa says.

"Krista's going to the training facility at the YMHA," Axel adds. "We believe there's a lot more there than meets the eye."

As the men exchange conversation, I pass out plates with forks. Papa's eyes dodge mine. Anyway, I'm not scared since my father needs me around in order to seal the marriage deal with Axel.

"Sounds like progress! I'm proud of you, Krista," Führer Kuhn says, raising his cup. I fill it with tea water. He clacks his knuckles on the table and takes his place at the head. "Günther. Axel. We could use your help. Join us to discuss one of our biggest challenges. We need to create the image of a powerful Bund run by one leader. Not a bunch of vagrant cells." He serves himself a giant piece of pastry. The others copy him.

For a moment, I think the men have forgotten about me. I'm just standing here like the *k* in *know*. To be honest, the invisibility is liberating, like a green chameleon against a leaf that tricks his enemy to pass right by. Against my better judgment, I sabotage my escape. "Mein Führer," I call over forks scraping plates.

Heads snap my way.

My mouth sticks like cotton, but I force my tongue to click. "Perhaps Father Coughlin's radio show becomes your stage. Mail everyone and tell them to listen." The steam from the tea fuses with the stuffiness of the room. I'm not sure if I actually spoke up or not. But the perspiration on my neck confirms it. Geez Louise. Why did I do that? Maybe to prove I exist?

Papa seethes like a lizard shooting venom.

Führer Kuhn glues his eyes to me. "Continue, Krista." He drops four sugar cubes into his tea.

I clear my throat. "Father Coughlin. How many living rooms does your radio show reach?" I ask.

"Forty million to be exact," the priest says as he rearranges his priestly robe.

"At least a hundred million American mailboxes for us," the Secretary offers.

I veil a quiver. "Führer Kuhn. You could make all of America listen at the same time. You could build excitement for a message to America. They'll hear you as the leader of the Amerikadeutscher Bund."

Papa chews his thumbnail. His eyes are crossed trying to figure out what I'm up to. Axel drums his fingers on his thigh. He's waiting for the other shoe to drop. But this idea about the radio show just came to me, from my head, not my heart.

"Not a bad idea!" Father Coughlin bangs his fist on the table. His round wire glasses bounce on the bridge of his nose. "Not only will my radio show let Fritz speak to fascists, but he will speak to all Americans. Why wasn't this obvious before?"

Like a benevolent Santa Claus greeting a child, Führer Kuhn flashes a smile at me. "In this way, I will rule at the top of the pyramid, with Führerprinzip," he says. "Take notes, my Fräulein. There's paper on my desk."

His warmth means something. More than I can say about my father. My heart pumps. I have value. I shuffle through his desk.

CHAPTER 8

Club Fighter

YAEL:

YMHA Boxing Gym. 652 High Street. Newark, NJ

My hands are crampin'. I've been shadow boxin' to Nat's commands in the Y for an hour. Next to me, Harry's knuckles bleed from hittin' the speed bag.

"Stay in control!" Commander Nat Arno shouts as he strides past Minutemen in the boxin' gym. Dozens push their bodies off the ground hundreds of times. My arms burn just watchin'. Nat is the type of guy any soldier would want leadin' his troops into war. "Stay alert!" he commands. He taps his foot to men whippin' jump ropes over and across their bodies. Nat's not only the guy in the trenches who would save the squad when things got out of control, he's the guy whose squad would save each other. "Don't let anything dull your senses!" he orders. I read the clock on the wall.

There's a scrapin' noise above. I tilt my head up. Longie and his boys are in the open loft above the cavernous gym. Guys are movin' tables together. Looks like they're gonna have a meetin'. I wave.

Out of the blue, Maxie's jump rope smacks him in the face. "ROPE-A-DOPE!" he cries, pointin' toward the door. "Who's the German shiksa, Al?" Maxie asks.

Al stops jumpin' to look. "Wow! She can knock me out anytime."

I follow their gaze. My eyes pop.

"I'm jealous," Maxie says. His lips curl down.

"Don't be," Al says. "You, my brother, were never my cup of tea." Al snaps the towel on Maxie's leg. Maxie slaps Al's arm.

Puddy jumps in between. "Break it up, boys," he yaps.

Eyes burst out of Benny's head, too. He's spellbound by the blonde nemesis headin' toward us. Nat rubbernecks. Abie gawks. They're shell-shocked by none other than—Krista. She doesn't just appear under the spotlight, she presents in a long yellow raincoat, swingin' a drippin' wet umbrella. Raindrops sail through the air.

"This is gonna be interesting," Benny mumbles. "Gimme a ringside seat." He pushes through to the front. Others kinda float in from around the gym. They create a wall that I stand behind.

Nat spins around and confronts me. "Yael, she doesn't belong here."

Krista weaves her way through the wall of boxers and struts toward me.

With Krista still out of earshot, Harry intervenes. "She's not like the rest, Nat."

"Dangit, Yael. What the heck ya doin?" Nat shakes his head. "Being Jewish is tough enough without *that*."

"Your ma's turning in her grave," growls Abie. "You need her like you need a hole in your head."

"What if she's a spy?" Benny whispers. "I bet that umbrella shoots bullets."

Nat won't let up on me. "Don't be a putz. She's not just NOT Jewish. Maybe she's American, but she's a Nazi," he says.

"Nice to see you again, Harry." Krista offers a warm smile that breaks our huddle apart. Then she glances over at me. I comb my fingers through my hair.

"What happened to your eye?" Harry asks her.

She shrugs. "Just a little mishap."

"Trying to learn to walk and chew gum at the same time," Nat sneers.

"It's a good look for the boxin' ring," Harry's says, attempting to break some ice.

"Didn't expect to see you again," I say to Krista. I prop my foot on a stool to tie my shoe.

"I was in the neighborhood," she answers. "Are these gentlemen the Newark Minutemen I've seen in action?" she asks me.

Forget my casual coldness. It's boring me. I introduce my commander. "Krista. Nat Arno. Nat's a legend around here."

Nat glowers at Krista. "You enjoy the excitement at your Bund meeting the other night?" he asks. As he walks away, he glares at me over his shoulder. "Gey shlog dayn kop in van," he hisses.

Only Nat would curse me to bang my head against the wall. "Nat's a tough nut to crack," I say to Krista.

"You're a hard nut to crack, too," Krista says. She doesn't lose a beat. "I better get learning. I'm going to need to stick up for myself." She holds out her wet coat and umbrella. "You keeping your promise to show me a few things?" I don't hurry to ferry her clothes around like some maid. I'm not sure how I want to act. I'm still in shock that she's got the nerve to show up in here.

"What's your secret of getting a gorgeous dame to show up drippin' wet, Yael?" Maxie jokes. "Give me a few pointers."

"Zip it, Maxie," I say. My cheeks burn. If I don't stop him, he'll keep goin'. My own eyes can't help but notice how Krista's wet clothes cling to her body. She could be twenty-six for all of her teenage years.

"Rainin' cats and dogs out there?" Al asks her. He takes her things, but not before I see his eyes scan her sleeveless undershirt, loose shorts and red belt. "Next time kick twice at the side door so you don't get stuck in the crowds up front," he suggests.

Krista slips off her galoshes to reveal her ready-for-action sneakers. She opens her hands in front of her. "Where are my gloves?" she asks no one and everyone.

I watch Krista scan the boxin' gym. She looks up. She locks eyes with Longie in the noisy balcony. He pauses among colleagues who are movin' boxes, stackin' papers, and installing dozens of telephones. Her gaze lingers on a man snappin' shut a suitcase filled with dough. Then she glances back to Longie. He pushes back his jacket to reveal a holstered gun. That's a clear message if I ever saw one.

What's she doin' here, I wonder? Is she runnin' away from something? Or is she runnin' me for a song? I'll play along. Like the old Abe Lincoln sayin' goes, "Keep your friends close and your enemies closer."

"Benny," I say. "Get the girl some gloves."

Puddy cozies up to Krista. "Yael's a sucker for a right cross." He crosses his right hand toward her and taps her face.

Maxie points to his chin. "Leygn a Khsime afn ponem."

"Nice advice, Maxie," Benny says as he returns with the gloves. "He wants ya to leave your signature across his kisser." He pulls the gloves over Krista's hands and laces them.

These guys are startin' to crowd my style. I take control and show Krista the basics. Left. Right. Hook. But, the Newark Minutemen won't let me go it alone. They help me coach this fox in the hen house. In between my instructions, the dark, muscular men tilt her snowy, statuesque shoulders. They stretch her arms and swivel her hips. Abie sets her stance. Maxie raises her fists to guard her face. Al tells her to step on his shadows. Puddy guides her arm into a mean hook. Her awkward movements turn fluid, like virgin gears oiled for production. Are we trainin' the enemy?

Above us, I watch Longie squeeze his brow at the scene on the floor. He zeroes in on Krista as if he's measuring the width of her eyes compared to the distance between them. He hands a note to one of his men. I guess at his orders: trail this broad and delve deep into her people. Longie won't be a sittin' duck, waitin' for Nazis to shoot gullible Minutemen out of the water. Dangit, he thinks I'm lettin' my guard down. Not a chance. My gloves are up!

"Winnin' comes down to knowing what your opponent is afraid of," I tell Krista. "If he likes distance, pretend to move in. If he's afraid of the right, fake your right." I twitch my glove at Krista. Her golden braids don't budge. She's not fallin' for my tricks. "But always, do the unexpected." We are the unholy pair, I think with dark amusement.

She tries hard, succeeds, and fumbles. Benny gleams. Abie shakes his head. Harry pats her back. We laugh. Others smile. Some grumble. In the last few hours, more than a few bricks have tumbled down from the wall between us. As far as I can tell, she's still more American than Nazi, despite her family. I hope she'll stay that way.

The crowd thins as we train into the night, gaspin' and sweatin'. Finally, we decide it's time to give it a rest for the night. I take off my gloves and reach into my leather bag. "Hey, Miss K., come here," I say with warmth that surprises even me. It must surprise her, too, because she has trouble meetin' my eyes. I pull Krista in front of the mirror and hold up my camera. "I want to take a picture of us." The Star of David on my boxin' shorts brushes her shorts. I click the shutter. The flash of my camera shines in the glass.

"Take one for me, OK?" she smiles and runs her fingers through my thick blond hair, her bravado back.

A commotion above distracts us. We look up. I can't believe my eyes. Longie shakes hands with a man. Not just any man. J Edgar Hoover, head of the FBI!

"What's he doing here?" Krista whispers.

"Your guess is as good as mine." I can't start yappin' about our operations and how we're helpin' Hoover and his G-men root out Nazis. It's bad enough she's seen this much. Longie and Hoover have been workin' together ever since Longie helped with the Lindbergh baby kidnapping.

CHAPTER 9

Prep

KRISTA:
Shooting Range. Plattdeutsche Volksfest Farm. NJ

At Plattdeutsche Volkfest shooting range in the secluded farmlands of Jersey, Frank and Papa plant one knee on the green lawn next to Axel. The three of them fire automatic rifles at human cardboard cutouts. I'm close enough to see Axel's downy hair on his arms. Gunpowder stings my nostrils.

"Well done!" Führer Kuhn bobs his head. I agree with him. Axel is good. In fact, I smile as he shoots. But the Führer goes overboard with his compliments. "You have a sniper's eye," he says and elbows Secretary Wheeler-Hill to signal his pleasure.

"We've had the privilege of learning from the best executioner in the German Reich," Axel says. He stands and nods toward my father. "Herr Brecht vouches for our NRA membership so we can practice here."

My father's chest puffs out. He's never had a problem hiding his arrogance. "The boys have skill. They simply needed to learn detachment from the task. That's what creates the magic," my father says. "It lets you imagine your target already dead, like a hunk of meat." I've heard Papa's vulgar words many times before in our home. He reminds us that he was trained as an assassin during the Great War. That's where he learned what he calls quick and painless slaying. In fact, he bragged to Heidi and me one night at dinner. He explained, "One minute my man was biting schnitzel. Before he swallowed, maggots were chewing his lifeless shwanz." The image gnaws at me still. I guess my father is the kind of man Kuhn relishes beside him. Papa twirls the weapon in his hands.

"The government doesn't even know they are arming our men on Uncle Sam's dime," Secretary Wheeler-Hill says. His syrupy voice juxtaposes the violent conversation. He takes Frank's gun from him and strokes the wooden stock.

"We got a big discount on the NRA guns," Frank says. "We'll be able to supply every camper this summer."

Axel hands me his rifle. He expects me to store it. When no one is looking, I raise the gun and look through the sight. The frame parallel to the slide release is almost too hot to touch, but I squeeze it anyway. When it clicks, Führer Kuhn turns to me. I hold my breath. He smiles and takes the gun as if he's helping me. He places it on the rack. I'm not sure if he's treating me as a child, a woman, or something else entirely. The sense I get is he doesn't want anything to happen to me.

Papa whips around. "Wilhelmina! Keep these girls out of trouble! Bring us lunch!" He places his gun on the rack with the others.

Heidi grabs my sleeve. She pulls me into the storage barn with my stepmother.

"Krista! Don't forget the beer!" shouts Axel.

I'd rather be target practicing. I glance over my shoulder at Führer Kuhn. He's gone on to his next task. "Tell me, Secretary," he says. "What's the report on building our army?"

From inside the barn, I'm surprised when I hear the Secretary's answer. "We are leveraging American resources," I hear him say. "In addition to purging NRA weapons, our members register with the National Guard for free military training."

"The American government has no idea they are training their enemy," Papa sneers.

"We drill stormtroopers at the local gun ranges in cities from Philadelphia to Cleveland to Detroit," the Secretary responds. In Yaphank, we've enlisted German riflemen and machine gunners to train our soldiers at the Camp Siegfried facility."

I punt open the wooden barn door with my foot as I balance two trays of beer steins. Even before I stop at the table, the men seize the mugs. I compare their real-life faces to the ones in the *March of Time* film. The lens that once smudged my focus is now clearing.

My sister Heidi is right behind me. She places a tray of triangle sandwiches in the middle of the table next to a bowl of shiny bullets. As soon as Führer Kuhn takes a sandwich, Secretary Wheeler-Hill grabs one and stuffs it in his mouth. Wilhelmina decorates the table with two daisy-filled Coca-Cola bottles.

I choose a sandwich and stand a few feet away. I hear myself chewing. I wonder, are my friends and family the good guys or the bad guys? Does the answer matter? If I don't have a choice, then no matter what I think, my side must be armed and ready to fight the other.

Führer Kuhn startles me. "So tell us, my schöne junge Frau. What have you uncovered from the Newark Minutemen?" He touches his mug to his lips. "Heidi reports that you have made progress." He sips.

My eyes squint against the lingering scrutiny of the group. Each curious glare my way is an unspoken threat, a dare for me to not defy the mob.

I study them in turn—the way Axel's shoulder twitches when he's tense, how Führer Kuhn's forehead wrinkles when he frowns, how my father's nose flares when he's angry, how Heidi swipes her tongue across her lips when she's nervous. These mannerisms are familiar. They remind me of me. Just like these people, I come from an educated and civilized world of artists and intellects. We honor the same men, places, and holidays.

We voted for the same leader, Adolph Hitler. My children will bear their Germanity. Despite my growing dread and doubt, this logic and duty guides my answer. What am I without them? Who am I alone? No one.

The words fly out of my mouth like bees escaping a jar. "The Newark Minutemen not only train in the YMHA," I say. "I've watched fleets of men answering phones and passing messages to Mr. Zwillman. I saw money exchange hands there."

"So the YMHA is their ground zero," Secretary Wheeler-Hill says, rubbing his chin. "And at least one of their intelligence units."

"There was an interesting visitor as well." I unveil the shocking connection. "I recognized Mr. Hoover from the FBI."

"J. Edgar?" Papa raises his eyebrows. He doesn't believe me. I know it was Mr. Hoover from the news clip last year. He chased down John Dillinger.

"Hoover's a hypocrite!" says Secretary Wheeler-Hill. "He tells America he's sweeping the streets of gangsters. Yet there he is in bed with the worst of them."

"How sloppy of them to show their hand," Führer Kuhn says. He puts his arm around me. "They were not expecting an outsider. And a clever one at that." Führer Kuhn smiles. He squeezes my arm and turns to Papa. "If your daughter had been a boy, she would have made quite the stormtrooper. You should be proud."

My father gives me a disparaging look. But for the moment, at least, I feel relief. I've given my allegiance as a loyal American Nazi of the Bund. I have proven my selfless choice of nation first.

Secretary Wheeler-Hill isn't one to let the emotions of a single accomplishment steal his spotlight. "Nice update. What of our other operations?" He turns to the boys. "Is Camp Siegfried ready for the summer?"

Axel's arms hug his sides. "Supplies have been ordered and training scheduled," his voice clips. When I hear Axel's report, my relief wavers. All these tasks are being activated by something bigger, like ants shaken from their sandy hills by an approaching train. My skull vibrates. The buildup is ominous because there's no turning back.

"I expect weekly reports for the matching program between the junge Manner and Frau," the Secretary says. He shoves two more quartered sandwiches into his mouth. "I want an accurate projection," he muffles through his full mouth. He gives Heidi and I a shifty look as if we were eavesdropping on something we shouldn't have heard.

I shudder. Projection of what? Under my pounding temples, I sense a collision. I must stay vigilant.

CHAPTER 10

Wind-Up

YAEL:
Harry's Apt. Hawthorne Avenue. Newark, NJ

At Harry's Hawthorne Avenue home above the candy store, I lean over the large steamin' pot and slurp hot chicken soup from the ladle.

Harry's mother, Lena, swats my hand. "Shlekht eyngl!" she scolds. "Harry, vhy do you bring me this bum?" She's a tough one but has a heart of gold.

Harry crumples mail at the end of the kitchen table and fans himself with an envelope. "Ma," he says in his deep voice. "If you think I'm bad, you should see who Yael's hangin' out with these days!" A kitten jumps up on his lap and purrs.

I drop the ladle in the pot and embrace Lena, my second mother. "Sheyna muter," I say to deflect Harry's comment. "You know I lose my willpower when I smell your cookin'. It reminds me of my mother's matzah ball soup. She told me food's the glue between Jews."

In one swoop, she punches me in the ribs.

I double over. "Ma, you've been workin' on your right hook." She ignores me, grabs a bottle of whiskey from the counter, and dribbles it over the cat food. The cat bounces to the treat.

Harry shakes his head. "That's not gonna help the cat grow, Ma." He puts a penny under one of the table legs to keep it from wobbling.

Everything about Harry's home is what was taken from mine. I'm lucky to have this. But with the good comes the bad. Lena hooks my eyes in hers and guides them to the overflowing garbage.

I smile. "I got the trash, Ma." I hug my arms around a bag of garbage, escape out the door, and take two steps down the stairs. But then I back up. I bite my tongue and slide down the bannister, squealin' to myself the whole way down. All of a sudden, the dark landin' is crammed with people. Unable to stop, I collide with bodies. Longie's cologne prickles my nose. My eyes adjust. Rotten apple cores, bloody fish heads, flaky eggshells, and chicken innards are splattered across Nat's overcoat.

Nat curses up a storm. He swats away garbage and picks moldy berries from his collar. Stumbling to my feet, I meet the green eyes of Harry's little sister, Esther. She tries to stifle a grin, but we both burst out laughin'. Her lanky, pre-teen body bolts up the stairs. The typically composed Isaac slaps his thigh. Fat tears leak down Longie's ruddy cheeks. We untangle ourselves and follow Esther.

At the top of the stairs, Longie follows Isaac through the open door and I'm right behind. Lena greets the boss with a hug. "Sholem Aleikhem, Mr. Zwillman. I'm sorry it's so hot in here. Everyone. Sit."

Longie never breaks a sweat so I can tell he doesn't care about the steamy room. "It's been too long, Mrs. Levine," he says. He waves to Harry and opens the refrigerator.

I sit at the table and turn on the fan. When it whirls, I hum against the blades. Esther giggles and jumps into her father's lap as he spoons his steamin' tea. I gaze at the innocent girl, barely a young woman. The times around us are forcin' her to grow up too fast. Maybe we can help slow it down.

When Nat enters the apartment, the whirlin' fan casts the garbage smell from Nat toward Lena. Her nose flares. "Mr. Arno. Vat happened to you?" She forces the prize-fightin' Nat into the chair across from me. "Mr. Zwillman, hand me a towel. By the vay, take a dollar from my cookie jar and put it on number 426. I had a dream." Longie drops the towel into her hand. He reaches into the jar and pulls out a bill. Except I know the money came out of his own pocket. He never lets Lena pay a dime for anything.

As Lena scrubs Nat clean, Esther fills bowls with fluffy dough balls and dribbles soup over them until they float. I want to capture her virtue with a photo. As she serves us, I reach inside my pocket for my camera. But something cold and hard freezes me. It's the smooth amulet from the hopscotch game with Krista. My chest wrenches. The smell of spring dirt from the Big Yard mingles with the scent of garlic in this warm home. My aggravation wrestles with me. Is Krista my enemy or not?

Longie fiddles with the Victrola and I hear a record spin. My head turns as the voice of Benny Goodman scratches. His clarinet, which usually soothes my soul, grates my nerves. If Krista's the enemy, what does that make me? I force myself to spoon the soup into my mouth. I feel its steam, but it's cold. I taste the broth, but it's bland.

Longie's eyes yank me. Can he feel my detachment?

Nat slurps his soup.

My eyes flicker and I return from my world of self-pity. What's certain is that I can't be sure of my future. So for today, I'll imagine taking one barefoot step at a time across pebbles in the water.

Suddenly, Harry snaps a paper across the end of the table. "Pop. Listen," he says. He reads a letter.

"Dear relatives. My mother, who is your cousin, has passed, and the Nazis made us leave our home and go to the train station. At the train, when the soldiers flung open the cattle car doors, our father yelled so we could get away, and he was shot. A man snuck us away. I beg you to help my little brother and I to come to America. I promise we will not be a burden. Yours faithfully, Manya Hurwicz."

"Nazis won't admit to this," Isaac says. "Harry. Tomorrow, take that letter to Aunt Rose." No one ever speaks the words aloud, but Isaac's sister Rose has high-level government clearance. My lungs stir bein' so close to someone operating on the razor's edge. As a woman, Rose can travel among dangerous operations. In the past year, she has flown back and forth to Europe four times. Isaac eyes Longie. "Help us get those children out of there and bring them to us." The boss acknowledges the request with a nod.

"Longie. Please bring over the map in the box on the counter," Isaac says. The bowl on the table screeches when Isaac pushes it to make room. "Rose has told me there's a lot of movement in Europe." Isaac's finger rubs the middle of Europe. Everyone leans close. "Now that Hitler controls Austria, he flanks Czechoslovakia."

"Is he gonna pounce on Eastern Europe?" I ask.

"Good question," Isaac says and moves his finger north. "With Czechoslovakia, he'd control the center of Europe and the gateway to the East. He'd be on the Russian front. Starting another war would be easy."

Nat picks up his bowl and drinks his soup. "Does anyone think Hitler's plan isn't to rule the world?" Nat declares. "He's spending billions on guns."

"His weapon is more powerful than guns," Longie says. "It's German blood. Nazi-Germans around the globe are waiting for their super-god to unite them under him."

I shake my head. "No one here wants a dictator tellin' us what to do." Our country was built by different types of people from all over the world who want an equal chance. When the rights of even one of us is taken away, it affects us all.

"Time to quit punchin' feathers, fellas!" Harry bangs the table. A crunched envelope next to his hand uncrinkles and sends goosebumps across my arms.

Longie stands straight. "Harry's right. It can be ugly doing things the right way, but we must fight," he says. "Time to load apathy into our fists and fire like a Tommy Machine Gun."

YAEL:
Cemetery. Newark, NJ

In the cemetery where my parents are buried, raindrops splatter like pancakes against the cracked cement path. After dinner at Harry's, Longie and I walk through the graveyard. The water bounces into my shoes and soaks my socks. The night isn't on my side because then the wind turns my umbrella inside out.

"With all our modern inconveniences, you'd think someone would come up with a decent brolly," Longie says. He takes the umbrella from me and chucks it into a trashcan. I bury my hands in my jacket pocket, but my shirt sleeves have already turned soggy.

"In the olden days, these tombstones were aligned side by side," Longie says to me. "They were spaced and distanced like a marching band."

"Maybe these monuments had their day, but they beat to their own drum now." I flip my head and rainwater wings from the brim of my hat. "Half this place is crumbling away."

"Some of these poor folks got roots punchin' through their sacred beds," Longie says. "But some are restful." He tilts his head as if he's listening. "Thanks for taking me up on this night stroll. I haven't visited your parents' site in a while." Longie buttons his coat up to his neck.

We slosh over a few spring sprouts through the dark cemetery. "I figured ya wanted to talk to me about something," I say, tuckin' my chin against my neck as the rain whips me.

"I know a lot of folks buried in this place, Yael," Longie says. Across from the single headstone that marks my mother and father, we stand in solemn respect. Behind the stone, spiked black fences stand at attention, like trophies honoring their warriors. "There are good deeds in this cemetery that seeded many other good deeds," Longie says.

There's no feelin' inside me. It's more of a duty. "I dunno. Cemeteries depress me." I kinda wish Longie would just stop talkin'. His voice is muffled by the rain as it is.

"Sure there's sadness here," Longie says. "But also, cemeteries keep the stories alive. When someone dies, it often feels like we're falling into a hole without them. But the memories catch us and place us back around the table with them, listening to their voices tell the old stories."

Finally, the drops lighten. The wet brings out the smell of old stone buried in the air, like the iron in quarries. I rub my hands together.

"You're wearing the watches," Longie says. "Your father's and mine." He taps the double metal jewelry stickin' outta my wet sleeves.

"I try to when I'm not fightin'," I titter. Which isn't often, I think. That's my whole life these days.

Longie holds my left arm. "6:11," he reads from my father's broken watch. "Six plus one plus one. Eight."

"You never told me why that number was important."

"Now I will. Eight is one rung above normal." He plunges his hands into his coat pockets and huddles close with me. I smell his aftershave. That's the same scent that signaled my father's return home from the docks. "If you look around, everything is made up of seven. Seven days. Seven oceans. Seven notes in music and colors in a rainbow. Even seven holes in your head." He clutches the back of my neck. "Seven means things are complete." He smiles, not with spark. But with calm. With wisdom. "But eight. Eight is beyond. Like Chanukah is eight days long. Oil that should have lasted one day lasted eight and let the heroes beat the bad guys. Eight is courage that pushes men beyond normal." Longie touches his thumb and middle finger together. "Eight leaders of the Newark Minutemen."

For the first time, I examine Pop's watch crystal that protects the frozen hands. "I miss 'em," I admit. I realize the loneliest part is that I can't hear their voices anymore.

"You're here to visit them through your memories. Talk to them," Longie says as if he'd just heard my thoughts.

I widen my eyes and exhale. "I don't know what to say." My fists are numb. I open and close them to get the blood flowin'.

"You honor their memories by affirming their dreams." He winces at me, at what must be my pitiful face. "Years ago, your parents left a barbaric Russian Empire for a dream," he says. "They fled horrors of the Tsar's bloody programs, the rampant looting, brutal rape, and mass murder. Their families were slaughtered like sheep."

Longie chases my eyes. I don't mean to disrespect him. I'm just afraid I can't control my feelings.

"Every night, corpses lined the street," he says. "Life came down to one simple choice— survive or perish." Longie grasps both my shoulders in his hands before I can look away again. His warmth settles me. "They left everything behind—money, jobs, even their language. They carried each other into a new world."

He releases me. "They struggled when they arrived. Settled on the East side of New York in the tenements. I know your Pop told you stories, but you were too young to remember."

I squeeze back the wellin' tears.

Longie's wet face tightens, but he doesn't back off. "You can't imagine the life," he says. "Many packed into one room, sleeping on fire escapes to cool off in the summer, bundling together in one bed in the winter. Most importantly, Yael, because of their courage, you're here today. Do you understand they have shaped your purpose?"

My teeth clack from the chill.

"Keep their dream alive, and they'll be with you every day and help you know who you are. This is your legacy." He pats me on the shoulder and then withdraws into the darkness to give me light.

My throat tightens. I dig deep and push away a sick feelin'. I breathe in and then blow the rain away from my mouth. "Pop. M…mama," I stutter. I pause. "You're not here." My voice lifts. "So you must be somewhere else. I miss you so much." I shift from one foot to another. "Everything is a mess. Bad guys are comin'. We're tryin' to stop 'em, but we're criminals if we do. Innocent people are gonna get hurt. There's no avoiding it. Sometimes, I don't even know who I'm supposed to help or trust or if I can protect them." My body prickles. Then I remember something. I reach into my pocket. I pull out a stone and rub it between my fingers. I place it on my father and mother's headstone. "I hope I make you proud. Please accept me for the decisions I make." I glide my hand across the headstone. "Mama, Pop. I wish I could hear you one more time."

The ground becomes alive with more splashes than my eyes can see. The rain drowns out my cries. Longie grabs my shakin' body before it hits the ground.

CHAPTER 11

Feint

FRITZ KUHN:
Billiard Room. German Hall. Springfield Avenue. Newark, NJ

The wooden rack around the ten billiard balls feels silky against my palms. I lift it and the balls rest like a petrified triangle on the table in the Bund Pool Hall. One of my soldiers hands me a pool stick. His fingertips are blue from the chalk.

A full-in-the face hit on the nose will release maximum energy. But tonight, I take a different tack. My cue ball is positioned at the top corner pocket so I can leverage my power with a spin aimed at the second row of balls. I thrust the stick and the balls break. Everyone claps, just as I expect. Now, I control the next move.

Among us are forty of my most trusted men, including Günther. I am pleased that he has brought in our next generation, Axel and Frank and their friends. If my own father had taken me under his wing, I would be in Berlin running things right now. My heart tugs at my chest when I remember his fading smile. He gawked at my stricken face when I told him his alma mater didn't accept me. From then, it was downhill. No matter how much I achieved, his silence shouted his disappointment. Then he double-crossed me. Turned me in. Fool that he was. We could have risen in the ranks together. Now, I thank him. This path I'm on is bigger than him.

"Mein Führer. Those magnificent portraits of Hitler facing one another across the pool tables are inspiring," Axel says. His voice brings me back. My eyes rest on this perfect specimen for a few moments. Why does he excite me so? Because he reminds me of myself? Or because he holds my future?

Interrupting my thoughts, Camp Nordland's Führer Schwartzman gushes. "Congratulations on taking down the House Committee, mein Führer," he says as he chews on peanuts and hotdogs. "How dare that Senator Dies calls us Un-American." There's no doubt that Hermann will do wonders training our stormtroopers at Nordland, but he's going to have a heart attack if he stuffs any more pigs-in-the-blanket in his mouth.

"We sent home the investigators with their Schwanz zwischen ihren Beinen." Camp Siegfried's Führer Vandenberg covers his crotch to emphasize his point. He proves to me that he's going to run his camp with the vigor of a lion tamer.

I place my hand on his shoulder to embrace the gravity of our win. "Their mission to destroy me has failed. Just like they failed to prove our orginal Nazi party here was a fascist fifth column."

"Dumpkoff! Of course Friends of New Germany was a fifth column and so are we," Dinkelacker guffaws. As my director of youth, he's going to pave the way here. Who wouldn't follow such a movie star face like his?

I chalk my pool stick. "I screwed them! The whole Commie, Roosevelt, *unamerikanisch* Inquisition," I say, brimming with pride.

"They have their heads up their arsch," National Secretary Wheeler-Hill says as he turns toward our young members. He doesn't disappoint me when he slips his hand into his jacket like the old French Emperor. "Years ago, we hung everything out of our shorts for the *Times* and they looked away like little girls. They covered their ears when we told them we were going to destroy the Moscow Red madness and its Jewish bacillus crawling from American sewage." No one can accuse Little Napoleon of talking about the bush. He gets straight to the point.

I thrust my stick and drop two balls into corner pockets. But no third shot opens, so I shoot the cue ball behind two of mine. Now, no one has a shot.

Hermann stomps around the table searching for an angle. "When our brilliant Führer Kuhn changed the name from *Friends* to the German American-Nazi Bund, their heads spun," Hermann says. He grunts when his balls ricochet off the sides without dropping in a pocket. He lobs his pool stick to Frank for chalking.

Meanwhile, I overhear my Camp Nordland professor, Kunze. He speaks to the young men. "Many trivialize our rising power here," he says. "But *The Nation News* gets it. They warned everyone a while back that we are a replica of the rising Hitler regime." I'm pleased he will be teaching the stormtrooper recruits.

"We pulled the fur over their ears," Vandenberg adds. He loops his thumb underneath his Sam Browne belt.

"They think we're a bunch of American boy scouts," Frank sniggers, throwing in his two cents.

Günther grabs the pool stick from Frank and circles the table. "Even FBI Director Hoover can't find a law to corner us," Günther says. He overshoots the ball and misses.

The government has wasted my time and theirs. "Next time they ask me if I think there are any good Jews, my answer will be, 'If a mosquito is on your arm, you don't stop to ask if it's a good mosquito or a bad. You just smash it.'"

The men in the room gurgle.

Axel stands next to me. We watch Dinkelacker place the cue ball off center behind the baulk line. He slides his stick back and powers the weapon. The white ball shoots across the green wool, collides with the head ball, and sends the two balls behind the head sailing into the side pockets.

Onlookers shake their heads. Dinkelacker is calculated, never to be underestimated. After all, he threatens Bund members who don't send their kids to our camps. He offers them a one-way trip back to Germany.

The attention on Dinkelacker gives me an excuse to talk to Axel. "Günther told me you took your destiny in your hands tonight and put an engagement ring on Krista's finger."

"Yes, mein Führer. I stopped by her house and caught her right before she went to sleep," Axel answers as that Frank Schenk ogles us.

"Good timing for reinforcing obligations to bear children for the Reich," I say. "Krista has all the qualities you could ask for. I expect you will take care of her."

"I would have bedded her on the spot, mein Führer," Axel says, his lips tightening. "But we argued because she wouldn't tell me who hit her. She insisted it was the door." He rubs his temple. "I told her Axel would kill whoever hurt her."

"Your suspicions run to the Newark Minuteman, I presume?"

"Who else?" Axel is quick to say. "Krista knows no one hurts what's mine."

"Gut," I say. I'm proud of the boy for assuming his rule. Now he must convince her of her own value. She will be a big asset for us if he can.

"We will live the perfect life in Germany." Axel's vision is crisp.

He warms me as he basks in predictable rules of right and wrong. "You will make pure Aryans for the Reich, Axel!" I know this man will exceed and succeed at all costs, and I will ride his coattails. Axel is key for our success. He will learn that Krista unlocks the potential for the future.

YAEL:
Yael's Apt. Hawthorne Avenue. Newark, NJ

The doorknob clicks and the door to my Hawthorne Avenue apartment creaks. I swing the door open and raise my fists. "Son of a gun," I cry. I should have known.

Longie winks and kisses the tilted mezuzah affixed to our doorpost, the daily tradition that brings watch over the home. Tonight, he enters like family.

In the kitchen, my brother Dov waves at Longie. He turns up the radio to drown out the downpour outside just in time to join the opening theme of our favorite radio show.

"Who knows what evil lurks in the hearts of men?" Dov and I chime with the announcer. "The Shadow knows!" We laugh along with the ominous cackle on the radio. When our parents died, my brothers and I clung together. Most importantly, we never lost the sense of humor between us.

Longie flashes his smile that reaches places the sun can't.

I tap the top of the radio. "I gotta get some of those invisibility powers," I say.

"From what Longie tells me, you're doing just fine sneaking up and terrifying the bad guys," Dov says. His bright eyes tell me he'd like to be out there with me. But we both know he's gotta keep gas in the family tank. "Keep your head down, but keep it up, little bro." Of course he's a big part of why I'm out there avenging.

I unscrew a bottle of milk from the refrigerator and slurp the cream off the top. But I guess my stealth skills need some work. Dov's wife Sarah charges out of the bedroom bundling the sleepin' baby Abner in her arms. She flips off the radio and snatches the bottle from me with her free hand. "Yael!" she yells in a loud whisper. "How many times have I told you—"

"Sarah," I interrupt as I put my arm around her. "I cherish the way these moments bond us." She tries to squirm away. But then, uh oh—the baby whimpers and kicks his feet.

Longie supports me with a shrug of his shoulders. He steals baby Abner from Sarah and sits down in the chair. The tiny hand of the snufflin' baby wraps around Longie's finger. He strokes the silky black hair on the delicate head with his thumb. Then Longie closes his eyes and sways his body until there's soft breathin' from the baby. Just when I think Longie's decided to nap in that position, too, he slips his hand around the infant and retrieves an envelope from inside his jacket. He flings it at Dov. "Here's the visas for your brother Marty and his wife to get the heck outta Germany. Compared to Hitler, Kuhn's a mouse." Is there anything Longie can't do?

"Thanks, Longie. Hey, is this Kuhn really a threat?" Dov asks. "A lotta people call him a Chaim Yankel or a guy who just fell off the turnip truck."

"A dog with sheep schlepping behind him," Sarah says as she scrubs the dishes in the sink.

"Do not underestimate this man," Longie says. He brushes the baby's head with his lips. "Kuhn's a former German machine-gunner who fought with men who are now high up Nazis. He's a university man from Munich with a masters in science. He was clever enough to escape Germany when he shoulda gone to jail. He's a family man with two kids, and he worked for Henry Ford."

I hop up on the counter next to Sarah. Wrong move. She hands me a dishtowel.

"And now, he's addressed as BundesFührer," I say. "I don't get how German Americans fall for Kuhn as their Hitler proxy." I snap the towel at Sarah, she snags it between two fingers and hands me a pot to dry.

Sarah trades Longie a plate of warm chocolate pastry for the baby. "People claim he's a liability to Hitler, calling too much attention to the Nazi party in America," she says.

"I don't see how," Longie answers. His chest swells as he inhales the richness of chocolate and butter. "Fritz Kuhn owns land, runs camps, controls business. He heads up six companies with a militia and propaganda unit." Longie peels the icing off the cake and eats it.

"His Settlement League is a front against boycotting German goods," I explain.

"Yael. Where are Kuhn's newsletters ya showed me?" Dov scrounges through a pile of papers on the table. "I remember something about shortwave broadcasts from Germany. I can help listen to some of them, Longie." Dov's achin' to help anyway he can. I fish out the newspaper he wants.

"Everything helps! The paper is part of the German underground," Longie says. "Harry's been catching hidden codes in it."

"He's gotta gift for it!" I say. "He found an advertisement that recruited spies." I toss the dishtowel in the sink.

"What gets me is that Mr. Kuhn heralds himself as America's hero," Sarah says. "The next George Washington." Sarah shifts and the baby's leg dangles out of the blanket. The difference between the bracelets of fat around his calm ankle versus the kickin' heels is liberating. She pushes the bottle between Li'l Abner's lips.

Longie shakes his head. "He dodges our bullets. As you've heard, Congressman Dies is trying to put Kuhn in jail for treason."

"Dies runs the House Committee on Un-American Activities, HUAC," Dov explains to Sarah.

"How many of these Bund members does he have?" Sarah asks.

"We don't know if Kuhn has fifty or five hundred thousand members," Longie answers. "But I can tell ya, the momentum is building for what he calls der Tag, The Day." Kuhn and his Hitler-cronies are gonna turn our lights out if we're not ready.

"Can the Minutemen stop him?" Dov plants his teeth into an apple and tears away its flesh. He tosses the fruit to me. I catch it and crunch the other side. Since we were little, Dov always shared his food with me.

Longie hesitates. "The FBI wants us to get into the inner circle and rub Kuhn out," he says.

Suddenly, a knock on the window from the fire escape turns our heads. In one motion, Sarah passes the baby to Dov, seizes a baseball bat and shoves up the window. The room jingles with pings of rain thrashin' off the iron platform. I hadn't realized how insulated we'd been.

My jaw drops. Krista's face surprises me. Water drips down her cheeks over her puffy lips.

I leap up and dash over before Sarah can do damage to her. "Sorry about the invader, guys," I say with a grimace. I grasp Krista's slippery hand through the window. "She won't harm anyone." Rain drops onto the wooden floor. "Right, Krista?"

"No, of course not. Yael's a good pal," she says through the open window.

Judgin' by my family's gawkin' faces, they aren't convinced. With Krista's soaked blonde braids, there's no chance of disguising this German broad hangin' off my house. Behind me, Sarah grabs the baby, disappears into her room, and slams the door behind her.

"Uh. Krista," I quaver. My hands cup open and flutter. "Meet my brother, Dov, and my, yeah, Longie Zwillman." The collision of my two worlds rattles around inside me like broken glass digesting inside my stomach.

Yiddish curses burst out of Sarah's room like confetti.

My shoulders shrug to my ears. "I guess, um ... it's better if I talk to her outside."

Dov gives a short, "Yup."

Longie knows Krista from the Y, so he rolls with the punches. "That's probably best," he says.

"I'll, uh, be right out here if ya need me." I follow my pointed finger through the window into the rough weather to face Krista. "Nice of you to drop by," I shout over the pangin' rain.

Krista wastes no time. She extends her shadowed hand. "Axel gave me this ring." The wet rock reflects the light from inside the apartment into my eye. I whisk my neck sideways.

"It's huge," I say. "We could buy the Statue of Liberty with that thing." I nod my head east toward New York Harbor and complete the triangle with a nod north toward Manhattan.

"Axel wants to prove how much he can give me." As she speaks, her cheekbones move like two pyramids built by slaves in the desert.

She and I both know that indulgences from Axel will become her norm. "You'll have a nice life, won't ya?" I say to her. My breath steams from my mouth. "Obedient servants, enchanting castle." The burnin' inside me betrays my cool act. "A man who worships you as long as you follow his orders."

"Look, Yael. I don't have a choice." Krista's whinin' infuriates me. I stare at her wet, plastered hair against her head. She looks callous and she looks fake. "This marriage helps my family survive," she says.

"Well, you should have a choice. We all need choices. But rules in your world seem carved in the shape of a swastika, don't they?" Dang! How do I rescue this woman and pull her from the abyss? I pluck my wet clothes away from my sweltering chest.

"Choice is a vice," Krista says. She gazes at me with soulful eyes. "The party helps us live deliberately so we won't feel lost." Is she beggin' me for some permission? Krista blinks hard, as if she's just cleared her thoughts. But I know she still can't see the alternatives. She turns away. "Honestly, sometimes I do feel less lost when I'm with a vagrant like you."

"Aww. That's the nicest thing you've ever said to me," I say. She can't even be tolerant when she's tryin'. At least she's tryin'. My knuckles whiten as they grip the fire escape rail. Part of me wants to jump over and escape from her. On the other hand, I'm achin' to bulldoze the wall between our worlds. But how?

Krista tries again. "I mean, in normal times, I could be with someone like you and be happy." She shifts her eyes to see my reaction.

A hiss from a car passin' below through the rain distracts me. I lean over the rail. "It's a hard life for Jews. The coal man forgets us. You wouldn't last through the winter." The cold drizzle drains the heat from my body.

"I guess I'd need to learn how to knit heavy sweaters from an Irish woman," quips Krista as she leans against my side. Is she hoping we heat each other up?

"If you got stuck with me, you'd have to look at life differently."

Krista gazes at me, and I'm overwhelmed by the beauty. Her lips part, as if she wants to tell me something. But then they close. "Always open to learning new things," Krista says. "How would I look at life differently?"

I catch the glint of her ring. Usually, the rain against my face on a warm night calms me, but not tonight. The wet grates me like nails scratchin' chalkboard. I'm not sure this conversation is worthwhile, but I continue. "That's not for me to answer. You need to ask yourself how you would look at life." I tug my sleeve over my hand and wipe away the water on her face. Her eyes meet mine and time swallows me. My mind blurs between where this woman came from and the future she represents.

"OK." Krista pauses. "I guess I'd have to believe in different things?"

"Actually, being from my world isn't about beliefs. It's about actions. So, you'll have to do different things." The only way to make her understand is through reality, not emotion.

"Can you tell me if I'm hot or cold?" asks Krista. "I'm new at this."

I tighten my lips to hold back my smile. But she can't have it both ways. "For one, accept people for who they are," I say. This make-believe conversation annoys me. Even if Krista wanted to, which she might, her inner circle won't let her take the risk. "As Mama used to say, 'You can't dance at two weddings.'"

She tilts her head. "Tolerance is what I want in my life more than anything," she says with a cringe. "My father barely accepts me, I mean with all the stuff about my mother."

So far she's sayin' what she thinks I wanna hear. "Also, we take care of our own, in a different way than your crowd." Maybe I should feel sorry for Krista rather than judgin' her so. Her fluttering eyelashes brush my heart. It's gettin' harder to keep my hands off her. I bury them in my pockets and fondle some crumpled money that I'd forgotten was there. "Takin' care of each other makes us bigger than ourselves. You'd have to fight to be part of a chain of generations." If she opens her eyes even a little, this effort will have been worth it.

"I'm not afraid of fighting." She shivers, but her eyes stay steady. She's got that raw nerve. I think she's tellin' the truth.

"That's why I invited you to the Y to box," I say. "But you'd have to fight against more than just people. By the way, I don't blame you for bein' loyal. Your people want to make lives better. They want you to be proud of where you're from." She's thinkin' about my words. There's no pinkness in her cheeks betraying her integrity. Now I tread carefully because she'll turn brittle as cast iron at my next comment. "The problem is you believe some lives are more important than others." My throat narrows. "You sacrifice the less important ones for the good of the country." I'm surprised that she holds my stare. "If you ever wanted to break away, you'd have to both fight yourself and hold on tight with your own two hands."

Krista's teeth chatter. The warmth from her body has drained. "The problem is my two hands aren't mine," she whispers.

This knocks me for a loop. I grasp her and take her into my arms.

CHAPTER 12

The One-Two

YAEL:

Hitler Park. Montgomery Hall. Montgomery Avenue. NJ

There *he* is. Among the boisterous crowd, Führer Fritz Kuhn poses for photos with children and signs autographs. How appropriate. Adolph Hitler's May birthday celebration is here in Hitler Park. How inappropriate. Hitler Park is located in the middle of Newark, New Jersey.

We didn't expect to be bringin' down Nazi celebrations today, and maybe we should stay out of the limelight, but this opportunity is just too temptin' to pass up. We're aimin' to strip the swastika flags that are wavin' up there at the top of the flagpoles. Without attracting notice, Harry, me, and a group of Minutemen zigzag through bouncy polka dancers and swingin' beer steins. The scene is underlined by a general snarl of German. We spread out among Nazi-uniformed soldiers who are busy rollin' sausage on grills. The burnin' grease makes my mouth-water and I hesitate. Harry doesn't miss a trick. He elbows me forward. We slip between portable tables filled with families and hop over food baskets weightin' down the corners of wool picnic blankets.

The sudden clattering noise on the stage makes my teeth clamp. I swing to see four boys dressed in their mini-Hitler outfits chase each other in front of the brass band playin' "Deutschland Ueber Alles." The rabble-rousers don't even try to avoid an older couple twirlin' in their Bavarian costumes. An old man falls back into a tuba player. The clankin' instruments send the onlookers into mayhem. Women scream, men wave arms, kids cheer, and tight-pants uniformed officials dart after the terrorists.

The distraction helps us. I move with our boys into a cluster of women dressed in their traditional get-ups. I follow the group's glare toward a plump, plaited-hair woman on the platform next to the bandstand. Her loud tap thumps through the microphone. "Bitte! Beachtung," she screams so loud that people cover their ears. "Please!" She waves her hand in sync with a banner fluttering over her head. It reads in German, "Your Homeland is the Other Home of your Life." That's a head full.

Finally, Fritz Kuhn appears at her side. The mayhem calms to a silence. "Willkommen!" he shouts. "Today we celebrate the birthday of our great leader. Tomorrow we sit in Washington, D.C."

"Why would we assume his ambition would be less?" Harry says, clamping his lips. I can almost hear his blood hum.

A boy not more than six attacks the platform. He raises his uniformed arm. "By our fist we smash whoever stands in our way," he shouts. His blond hair swipes his eyes. Kuhn beams. The crowd guffaws and raises a right-armed salute. "Heil Hitler!"

The emcee licks her lips and then plunges her hand into a large jar filled with coupons. "Our own Führer Kuhn will present the winning raffle for our prized Bible, *Mein Kampf*," her raw voice yells. She pulls out a ticket and reads it. "And the winning number is—"

You can hear a pin drop.

She moves the paper away from her eyes. "It is 1-3-9-1."

A woman dressed in a tight German outfit leaps up and down and screams with joy. As she waves her ticket, we advance toward the flagpole.

I look up. The red and black flag jerks against the blue sky, like it's taunting it. As Benny unwinds the rope from the cleat to free it, I keep watch. Through the swarm of people, I think I notice Krista's parents eating on a plaid blanket. Just as the man opens his chops around a sandwich, the woman elbows him. Uh oh. Is that Mrs. Brecht pointin' at us?

The man squeezes his temples. He frowns at Benny. We're caught red-handed. The man rolls to his knees and springs up as fast as someone his size can do that. His sauerkraut sprays across the blanket. He cups his hands around his mouth. "Führer Kuhn!" he screams. "We have some goons on our turf!"

I don't wait to get a good look at him. I drum Benny on the back to speed him up. He squeezes the rope and flashes his hands up and down likes he's milkin' a goat. My heart's racin'.

Kuhn raises his arm to nearby stormtroopers. They whip out iron bars and rush at us. I have to admit, his system is greased. But we are one step ahead. From behind a tree, Harry extends his leg. In the next moment, I understand his plan. He trips a soldier runnin' toward us. And that's not good for the bad guys. The soldier grabs onto a white tablecloth, draggin' food, plates, and flower pots behind him. The man hits the ground. A red icing swastika cake slides off of its platter and splats across his uniform. We couldn't have choreographed a better vaudeville show.

Across the park, Al pours fuel across hot BBQ coals. He fans the flames. Heads turn *that-a-way* with a stampede to follow. But we aren't outta the woods. With a battalion pushin' through the crowd toward us, I unhook the flag for Benny, tie it in a knot, and throw it over several heads to Abie. Abie pivots, dashes, and tosses it onto a hot BBQ. Like clockwork, a lyin'-in-wait Puddy squirts fuel on the coals and the flame whooshes. Maxie runs by and pours on some extra gas. The fire rumbles and swings at his chin. He dodges. "KAY-O!" he cheers.

The befuddled Nazis lunge at the Minutemen, but our gang escapes before the raffle-ticket winner sways back to her seat.

FRITZ KUHN:
Cohen's Deli. Hawthorne Avenue. Newark, NJ

"Longie Zwillman is like a rotting fish. He starts stinking from the head." I jab my fork through the bulging eye of my smoked cod at the counter at Cohen's Deli. "His goons ruined our Hitler Day. He's going to dread the day the Newark Minutemen touched a canvas."

Delis aren't my choice for lunch, but Günther was craving a pastrami sandwich, and Cohen's is right around the corner from my Newark Bund office. When we arrived, the line was out the door. Always thinking, I led the way through the pushy patrons to seize the counter seating. All I can hope is that I'll escape soon because this place racks my head. Even now, the busboys clank dishes and servers yell like fish ladies.

The mix of people in the deli disgust me, too. Jews, Italians, Poles, and even some of these Americanized Germans. It's like too many ingredients in a stew that ends up tasting like nothing. But if you can get past the riff raff, the food is okay.

Günther forces an overstuffed pastrami sandwich into his mouth. As he bites down, the sauerkraut erupts past the edges of the rye bread. "Günther. What does that Mobster Zwillman care about most?" I ask him. If I'm going to beat the crook, I need to understand what drives him.

His muffled answer bubbles through his ballooned mouth. "Family."

"Family?" I ponder this. "So, should we mow down his mother?" I shake my head. Even I draw the line here. Plus, we could never get to her. A bone from my fish pricks inside my cheek, and I pluck it from my mouth.

"He also cares about image." Günther wipes his greasy face on his sleeve.

"What do you mean?" I ask. "Like fancy clothes and nice cars?"

"Nah. Zwillman's different. He's a gentleman," Günther spills mustard-covered sauerkraut in his lap and gets distracted. "Frick!" he curses. I watch him wipe his pants. The crowd is pushing up against us. Faces of Jews and Italians yammer away. I sense another cluster of god-forsaken creatures ramming their way into the deli. I knew we shouldn't have come here. I sneeze from the stench in the air.

LONGIE ZWILLMAN:
Cohen's Deli. Hawthorne Avenue. Newark, NJ

From the counter at Cohen's deli, I hear Nat order our sandwiches. "Extra fat on the pastrami, Mrs. Cohen." He's up there with Harry and Abie while I wait at our table near the door. My stomach rumbles from the sweet and pungent smells seeping from caramelized gribenes and pickled vegetables.

Over my grumbling stomach, I hear my name. But it's not said with the familiar ring of my men callin' or my Ma. It's bastardized by a German accent. My eyes circle the deli. Bingo. It's comin' from a large man in a Nazi uniform eating at the counter a few feet from Nat. The guy's back drapes over his crossed Sam Brown belt like an overpoured muffin. Next to him, his equally full-figured cohort hacks spit into a napkin and rubs his khaki pants. I strain to hear their conversation. It's a rare day that a Nazi hangs out at the deli.

Steam streams from my ears when I realize who it is. Kuhn. The last thing I expected today was to bump elbows with this enemy. It's true, in Newark, you plan your day around a row with an Irish or a Pole or an Italian. But of all the nerve, one of my vilest enemies dares to infiltrate my neighborhood sanctuary. And there he sits, the self-proclaimed American Hitler talking trash about me. Well he's not sitting here for long if I have anything to do with it. I wedge through the crowd and park myself over the pathetic man.

Kuhn ignores my presence. He turns to his mate. "Zwillman's a con man who controls jobs, cheats people out of money, and makes his friends indispensable," the low-life says.

"More than family, Longie Zwillman cares about being legitimate," the German with the stained pants explains. There's my name again, and he's wearing it out. I roll my right fist in my left palm. "Sure," the guy says. "Zwillman brags about his old bootlegging empire. But now he claims he's on the up and up. He covers up his racketeering by throwing money at hospitals and opening up soup kitchens." He finally swallows the grotesque amount of food in his mouth. "Fritz, remember when he put up a reward for the Lindbergh baby in '32? He wants to whitewash his rep and be a hero to his people."

From my elevated vantage point, I swipe the elbow of one of my best suits against the shoulder of Kuhn's brown military blazer. He tilts up his peachy forehead and shines me with his widows-peak. His mouth drops and so does his fork.

When the fork stops bouncing, I crush the weak metal with the heel of my shoe. "Mr. Kuhn," I say with a grin.

Kuhn rises. His pasty face meets my ruddy one.

"Fritz. We're … we … we're late." His companion stammers as he swipes grease off his chin and joins his boss.

An imposing Harry, Nat, and Abie triangulate behind me.

"Mrs. Cohen doesn't like Hitler's soldiers eating her food," I say.

"We have no ties to Herr Hitler," he responds. "We are good Americans, just like you, Mr. Zwillman." He dares to crack a smile.

"Fritz. We need to go. Now!" His companion pleads.

Kuhn grabs his garrison hat from the counter. He stares me down. His friend jams him through the crowd and pushes him out the door.

Across the counter, Mrs. Cohen waves the bill and yells at the dodgers.

"The check's on me, Mrs. Cohen," I say. "And please, add chocolate rugelach to our order today."

FRITZ KUHN:
Outside Cohen's Deli. Hawthorne Avenue. Newark, NJ

Outside Cohen's Deli, I fume. "Zwillman's got blood on his hands, and we'll unmask this monster and his Commies before they bring down

America." I throw down a coin from my pocket and stomp on Lady Liberty's head. With both hands, I straighten my cap and walk.

Günther struggles to keep up. "We need to make Zwillman the poster boy for evil, the one Adolph is warning the world about," he says, offering an inspired suggestion for once.

"Superb!" I say. "Pay off our German cops in town to feed us every tip they can. We will unmask these outlaws."

Anger fuels my day with purpose. I stop in front of the candy store. I bang my knuckles against the window. Inside, the Jew behind the counter widens his brown eyes at me. "Just wait until Hitler gets here," I yell. I don't wait for his reaction. "Günther. Get a story about Zwillman for the DWJ going. Let's show the Germans of Newark that his breed stands for criminal no matter how much batter on the weinershähnel."

We charge back toward the office. Günther holds the door open for me. "We'll round up these pickpockets of the world," he says.

"Der Tag is coming," I say. "We will fry them all and melt the gold from their teeth to fund our mission."

CHAPTER 13

Red Boxing Gloves

LONGIE ZWILLMAN:
Ben Marden's Riviera Club. Fort Lee, NJ

"When God builds a nightclub in heaven …" I say to my gangster-in-arms, Meyer Lansky. "It'll be the spitting image of Ben Marden's." Ben Marden's Club is the highlight of Fort Lee, New Jersey. It still holds court for the who's who of every eggcrate-grill, high-fender, Cadillac owner from Hollywood to Manhattan.

We are upstairs decked out in tuxedos, sippin' martinis in the hidden casino of the lush Cabaret and Casino Club. My partners and I built the club on the cliffs of Fort Lee. It was the original Hollywood before the studios ran away to sunny California. "Remember when we were kids," I say to Meyer. "All the biggies hung their shingles here—Universal. Goldwyn. Fox. Selznick. To name a few."

"Those were the days! For all of us Jews, Negroes, women, and underdogs. The business gave us second class citizens a chance to make a buck." Meyer clicks his gambling chips into a pile and sips his martini. "Now we get it all to ourselves."

139

I check my watch. "By the way. Yael and his Bund-girl should be arriving for dinner downstairs," I tell Meyer.

"That's gotta be a powder keg of a partnership," Meyer says.

"It'll end soon," I grumble. "The chasm between them's not made for crossing. They're both devoted to their own worlds, and I don't see that changing."

YAEL:
Ben Marden's Riviera Club. Fort Lee, NJ

Three hundred feet up, on the cliff above the Hudson, the maître de receives Krista and me. "Welcome to Ben Marden's Riviera Club," he says. He checks our coats and my hat.

Krista's arm rests on mine as her high heels sink into the pink carpeting. My white dinner jacket flaps as we weave through fourteen hundred buzzin' socializers. I nod to a familiar judge smokin' in the lounge. Krista nudges me to notice the prince and famous actress clinkin' glasses. A boxer buddy smiles at me as his girlfriend corrects the way he pokes his fork through his brisket. On the way to our table, a neighborhood barber waves a comb at me as he trims the hair of a movie star that I can't remember the name of, a masseuse closes a door to a private room and winks, and the shoe shiner's muscles bulge as he wicks his rag back and forth over black shoes.

Krista agreed to join me for this goodbye dinner, even though we know we can never be friends in today's world. The truth. I'm not done with her. Krista believes she has no choice but to follow her Bund rules. Deep down, I don't think she believes the slop she's served. At least she has yet to do anything vile. On the other hand, I'm a vigilante who takes the world into my own hands and makes my own rules. So tonight I'm dazzling her with the tinsel side of my life. Maybe it doesn't have the moats and towers of German castles, but it has a splendor that would make any dragon spit fire.

The maître de seats us at a window table overlooking the new George

Washington suspension bridge that sweeps across the bay to the towers of Manhattan. Suddenly, my image in the glass free falls as the huge windows slide down into the floor and connect the entire restaurant with the sky. I adjust my crooked bow tie before my reflection disappears. Krista gasps as she sinks into her plush chair. The same warm wind that drives the waves against the rocks below showers us. We watch the white foam spray high up the cliffs.

Krista places a white linen napkin on her lap, and I follow her lead. "Well, Krista," I say. "You're off to the next chapter. Summer, then across the ocean to Berlin. I'll visit." I shake my head. "I'll visit camp. Sorry. Not Berlin." The corner of my mouth turns up.

The waiter sets down a basket of bread rolls wrapped in cloth.

I reach into the basket and bounce the scaldin' hot bun between my hands. "Be ready. When the town baker gives you two bread rolls, that's the signal. I'm comin' that night." I nip the roll. "Where did you tell Axel you were goin' this evening?"

"He didn't ask. He and my father are at a Bund meeting." Krista's posture stiffens. "What do you mean? What about two bread rolls?"

"It's the signal to meet me at the Siegfried Lake. 10:00 p.m. I'll find ya." I bite into the roll. Let's just call it a nod to my Russian grandmother who baked explosives into her bread for the Cossacks to sink their teeth into. I sniff at my own wit.

"No, Yael! You mustn't." She sounds startled, scared even. "While I wish this were different, it's not. We agreed this couldn't work. My life is carved in stone. If I try to change anything, people will make me disappear." She hiccups. She's nervous. "Plus, Führer Kuhn and my father are pushing me to spill the beans about the Newark Minutemen. They'll stop at nothing to strip information from me." She scans the room "They're probably spying on me as we speak." The forlorn defeat in her eyes tugs at my heart. But more, it ignites my determination.

"Then we'll out-box 'em," I say. "Throw a fake one-two to the body, watch their eyes drop." I swing my fist. "Then a big left hook to the noggin." Krista's got another thing comin' if she thinks this is our last night. Don't count me out of nothin'.

She smiles. "Light fast punches until they're helpless." Her eyes glimmer.

"There ya go! You're learnin' fast at the Y. Hey! You can even help me spy on 'em." It's a joke, but it can't hurt to test her mettle. That poker face is hard to read. Or is she just innocent? Dang! She's an enigma.

"If I can curb the violence that's coming and share a little intel, it's no skin off my neck," Krista finally replies. "In fact, don't know if it means anything. But there's something I keep meaning to share. Führer Kuhn writes a lot of checks to himself." She opens her purse and hands me one. I snagged one the other day when I was working in his office." No, she's not innocent.

"Hmm. Thanks. Could be helpful." Maybe he's payin' himself a salary or something a bit more underhanded. I store the check in my wallet. "Look, Krista. It's time I let some good into my life. Cause there's been a lot of darkness."

"I doubt either one of us can compromise, even if we wanted to," Krista says.

"You're right. I won't compromise." I look outside, down the river against the spotlights on the cliff. They're beamin' at us. On cue, a waiter approaches the table and hands me a box wrapped in white paper tied with a blue ribbon. "It's not a diamond ring." I hand the box to Krista. "But it proves what I have to give ya." Maybe I'm not what she wants. But I believe, deep down, I stand for who she is. She just can't hear herself yet.

As Krista slips her finger under the blue ribbon, I stop her. "If ya open it, ya must believe in it."

Krista drops her hands in her lap. She hunts my eyes for a hint. "I can't just accept that." There she goes again, provin' her autonomy.

"Well. Whether you open it or not, it's yours." What Krista must accept is that I'll give her not just a life but the right to choose her own life.

The fifty-ton dome roof of the restaurant rises and slides open. The space above us moves with a life of its own. The salty air brushes our cheeks. I know it's only a hint of the power the breeze holds. Reminds me of my fists restin' in my lap. My lip curls.

On one stage, the nightly Riviera Follies featuring *America's Loveliest Girls*, energizes the room. It's all I can do but hold myself in my seat as we eat dinner. Finally, I toss my napkin on my plate. I take Krista to the revolving dance floor under the open roof. To the tunes of the Tommy Dorsey Band, we continue that dance we started those nights ago at the Newark Bay. At first, Krista resists the classic American music, as if breakin' the rules. But then, she doesn't just follow my lead, she interprets it and shapes it all on her own, like a conversation.

After the Dorsey song, a waiter approaches us and whispers to me. I take Krista's hand in one of mine and the gift box in the other. We follow the escort to a hidden door and enter a stairway.

Upstairs, the plush gambling casino of the hidden Marine Room opens to us. I hear the soft bounce of dice against felt. In the center of the room, Longie flips chips onto the crap table. They land on five and three. He's with New York Jewish Mob King Meyer Lansky. Flanking them are Newark Minutemen Nat Arno, Puddy, Harry, Abie, Benny, Maxie and Al.

Longie waves me over. "Welcome to our quarter-million-dollar holy shrine." Quarter-mill was the shockin' price tag last year to rebuild the Riviera after the fire burnt it down. He hands me the dice. Chips click from bettors covering the board. I roll two fours.

Just steps away, Nat and Abie glare at Krista. Nat lights a cigar. "Mind if I ask you a question?" he says, puffing smoke next to her ear.

The hairs on my neck prickle. "Nat. Leave her alone," I say.

Harry shifts next to me.

"It's okay," Krista says. "What do you want to know, Mr. Arno?"

Nat circles to her right. "At the end of the Great War, your Fatherland was lost when Germany surrendered," Nat says. Krista twists her neck to follow. "Hitler and Kuhn, your father and all the Germans had a crying fit. Why are Germans so boorish?"

Krista snatches a drink off the tray of a passin' waiter. Is she gonna toss it at the weasel? She gulps. "Germans are direct people. We didn't understand why our undefeated army would lay down their arms." Her comment makes sense to me.

Smoke wafts as Nat puffs on his cigar. "Oh, right. You claim someone stabbed you in the back." He smiles. "What's your opinion? The Allies or the Jew Communists?"

Harry clamps his strong fingers around my arm. I hand the giftbox to Krista.

"Germany is a proud nation," she says. "The Versailles Treaty chopped us up. It starved our population and suffocated a noble military."

Nat digs in. "So then you had to choose between being a dictator's puppet, sub-human Commies or, *ta-da*, the winner, Nazi slaves." Nat spreads his arms.

This time Harry surrenders. My fist finds Nat's chin. I hear the smack. Harry, Abie, and Benny drag me away. Longie escorts Krista toward the door. My knuckles burn.

Nat swings at the air. "Eizeh balegan!" he yells loud enough for me to hear it from across the room. "What a crap show."

I'm both boilin' mad and ice cube cold. Why do my choices in two different directions look the same? All I know is when I choose one, the other disappears.

YAEL: YMHA
Boxing Gym. 652 High Street. Newark, NJ

My eyes swoop around the YMHA boxin' gym. It's empty except for the late-night broom-pusher sweepin' the floor. After hittin' hundreds of bare-knuckle punches against the boxin' bag at the Y, I unpeel my drenched shirt.

Tonight at Ben Marden's was a jumble of emotions. I went into the night thinkin' I was gonna keep Krista tethered to me until I could figure out a rescue plan. But the fight on multiple fronts—Nazi Americans in one corner, my own gang in the other—isn't makin' it easy. Dark clouds are fillin' my skull.

I feel empty after sneakin' Krista back to her apartment. I didn't get to say goodbye. Her father's car drove up and she rushed inside. Now she's disappeared like ice meltin' in the sun. She's the first person I've let myself care for. She made life seem like there were good guys out there. Even though she might not be one of them. She has a duality about her, an innocence that lets her twirl when she's happy, yet stamp her foot when she's wronged. I hate how I feel for her. All I know is there's a pitch black hole in my chest. It'll ache until I see her again.

My knuckles look like the inside of a grapefruit, but I punch the bag more. With each hit, I repeat the Newark Minutemen creed: "We train to gain control over our bodies. But to triumph, we wrap our bodies around individual will. With each trial, pain becomes more bearable, motions more familiar, waitin' more calm. Then it's our way. Then we are Newark Minutemen." My limbs begin to feel reconnected to my body. I start to feel whole again.

KRISTA:
Krista's Apt. Nye Avenue. Newark, NJ

On the rooftop of my apartment, I hold the white gift box that Yael gave me tonight at Ben Marden's. I didn't get to say goodbye to him when he brought me home. I'm lucky I got inside before Papa saw me. Tomorrow I leave for Camp Siegfried, and they'll be no looking back.

Through my hearing ear, the chaotic streets rumble below. Through my deaf ear, there's calm. I untie the blue ribbon around Yael's gift, unwrap the paper, and open the box. I gasp. Two plump, red boxing gloves rest in there like a Cavalier spaniel on King Charles's lap. Better, like a symbol of Yael's respect for me. It's a shame. I've yet to feel that from Axel.

As I lift the gloves, their weight empowers me. Whether I'm American or Nazi or American Nazi, Jewish, or Martian, this feeling buoys me. I read the card in the box, "We train to gain control over our bodies. But to triumph, we wrap our bodies around individual will. With each trial, pain becomes more bearable, motions more familiar, waiting more calm. Then it's our way. Then we are Newark Minutemen."

With the card, there's a photo of us from the day Yael taught me to box. The selfie in the mirror. I gulp at the image of our bodies together. My heart feels like its pumping tar through my veins. I wish I had the power to free my hands and shape my own life. But I don't.

CHAPTER 14

Body Shot

KRISTA:
Woods. Camp Siegfried. Long Island, NY

My five best friends and I trek in a line through the dark woods of Camp Siegfried. I smile for the first time since I arrived here. Leaving Yael shredded me, but the more time that goes by, the less I hear him in my head. Most of all, seeing camp friends from last summer band-aids the wound.

Sneaking out of tents with besties Daggy and Greta in the middle of the night is risky but worth it. It wouldn't be the same without including Klaus, Penn, and Cort. The boys bring out the carefree side of me. Plus, it's nice not to have Heidi breathing down my neck. I feel lighter when she's not around.

It's brisk for the beginning of summer, but the mosquitoes don't seem to notice. I slap my neck again. Even though I complain about camp, once I'm here, I wish I could freeze time. Yael wouldn't get it. I don't know, though. This year, it seems like it's going to be less neverland and more a place that we'll never return from. I think I'm going to grow up fast.

Behind me, Klaus's voice booms through the inky darkness from the end of the line. "If you forgot the booze we're counting on to get us through summer camp, I'm going to beat the crapola out of you!" he shouts over Greta's shoulder to Penn. Penn stumbles forward and steps on the back of my heel.

"Mission accomplished, Klaus!" Penn says. His foot snaps a branch right behind me. "Pop's shop won't miss our summer stash." I hear the slosh of vodka. Drinking's not my forte, but my juices swivel, anticipating this rare night ahead. I know that freedom is all downhill from here. Daggy is right in front of me. I rest both hands on her shoulders. She squinches them up. What would I do without Dags?

Klaus lunges past Greta and reaches for Penn's bottle. I'm worried Klaus is so big he's going to crush him. He's as stout as Penn is wiry. But Penn sidesteps him. Only thing, Penn doesn't apologize when he bumps me sideways.

Penn rights himself. "Heads up, Cort!" he calls. He lobs the bottle over Daggy's chocolate brown hair. Even in the darkness, her to-die-for caramel highlights gleam. The bottle lands like a football in Cort's outreached arms.

The screech of a twisting metal cap makes my teeth ache. "Here's to drowning out today's opening day anthem at Camp Siegfried," Cort says. There's a gurgling sound. I couldn't have said it any better myself.

Penn grazes my back when he tugs out another bottle. "And here's to the breeze that raises skirts above girls' marching knees," he says. The girls and I groan. I hear Greta's long slim hand slap Penn's back as he drinks. I twist my neck. Vodka spurts out of his mouth and onto his shirt. "You got my nice clean uniform dirty," Penn whines.

"Shh! Let's not wake up the lions and tigers and bears out here in the middle of the forest," growls Klaus. He reaches past Greta a second time and snatches the bottle from Penn. Klaus's growl is worse than his bite. His toughness protects him from the heartache of losing his ma to polio two years ago.

"Klaus, you're the only wild animal within a mile of the lake," Greta says. She kicks up the undergrowth of the trail with her boot and pebbles ricochet against my legs.

Up ahead, Cort stops. "Daggy, careful not to scratch your guitar," he says. He bends back a branch for her to pass through. His dimples frame his smile. As the only boy of a family of seven, he's got manners. Cort watches out for Daggy here and at home. He lives in the apartment right below Daggy's. She lives with her wretched aunt. Cort and Dags have never admitted it, but it's obvious they have a thing for each other.

I see Daggy's tendons stiffen as she lifts her Gibson guitar above the tree branch. She slides past Cort and reaches back for my hand. He holds the branch for me as well. I get what she sees in him. Then his tongue pushes against his cheek. He's up to some mischief. He bends the limb tighter, waits, and then lets it swing at the unsuspecting Penn.

"Dagnabbit!" Penn snips. He darts forward and grabs the booze out of Cort's hand. Penn doesn't need the teasing. He's the middle child of five and victim of an abusive father. His father was a crewmember during the ill-fated Hindenburg airship disaster last year. He hasn't been the same ever since. Penn's become the breadwinner of the family, if you call pickpocketing a way of life. For Penn, camp is a sanctuary, as long as he can bury the guilt of being away. But he's a survivor. Out of all the guys, I'd put my life in his hands.

"This spot looks good," I hear Penn say through the darkness. We move toward the gray dust that rises when his backpack thuds to the ground.

By the time we reach the spot under a canopy of trees, Penn is gathering sticks for a fire. He throws them down and hands the bottle back to Cort. They grab each other's forearms in the Roman tradition of peace and shaking out any hidden weapons. They are, after all, brothers-in-arms. Cort settles on a rock and sips the alcohol. A muted light from the sky lets me glimpse a rare calm across his baby smooth face. Penn nurses a flame, blows the sparks, and the heat sucks the summer night chill from the air.

We unload our packs on the silky dirt. As the flames grow, long shadows swaddle me.

The camp camaraderie among us like-minded German-Americans is fierce. This summer, we will share tents, race each other, and splash lake water together. Our conversation will come through our mother tongue. Patriotic songs and rituals will bond us. And as Heidi says, we will become disciplined Aryans with a responsibility for the German culture. She repeats it so many times, I can say it in my sleep.

Daggy sits down cross-legged and places her guitar on the ground. "Hey, Cort, pass the bottle this way," she says. Daggy twangs the guitar strings in beat with chirping crickets. "One day down, and like eighty-nine more to go until we're back to civilization, Cort."

Greta leans against Dags.

Cort chugs and gets to his feet. "This is nobby compared to our tenement stuffed with my herd of sisters. Here you go, my beautiful Daggy," he says as he hands her the bottle. Daggy is beautiful. She has that combination of strength and softness. But it's her safe eyes that wrap around you that make her extra special. "Hey, Penn. Where's our fire?" asks Cort.

"Your slave is working as fast as he can, master," Penn says. "Klaus, give me a hand, you lazy bum."

Klaus hops up and heaves two heavy logs onto Penn's sticks. He grabs some dry straw, shoves it under the handiwork and the fire crackles like cellophane packaging. For the moment, the popping wood is all we hear. We applaud Klaus, our claps echoing against the night air like boots on crisp snow.

The defeated Penn retrieves another bottle of vodka from his bag. He snuggles between Greta and Dags, tilts his head skyward and coats his throat with liquid.

Klaus nurses the campfire with a long stick. The fire delivers a circle of light and mesmerizes me. The orange and red swim together. The yellow infiltrates, like a rising tide. In the center, the white ebbs the colors. Could

Yael and I ever fuse together like this? There's a fire that burns between us, for sure. But is it the gift of warmth or the curse of destruction?

Cort plops down on my lap and breaks my muse. My arms wrap around him, and I rub my cheek against his smooth face. I warm to his wide eyes that devour life. But I disappoint him. "Sorry, guy," I say. "My legs are killing me from drills today." I shove him and he rolls through wet leaves. His head lands in Greta's lap. She's getting a double dose of warmth with the two boys lounging on her.

"Dags, my turn. Pass that bottle," I say.

Daggy stretches her arm toward me, but Greta swipes the bottle. Cort opens his mouth. Greta side-eyes Daggy and drizzles liquor into Cort's mouth. Daggy gives Greta a double dare look for nabbing her booze and boyfriend. But Dags wouldn't hurt a fly.

Penn comes to my rescue. He hands me his bottle, freeing me from the drama. Daggy scoots around next to me. "Krista. I've missed you so much!" She makes my night. "What's the gossip about you and Axel running off to Berlin?" she whispers.

I breathe in the sweet scent of soil. "I love ya, Dags, but that subject is off limits tonight." The vodka sizzles my throat and cools me off. "I promise to spill the beans tomorrow. I need to get your advice."

The firelight flickers on Daggy's face and camouflages her next move. She pulls something out of my pocket. "Who's this keen boxer?" She studies the photo of Yael and me. "Hmm … a star of David?"

"Gimme that!" I snatch it back. I had almost forgotten the shape of Yael's face but there it is. Thank goodness, no one else saw it. "Mind your own business, Freundin." Dags soft gaze tells me I can trust her. But I better hide this.

Suddenly, there's a loud squeak. We whip our heads toward the crying baby noise. There's a thunderous rattle like a dozen dogs wagging their tails against a door. Small black rubber balls bombard us. Flapping wings slap us and we flail our arms in battle. As quickly as we are attacked, we are freed.

"Bats!" Klaus says. "Strange. Something rattled them. Bats don't usually attack. There's something over there." He narrows his eyes at the prickly brush. A twig cracks.

"You're nuts!" Penn says to Klaus. "I'm cutting you off."

Klaus sways between fight or flight. He strains to see what he can't.

"Hey! Relax," Daggy says. She picks up her guitar. "We came out tonight to unwind before torture-summer." She strums "Jeepers Creepers." It unlocks my smile.

Klaus spreads his legs. He opens his mouth and bellows the American words. The embers popping from the damp kindling clap to the music. Penn's deep baritone harmonizes with Klaus's tenor. Then we get a wake-up call. Cort's tone-deaf voice ricochets like a bullet in a steel room. Greta punches his arm. Our laughter rumbles. It feels like a splash of river water against fevered eyes. It's funny how honest it makes me feel.

"It's a relief to get away from the mumbo jumbo at camp," I say when we finish the song. "Don't you think?" I wrap my arm around Dags.

"Sure, but this is an important summer," Greta says. "Germany says the Bund is preparing American youth." Greta's either had too much to drink or has been listening to shortwave radio shows. But she's not wrong. We're being groomed.

"My step-aunt couldn't wait to toss me into Camp Aryan away from my friends," Daggy says. "She claims the locals in Newark brainwash me with red, white, and blue hogwash." She laughs, and it's good to see her do so.

"As Führer Kuhn says, Supermen on one side, the rest on the other," Cort says with a German accent. He moves next to Daggy, where he should have been in the first place. He flexes his muscle under her chin.

She bites his arm and the boys laugh.

"Ya. Especially since Übermensch Superman is going to free our country from mutant Jews and Jesuits," Klaus says. He clenches his fist and ups Cort with his impressive biceps.

I open my mouth to challenge Klaus, but Cort hushes me. He cocks his head. We hear strange sounds. It's a mix of animal screeches and grunts coming from beyond the dense brush. Klaus and Cort spring up and smother the fire. Penn and Daggy scramble behind trees. I think Greta is frozen.

"Keep still," I hiss. I crouch low and wave the campfire smoke away. "Penn. What are they doing?" The smoldering wood singes my nose.

He runs his fingers through his hair. "I'm not sure. Let me find out." Penn pushes aside some branches. He stops short and his head locks. "I see bodies and dust flying everywhere. I think they're having like an orgy."

"What?" I whisper with indignation.

There's a muffled cry.

"Let's help," Daggy murmurs. "Sounds like someone's being hurt." That's what I like most about Daggy. She acts when someone needs her.

"I see guards with guns." Cort peers through the bushes. "But I gotta gun, too." He pats his pocket.

"Cort!" Daggy whispers in a worried tone.

"He's kidding," I say. "You are kidding, right?"

A smirk crosses Cort's face.

"Krista!" Greta calls to me, covering her mouth with both hands. Is that Sascha? Our friend from school."

"There's definitely a guy on top of someone," Klaus cries. He swoops up backpacks. We take his cue and grab the rest of our belongings. "Let's get out of here!" he says.

A twig behind us snaps. My shoulder blades prickle. I spin around, but I'm devoured by only blue blankness. Is my mind playing tricks? Whether it is or not, the night has exhausted its nostalgia. I can't help but wonder what else is in store for me this summer.

CHAPTER 15

Saved by the Bell

KRISTA:

Archery Course. Camp Siegfried. Long Island, NY

On the way to breakfast, I hurry behind Axel as he sets up the archery station for campers. If he stops me, my pounding head will defy my best behavior. Last night was fun, but it's making me pay this morning. No luck! Axel's blue eyes hook me.

"Krista, gut Morgen," he calls to me. He straightens his thin black tie. "My Leibling!" he says. "Why didn't you visit Axel's room last night?" There he goes again talking about himself in the third person. He hands me an arrow and bow.

I ignore my fiancée's question but accept his weapons. I twist my uniformed torso toward the target, but the blazing sun makes me squint. I set the arrow in the bow and stretch the string. A twang kicks when my fingers release the arrow. The point lands in the chest of the dummy. Right through the heart! A shiver of pride ripples through me.

Axel plants his fists on his hips and raises one eyebrow. He wants an answer. My skin twists. "Last night, I was tired," I say.

154

"Drinking all night with your friends will do that to you," he responds.

My chin drops. Dagnabbit! Axel knows. My hand squeezes the bow. A breeze against my ear nudges me. *He* was the someone in the woods last night. "So now you're spying on me?" I snap. My temples thump.

Axel's body blocks the sun. He leans in. I feel his clammy breath on my face. His glower pierces me like the arrowhead in the stuffed body across the lawn. "You will never behave like that again. That's an order!" His angled jaw bulges.

My annoyance turns to frustration. "You mean doing what I want?" The words roll in my throat.

Axel kicks the container of arrows, sending them scattering across the ground. The noise hammers my skull. He picks up one and pokes the point of it into my chin. "Obedience is the path to reward. Axel will be merciful if you fear him. He will honor you when you serve him." He lowers his weapon. "On the other hand, Krista, if you disobey, you bring disappointment. Mark my words, you will be punished." He's starting to sound like Papa.

Words spark off my lips. "I'm not some cadet you can command."

"Yes, you are! I am your superior!" shouts Axel. "You must obey Führerprinzip and follow with blind obedience." Axel recites the rules of our hierarchy. He's full of himself. But if I'm going to live in his world, his words ring true. He's a master at painting me as the villain.

My stomach prickles like it's crawling with spiders. Under our laws, there's nothing for me to criticize. I accept defeat. "OK, OK. I'm sorry, Axel." My weakness gnaws at me like a vulture noshing on a dead deer.

My submission hits Axel like a snowball in the face. Red blotches cover his neck. "You are my property," he says. "You'll not make me a fool. I'm an officer in the German Reich!"

Now he's crossing the line. Property and hierarchy are two different things. My strength returns. "Maybe you should find someone else who will follow your orders."

"Maybe Axel will marry a woman who doesn't play in garbage cans with Jews." Interesting. Axel's face tints green when he refers to Yael.

Frank appears with Heidi and Daggy. "Everything okay?" Frank asks.

"Life's perfect!" I say, my shaky voice betraying me. I need to get away from Axel. Now. "Let's get something to eat," I say to Heidi and Dags.

Dags takes my hand. We walk away.

Behind us, I overhear Frank. "Don't worry, Axel. A little discipline will fix her right up."

A muffled thud stops me cold. I whip my neck around. Axel's back faces me. I hear him breathe in through his nose and exhale through his mouth, like a lion. He stares at the weapon he just launched. It's in the target next to mine. Right inside a Jude symbol painted on the stuffed human's chest. How did I miss it? Is that a cruel joke?

The only discipline I'll follow is my own. Just gotta decide my path.

KRISTA:
Cafeteria. Camp Siegfried. Long Island, NY

I hope these scrambled eggs will cull my hangover because the ruckus of campers under this mess tent bores into my brain like a drill. At least sitting at the end of the table gives me space to stretch my legs into the aisle. Across from me, Heidi rolls her eyes. She always knows when I've been up to no good, as she puts it. I escape a scolding because she's glued to a pamphlet about the German Nazi Youth leader, Balden von Schirach. Any girl with eyes drools over his good looks.

Across the cafeteria, steam from the grill scrubs Dags's face as she cooks. She winks at me. She knows the pieces of my puzzle. Wonder what she thinks I should do? As I scoop food into my mouth, a boy bumps my elbow. It's not my day. As he steps back, the reflection from his belt buckle, the one inscribed with *Blood and Honor*, stings my eye. I swing my head just in time to see Führer Vandenberg and the Head of Youth Herr Dinkelacker swagger into the cafeteria. Führer Kuhn shadows right behind his Camp Siegfried officers.

The officers' necks, strapped in tight uniforms, shift to inspect the youth. Papa told me the campers wear Hitlerjugen uniforms that were smuggled on German ships. The buckles and shirts are stamped with the same Runic lightning bolts as the ones in Germany.

I track our leaders. I see Führer Vandenberg studying Daggy as she scrapes sausages off the grill. Cort notices him stalking, too. His head shakes at me between the dishes piled in his arms. Next to Cort, Penn swings an axe into firewood. Führer Vandenberg dodges the wood chips splayed toward him and gleers. What does he expect? Penn's grit crams into everything he does. Good thing Cort wasn't the one with the axe.

Steps away, Herr Dinkelacker loiters over Greta's shoulder as she scrubs pots. He plucks a berry from a jar. She blushes. He tosses the fruit in the air and catches it between his lips. Herr Dinkelacker blasts a white smile and Greta giggles. Geez Louise, that was predictable. But it embarrasses me anyway. I spoon eggs into my mouth. After that spectacle, if the eggs were rubber, I wouldn't taste the difference.

Führer Kuhn joins Herr Dinkelacker. Here they come toward me. From the opposite direction, a boy in a white apron is moving too fast. I see it coming. He smacks into the front of the Führer's jacket. The poor boy. His face grays and his covered basket swings.

The Führer scoffs. He sniffs at the basket. He lifts up the red-checkered cloth and flips over the small loaves as if he's searching for tripwires. Führer Kuhn strokes his finger across the swastika insignia stamped into each roll. "Herr Dinkelacker, help yourself," Führer Kuhn says.

The attractive head of training selects a bread. The malty aroma makes my mouth water even from several yards away.

"Your Hitler youth model is working well," I hear Führer Kuhn say to Herr Dinkelacker. "Health, Hitler, heils, and hatred."

Heidi must have heard the Führer's compliment, too, because she bats her eyes at Herr Dinkelacker. The bread boy places a biscuit on her plate.

"What can I say, mein Führer?" Herr Dinkelacker grins, showing off his white teeth for Heidi. "Blind obedience forms a nice grip on the

157

individual."

"In our program, there are no words for weak," Führer Vandenberg says. "This summer, our youth thanks us for the pain they bear." As girls pass him, his eyes wander around the curves of their bodies.

"And here comes our trophy boy right now to join his friends," Führer Kuhn says. He flips his head toward my own lord, Axel, whose tray is piled high with eggs and sausage and potatoes.

Axel doesn't notice the gawking officers. He sits next to Heidi and dives into his food without so much as a hello.

The bread boy places one roll on Axel's plate. He places two on mine. I hand one roll back, but the boy spreads his fingers and touches my eyes with his. Two rolls? My chin drops. Two rolls. This is the signal. How did Yael do it? My heart pounds. He will visit me tonight at 10:00 p.m. sharp. I told him not to risk this. And for what? A fantasy that can never be real? My eyes flutter. Of course, I was wishing he would come. I hope no one can see the dark grin inside me.

"I'll take your extra bread," Axel says. He snatches it.

"Gut Morgan, Freunde," Frank says as he appears at the table.

"Looking forward to the hike tonight?" Axel answers. He tears his bread, shovels scrambled eggs inside, and devours it. He winks at Heidi.

Frank sits next to me and flings a pamphlet down. "I brought you girls a present. It's information about sterilizing women who marry undesirables. You know, like Jews and Negroes," he sneers. The cover shows the tubes of a uterus tied together. Frank stretches across the table and brushes Heidi's cheek with the back of his hand. She leans into him. I gulp. What does Heidi see in the vulgar man? His propaganda paper is revolting. People have the right to be with whoever they want. Does Heidi think about this? There's a knot inside of me. I hate her weakness.

"Our Fräuleins know better," Axel snorts. "They're not foolish enough to fall for charlatans charming themselves to get under Aryan skirts."

Axel's words have merit. Jews do not marry outside, so why would Yael even want to date a non-Jew? I think of the photo he gave me and our time dancing together. I ache for the few moments we had, the connections. Were they ever real? Am I who I think I am, or who I remember I am? I guess I'll get a glimpse tonight.

"We know that Minuteman wants to get under your skirt for more than fun, don't we Krista?" Frank tries to provoke me. "He peers up your rear-end to discover the secrets of Aryan perfection."

The guy is incredibly foul. I ball my fists to hold my temper. But my temper beats me. I punch his stomach with a right cross. He sucks air like a vacuum cleaner.

Behind me, hands clap. "Where did you learn to box, Fräulein?" Führer Kuhn asks. Axel, Heidi, and I jump to attention. "Heil Hitler!" We salute.

Frank unbends himself and stands. His face is beet red.

Führer Kuhn sneers. He presses Axel's shoulder and lowers him back into his seat. "May we join you?"

"We are flattered," Axel says. He knows the way his bread is buttered.

The officers join us. Greta and a girl rush to the table and serve them plates full of eggs, potatoes, and sausage.

Herr Dinkelacker addresses the boys as his eyes chase Greta's movements. "What are your goals this summer?" he asks the boys as he chews.

Greta brushes against Herr Dinkelacker. Geez Louise. That was not an accident. Her cheeks are as red as a bullfighter's cape. "Fräulein." He licks the eggs off of each finger. "Glass of milk. Bitte." Greta stumbles backward, then dashes. It's clear she's falling for his game.

"Yes, you boys are leading the German hour in America. What's the plan?" Führer Vandenberg asks, shaking enough salt on his eggs to make a slug curl.

"Simple. To train brave scouts," Axel says to the doting officers.

Führer Kuhn purses his lips at me. "Speaking of bravery. Krista. Your bravery against the Minutemen will serve as a model for the youth this summer." Everyone looks at me. I wish he wasn't doing this. Is he going to fly me from a flagpole?

"We'll have Krista share her tactics with the girls, mein Führer," Frank says. I'm about to punch him again. I know he's sneering underneath. On the other hand, Axel wrinkles his forehead. He wants the Minuteman story put to bed, so to speak.

Führer Kuhn waves his head. He actually thinks that's a good idea. I stare at a bee buzzing around the pancake syrup. Maybe they'll forget about it in a few days.

In that moment, the bugle sounds. The room rumbles. Plates clatter and boots stomp against the floor. Axel and Frank walk ahead of us with the officers.

"Update us on Secretary Wheeler-Hill's program," I hear Führer Vandenberg ask Axel and Frank. "The one to accelerate the Aryan race in America." I tilt my hearing ear toward them.

"It's scientific, yet simple," Axel says.

"We schedule males and females according to cycles. Each night, we have a night-hike to maximize success," Frank explains.

My internal radar beeps. I struggle to decipher Frank's remark.

Führer Kuhn claps Axel on the shoulder. "You're both doing a fine service for your country. Let's get to the drills," he quips.

Heidi and I join the crowd in the exodus. But I don't get very far. Klaus's boxy body blocks me. "Krista. Frank needs completed paperwork from your exam. We need your hereditary history." He hands me a pen. "Any sickness or mental issues in your family?" He pushes dirty dishes aside and places papers on a table.

"My father's controlling." My self-honesty refreshes me.

Klaus tries to stifle a laugh, but air spurts between his lips.

Heidi answers for me. "Our family has *no* mental issues."

Klaus points. "Gut! Sign here."

I hover over the paper. "I can't read all the German."

"Jiminy Cricket, Krista. Don't get me in trouble," begs Klaus.

Heidi orders. "Krista. Sign!"

Not worth the argument, I obey. My pen-scratch proves I'm racially valuable to the Reich. Good thing racial truth doesn't show up in blood tests.

Klaus whisks the paper away from me. But he's not so smooth. He knocks a glass of milk onto my clothes. "Scheisse!" he says. "So sorry, doll." Klaus grabs a napkin and swats my drenched skirt. Heidi snatches the napkin away.

Dags pops up from nowhere. "Krista, I'm done with work. Go change before drills," she suggests. "I'll cover for you."

How is Daggy always so there and here? Couldn't imagine life without her. "Thanks, Freundin! Hey! I get dibs on teaming up with you in the relay race today." Last summer we won.

KRISTA:
Bunkhouse. Camp Siegfried. Long Island, NY

In the bunkhouse tent, I bury my head into my sun-warmed skirt. Feels good to be out of the wet one. Something in the pocket crunches in my hand. I shake my skirt and the crinkled photo of Yael and me drops to the floor. I smile for a moment. Then my throat parches. If someone finds this, my next breakfast will be on a submarine to Germany. I tear a small opening on the underside of my mattress and slip the photo inside.

Out of the blue, a heavy breathing outside my window jars me. I cover myself with my clothes. I peer out the window and rub my eyes. Führer Vandenberg is scurrying behind nearby tents. Gott im Himmel! Was he with someone or alone?

Dressed in a clean uniform skirt, I'm about to leave, but another noise stops me. There is sobbing from the back. From under the cover in a bunk, Sascha's strawberry blonde hair bows out like a scoop on an ice cream cone.

I sit on the edge of her bed and rest my hand on her back. "Sascha? What's wrong?"

"I'm so tired," she groans. Strands of hair ribbon across her face.

"Were you up late?" I ask her. Of course she was. We all had activities last night that have left our eyes red-rimmed.

"We took the Reutli-Oath last night. We unified with Germans around the world." When Heidi and I were young, our father told us the medieval tale at bedtime about three men from different cantons who swore to unite against the Austrian-Hapsburg empire.

"We swore to all stick together in America and to eliminate enemies of the Fatherland." Sascha yawns so big I see her tonsils.

They want us to stick together as Germans? "But aren't we Americans?" I ask.

"Oh! They say it will all be the same very soon," Sascha answers.

"What will be the same?"

She changes the subject. "And they matched partners last night."

"Matched partners?" The pieces of a puzzle click in my head.

"Yes," Sascha says. "They said not to feel ashamed if we get pregnant. Our duty is to have children so Germany can grow."

I close my eyes. "Sascha. What exactly are you saying?"

"It was my first time and it hurt," Sascha says. "Coupling for the Führer." She forces a crooked smile. "Like Lebensborn in Germany. Giving babies to German families. Only here, it's mostly for German-American families, of course."

"You had sex?" My chest constricts. That *was* Sascha in the woods.

"Well, yes. It's my duty to populate America with Aryans," Sascha says. She hugs me and her damp face feels cold against my neck. "The nice part, they say, is we will all have babies together."

With the sudden sound of a flock of geese scattering, Frank and two officers burst through the door flap. "Krista, you're late for drills. Schnell!" Frank barks.

"Sascha isn't well, Frank. She needs my help."

"You will not interfere!" His plebe shoves me out the door. Inside, I hear Daggy's guitar bonk against the floor.

162

"Please Frank, not now, not again," I hear Sascha beg. A crime is happening under my nose, to my friend. Who do I tell?

Behind me, I hear Frank yelling at his officers. "Hold her down."

The soldier's silence buzzes over Sasha's pleas.

"Don't look at me like that! Hold her down!"

Across the lawn, paramilitary exercises begin. I watch the goosesteps snap the gray drill grounds. The sun reflects off Führer Vandenberg's spectacles. Scouts raise their daggers as one. "When Jewish blood drips from the knife, then will the German people prosper," I hear the battalion chant in front of me. Behind me I hear Sascha moan.

CHAPTER 16

Overhand Punch

YAEL:
Woods. Camp Siegfried. Long Island, NY

Until it's dark enough to meet with Krista, I lean against a tree in the Camp Siegfried woods lookin' through the viewfinder of my camera. Through my lens, scenes unfold across the ramblin' camp below. The place must be a couple hundred acres. The bittersweet smell of the freshly cut grass from the field wafts into my nostrils. I twist the lens to zoom in closer. Through my viewer, I watch a round-faced girl extend her elbows and send a volleyball into the air to a long-legged teen who whips her wrist down on the ball, sending it over a net. *Click.* In a glassy pool, bony ankles of boys splash white froth in a race to the finish. *Click.* Scrawny arms and knobby knuckles box against rocky ribs. *Click.* Boys mount themselves on their teammates' shoulders and yank their opponents' arms in a game of chicken. *Click.* Teams launch rubbery bodies into the air with wool blankets and catch them like eggs.

But as I adjust the closeup focus, I discover that the camp isn't what it first appears to be. On the field, there are rows of campers dressed in uniforms that resemble Germany's Hitler youth from *Time* magazine. My chest tightens. Watchin' German-American Nazi Bund soldiers march in Newark past Macy's department store is one thing. But this is different. I've never seen so many kids outfitted together as a miniature Nazi war troop. *Click.*

Mosquitoes buzz near my sweaty neck, but I'm too busy to swat them. Marchers goosestep until they faint, small children disappear into the deep holes they dig, swollen hands drop hammers they can no longer pound, bleedin' knees chafe from scrubbin' wooden floors. *Click. Click.* My finger releases the shutter. Commandos crawl through rough terrain, aim rifles at mock enemies, throw mock grenades. *Click. Click. Click.*

The sweat dribbles down my face. The bug attack becomes unbearable. I smack my neck and examine the flattened insect against my blood-smeared hand. But a rumblin' at the camp entrance distracts me as suddenly as if a stinger jabbed my vein. I snap my camera at the helmeted guards directing military trucks with their lances.

I slip my camera inside my jacket pocket and lean against a tree. Am I dreamin'? Will the photos prove my nightmare is real? I rub my grimy hands inside my pants pockets. My wallet falls out and lands on the ground. The flaps open and a photo juts out and lands on a fuzzy dandelion. It's the image of Krista and me in the mirror. I flick the paper so it won't disrupt the ball of snow. I return the photo to my wallet for safekeeping. Krista has an almost identical image of the two of us preserved forever. At least, I hope she opened her boxin' gloves and found the photo I gave her. I pluck the weed from the ground and blow the seeds against the settin' sun with a silent wish.

My wristwatch shows 10:00 p.m. and, as if on cue, a noise startles me. I hide behind the tree. Through the tree cover, the moon reveals a silhouette of a uniformed young woman approaching the lakeside. She seems so anonymous, like a cut-out from black paper. In the darkness, she brings my face warmth like the sun. I slip behind Krista before she sees me.

Before I can duck, Krista's balled fist swings at my face. She clacks my jaw, throwin' my neck backward like an apple branch in the wind. "Yael! Holy moly! You frightened me."

I rub my chin. "Never saw your boots shake before."

"I'm so sorry." She covers my hand. "I told you not to come."

"Nice shot," I goad, tryin' to ignore the throbbin' in my jaw. "I told you I would."

She steps back. Fear beats in her green eyes. "And I told you it was dangerous." She refuses to meet my gaze. Do I approach or retreat?

I keep it light. "Nice camp ya got down there. It's very, very, German." I'd really like to say it's a teenage war machine, but this is her world so I step carefully. "Reminds me of a countrified Hitler Nazi Youth Camp." I just stuck my foot in my mouth.

"Not really. We simply practice our traditions." Her eyes bat at me.

"But everyone speaks German."

"That's our culture. Your people speak Yiddish." She wrinkles her nose. "Were you down there in the camp spying?"

I dodge the last question. "True. But military drills, swastikas, Heil Hitlers, Nazi flags flyin' above American ones. The whole scene seems, well, kinda un-American." My steppin' carefully may be more like stompin' because daggers shoot from her eyes. I sit down on a broken tree to calm things down. Luckily, she joins me. The moonlight stamps leaf-shaped shadows across her face.

"We learn discipline," she says. "They work us." Krista raises her eyebrows. "It's hard, sometimes painful, but we learn responsibility for our mistakes. Obedience improves us." Krista sounds mindful, yet her machinelike drone hints that her words aren't her own. It makes me sad. She's heard these words so many times that they've become automatic. "All a process to become one with the Fatherland," she says, finishing the rhetoric.

"You're not one of them. There was a mix up at the hospital," I say with a smile. Her face is blank, distant. Will she come back to me?

"My parents are coming next weekend for Götterdämmerung," she says without meetin' my eyes. "We celebrate burning the old world for the new."

"That sounds peaceful," I quip.

"A hundred thousand people come to hear Führer Kuhn." Krista's eyebrows lower. "Axel and I will be presented the night before. The most important party members will honor our union."

I tuck my hand under her chin and curl her face toward me. She can't hide the haunted look in her eyes. "Are you okay?" I ask. No matter how old she gets, those eyes will always look the same.

"I've accepted my fate with Axel, so I'm okay for that," she says. I flinch. "But there's something else. I didn't believe it was true until today," she says under her breath. Krista inhales and palms her forehead. "Have you ever heard of Lebensborn? Germany's way to raise the birth rate of Aryan children."

"Some kind of new superfood for the super race?" I flex my arm to try and get a laugh out of her.

She bats my arm down and sighs. "No Yael, listen to me. The most valuable contribution Aryan women can make to Volksgemeinschaft ,or Community, is to have many children with another Aryan. Our American leader, Führer Kuhn, duplicates Hitler's program." She exhales sharply. "Girls like me are forced to make little Aryans to backfill the soldier shortage from the last War."

Longie has told us about baby-breedin' in Hitler's Germany. But crankin' out babies right here in America for Germany has never been imagined. "A human farm?" I frown. "Is that what you're tellin' me this so-called summer camp is?"

"My friend Sascha was attacked by an officer who was determined to sire a child," she admits. "He told her it was official policy from the very top."

I'm dumbstruck. "What if she gets pregnant?" My stomach twists in disgust and a growin' horror for what Krista might be facin'. I don't wanna hear the answer.

"Either an American-German Bund family adopts the baby here or we export it to the Fatherland."

From close by, I hear a rustle in the bushes. "Krista? Krista!" I recognize Heidi's voice. "Are you out here?"

Krista mouths she has to go. She brushes my cheek with her lips.

I grab her elbow. "I'll return to get you," I mouth back. Why am I so drawn to her?

Krista shakes her head no.

She pulls away and ducks out from the branch cover. She walks toward her sister. "Geez Louise. I'm right over here," I hear her say.

"What are you doing out this late?" Heidi says. "Are you with someone?"

"Nope. Just getting some air," Krista says.

I peek between the tangled branches. Heidi darts her head like a peckin' chicken from the market. "You better not be with that vile Jew. I forbid it! The match with Axel will ensure our positions in the Reich. We must all sacrifice."

"I know. But it's not fair," Krista says.

"We're women. Of course it's not fair," snaps Heidi. "I'm tired of keeping you in line."

"What have you turned into? Where's your heart?" asks Krista.

"How dare you! I'm what we deserve to be, little sister."

"I don't know you anymore," Krista declares.

"Nor I, you." Heidi retorts. "Frank needs to meet with you right now."

"For what? I thought we had the night-hike." I hear fear in the sudden rise of Krista's voice.

"I don't know what you did now. I'll meet you at the hike," Heidi says.

I cross my arms in front of my chest to hold myself back. I don't dare intervene, or I'll never be able to help in a bigger way. I don't doubt they'd have my neck, too.

KRISTA:
Officers' Quarters. Camp Siegfried. Long Island, NY

I peer through the window into the Camp Siegfried officer's quarters. Frank is alone at his desk, facing the wall behind him. Light from an overhead lamp shines on the back of his head. Under his razor-cut hairline, bumpy red dots spot his bare neck. I imagine flesh-eating mites chewing under his skin. My stomach growls, but not from hunger, and certainly not from fear. Once inside, I approach him.

"Krista," he says without turning. He thinks he's intimidating me, making me wait like this. It has the opposite effect. He will never scare me. He spins and sprays me with his cold blue eyes. "It's late, but we must do this now."

"Do what?" I ask with a dread that pushes me backward.

"You're ovulating," Frank says as if he's announcing the time. He slaps a folder down and points to the desk. "The less you resist, the easier it will go. I know you're a woman of duty."

Before I digest what Frank is saying, he lunges at me. His foot bangs the chair leg. "Frick!" he swears. He hobbles toward me. "As your good friend, I would give you compassion if I could," he says. "But as you know, in our Nazi rise, compassion is outlawed."

I swerve away, seize a pile of *Mein Kampf* books from the table and hurl them at him. One smacks him in the cheek. Yet he seems unfazed.

"I understand there's some interesting tidbits not included in your file," Frank says. He smirks as he gallops to the door. There's only one thing that could amuse Frank like this. Does Heidi know my secret? Papa tells her everything. She must. But I do not believe my sister, my mentor and best friend, would ever betray me.

The door squeals as he closes and locks it. "Heidi told me about your real father, the Jew," Frank snickers.

I'm wrong. Heidi did betray me.

"You're not as pure as Axel thinks. I guess you're still part Aryan. But it can be our special secret." He licks his lips. "You're lucky you have Heidi. She shared it with me for your own good."

Suddenly, the years of conviction I've had toward my sister slaps me in my face. Growing up, I've always had this excitement being sisters with Heidi. We braided each other's hair and played hopscotch. We shared stories about boys. As my big sister, Heidi helped me figure out things. She taught me multiplications. She simplified the good from the bad. I remember when she explained good art to me. She stressed the beauty of muscular white men versus the lifeless, formless modern art threatening the world. I trust her so much. But she's tearing me apart. She has one opinion. And that one isn't even her own.

Frank grabs my shirt. "Frank, Stop!" I beg.

"It's my duty." He drags me to the desk.

"You're not thinking clearly." I thrash, but the guy is stronger than I think. I can't tell if he's just filled with lust or has really turned maniacal.

"You're wrong. I'm thinking about the most important thing we've learned—how to preserve the Aryan race so the world's a better place." He holds my neck with one hand and unbuckles his belt with the other.

Abruptly, he stops. I hear keys jingle outside the door and so does he.

"Frank, you in here?" Axel calls out.

Frank shoves me onto the couch. My face bounces against the cushions. He leaps behind his desk. I hear his belt buckle clip.

I hear Axel turn the key in the door. It opens. "Hey, pal," he says to Frank. "We need to get to the night-hike." He spots me disheveled on the couch, hair dangling in my face. He eyeballs the books scattered on the floor. He scrutinizes Frank's sweaty brow.

"We're coming." Frank sighs. "Krista took a tumble and I made her rest while I finished some paperwork." Frank approaches the couch. His stare twists into me like a corkscrew. "Krista, you feeling better?" His hand grips my hand hard, warning me. I'm so upset, I can hardly move much less speak.

Axel smiles and thumps Frank on the back. "Thanks for looking after my girl, Frank!"

"That's what Kamerads are for," Frank replies with a grin.

I glare at Axel, then Frank. Their bodies merge into one monstrous being. *You're playing a dangerous game, Frank.* I'll protect my flank. This is war.

KRISTA:
Woods. Camp Siegfried. Long Island, NY

Just after midnight, Axel walks backward down the dark path through Camp Siegfried woods. Soft thwacks push off the heels of his boots. "You scouts are preparing for the next phase of world civilization," he shouts in a gritty voice. Eighteen of us follow him on the compulsory night-hike. "The youth is the future!" he chants.

"The youth is the future!" we chant back. By now, we know the rumors about night-hikes are true. The program breeds children for Nazis. Heidi says if we're going to be part of the super-race, we must secure its future. She says her goal is to win the Iron Cross for breeding the most babies. I'm in this club whether I like it or not?

Frank, carrying up the rear, pushes the line hard. We each carry thirty-pound backpacks and forage through brush. The brambles slice our skin like paper cuts. We must ignore pain. Or else. We arrive at a staging area.

"Greta and Daggy!" Axel orders. "Empty the crates we carried up here. There's kindling inside to get a fire roaring. Heidi, have the girls set up bedding."

Frank commands the boys. "Klaus, Penn, Cort, and the rest of you. Move those logs." His hands teeter on his hips.

The boys are aloof, barely looking our way. There's a charge in the air. Relationships will change after tonight. Even with Cort and Dags. They're matched, but Dags told me they have an agreement. She said she couldn't bare getting pregnant only for some Bund member to steal their child. I know Axel's got every intention of following orders with me. With his status, we'd keep the child. I can't get my hands around any of it.

"Start the fire," Axel orders Frank.

Frank scowls. I know he hates that Axel is his superior. It's the one time I don't mind watching the bossy side of Axel. I sneer at Frank. He brittles. At least there's some upside to being Axel's partner. After many attempts, Frank starts the fire, but it barely licks the logs.

Axel prods Frank. "C'mon. I'll help you get more wood." They disappear into the trees.

Meanwhile, Heidi shouts orders at us girls. We do as she says. Sascha and I unload our backpacks and join Greta and Daggy next to the fire. Flickers from the campfire stroke Sascha's freckled cheeks. She tosses a tinder into the fire.

"Sascha. What are you doing?" I gasp.

Sascha holds the items close to her eyes. "Applesauce! These are books."

I read one of the titles and pick up another. "These aren't just any books." No it can't be. *Emil und die Detektive.* Nostalgia twists my belly into a knot. It's a childhood story, haunting me again, about a boy lost in a city until the city sticks up for him.

Sascha reads another cover. "Gertrude Stein. She's a famous Jewish author."

Axel reappears with Frank." Move it! Let's make this fire growl," Axel orders. He screws my wrist around until the book drops from my hand. I shake the throbbing pain away. "What are we waiting for?" he barks. He shoves me against a tree. My hands grasp the trunk behind me. My wrists rip on the fishhook-thorns. The pain couldn't be worse if someone had poured hot alcohol into my sliced skin. I shiver.

Daggy clutches my arm. "Are you okay?"

"Daggy. Stop!" Axel shouts. "No pity. Aryans ignore pain." He rips the pages from a book and feeds the fire. The reflection of the roaring light twists his face into an ogre. He and Frank walk toward the boys.

"Stand up straight!" Frank yells at me over his shoulder. "If you can't be tough on yourself, you'll never be tough on enemies." I hobble and settle on a log next to Greta.

"Krista! Demand more of yourself!" Heidi yells. Why does her voice sound far away? She's right next to me.

My head throbs from the plant's toxin. I squint at Heidi. "You have a nerve!" I say. "Demand more of myself? Like the demands you put on yourself working overtime with Führers."

Heidi raises her hand to slap me. Why does she hesitate? Maybe my puffy face scares her? Maybe there's some loyalty left? She swings toward Greta. "Why are you groaning?" she foams.

Greta's bottom lip quivers. "Tell them, Dags," she says.

"Herr Dinkelacker wouldn't leave her alone," Daggy seethes. "She's pregnant."

A few of us gasp.

"He's the handsome leader of Jugend of America," Sascha says. Her voice sings his praise. "How could she deny him?" I can't believe my ears. I knew Sascha was drinking the Kool-Aid, but I didn't know she was drowning in it.

"Your parents will be honored that you did your duty," Heidi exclaims with a smile. "Only four more children to meet quota for the Reich."

"They're proud I'll bear a child for the Führer," Greta says.

I search my other friends' eyes. Am I the only one around here who seems upset? My swollen tongue slurs my voice. "This is barbaric," I argue. "We must stop this for all of us."

"Turn your humanity off, little sister. This is our duty! Keep your mouth shut and be a good soldier." Heidi's words spear me deeper than the daggers did. But maybe she's right. After all, Führer Kuhn and my father praise Heidi as the pure German woman. I scan my squad. Everyone around me seems to be joining the battle. Am I wrong? Maybe I'm confusing darkness for righteousness? Who's to say what's moral when it comes to survival? Did Yael fill my head with lies like Heidi warned? Was he just trying to use me like the repulsive Frank claimed? Was he jealous of Axel? Seems like it doesn't really matter what I believe. This is my life. I might as well embrace it.

"Inbound at three o'clock," Daggy whispers. "Here comes you know who."

But the warning is in vain. At the moment, I can barely hear out of even my good ear. Axel grabs me. I watch his lips move. "Axel is ready." He drags me through the woods like a cat lugging a half-eaten bird. My head sways. My lungs fight to breathe as if I'm being tugged through water. He flings me down on a blanket. When he unlatches the shoulder strap of his Sam Brown belt, the leather swings like a tail and swats my thigh. He clicks his metal belt buckle, threads his strap back, and releases the teeth. My legs scurry, but not fast enough. He clutches my knee and yanks me under him. The pungent smell of iron from my own blood breaches my lungs. I squirm.

"Come my darling, wife," he says to me under his breath. "We must groom you for the Reich's three Ks: Kirche, Küche, and of course, Kinder."

"Church, kitchen, children," my voice mumbles, unbidden. "But I'm not your wife yet."

Axel's mouth is right at my ear. "I love when you fight Axel," he whispers. He digs his fingers into my wounds, rippling pain all the way to my ears. He flips me on my knees. With his other hand, he pulls up my skirt and shoves his shorts down. "Axel will have a child in you for the Führer before we're in Germany." He slips his cold hand up my skirt and moves my underwear aside. He rams inside me, babbling as he thrusts. "We're perfecting the German race. Tell Axel you worship him."

Over the *Horst Wessel* National anthem humming from nearby voices, I can't control my brain. "*Church, kitchen, children. Church, kitchen, children*," I cry to myself. I'm no longer me.

CHAPTER 17

Brawler

YAEL:
YMHA Bowling Alley. 652 High St. Newark, NJ

"Thanks for inviting us to massage the maples with ya tonight, Boss," Puddy yells to Longie as he swings open the door of the basement bowlin' alley of the YMHA. Harry, Benny, and I roll in right behind Puddy. I hike up my cuffed pants and pull my V-neck over my tight, short-sleeved shirt. We plop down on a blue couch across from Longie and Isaac. As sure as a bad penny turns up, Puddy props his feet on the table.

Longie's gathered us boys tonight to get some smarts from Harry's pop about what makes Kuhn tick, all drinks included. I smile to myself. We sure got it made with the benefits that come along with workin' for Longie. Not a lot of guys are this lucky in these hard times. I've also decided to ask Longie to help me with Krista, but tonight's not the night.

Nat enters the basement alley and heads straight to the bar. At his heels, Al's barely through the door when a shoeless Maxie sideswipes him. Maxie leaps onto the alley and slides down the lane. He runs back to the balls, launches one down the lane and clears the pins. "KAY-O!" he shouts.

Al recovers and greets Longie. "Hey, Boss and Mr. Levine." He slaps Puddy's wigglin' feet. "Sheez, Puddy," he says. "Those your religious socks?"

"What's ya talkin about?" Puddy looks down at his feet.

"Your socks are full of holes," Al says. "They're *holy*." Al picks up a ball, steps with a backswing and lets the ball fly forward. It arches into the air, bounces twice with a bang and knocks over three pins. He raises his arms in a V for victory.

"We're here to relax, boys," Nat says. "But we also got a special guest." He extends his arm toward Isaac. "Grab a seat, everyone!" He passes drinks as the gang settles around Longie and Isaac.

"Thanks for comin' down today, boys," Longie says. "Things are heatin' up on our turf with Kuhn and the Bund. Yael was out in Long Island at their camp and uncovered some disturbing stuff." He pauses until everyone stops talking. "We're just startin' to understand the swell of Mr. Kuhn's organization."

"If we know how the bums think, we can hit 'em where they're weakest," Nat says.

"My pop understands how these guys tick," Harry says, raising his eyebrows. "He escaped a mad Russia and marched against Germans in the Great War."

"The floor is yours, meyn Chaver," Longie says to Harry's Pop.

"Danks, Longie," Isaac lights his pipe and puffs.

The cherry scented tobacco from his pipe brings back a memory and I smile. Longie and Pop used to smoke at Friday night dinners. No matter how cold it was, Mama made them go outside on the fire escape.

Isaac squeezes his brow. "Understand," he says, peering at us through his round glasses. "Kuhn and his people weren't always bad. Their minds have been hammered into pieces and glued back together.

People at the top convince them they are now special." His rare black eyes, the ones that have seen so much, are motionless. "They are like children who can't function without rules. They are dependent on the leaders." He puffs his pipe. I've seen the reliance he's referring to with my own eyes. My fellow Troopers can't even tie their own shoes without a lesson. "The saddest part is that the manipulators exploit the vulnerable," Isaac says.

"Ya mean the kids?" Nat growls.

Isaac combs his thick gray mustache between two fingers. "Yes," he says. "Germany's youth. Textbooks teach that Aryans are superior. I didn't believe it until I read it with my own eyes, but from the smallest child up, they are taught a gospel."

"What do ya mean?" asks Al.

"The first page of their books say, 'In the beginning, God created the German. From ice he created him," he explains. "They are taught that they are divine."

"Didn't Greek Spartans teach their kids they were superior, too?" Abie asks.

"Spartans?" Puddy interrupts. "The Spartans were nuts. I saw them in that *Three Stooges* movie where the Stooges go back in time to the Greeks."

Al throws his socks at Puddy. "Get a life."

"Listen up!" Nat yells. The boys' shoulders sink. "Sorry about these wise guys, Mr. Levine. Please go on."

Unshaken, Isaac continues. "You are correct, Abie. In the eighth century, Lycurgus built a nation with an elite military supported by serfs. He demanded lifelong loyalty to Sparta."

"A war culture," Harry says.

"Yes, son. And a brutal, merciless one at that." Isaac says. "Only those with noble lineage *and* athletes were granted citizenship."

"A powerful racial elite," I say.

"Yes, Yael. Their Krypteia secret police terrorized lower classes into slavery."

Nat downs the rest of his drink. "This is too close to home. Let's take a break and roll some balls." Nat claps Benny's shoulder. "Let go of the ball this time, pal."

We move from the lounge area to the long wooden seats facin' the bowlin' lanes. I walk up to the foul line. "The key is concentration, boys." I grip the ball with my fingers. "Bowling is like learnin' to walk, Puddy."

Puddy wobbles and falls down on purpose. The boys laugh.

My ball rolls down the lane. It knocks down all the pins. I spin around and Puddy bows down. Longie and Isaac smile. They join us on the benches.

I sit down next to them. "Whatya think?" I ask. "Is Kuhn workin' on his own or takin' orders from the big guy in Berlin?" Krista's smile flashes in front of my mind, but I shake my head.

Nat, never off duty, hands me another drink.

"Here's my opinion," Isaac says. "Kuhn thinks he's Hitler in America. In fact, he's called himself that. He could be insane. But I don't think so." He takes off his glasses and rubs the lenses with his handkerchief. "There is too much entitlement shining from the holes in his head. That comes from the authority he's been given and the money behind it." He slips the glasses up to the bridge of his nose.

At the end of the bowlin' lane, Maxie resets the pins by hand. "Hey Prof," he calls out to Isaac. "Is it true Hitler has a bowling alley in his Berghof castle?" Maxie adds four extra pins to the ten for a game of fourteen.

Isaac nods. "That's what they say, Maxie."

"Kuhn. Nazis on the rise. They run a brutal world," I say. "Brainwashing kids. Ancient prophecies. Sounds like a recipe for destruction if you ask me." Krista's been primed from the start. I hope I'm not too late.

CHAPTER 18

Left Hook

KRISTA:

Classroom. Camp Siegfried. Long Island, NY

Around me, noisy students take their seats in the Camp Siegfried classroom. The spitting noise that erupts out of the mouths of my kinsmen is anything but arousing, but the color of the German voices wakes me up.

My elbows rest on the desk and my hand pillows my chin. With my other hand, I glide my finger down the three books piled in front of me. I notice the clock on the wall is stopped at ten before six. Below the clock, Führer Kuhn and Secretary Wheeler-Hill add numbers on a blackboard. They smile when they get a total of five-hundred-fifty.

I tilt my hearing ear to eavesdrop. "Educating Germans in America is turnkey," I hear Führer Kuhn say to our guest teacher. "We simply steal from the masterminds in Germany." I have to admit. It's hard to tell the difference between lessons about our native culture and the new ideas being rammed down our throat.

Axel slides into a tablet-arm desk in front of me. He taps my desk and smiles. I've been avoiding him, but he owns me and knows it. I send him a crooked smile back. That's the smile Yael used to give me. Geez Louise. Why did I do that?

Secretary Wheeler-Hill clacks his stick against his desk. In unison, students snap to attention and we recite the pledge: "Under our Father, Adolph Hitler who is our savior; For Hitler we live and die; Hitler is our lord who rules a brave new world."

Our teacher clacks again. We stiffen our spines. With everyone in uniform standing the same way, the room reminds me of the mirror maze on Coney Island at the seashore. Last summer, Heidi and I got lost in it. I can't help smirking when Secretary Wheeler-Hill takes giant 'mother may I' steps down the middle aisle of desks. Did he catch me laughing? His eyes make me fidget.

"Germans do not choose to rule," he shouts in his high tone. I'll never get used to that voice. "So why do Germans rule?" His stick whistles when he swings it near Axel's torso. Whew. I'm in the clear.

Axel stands with his chest out. "It's our birthright, like the lion," he says, twitching the back of his head. I twist my engagement ring. Am I starting to get used to this thing?

Führer Kuhn's eyes sparkle. I think he believes Axel is the chosen son who can do no wrong. But I notice something more than admiration. There's adulation as he scans Axel's long legs.

The Secretary waves his fists. "Class. Who is our Lord and leader?"

"Hitler is our Lord and leader!" we respond.

Across from me, Secretary Wheeler-Hill takes a textbook from Heidi's desk. He marches with it down the aisle. "The German Ministry of Education has sent these books. Open to page eleven." At the back of the room, his boots scratch the floor next to Klaus.

Klaus jumps up. He has that loyal look, the one with eyes looking at nothing straight ahead. He balances the open book in his hands. "The collapse of German society was the deliberate result of Jews and non-Aryans," he reads. "When will the savior come who will do battle against these evil forces?"

The secretary glides around the back aisle and nods at Sascha.

Sascha jumps to attention with her book. "Now we hear his footsteps," Sascha reads. "Awake, Germany, the redeemer has come. The Nordic Aryan race shall yet rule the world."

Secretary Wheeler-Hill raises an eyebrow at Führer Kuhn. The Führer curls the corner of his mouth. In front of Sascha, our professor taps Greta.

Greta rises and reads. "When Germany was on the brink of an abyss, divine providence sent a descendant of the Nordic Aryan race. Adolph Hitler. He will restore a Germanic-way of living, free from Christianity."

"Perfekt!" Our teacher rubs Greta's stomach. I groan inside. She has gotten a lot of attention since her pregnancy. The Secretary marches forward and clacks his stick on Penn's desk.

Penn jumps up with his open book. "Give yourselves for the sake of the Führer," he reads, forcing a strong voice. "Do not forget that treason against a divine leader will bring perdition down on you." Poor Penn. His knees are shaking. He's never like this.

A row away, Secretary Wheeler-Hill points at Frank.

Frank stands. "Only Germans can understand his sublime language," he reads as the Secretary saunters up the next aisle. "Now, blessed children, so can you."

Our teacher stops in front of Heidi. He places the book back on her desk. "Fräulein Brecht." Heidi leaps to attention. "To rule the world, how must Aryans remain pure?" he speaks softly at her.

"Not mingle with other races," Heidi snaps with the verve of a soldier. In that moment, she doesn't seem like my sister. She seems like a leader. It takes me off guard. Yael would not understand, but I'm proud.

Secretary Wheeler-Hill does an about face. "Gut!" he barks like a miniature dog. Heidi sits. He combs the room with his eyes. "Who will explain Horst Wessel?" Several hands shoot up. He hunts. He glances at me. Geez Louise. I hold my breath. He glares past me. I follow the angle of his bulging eyeballs. Daggy is scribbling on a paper. Too late to warn her. She's probably writing advice to me about choosing my life. Last night, I told her about Yael. She thinks going to Germany with him is bananas. "Daggy Schmidt! Horst Wessel!" he calls. "Explain the history!"

Daggy's pencil flies in the air. She springs to attention. "Horst Wessel, he, he was a boy," she stutters in English. "A boy who, he was shot, by Communists and then—"

From the front of the room, the clap of Führer Kuhn spreading his boots against the wooden floor bombasts the room. The class jolts. Führer Kuhn's eyes stare like those mannequins in Macy's department store window.

I can feel Daggy's frosty fear.

"How dare you disrespect our German tongue with the English foreign language," Secretary Wheeler-Hill snaps.

"I … ich bitte Sie." Daggy falters through a German apology.

"You slander your devotion toward our Führer," our teacher rants. "Is he invisible to you? For one week you will be treated as no one, just as you treated our Führer. You will be stripped of your identity. Turn in your uniform! Out!"

You can hear a pin drop. Daggy hugs her books and rushes out. I've never seen her crushed. She slumps like a flower that was stomped by a cow. I'm so worried for her.

Next to me, Cort's knuckles whiten around the edges of his chair. I know he wants to run after his girlfriend. His pale skin turns ruddy.

Secretary Wheeler-Hill notices and points at Cort. "You're answer, Herr?"

Cort jerks to attention. "Horst Wessel. A German stormtrooper, murdered by Communists," Cort grunts. "Just like Abraham Lincoln, he fought for union during a Civil War." His German is laced with fury.

Our professor and Führer Kuhn exchange a satisfied glance. Cort has just recited the only acceptable answer. Führer Kuhn dusts a thread off his jacket. We are wound-up mechanical dolls. It's spellbinding and nerve-racking at the same time. Why do our lessons tick like a timebomb?

"Who is SS Wilhelm Bohle and what is his message?" The Secretary lashes at Cort. He's making him suffer for his association with Daggy.

"German State Secretary," Cort says, his voice shaking. Knowing Cort, it is more from the dread of Daggy's punishment than the Secretary's wrath. "And, he believes, um—"

"Sitzen!" The secretary spins to the reliable Axel, of course. "Officer Von du Croy," he calls. "What does SS Wilhelm Bohle want us to know?"

The hands of my fiancé thwack his thighs when he stands. "Bohle promotes Volks-Genossen," Axel says. "This means Racial-Kameradship."

"Gut!" Führer Kuhn says from the front of the class. "So tell me class. Does this mean we are a community of many different Germans?"

There is a mixture of yes's and no's.

"Nein!" His voice seems to shake the walls. "The lines of a German aren't drawn between rich and poor, rural or urban, living inside Germany or abroad," he says. "We are a living breathing soul of one German. We are a part of a great whole. A whole that's worth dying for."

Sounds nice to be one, I think to myself. Then, I think of Yael. He's not German. Anyone who isn't a German can't live on the inside. A shame for outsiders. Who wouldn't want to be bigger than ourselves? An invisible wire pierces my chest, and I feel the connected vibration of our class.

"And which exact meaning of Racial-Kameradship does Bohle hammer into us?" the professor asks.

"Germans can't choose to be German," Axel replies. His pupils quiver. "We are sent by God to be German." In his answer, I hear Axel define the moral character of the German—the character expected of us.

"Perfekt, Officer Von du Croy!" Kuhn exclaims. "Nations will no longer absorb Germans as cultural fertilizer, not in Europe or Asia, and especially not here in America. Germans will take what is rightfully ours! Where a German lives, is Germany." He motions for Secretary Wheeler-Hill to continue.

"Pencils to paper! Write Hitler's Nuremberg Laws," Secretary Wheeler-Hill says.

I know the first one. It's about protecting German blood. Marriage between Jews and Germans is forbidden. And it doesn't matter if you live in Germany or not.

Head down, I peek at the Führer. His chest rises. He's inhaling the sight of us doing his bidding. I can imagine what he must be thinking. "We are sowing our Fatherland in the soil that we will reap." The rhythm is captivating, even for me.

KRISTA:
Camp Siegfried. Long Island, NY

"Daggy's disappeared into thin air," I say to Greta and Heidi as I scrub the grime off the long wooden table in the Camp Siegfried mess tent after dinner.

Sascha rushes toward us. "No luck. Cort has searched the cabins and tents, everywhere," she says. She chews her nail.

"She hasn't disappeared, Sascha," Heidi says over the scratching of our horsehair brushes. "She simply didn't come to dinner. Daggy is ashamed of herself."

"She's probably back at our cabin," Greta says.

"No, she's not." I point my brush at a shadowy figure across the drill field in a remote area of camp. "She's over there, by the old campsite." I drop the brush and race through the long shadows, swatting away black gnats pricking at my sweaty face. Over chirping crickets. I hear the girls trample behind me.

"Come on!" Greta calls to the others.

At the dead camp site, my mouth drops. Daggy is covered with gray soot. The ash coats her street clothes. Her arms and legs and face and hair are white. She's shoveling ashes of a campfire into a crate.

"What did they do to you?" I choke as I ask.

Stone-faced, she says nothing.

I tussle the shovel away from her hand. "Daggy, tell me!" Something dreadful has happened. I look down at her clenched fists. Metal strings jut from them. "Oh, no," I mumble. I uncurl her fingers and follow her catatonic eyes to the rubble pile. Silent smoke rises from her charred guitar.

"They said American music polluted me," Daggy says in a monotone. Her fist tightens around the strings and blood smears between her fingers.

Heidi, Sascha, and Greta surround us.

Greta guides Daggy to a log where they sit.

Daggy touches each of us with the sunken dark eyes. "After the closing ceremonies," Daggy whispers. "Two scouts took me to Frank's office." She chokes down a sob and covers her face with her hands. Sasha sits next to Daggy on the log and rubs her shoulder.

"You mustn't tell Cort," begs Daggy. "He will get himself into trouble if he knows."

"Continue, Daggy." Heidi barks.

"Geez Louise, Heidi! Give Daggy a moment, okay?" Why must my sister play the big bad wolf with this slaughtered lamb?

Daggy inhales. "Frank read my charges. He said, 'I affronted Secretary J. Wheeler-Hill by slandering our Mother Tongue with bastard English and disrespecting our culture.' Then he told the two scouts to ..." She coughs. A tear washes a line down the white ash on her face.

"Spit it out!" Heidi says. She grabs Daggy's shoulder and shakes her. Greta pushes Heidi's hand away.

Daggy brushes her grimy face with the backs of her hands. "Frank told the boys to play rock, paper, scissors to decide who would punish me." Her voice turns cold. "The older scout, I think he was fifteen, beat rock with paper."

Greta smooths Daggy's hair. "Did he hit you?" Greta asks.

"Greta. Geez Louise!" I say, kneeling in front of Daggy. I put my hands on both her cold knees. "Don't you get it? Dags has been—"

"He took me to the couch," Daggy interrupts me. "He got on top of me. I tried to push him off. He stuck his tongue in my mouth and pulled up my skirt and moved my underwear and then put *it* in me. Frank told him to slow down. But he finished fast. He got white gook all over me." Tears well up in my own eyes as I watch Daggy grind her teeth. My hand shakes on Daggy's wracking legs.

Populating the Reich is one thing. But this is barbaric. "What they did to our friend is cruel," I say as I give my sister Heidi a lethal look. I take Daggy in my arms and let her cry. As God is my witness, I'll find a way to stop these animals.

Daggy's chest heaves. "Frank made the younger boy watch," she says. "And then Frank made the boy touch him down there."

"You don't know what you're talking about," Heidi says. She glares at Daggy. "I'm sure Frank was punishing the boy for something."

I cringe. Heidi is trying to justify Frank's sick behavior.

"Maybe." Daggy rolls her eyes up at Heidi. "Frank pushed the boy onto his knees and grabbed him by his hair," she whispers. She's obviously never witnessed anything like this before. "Then Frank unzipped his own pants with the other hand and forced the boy against him. Afterward, he made the boy say he enjoyed it." Daggy closes her eyes and shudders. "Frank told the kid he will ask the Gestapo to check the *Reichszentrale,* the list of homophiles, to see if this runs in his family."

"Hideous," Heidi says. "Obviously, the homo deserves everything he gets." She holds up her hands in retreat.

Loathing for Heidi razors through my veins. She's looking the other way to protect Frank by putting the blame on the poor kid. At the same time, pity overcomes me—pity for what Daggy endured, pity for the younger boy, pity for Frank who blames everyone for his own pain. I feel pity for Heidi's spineless selflessness. I glance down at my own hands. Did this intolerance pass throughout our generations? After all, my hands look just like my older sister's.

CHAPTER 19

Combination

LONGIE ZWILLMAN:
Office. Hotel Riviera. Clinton Avenue. Newark, NJ

On the couch in my Hotel Riviera office, Nat balances his cigar in one hand and dips his Twinkie snack cake into his coffee with the other. He shoves the whole thing into his mouth. "Hey! Isaac," Nat calls across the room to Harry's father.

Isaac rubs his forefinger across the books in the long bookshelf in my office.

"I just heard on the radio the Nazis sent some loser to Tibet to find proof of their Aryan ancestors," Nat says. "They're supposed to find giants with powers who came down from a place called Thule." Doughnut pieces fly from Nat's mouth.

As I lean forward in my desk chair, Nat waves me down. "I got this, Boss." He picks up the crumbs from the floor and drops them into the coffee cup.

Isaac brushes his fingers through his wavy white hair and walks to the world globe on a side table next to Nat. "You are correct about the

Tibet news, Nat." He spins the globe and points. "Hitler's man Himmler launched an expedition." Isaac's heavy Yiddish accent brings credibility to this farfetch'd tale." He moves his finger to the top of the globe. "Thule was a place near the North Pole where these Giant Aryans lived for a thousand years. A catastrophe destroyed the world and they scattered." His finger slides around the globe as if he's painting.

"Holy mackerel!" I say. "Hitler's out to prove that the bones of the German and original humans are the same."

"They believe their ancestors are from another galaxy and they are destined to control earth," Isaac says. "I'm not kidding."

"A bunch of Looney Tunes, if ya ask me," Nat says. He points to his mouth to reassure me that crumbs are contained.

"The lost Thule is said to be the capital of Hyperborea," Isaac explains.

"Never heard of it," Nat snaps. He chugs his coffee.

"The place is mentioned in ancient stories, including Homer," Isaac says. "The logic is that the pure Aryan race lost their powers when they interbred with minderwertigen, the lower form of humans."

"They're referring to the likes of Jews, Catholics, Negroes, and cripples?" I ask.

"Exactly, Longie," Isaac says. "They believe that as soon as the mixed breeds are exterminated, the pure Aryans will resume their powers."

"A regular pagan sacrifice," Nat spouts. "Whackos."

"Actually, less of an offering and more of a cleansing." Isaac checks his watch. "I must be going." He stands and plucks his coat from the rack.

As I watch Isaac open the door, a bad premonition raises the hairs on my arms. I hope it's not as dark as my quivering gut suggests. "Too bad you'll miss Yael and Harry," I say to Isaac. They should be here any moment."

YAEL:
Longie's Office. Hotel Riviera. Clinton Avenue. Newark, NJ

Isaac brushes shoulders with me as he exits Longie's hotel office. He squeezes my arm. "Gotta run, boys!" Harry enters behind me and hugs his pop.

Longie stands up behind his desk. "I'm gettin' extra smart from your pop so I can rough up candidates who come askin' for dough," he says to Harry. He shugs us, his signature half handshake, half hug.

"You already got the smarts, Boss," I say.

Nat Arno punches the air. "I teach ya how *not* to think."

"Sit, boys. My mishpuch, family," Longie says. Longie and I sit in the two big armchairs and Harry joins the cigar-puffin' Nat on the leather couch. "Yael, your father was a good man and he shouldn't have died under my watch."

"I'll get his killer." My eyes don't mist anymore when I think about Pop.

"You know what Longie always says," Nat says. He takes out his pistol and twirls it around his finger. "Retribution knocks out the bullies."

"From the time I was a boy, they beckoned me—Reef der Langer, the long one, they'd call. Ever since, I've fought against the creeps in our streets," Longie says.

"Longie's gang, The Happy Ramblers, protected the Jewish peddlers from the thugs," Nat tells us.

I nod. "Pop used to say you gave us what the Third Ward needed."

"Back then, boys, Newark had no fight, no family, no law," Nat explains. "It's simple. Longie made us stick together. Even our cops don't look the other way. They protect us and our businesses. He's earned everyone's gratitude."

"I'm lucky to be family," I say. "There's a favor I need. And ya might not wanna help me this time, Longie." I lock eyes with Nat. "I know Nat won't."

"What?" Nat loosens his tie. "The Nazi shiksa? You're leadin' with your chin, pal. Wide open for a KO." He swings his arm and taps Harry's chin.

Harry puffs his chest at Nat.

"Marriage outside was a line your parents drew in the sand," Longie says without movin' a muscle on his face. "They knew life was hard. Why make it harder?"

Is Longie appealing to my guilt or to my ego? He's wise. He's makin' this about me. "I get it, Longie," I say. "But I wanna rescue her. Her people will destroy her. Already they're forcin' girls to be incubators for their sicko cause. I gotta—"

"Why the heck would you risk everything?" cries Nat. "Ya gonna wheel the Trojan horse right into the command center? Our fall will be on your shoulders, pal."

"She wants out. She despises her father for forcin' her into Nazi life," I argue. But my words chafe my insides like a knee scrapin' gravel.

"Why are you the one to rescue her?" Longie asks.

"You got plenty of choices, Yael," Harry says. "Jewish girls pant when you enter the room."

"Why the heck invite trouble?" Nat asks. "You know she's a spy. They all are. In my experience, the best lookin' dames are the most dangerous."

"When have you ever had a good lookin' dame?" Harry says with a smile. Nat's lips twist toward his ears like he just smelled someone's underarm.

"You're right, Nat," I say. "A knife twists in my chest when I think of what she is. But when I'm with her, I see her for who she is. My gut tells me she's a good person." I force myself to look into Longie's eyes. "If you won't help me, then I'll do it myself, even if I die tryin'."

Longie kneads his chin. The dilemma is written in his weary eyes. His mouth tightens to a thin line. He protects me like I'm his blood. But he wants me to be who I'm supposed to be. "You trust her?" he asks.

"She's not part of what I hate, Boss. So yeah."

Longie breathes a long sigh. "That's a risky assumption. Fighting Nazis is dangerous business, Yael."

"She's bein' brainwashed at Camp Hitler. I need to get her out," I say. I don't think those words lend comfort to my guardian.

"Why are you doing this?" Longie lobs a stare at me. I know he trusts me with his life, but he doesn't trust himself with mine.

"Why?" I puzzle it. "Krista's a hostage," I sigh. "She's bein' abused and she's mixed up." I scrub my head with my fist. "You should see what they do to these kids at their camp. Teenage girls are forced to make babies. It makes my blood run cold." If I don't rescue her in time, the confident young woman with my boxin' gloves will be wide open for a knockout.

"What exactly are you fighting for, Yael?" Longie asks.

My chewed down nails dig into the leather armchair. "She's forced into the Hitler way, to marry a Nazi, to go back to Berlin," I say. Krista's reality is gonna break her. Does she even see a way out? Her choice is bein' robbed.

"This fight started for you long before her. Think. What are you fighting for?" Longie asks me.

I try to slow down my racin' heart. "Nazis are rootin' in our soil and everyone's ignoring how big it is," I say.

"That's right," Longie says. "Don't forget. You watched Nazis carve a swastika into your father's skin." He knows I could never forget this.

I stand and walk to the window. Below, the cars on the street bait one another. Metal scrapes metal. The sound brings back a memory; *Five years ago, a foghorn, like a low mournful bellyache muffled by a blanket rattles my heart. Nat and Longie stand with me. Below us, my pop's bobbin' boat slits the moving water. Men tug my lifeless father and Ruby from the green bay water onto the dock. The flaps of spongy skin wave on my father's chest, revealing a hideous swastika.*

I turn toward Longie's desk. In one corner, there's a framed photo of Longie in his white tux jacket. His warm smile reels me in. In the other corner is a picture of my father and I on the wharf at the docks. Pop's arm is wrapped around my shoulders. In the photo, my father is smilin' down at me. I remember more: *From the dark hollow womb in the front of his father's bootleggin' boat, I hear German men order my father to hand over the hidden booze.* That awful night was the first time I understood my father's job and the risks that went with it.

191

My eyes sting like they've been squirted with lemon. "OKAY. Tell me the way," I say. "What would I have to do?" Maybe fightin' the enemy and savin' Krista is one and the same? For both, I'm pushin' against the wind, riskin' my life.

"Last year, two friends of mine spied on the American Nazi Bund for the FBI and *Chicago Daily*," Longie says. "They went undercover."

Nat, always the plotka-macher, stirs the gossip. "James and John Metcalfe became stormtrooper goons like the ones us Newark Minutemen marinate. John is a newsman. Jamie is FBI. His bullet put down the gangster Dillinger. When their story hit the newsstands, the Bund tried to mow 'em down with a machine gun." By the roll of Longie's eyes, I'm not sure he thinks Nat's helpin'. But I gotta know the truth.

"Sometimes you gotta use a thorn to take out a thorn," Longie says. "Just like those boys, you go undercover and spy for us. You train. Gain trust. Feed us intel."

Fightin' Germans is one thing. Bein' them is another. They took everything from me. My face clenches as cold memories flood my mind: *My hand slips from Longie's. I run into my grievin' mother's arms. A noise from deep inside shakes her body. She squeezes me tight and then deflates like a balloon. She clutches her chest. My frail arms struggle to hold her weight. Her lifeless body pulls me down. My tears freeze in my eyes.*

Longie continues. "We've caught stormtroopers with plans to murder one powerful American after another. People like Jack Warner, Charlie Chaplin, Catholic bishops. Even FDR." My brain stutters. These names bounce around my skull like a pinball game at Asbury Park. I turn toward Harry. His dark eyes calm me. My thoughts catch up.

Cigar smoke slips through Nat's lips. "The German plots are gettin' more ballsy. Just last week, our guys in Chicago diverted plans of blowin' up a military site. Americans won't swallow it. They think it's fake news."

Longie rises and steps toward me. He points at the wall mirror. "When you look at your reflection, you see who you are. But when I look at you, I see who you can become." His bleary eyes scour my troubled face. "And you will become way more than a boxer," Longie says.

"I'm not afraid of silencing people and dodgin' machine gun bullets, Boss," I say. My fists clench. "I'm afraid of myself. If I'm in their inner circle, I'll kill 'em."

"You know how many Nazi spies the FBI caught last year?" Longie quizzes me.

I shake my head.

"Thirty-five," Longie tells me. "Ya know how many this year? Six hundred. Germany disguises them as tourists, students, and workers. We let them mosey in on red carpets. Indifference is our greatest enemy." Longie places his hand on my shoulder. "Our enemy is unworthy of our fear or awe. It's time to fight back. We must not stand aside while our innocent blood is shed." Harry and then Nat stand at my side.

I consider my life. Each night, as soon as I close my eyes to sleep, the splash of my father's boots against water douses me. My nightmares have put me on a path of destruction. Do I suddenly have a choice? I feel calm. Or do I feel insane? It doesn't matter. At this moment, I let go of who I am.

"I have nothing to lose," I say.

"Then the enemy should be terrified," Longie answers. He breaks a smile.

"They can't win," Harry says. He gives me a thump on the back. "Because you won't let them take our will to live. And I don't mean just be alive. I mean live."

Longie wastes no time. "We'll load ya up with a new identity, a uniform, and the all-important Certificate of Aryan blood," Longie says. He nods to Nat to carry on.

"You get to change in phone booths like that new comic book guy *Clark Kent*." Nat says. He slaps Harry's back. "Harry, call your Aunt Rose to fire up her contacts in the underground. I'll take care of the other stuff." Nat and Harry take off.

"Hey, at least I don't have to wear Nazi Superman tights," I shout after them.

"This Sunday, join me at the Newark Bears ballgame with Mayor Ellenstein," Longie says. "He'll fix everything for training at the camp down in Andover. We'll talk about it at the game."

My bravado is real. Sacrifice has been erased from my vocabulary. But my years of blood blistering revenge still simmer close to the surface. I hope I can control myself livin' like a sardine in a can of Nazis.

"You're making history, *now*!" Longie tells me. "You're going to wake America. You're going to make citizens see the threat to liberty standing on our doorstep. Your father would be proud. My own father used to tell me, 'Az me muz, ken men'. It means, if you have to, you can."

LONGIE ZWILLMAN:
Bears Vs. Orioles. Ruppert Stadium. NJ

"What the heck's gotten into our Bears today, boys?" Newark Mayor, Meyer Ellenstein, shouts across me to Harry and Yael. We're at Ruppert Stadium watching our Newark baseball team getting creamed by the Baltimore Orioles. "Ya'd think they were still hibernating from the cold," Meyer says with his colorful charm.

I look at Meyer pouting at his precious Bears like a disappointed brother. But that look doesn't last long. He's got hope like a bird's got wings. Meyer's as talented a guy as I've ever met. Four years after the crash, against twenty-nine candidates, we put him in the Newark Mayor seat. He's one of us. Puts people in jobs, fights big biz, loyal to a fault with his friends. Meyer is the guy who Webster should list as the definition of *charisma*. A charm that brings devotion.

We set Meyer in motion before the Great Crash. I must've been barely twenty-three when I opened the Third Ward political club on 88 Waverly Avenue. One night at the club, we decided to make Meyer our Mayor. Newark had lost its identity. It was gritty, stagnant, and entitled all at once. I swore to give it what it needed most—goodness and power. The club united us and today stays true to its roots. We have a place to do business without a lot of red tape. A place where a decent businessman can talk plain to judges and cops. A space to get the right guys elected and name a state attorney or two who will make a difference. Without these straight shooters unclogging the pipes, we would drown in these hard times of the Depression.

Maybe Meyer and I connect because we come from similar legends. He worked ten hours a day as a kid in a silk mill. He played ball and fought at the boxing ring in his free time. Kid Meyer they called 'em. Coulda been a great. But his pop died, and his ma needed help raising five kids, just like my life. I'd never admit it to him but he's a better guy than me. He became a dentist and an attorney.

A cheer jolts us. Like blood and thunder, 17,000 fans cheer a home run by the Bears. I can't restrain myself. "The Bears are gonna beat their '37 pennant record!" I elbow Harry on my left. "Make sure I put more money down on the series."

"The pennant won't be easy," Yael says. "Last year's twenty-five game lead was historical."

"Problem is the boys are so darn good. Yankees call 'em up faster than they can get plate time," my sidekick, Meyer, calls it like it is.

I startle at a noise that sounds like the sky clapping its hands. We spring up. Harry bare hands a foul ball bullet off a wooden bat before it crushes my head.

The Mayor blurts at Harry. "Why're ya a boxer, bum? Let's get ya out on the real field. I bet a guy your size could wake up the air around home plate."

"Yeah, Meyer, look where baseball got ya," I joke.

Harry and Yael laugh with deference. After all, Meyer's a powerful guy.

I turn the conversation to business. "Governor Hoffman was at my shore house last week," I say to Meyer. "Between the two of ya, seems everything's set for Yael and his new station in life."

Yael's eyes glint with curiosity.

The Mayor reaches inside his jacket pocket and pulls out an envelope. He hands it across me to Yael. "This is your ID and medical exam, son. Rike Saxon's your alias name. It maps to public files if anyone comes snooping." He holds up three copies of a booklet and hands one to each of us. "Here's a translation of the *American German Volksbund Rules and Regulations*. Good toilet reading."

We all chuckle.

"Be careful not to confuse your Yiddish with whatever old German your mama taught ya," Harry cautions.

"You'll prove you're a German national of Aryan descent," I warn Yael. "And you'll swear you're free of Jewish or colored-tainted blood."

"I'm gonna have to practice my straight face," Yael says, flashing his teeth.

Harry shakes his head and frowns.

Meyer smiles. "Good for you. Keep your sense of humor, Yael. It might be the only thing that keeps you sane. The German-American Nazi Bund worships the fanaticism that's cooking in Germany."

"Our cronies have no doubt that the Bund is going for America's jugular," I say, catching Yael's eye and holding it.

Meyer rubs his hands. "The organization you're joining, the Ordnungs Dienst or O.D. is modeled after Hitler's stormtroopers and designed with mathematical efficiency. They wear the same uniform, march the same drills. Have the same purpose."

Harry thumbs through the document. "This is worse than the Torah. There must be ten-thousand steps," he says. The attention to the details shows the discipline behind the American Nazi movement.

"Just do as they say, no matter what," Meyer says. "They are whizzes at sniffing out spies. And they take no mercy to the ones they find."

"There's a ruthless efficiency to the mounting machine overseas. We're pretty sure they're gonna start a war. No one wants to admit it, but it's creeping into America," Meyer says. "You're doing a good thing, Yael."

CHAPTER 20

Stick and Move

KRISTA:

Main Hall. Camp Siegfried. Long Island, NY

T he main hall at Camp Siegfried hums with guests celebrating the Götterdämmerung holiday weekend. Overhead, light splits through the chandelier crystals and sprays colors across the pamphlet in my hand. The cover shows the world burning. I read about Ragnarok, the end of the world. I think that's supposed to be a good thing?

"Ah! You've found some good reading material," a voice behind me says. Herr Dinkelacker leans over my shoulder and investigates the brochure. He lets the fan spinning in front of me blow against his face. His cologne smells like limes and spices. Caught off guard, I'm tongue-tied. As I turn toward him, my cocktail dress crackles.

Herr Dinkelacker plucks the paper from my hand. "Today we celebrate cleansing the world," he reads loud enough for me to hear over the crowd. "If we mate with our own, we can end evil mutations." Despite his challenging comments, he has the physical goods for selling the image of the perfect male. The chiseled jaws of his symmetrical face gyrate as he

197

gnaws his chewing gum. No wonder Greta didn't have the willpower to say no.

My daunted voice is caught in my throat. I'm thankful when Papa cups his hands against his mouth and calls. "Dinkelacker! What's the total count for the event?" My father is flanked by Führer Kuhn and Secretary Wheeler-Hill. The mirror on the wall behind them reflects the matching diagonal leather belts across their backs. It's like three scratches across a tic-tac-toe grid. I fear their real game won't be that bloodless.

The head of youth escorts me to Papa. "An army of fifty thousand are coming tomorrow for Götterdämmerung to hear you speak about the future of Amerika under the swastika," he says to Führer Kuhn, flashing his fairy-tale smile.

Axel appears by my side and puts his arm around me. He's aroused by the earlier announcement of our engagement in front of everyone who's anyone in the American Reich. I have to admit, the attention lifted me. Frank and Heidi join our huddle. Frank better stay out of my right cross distance. It's all I can do to keep my fists away from his nose.

"We've raised a million dollars for the our Nazi colony in America," Secretary Wheeler-Hill says. He hands Führer Vandenberg his tabulation. "Even the big guys across the ocean are impressed."

"And there's cream on the top for us," Papa says as he taps his pocket. "Just thinking about reaching a million members makes this muggy night a little cooler."

Geez. Papa just said a million. It's amazing how fast we're growing. Maybe Yael is mistaken about the American Bund. How can so many people be wrong? Papa hands me his empty glass. I place it on a nearby table.

"That makes the Assembly our biggest revenue stream after the Camps," Führer Kuhn says.

"Just wait until Machtergreifung," Führer Vandenberg says. "When a Nazi President sleeps in Abe Lincoln's bed in the White House, the real money will flow."

"Enough politics for today!" Führer Kuhn smiles at Axel and me. "You're all enjoying Camp Siegfried?" he asks.

"It's an Aryan paradise in America," Frank responds like a mutt in heat.

"Our camps are our homes away from the Fatherland," Secretary Wheeler-Hill says. "It's time to make all of America just as great."

"Here's to America first," Frank says. His fawning disgusts me, as well as the sweat rings under his arms. Whether I stick with my own people or not, Frank is going down.

"Amerika Verpflichter, Deutschland Dernunded," Axel says. How does he think we stay obligated to America but always tied to Germany? Axel's white teeth shine against his golden answer. If I have to be stuck with a Super Aryan, I guess it might as well be him.

Führer Kuhn's eyes light up. "Refreshing. In Berlin, they're applauding our youth program thanks to you, Herr Dinkelacker."

Heidi smiles at the dashing Herr Dinkelacker. My stomach turns when he licks his lips. But should I blame this indoctrinated Nazi? Heidi is his idyllic woman—tall and slender, blonde pigtails framing her perfect pale face and cornflower blue eyes.

Führer Kuhn steps toward me. Axel and Frank part, like foot soldiers clearing the path. "What do you think, Fräulein?" he asks. I look at the Führer's staunch face and wonder what it's like to be him. Does his head spin with ways to expand the Bund? Does his back itch, fearing an enemy from behind? Does his heart burn worrying his own children could report him for not following the party line? Are his lips cracked kissing up to bigger fish than him? I smile with that thought. Führer Kuhn gazes at me, with his hands behind his back. He must be trying to read my mind.

"Your question for me, mein Führer?" I ask.

"In Germany, Hitler wants to isolate Aryan blood from other breeds," he says. "What do you think about this idea for Amerika?"

Heidi nudges Frank. She's fearful of my blunt words. "America could benefit from less disease that comes from interbreeding," Frank answers for me.

"My question is for the Fräulein," Führer Kuhn says, ignoring Frank.

After a long pause, I say what I'm thinking. "What I've learned from you, mein Führer, is that Hitler believes in survival of the fittest. In this way, he's a naturalist. He believes humans, like all animals, are strongest when they do not crossbreed with another kind. He believes he will help nature to purify a strong race for our survival. You believe his vision for evolution is violent but necessary for America."

Führer Kuhn smiles. "I believe what the Fräulein is saying is this: mixing Aryan with Asiatic, African, or other sub-standard race in a Frankenstein experiment is madness anywhere in the world!" Even if that's not exactly what I meant, I'm pleased the Führer Kuhn is impressed.

Axel puts his arm around me. It feels nice for my fiancé to acknowledge my contribution for once. But I'm not ready to relinquish my spotlight. "With all due respect, mein Führer. A question," I say.

Heidi shuffles her foot. Axel scratches behind his ear. I let them stew for a few seconds. Then I speak. "Today, the world is everyone's business. Shouldn't we take care of it together?" An awkward silence swallows the group. Axel drops his arm off my hip. Heidi glares at me, but I don't care. It feels good to speak my mind.

Führer Kuhn nods. "Excellent question. Hitler's world will benefit the entire world," he says. "By breeding the healthy and strong, we stop the suffering. We free the human race." His eyes are glassy. "Führer Hitler resurrects the Reich. I deliver the Germanic brotherhood to Amerika." I can't help it. He makes me believe.

"We serve you as guardians of the U.S. Constitution," Axel smiles. When he's not bossing me around, his boyish charm does excite me. I catch my reflection in the wall mirror. Am I accepting my destiny? Maybe it was Herr Dinkelacker who woke me up earlier with his charm?

Secretary Wheeler-Hill raises his arm. "Heil Hitler, to loyal Amerikans with Hitler's vision," he shouts. "Our victory brings world prosperity."

With the group conversing, Führer Kuhn turns to Führer Vandenberg and my father. I eavesdrop. "Führer Vandenberg. I'm pleased that Camp Siegfried is preparing my daughters well for the Reich," Papa says. "You are to be commended."

"Your girls are lovely," Führer Vandenberg side-eyes Führer Kuhn. "And you must wonder what other patriotic duties you can offer," he says." He glances at my sister. "I invite you to further demonstrate your loyalty. Your worthy daughter, Heidi, is qualified to contribute to the Reich with me. You know what I mean?" He winks. Führer Kuhn puckers his lips.

My father grits his teeth.

Is Heidi hearing this? Geez Louise. She's busy popping Herr Dinkelacker's bubble gum.

Papa fidgets. He crosses his arms against Führer Kuhn's gape. "I understand the sacrifices that Germans must make," he says. "You have my unfettered approval."

Führer Vandenberg blinks at Frank's gawk. He nudges up his glasses. There is a chess game in motion with my sister as the pawn. I'm tempted to warn her of the players. If I did, she would only chide me for not accepting everything young ladies must endure for the Aryan cause.

Führer Kuhn places his hands on his hips. "I am honored to receive every German-Amerikan father who brings their daughter to me," he says. "I'm ready to expand."

Axel squeezes my hand. He walks me toward the large glass window facing the parking lot. The space is packed with cars. I guess one advantage of being tied to Axel is avoiding the horse auction Heidi must now parade.

YAEL:
Parking Lot. Camp Siegfried. Long Island, NY

The croak of matin' bullfrogs at night covers up the noise of our covert mission in the Camp Siegfried parkin' lot. I slide my body along the cold car metal. Wonder how many license plate numbers from this Nazi gala I'll record for the feds? Close behind, I hear Nat crackling gravel. From my crouched position, I have a view into the chandelier-lit main hall. The room is bustling with Germans in their Nazi best for the Götterdämmerung cocktail party. Krista did me a favor lettin' the cat outta the bag. With any luck, I'll catch a glance of her tonight.

"FBI's gonna have a Nazi field day," Nat whispers over my shoulder. "There must be a thousand cars parked here for the Gotter-dam party. Ouch!" he says when he bumps into me. "Can't see a thing in the dark." All the better to know he's close.

I imagine Krista sulkin' in a dark corner inside, waitin' for the boring festivities to come to an end. Maybe I should sneak in and drag her into a closet. Or better yet, outta that prison. Suddenly, there's a thump against the main room window. I can't believe my eyes. The back of that red dress I know so well is flattened against the glass. The dirty rat of a soldier-boy is pressin' her. Envy shackles me as I watch his hands movin' down Krista's sides. Dangit! She's huggin' him back. My blood boils. I wanna punch my fist through the glass and snatch her out of his gropin' arms.

My nerves jump like my finger's in a socket. One eye's trackin' the pork knuckles rubbin' Krista. The other's on the guards zig-zaggin' through the cars. I force myself to work. I curl around the back fender and hunker close to read the plate. As I raise my pencil over my notepad, a huge shadow blocks my light. I swing my elbow at the lurkin' figure, but the attacker catches it in his huge hand.

"Ease up. It's just me, pal," Harry growls as soft as his deep voice will go. Does he know I spied Krista?

"Sugar! Don't sneak up on me like that," I snap. I stretch my neck back toward the window, but Krista's gone.

"Stop flappin' your lips, boys!" hisses Nat. "This place is crawlin' with Ratzis."

The clack of boots kickin' pebbles grows closer. Schnell! Over there!" German voices shout.

"We gotta get outta here," Harry says. "Puddy's on the hood of Maxie's car. He's wavin' us over."

All I can think about is Krista hunkered down inside with that beast. She must be playin' along to survive. A pain like a paper cut gashes my chest. Or has she forgotten me? As I losin' her like money on a bad horse race?

Harry shakes me. "Yael!" he snaps. "Stop brooding over the dame!" He drags me toward the escape route. He's right. I can't let Krista goose-step over my heart.

Suddenly, lights beam on Abie and Al. They run.

Puddy flattens against the car-hood and grips onto the wiper canal. "Time to bob and weave, fellas." He whistles. Gravel churns under Maxie's spinnin' wheels.

I hear gunshot pops and gritty German commands. I see Benny hop onto the car bumper. Clouds of dust whip around us. Benny grabs my arm and pulls me onto the back of the car. Harry and Nat jump into the backseat. Maxie floors the gas. Dirt pangs against parked cars. Flashlight-beams drill through the darkness. Exhaust jets down my throat. Maxie gains traction. Gunshots ring out as we squeal to the exit.

FRITZ KUHN:
Bund Headquarters. Nye Avenue. Newark, NJ

I'm exhausted from Götterdämmerung weekend. But fulfilled. And happy to be back in my Newark Bund office eating lunch with Günther. The celebration lived up to its apocalyptic legend. As I told my followers, the cataclysmic downfall of democracy is right around the corner. Soon we will rise.

Through the intercom on my desk, Günther and I listen to the crackling voices from the Camp Siegfried office. During the weekend events, we installed a hidden microphone under Vandenberg's desk to eavesdrop on important meetings. This is a trial run.

I hear a girl's voice. "My father told me you met Führer Hitler at the Olympics," Heidi's voice crackles through the box into my office.

Günther arches his eyebrows. He shovels spaetzle dumplings into his mouth.

"Adolph, yes. He's a kind man with deep humanity," Vandenberg says. His voice sounds like sandpaper as it dribbles through the equipment. "He has your father's penchant for watching movies."

Günther smiles at me. We both lean in closer to the speaker.

"Führer Hitler is obsessed with Clark Gable," Vandenberg says. "So while there, we watched *Mutiny on the Bounty* in the viewing room together."

"My father swore an oath to Führer Hitler," Heidi says. For a girl, she's got confidence.

"As have I, sworn an oath," Vandenberg says. "There's nothing I wouldn't do for my country."

"I am also ready to serve, Fuhrer Vandenberg," Heidi says. Her gravel-voice through the intercom makes her sound like a machine.

"Yes. Your father is generous to offer your assistance to me," Vandenberg says.

Günther squirms. This dry run test has turned into a spying affair.

"You must give me your word that you'll not share secrets," Vandenberg says.

"Oh, you can trust me," Heidi says. "Please pass the salt."

"Führer Kuhn and I have great confidence in you," Vandenberg's voice creeps through the speaker. "We are assigning you to the Bunaste."

"The Bunaste? You mean there really is an organization that reports on Germans in America? I thought this was propaganda." Heidi's voice shakes.

"Most German-Americkans, like your family, support Hitler's New Germany. Bunaste protects us against German-Amerikans who might be a little confused."

"You mean traitors!" Heidi says. There's no mincing words with her. She has the bite of a viper. We have chosen wisely.

"Your father has helped create a pipeline of informants," Vandenberg says. "Now you will manage their research and profiles. We keep them stored at Camp Nordland."

"I'm honored to serve the Reich," Heidi's voice toughens. "I'll fulfill my duty in whatever way the Bund requires."

"Not everyone is as devoted as you, Fräulein. You will rise to the top with your talents." There is a pause, most likely a smile of gratitude. "You can also serve Führer Hitler in another way. I'll not beat around the bush, Heidi. You're a beautiful Aryan. You can serve by comforting me."

"Führer Vandenberg, your hand is on my thigh." I hear Heidi's fork drop. "Is this such a good idea, I mean, how would your wife feel?" Heidi asks.

The sound of a chair scratching the floor squeals through the speaker.

"I have not had sexual intercourse with my wife for an entire year. These are natural instincts to be fulfilled for the cause. And to increase the population with good stock like yours." Vandenberg says.

The sound of a door locking vibrates through the microphone.

"Our Führer believes it's pure to follow these instincts. No need to be timid," he says. The clicking of his belt buckle echoes into my office.

Günther chokes on his soft pasta.

That's enough voyeurism for even a devout soldier. I turn off the receiver.

CHAPTER 21

Go the Distance

YAEL ALIAS RIKE:
Training Facility. Camp Nordland. Andover, NJ

Under overcast skies at the Camp Nordland trainin' facility, a uniformed officer prods me like an animal. I stand in formation with other trainees as the alias, Rike Saxon. There are four lines of eight uniformed young men surrounded by dozens of officers who wear identical uniforms: gray shirt, black tie, black boots, Sam Browne belt, black cap, OD Stormtrooper elbow armband. The air feels cool against my bare neck. Irving buzzed my hair short to blend in. I've been processed as an American Nazi Bund Stormtrooper. Finger printed, photographed, and issued a pistol.

By the time I made it down to the small town of Andover at 5:00 a.m. for the first day of trainin', I'd downed three cups of coffee. They're barely keepin' me awake now. I was up way too late with Harry studying all those regulations. I spewed my guts to Harry. I made him swear not to tell Longie. I told him I'm not sure how long I'll be able put up with these guys bustin' my chops.

In front of the muster, the stocky, fortyish-lookin' leader, Führer Hermann Schwartzman paces. He screams commands in German. "From this day on, personal opinions are ausgelöscht. You are warriors, who die like Spartans rather than accept defeat." His demands pinch every nerve in my body.

At the top of my lungs, I strain to answer with the others. "Free America! Loyalty until death!"

Our commander's leathery skin stretches into a frown as he passes me. I hope my eyes are blue enough to avoid suspicion. He continues his military sermon. "You sacrifice your life against non-Aryans. You refuse Jesus since he was the son of a Jew," Schwartzman shouts without takin' a breath. "You eradicate red pestilence in America."

It's a good thing Isaac helped me brush up on German, or I'd be marchin' in triangles.

Schwartzman's veins bulge at his temples. "At initiation, you will take the Führer Oath, a personal bond between Hitler and the soldier," he says. His face ratchets red with each order. "Just as all German soldiers, you swear allegiance not to Germany, not to the flag, not the head of state, but to the one who holds absolute power over the German people. Adolph Hitler."

I peer into the nearby woods. Wonder where my trusted lookout guy is? He's supposed to have my back. Did Nat set up the dead drop behind the Bund Hall in town? Even with all these safeguards, I'm shakin' in my boots.

"Bund salute!" Schwartzman shouts. He demonstrates mechanics. "Right arm forward by shortest course, hand level with forehead, arm parallel with right foot." He eyes me. Like a bull out of the gate, he rushes toward me. Before I can protect, he grabs me. Son of a gun. My cover's blown. He twists my arm up. "Arm parallel, soldier. Fingers stretched. Thumb touching." He steps back and drops his chin against his chest. Somehow, I remember to breathe. My skin burns from the residue of his cold hand. The feelin' takes me back to the mornin' with my pop on the boat. *A cold gun scalds my skin as it turns me around. The Nazi's snow colored teeth readies to bite.* That was right before they roughed Pop up.

"Left hand on belt, left of collar, fingers extended over belt, thumb behind. Again!" Schwartzman shouts as he paces down the line. The extra flesh under his cotton jacket flaps.

We repeat the movements again and again. My arm sags like it's gained twenty pounds.

As the sun disappears, the Führer heaves out his chest. "You will guard our American colony! To die for Germany is to live for Germany," he roars in his deep voice.

"Loyalty until death!" we cry.

My lungs are gonna burst. I have a feelin' the torture has only just begun.

FRITZ KUHN:
Office. Camp Nordland. Andover, NJ

Through the screen window of my Camp Nordland office, I inhale the greasy sausage scent oozing from the mess hall. I peer out the mesh and scan the remote 204-acre resort facility located in Andover Township, New Jersey. My gut was right to build camps across the country with facilities for rallies and training and all the necessities for youth camps. I've ordered my men to stop threats against the camp. We got wind of a newsman snooping around. The officers were able to stage our activities. Now, the press thinks we are a bunch of boy scouts. But next time, spies will not get away alive. If the Amerikan Nazi party is to last for a thousand years, we must nurture and protect a new generation of Nazis.

Führer Hermann Schwartzman enters my office. He cocks his head my way. "We put the Trooper recruits through the paces today, Fritz."

"Did we lose any?" I ask.

"Not one soldier believes he can survive another day," he caws. "But I wager my right arm that all will return." He stands by my side and exhales. "Can you believe we opened less than one year ago, mein Fruend? 18 July, 1937. Already, we've produced hundreds of Gestapo troopers for Amerika."

"Impressive," I chortle. "Breaking even the most rigid man's spirit is so simple."

"Even more easy is molding him back into our image," my loyal friend says. "Just force his limits and compliment and you've got him by the balls." Hermann has such a way with words. "By the way, I've thought of a way to identify our top recruits," he says to me.

"I'm all ears." I raise my eyebrows.

"We tell the recruit to spit on the swastika."

My forehead wrinkles at the thought of the horror.

"Hear me out, mein Führer," he says, waving his hand. "If he won't spit, we reward him for his faith."

"And if he will?" I roll my fingertips on my thigh.

"He has shown discipline and we advance him." Hermann grins. "The ancient Knights Templar tested authority this way."

"You are a true leader!" I clap my officer on the back. "Listen. Keep our stormtroopers and officers isolated in North Camp this summer, away from the campers. The private suite will host my officers and a personal friend or two," I say with a wink.

"Most commute to their jobs and families, so there's only a few boarders," Hermann says.

"One of the boarders is the nephew of an important German Nazi and a close friend," I say. "His name is Freddy Schafspelz. Treat him well."

YAEL, ALIAS RIKE:
Training Facility. Camp Nordland. Andover, NJ

I didn't know days could be this long. In the empty locker room, my fingers tremble as I unlatch my locker. I'm exhausted. The cotton of my own khakis cool my legs after wearin' that scratchy uniform all day.

I feel like I just shucked off an old snakeskin. I put my boots, hat, and pistol into the cubby and toss the dirty uniform into a washin' box. I grab my jacket and whirl around to leave. My getaway is thwarted. A trooper trainee blocks my path. His cotton-colored hair cuffs me like a hookshot.

The soldier thrusts a black book near my face. "You forgot your stormtrooper manual. You think this is a joke, soldier?" His steel gray eyes seem to slice my throat.

My first instinct is to knock him out. But I relax my muscles and raise my hand in retreat. "Where's my head?" Dangit! Getting kicked out the first day isn't gonna make Longie happy. I wish I were somewhere else.

"This book comes directly from Hitler," the guy barks. "What if you screw up while you're protecting our Führer?" He steps back. "You know my obligation?"

"To report me." I hold my breath. This guy's gonna get me killed. It's too late to reach for my gun in the locker. I ball my fists by my sides.

"No! Worse!" The trooper hurls the book against the floor. "It means you owe me a drink for saving your butt." His smile blasts me like a light turning on in a dark room. He puts out his hand. "I'm Freddy Schafspelz. From a long line of German military men. This stuff runs in my blood so I know a thing or two, good and bad." His powerful grip defies his wiry appearance.

Saved by the bell. "Rike Saxon." I curve up my lip. "Can I pay my debt now? You could teach me the ropes."

"Happy to tutor you. You choose. A lesson on Lebensraum, taking land to feed us Germans or ... our fringe benefits with Fräuleins." Freddy claps me on the back and we walk. "Who knows? I might even introduce you to a girl cousin my uncle wants me to meet."

"You don't know me but a day, and you're tryin' to pawn off ugly relatives on me? I see what kind of friend you're gonna be." The guy sprouts dimples on his handsome face. I hoodwinked him, but that was close. I gotta stay on top of my game.

CHAPTER 22

The Ring

YAEL:

Lewis vs. Schmeling Boxing Match. Yankee Stadium. Bronx, NY.

I maneuver through eighty thousand zealous fans in Bronx Yankee Stadium. The air vibrates from the cheers. It feels good to be in the city with my homeboys to watch the boxin' rematch of the century. And good to have a break from the merciless trainin' in Andover.

The heat of the June night adds extra tension to the already nail-bitin' fight between black American Joe Lewis and Hitler's darlin', German Max Schmeling. With fans packed like sardines in a can, the only way to get to my seat is steppin' across the chairs. I hop up on one. I get a clear view of the Minutemen gang just a few rows down from Longie and the mayor's box seats. As I make a beeline, Nazi soldiers smack me with salutes aimed at their boy Schmeling. It takes everything I have to nail my fists against my ribs and hold back my swing.

The announcer blares, "Joe Lewis, the Brown Bomber, misses with a right and then follows through with a jolting swing to the jaw." Thousands of fists shake in the air.

Al and Abie see me and shove two guys aside. I squeeze through and lean on Harry. From the row below, Benny, Maxie, and Puddy slap my hand.

"Schmeling is hurt. He holds on to the ropes," calls out the announcer. "There's a ripping right to the thigh by Joe Lewis."

"Was startin' to think ya got clobbered by Nazis," Harry growls at me under the noise.

My bloodshot eyes blink at his narrowed ones.

"It's all Joe now!" the announcer shouts.

"Yael, ya missin' the biggest fight in boxin' history—Captain America vs The Ratzi," Maxie says. He tilts his head up toward me.

I'm transfixed on the ring. The Brown Bomber is rainin' punches. Max Schmeling's jaw is jiggling like a skeleton in a doctor's office. My chin drops as Schmeling sinks to the canvas. "Get a load of that!" I shout.

"Joe wants to finish in round one," the announcer rants. "An explosive right, Schmeling to the canvas!"

Benny leans our way and yells over the noise. "The Nazis been bragging that Schmeling's winnings will go to buy German tanks." He snaps his fingers. "Looks like they're comin' up a little short." He grins.

"Max is on the canvas," the announcer shouts. "He rolls over and is up at the count of two."

"One hundred million listening on the radio tonight," Harry yells over the earsplitting clatter.

"Another right to the jaw," the announcer says. "And Schmeling is in desperate trouble."

"Yikes!" Al exclaims. "Five left hooks from the Bomber. I'd be crying, too."

"What a bombshell! He's holdin' the ropes after a minute and a half," Abie says.

"Max goes down for the second time!" the announcer says in a boomin' voice.

Joe's gonna take down Schmeling in one," Harry cries. He claps me on the shoulder.

"Now it's the Brown Bomber at his dynamite best," the announcer says.

Harry wraps his elbow around my neck. "I was worried as heck!" he says. "Next time, signal me. Hang the gloves in the window. Something." Harry's not gonna let me slide, and he's right. It's just hard to explain. I've been sucked into another world thirty hours a day.

"A right to the body!" cries the announcer. The place is deafening one second, silent the next.

Here's my chance to give Harry a quick update. I lean close to his ear. "Stormtrooper trainin' is brutal, pal. They compare it to the German Gestapo."

"Ya gonna be able to rescue the dame?" Harry asks.

"First, I'm focused on slappin' the American Hitler behind bars." My stomach pushes against my heart.

Harry hands me his beer. I guzzle it down without a breath.

"Hey, you guys," Maxie bellows. "Look! Schmeling's hitting the canvas."

The crowd roars for Joe. I've never heard such a rib-rattling cheer. My spirit rises out of my chest.

A stormtrooper in front of Puddy punches the air. "Hit that Negro already!" he yells.

Puddy reaches forward and taps the guy on the shoulder. When the soldier turns, Puddy shoves a lit cigar in his face. The trooper's eyes spin like saucers. His arms flap. Fists fly. In a matter of seconds, Benny and Abie put those Nazis down for the count.

"Geez. Schmeling is up," Al howls.

"Nope!" Maxie says. "Joe's not letting up."

"Another jolting right," the announcer cries. "Max is down for the third time!"

"Jumpin Jehosaphat!" Al twists his fists in his eyes. "Max is hitting the canvas."

I point to the ref. "Look! Ref Donavan's stoppin' the action."

"Throwin' in the towel in the very first round," Benny says. "Anyone bet on that?"

"It's over, a magnificent knockout for the Brown Bomber," the announcer says.

The crowd hollers amid the thunderous applause. The clamor rings my ears.

Al flexes his muscles and tap dances. "The Brown Bomber destroys the Aryan master race!" he cries.

I turn and salute Longie and his gang up in the box seats. He sees me and waves me up. When we enter the suite, Longie tosses Harry and me a bag of Cracker Jacks.

"We just lived history!" I say. I tear open the molasses popcorn with the sailor boy and his dog. "Good to see ya, Mayor Ellenstein." I pull out an Uncle Sam soldier prize.

Harry crunches his candied popcorn. "The Brown Bomber just rang the Liberty Bell for Americans against the Germans!" he says.

"Yael. Good to see ya in one piece. How's the mission going?" Mayor Ellenstein asks.

"Stayin' in character isn't easy. They've almost tripped me up," I say.

"Longie says you're the best undercover we've ever had," he says.

I steal a glance at Longie. I know he's proud of me, but the comment takes me off guard. I hope I can always meet his expectations. "I'm learnin' secrets about the scumbags," I say. "The Bund has hundreds of Nazi cells across America. The orders come directly from Berlin."

"Kuhn's a Hitler copycat," Meyer says.

"Worse," I say. "He's doin' dangerous stuff in America with Hitler's ideas."

"From what Yael's found, they're fanatics," Harry says. "Even more than we thought. They believe they're American patriots who are defending the Constitution."

I nod. "Yes. Kuhn has his folks singin' the *Star Spangled Banner* with an outstretched salute."

"He's painted the swastika red, white, and blue," the mayor says. His visual makes my gut clench.

"We're gathering proof that Kuhn and his henchmen are takin' over from the inside out," I say. "And we won't stop until we have enough to bring 'em down."

"We've got a system in place to draw blood from their inner circle," Longie explains to Meyer. "Yael and Harry are the most strategic for us. Harry's the conduit between Yael and me." I pick up Longie's hint that there's other moles in the holes. My adrenaline sizzles. We're gainin' strength against the enemy.

"Always in your corner, pal," Harry says to me. "Just say when and where."

"You'll see the boxin' gloves in my window to signal any pick-ups," I tell Harry. "There's a loose brick in the Big Yard we'll use as a dead drop. Ya never know who might be watchin'."

CHAPTER 23

Outside Fighter

FRITZ KUHN:
Training Facility. Camp Nordland. Andover, NJ

"We have a stellar group of stormtroopers at Nordland this year," I say to Hermann Schwartzman as each recruit marches past and salutes. The sound of marching boots fills me up like warm apple strudel on a winter night. I'm proud to be their Führer.

"We're ready to put Amerika and the world on the right axis again," Hermann says. His eyes scan each soldier from boot to cap, like a parent checking that his child has colored inside all the lines of a picture.

"I understand that Horst Wessel is providing a guiding star for our soldiers," I say.

Hermann's chest swells to recite the slogan of our national icon. "Here! … Wherever Germany is, there you are as well, Horst Wessel!" he chants. "A martyr after my own heart. Every German-Amerikan will worship him just as Germans did after the Communists slaughtered him."

"Excellent!" I say as Hermann follows me back to the barracks. "Any concerns?"

"I am pleased with our recruits." he answers. "However, there's always some who struggle to fit in." He describes one soldier in particular. "For instance, recruit Rike Saxon. He's awkward. The silent type. Not sure if we can trust him."

Interesting coincidence. This is the same recruit Freddy's taken so kindly to. I rub my chin. "I'll ask Officer Schafspelz to keep a close eye on him."

YAEL, ALIAS RIKE:
Training Facility. Camp Nordland. Andover, NJ

At Camp Nordland, Freddy Schafspelz takes me under his wing. He introduces me to fellow trainees. "Gentlemen. Meet Rike Saxon. He's a Stuttgart, Germany import. He hacks meat for a living in Newark," Freddy sneers. "And he's as cool as the other side of the pillow."

I dip my chin to the Nazi-outfitted squad and kick the worn grass on the secluded drill field.

"Rike. Meet your fellow troopers, Paul Ochojski and Herbert Mai, two Harvard men. Paul slid into Harvard for his brawn, not brains," Freddy says. My new Kamerad sure does like to find the splinter that gets under your fingernail. But people seem to like him. "Paul played for the Crimson ice hockey team, so you can appreciate his athleticism. All kidding aside, his family is friends with Harvard President Conant, a great supporter of the Reich."

Interesting. We have a good idea how deeply the Nazis have infiltrated the masses. Now I wonder how far they've weaseled into America's elite.

Freddy continues down the line. "Herbert Mai here is a Brit who disguises his hooligan ways with that posh chit chat and slicked dark hair. Never could figure out how he and his breed talk without moving their jaws," he rags. "He was in the Harvard band. The German British Ambassador, Joachim von Ribbentrop, had him toot his trombone on board his ship."

"Indeed," Herbert says. "Ambassador Ribbentrop's a good chap to know. He wants us all to join him for a trip to Germany after initiation. Says he'll sign us on as sailors."

"Sounds like a man who provides fringe benefits," I say with feigned complement. Wouldn't that be a kick if I rode the same boat sailin' Krista to her Fatherland at the end of the summer. I could push Herr Axel right over the edge.

Herbert stares at me as if I'm a shot of single malt. Can he tell I'm not German? On the outside, my face stays as freshly ironed as my uniform. But my insides dare him to cross-examine me. Finally, he speaks. "I like this man's thinking, Sir Freddy." He flashes his big white teeth at me. The air sifts between my lips.

Freddy gestures toward the next Kamerad. "Walter Schultz is a Cornell man. He came to America through the Nazi exchange program run by Propaganda Minister Goebbles. We call him ein Langweiler since he's so boring." Freddy sneers at the pale-skinned Walter. His face is as white as whipped milk.

"Nice to meet you, Kamerad Saxon." Walter's translucent eyelashes flutter.

Freddy circles the short but stout Hugo. "Then there's just Hugo Steimle and me. We are from Universität der harten Schläge, or the school of hard knocks."

Hugo's blocky fist slugs Freddy's shoulder. I can't help but join the others in a laugh.

"Hugo's hat das Pulver nicht gerade erfunden," Paul says.

I dare a literal translation. "He didn't invent gunpowder?" I guess.

Walter presses his lips together and laughs with his eyes. "Your common German is a little rusty," Walter says. "The Amerikan equivalent is something like … not the sharpest pencil in the pack."

Hugo thumps Walter's shoulder back.

The signal for drills blares and stops my heart like an alarm in the middle of the night. Our light mood shifts gears. We fall in, stand chest out, head high, eyes straight. We follow commands and goose-step, goose-step, goose-step. Camp Nordland's leader, Führer Schwartzman, and the other officers kick our guts. They push me so hard it feels like someone's squeezin' my organs until they're purple.

The day couldn't end too soon. Like grit finally removed from raw flesh, the drills are over. The pain is forgotten. We have only to thank our masters with a psalm and they will release us. Our battalion sings Horst Wessel's song, the holy grail of German spirit. I recite and translate the German anthem in my head.

Now for the Brown battalions! For stormtroopers clear road o'er land!
The swastika gives hope to our entranced millions,
The day for freedom and for bread's at hand.
The trumpet blows its shrill and final blast!
Prepared for war and battle here we stand.
Soon Hitler's banners will wave unchecked at last,
The end of German slav'ry in our land.

LONGIE ZWILLMAN:
Office. Hotel Riviera. Clinton Avenue. Newark, NJ

I click on the telephone speaker in my Hotel Riviera office. "Go ahead, Yael. We're listening." Harry and I hunch over the speaker. This is the first time in a week we've been able to speak with Yael. It's late.

"The regular trainin's been brutal," Yael's electronic voice rumbles through the intercom. "But yesterday, we had special schoolin'. Führer Schwartzman yelled his fool head off. We trained with German war vets at a shootin' range on a farm not far from Nordland. I trained with Freddy, the guy I told ya about, and these other kids, Paul, Herbert, Walter, and Hugo. We practiced shootin'." Yael's talking a million miles a minute. "They get free guns from the NRA. But this was not just target practice, Boss. Our training was advanced, like assembling guns while we're blindfolded."

"Slow down Yael," I say.

Yael's on overdrive. He keeps rattling on as if he didn't hear me. "So, Paul and I pair up, right. I'm behind Paul with my gun, an automatic. Paul raises his gun, shoots, and sends bullets rippin' through the bullseye." As Yael talks, I imagine his face, a mixture of control and chaos. "Paul admires his shots. He even says this prayer-type thing. Spouts off about something like 'The blood myth is real. Our martyred hero, Horst Wessel lives in me. I will die for Germany.' And then the bastard sings, 'We follow not Christ but Horst Wessel."

Through the phone, Yael inhales with a rasp and I feel his intensity crackling right through the line. "The back of Paul's head is staring straight at me," he says. "So, I cock my gun. I set the cold steel. I point the sight at Paul's head."

I choke on my lox bagel and Harry tosses me a handkerchief.

"I wasn't gonna do it, Boss. I was just practicing my aim. But Paul swings around. He says, 'Try to beat that round of shootin'.'"

"What happened?" I ask. "Did you run?"

"At that moment, I think he catches me red-handed. But I roll the rifle up and shoot at a bird," Yael says. "Dang if I didn't hit it. But how can ya miss with an assault rifle? The joke of it all was that Paul cheered for me and jogged over to fetch it."

I take my handkerchief from my pocket and wipe my brow. "Nice recovery, son." I shouldn't have doubted him. He's made of steel.

But Yael's not finished. "I probed Paul and asked him how many guns are scammed from the NRA for free?"

"What did he say?" Harry asks.

"They're armin' for revolution," the ratzi told me. "Everyone's stashin' five-thousand rounds each. Can you believe it?" Yael's voice is both incredulous and hard as nails. His heated breath seems to blow us right through the phone line.

"I know you're ready to blow apart the Nazi Kingdom. Be careful," I tell Yael.

"Aye, aye Boss."

He heard me, but I'm not sure it registered. Harry drums his fingers on the table.

FRITZ KUHN:
Training Facility. Camp Nordland. Andover, NJ

At Camp Nordland, I witness the warrior explode inside my new trainee, Rike Saxon. To think we were worried about him. No more. During boxing, Rike unleashes a vicious right hook, knocking Freddy backward into the ropes. Then, like a savage animal, he loses it and beats Freddy to a pulp. Others have to yank him off. Maybe the man sees something Jewish in Freddy? At any rate, Rike has proven to me that he's got exceptional fighting ability, off the charts. I have made a decision! Rike Saxon will serve as one of my elite guards in the Amerikan Bund. We must, however, remind him to use a modicum of self-control. Then there's always the option to temper him with drugs.

After the round, Rike talks to Freddy near the boxing ring. Rike sways his head. "Buddy. I … I don't know what got into me." Freddy shrugs as he rubs his bruised jaw. Rike seems embarrassed by his own lack of restraint. But I approve, for he will be a potent weapon for the party. If I order him to attack, this soldier won't just advance, he will annihilate.

I observe the two boys. Freddy puts his hand on Rike's shoulder. "Where did ya get that Bolo Punch? Your hook uppercut is like a machete."

"Got it at my day job poundin' meat for the butcher," Rike says, forcing a smile. "Didn't mean to bang ya so bad."

Freddy rubs his swollen cheek again. "Just glad we're on the same side, pal."

YAEL, ALIAS RIKE:
Training Facility. Camp Nordland. Andover, NJ

My first weeks at Camp Nordland in the undercover operation as Rike Saxon cream me. Yeah! Me, a prize-fightin' boxer. I've never felt so tortured, like a housefly pinned to a board, being forced to beat my wings without flyin'. The leaders use our power against us, makin' even the strongest of us feel useless. They humiliate us, like torturers who let a laugh slip while they run their hands over cold metal punishment tools. I feel unhinged, without a skeleton, as formless as icing spread across a cake. The grunts of my fellow troopers haunt my nightmares.

But something is happening to me. Each day when I awake, a mechanical power moves me. I'm evolving into a piece of equipment. For better or worse, I'm forming into a machine with these German soldiers. I feel the union. I breathe with them. I speak with them. "Without all of us, each of us will fail."

During the eighty-centimeter march at one-hundred-fourteen steps per minute, Freddy falters. l lift him to his feet. "Bite the bullet, Freddy," I caution. "Otherwise, they'll make you do five miles double time."

We chant as we drill. "Hate on the enemies, march 'til ya drop!" I ingest the daily discipline and the wrath that unites me with my Kamerads. I'm so devoted to infiltrating, that linking becomes second nature.

"You better always have my back," warns Freddy. "I'm counting on you, buddy."

I hope I don't ever have to choose between my mission and this one individual. I'm bondin' with Freddy. I like him, but even more, I care for him. It's true that we both signed up for this mission for the same high-minded purpose, to protect our countries. I should be countin' the days when I can pull the rug out from under this nemesis. But we grovel together in the trenches with the bullets flyin' past our teeth. Ya can't get much closer than when you share fear. Plus, there's something I didn't expect to happen. I respect Freddy for including me. And in the same way, he respects me for my devotion to excellence. Unfortunately, he got a taste of that first hand during our boxin' match. The fact is, we're bondin' to the point of protecting one another if it comes down to it.

Should I be worried? Dangit! I should just bust my own chops right now. I gotta shake this feelin' that I'll do anything for him. Because if he knew who I was, he would be knockin' me out for good.

Führer Schwartzman storms at us. "Five miles, double time!" Schwartzman turns on the fierce war machine inside me. The Führer scowls at us. "You will give three hundred percent! If you fail, I'll demand five hundred percent!" he screams, projecting from his diaphragm."

As my identity warps into a stormtrooper, my psyche struggles to hold on to the Newark Minuteman inside.

CHAPTER 24

Cross Punch

FRITZ KUHN:
Infirmary. Camp Siegfried. Long Island, NY

"If you're born German, you are always a German," I say to Axel and Frank in the Camp Siegfried infirmary. As leader of the Amerikan Bund, I have a military responsibility to the German Reich. Orders from Germany require that both German-born men, as well as descendants, register for the national army and fight for the Fatherland, no matter where they live in the world. "Let's make that clear today to boys old enough to register for the German Unified Armed Forces."

Axel and Frank assist two ship-to-shore military doctors. The doctors examine two lines of stripped boys for medical compliance as German nationals.

"We've set up this room to comply with Article 17, mein Führer," Frank says to me. He points to the eye chart, waves at one doctor listening to a boy's heart and nods at the assistant taking the weight and height of future soldiers.

Axel escorts me to the main desk where Vandenberg processes forms.

In front of Vandenberg, a young man stands at attention in his white government issued skivvies.

"Klaus is nineteen today," Vandenberg says to me. "He has completed the military qualifying exam." He hands me the paperwork.

"Gratulation!" I say to the boy. "After the summer, you will serve The Wehrmacht. Der Führer, Adolph Hitler, commends you for being one of a million Germans in Amerika to register this year!"

Danke, mein Führer!" Klaus salutes. "This is my duty." His face is flushed. "I'm proud to be a German-Amerikan for the Reich!" I watch him avoid the stares of two campers glaring at him.

I calm his fears of the envy of his friends. "You and all your Kamerads will rescue the world. You will taste invincibility," I say. The patriotism that the boys harness today is euphoric. Much different than the Great War of my day.

Vandenberg stands in front of the room full of boys. "As you all know, Führer Kuhn stood side by side with Adolph Hitler at the Beer Hall Putsch. It was there they fought to overthrow the German government," he says. Around the room, the chiseled faces atop the muscled Aryan bodies tilt toward me. "I don't have to tell you boys that the Treaty of Versailles chopped Germany into pieces and made us prostitutes to the world," he explains.

"Herren, the BundesFührer, Fritz Kuhn!" Axel leads the cheer and the room full of nude boys repeat him.

I reciprocate their honor and relay my story. "We will never forget that fateful November day in 1923," I say. "Adolph inspired thousands to fight Marxism and retake what belonged to us. With inflation through the roof, we plotted a coup to capture the leaders of the Bavarian government at the Burgerbraukeller Munich beer hall. Adolph jumped on the stage, fired gunshots in the air, and called for a Revolution. But then bloody traitors gave us away."

"Heil Hitler!" The room pulsates with the fresh coronation of the new generation taking the reins.

"As you were, men!" I order and the exams resume.

"How many have we registered?" I ask Vandenberg.

"We've registered ninety-five percent of our qualified soldiers," Frank sings with pride, until he sees my disappointed face. His face turns white.

"But of course we will increase that to one hundred percent," Axel says to save face for his friend. "We will see you at the dance tonight, mein Führer?" he asks me.

"Of course! German dance demonstrates some of the best sides of our culture. The Schuplattler is a specialty of mine." I learned the shoe-slapping dance steps as a boy despite my old man. He'd get so drunk, our family was thrown out of the town gatherings more than once.

KRISTA:
Main Hall. Camp Siegfried. Long Island, NY

The main hall at Camp Siegfried has been turned into a ballroom with German folk music blasting through the speakers. My dirndl fans open as I spin to the schuplattler dance. Heidi, Greta, and Sascha mirror my twirls.

Across from us, Axel leads a contest of machismo. Beside him, Frank, Penn, and Klaus stomp their feet, clap their hands, and slap their knees with a fervor that no American could match. Yael would laugh if he saw this foreign show of my life.

Klaus gives extra slaps to the bottom of his shoes and the back of his lederhosen shorts. He grabs Gretchen and twirls her with a flick. He's full of himself. Cort told Daggy that Klaus registered for the German army today. Reading from Cort's narrowed eyes across the room, I don't think he approves.

As the traditional dance goes, the boys are trying to rile up calves for mating. Axel's face flushes. He hunts me down in a march around the room. Axel seizes me and swings me around. The heat of our bodies rivals the heat of the night. He pulls me close enough to feel his loins. For the first time in a long time, I share an attraction to him. He moves me around with precision and zest. His determination excites me, and I mirror his energy. We dance-march around the hall in sync with every single other couple in the room. Even Cort and Dags are clapping now. I belong.

CHAPTER 25

Lead with Your Chin

LONGIE ZWILLMAN:
Office. Hotel Riviera. Clinton Avenue. Newark, NJ

The phone in my Hotel Riviera office rings. I pick it up.

"Hey, Boss, sorry to call so late," Harry says to me through the line. "Glad I caught ya."

I look at my watch. In my biz, my work-day runs twenty-four hours.

The phone crackles. "Was working out late at the Y with Nat," Harry says. "We had a skirmish with one of those stormtroopers."

I wait for the punchline.

"We were walking down the front steps of the Y. Suddenly, someone bumps us. There's all kinds of clatter against the sidewalk. Nat's fists shoot up."

"Did the guy give ya trouble?" I ask.

"Strange. The opposite. He apologized. 'My deepest apologies, sir,' he slobbered to us in a German accent. And then I noticed his trooper uniform under his jacket. The loser plucked up his hat from the ground with one hand and scooped up his notebook with the other. Then he

228

disappeared. But he left a paper behind called *Awake and Act*. The name scribbled on it was Walter Schultz."

"Walter Schultz? That's one of Yael's guys down at Nordland," I say. "*Awake and Act* is one of Kuhn's papers. What happened to the guy? This Walter?"

"We looked everywhere, Boss. No Walter. But we got something. Notes written on the pamphlet—*Andover Munitions Dump. WED. 2 AM.* Seems there's gonna be a rendezvous, some meeting at the ole' factory. In the middle of the night."

"Let's cross our *T*'s. Get a message to Yael. See if this is real," I say. Seems a little too convenient.

"I've left him the message, Boss. His gloves haven't been hanging in his window all week. I think he's deep in training," Harry says with a cough. It's a worried cough.

"Yael will get the message," I say.

FRITZ KUHN:
Sidewalk. Hawthorne Avenue. Newark, NJ

Günther and I swelter as we walk down Hawthorne Avenue.

"Hey, watch it punk!" I yell to a dirty Italian kid playing tag with God-knows-what kind of other mix-breeds. Too late. He knocks me into some fat Polish woman gossiping on her stoop. Two doughy women curse me and prop me up with their sweaty hands. I need a hot bath!

Günther hands me my smoldering cigar from the sidewalk. I swat the thing out of his fingers and stomp it out like I'm squishing a bug. The derelict kid hands me my officer cap. For a second, his doe eyes catch me off guard and remind me of my own boy in Chicago. "Grazi," I thank him in his native language. After all, Italy rides with the Germans.

The only real relief from the scorching heat is knowing that steps are in motion for a Minutemen fall. Günther hands me another lit cigar. A breeze from the setting sun cools my neck. I reveal my psychological warfare to him. "Sabotage comes in many forms," I say as we walk past a noisy diner.

"Does this have to do with the Andover Armory?" Günther asks.

"Yes. The burglary at the armory is a decoy." I puff smoke. "Don't get me wrong. We're hijacking ammunition for our arsenal. But I'm killing two birds with one stone."

"Stockpiling guns for our war here is child's play," Günther says with a chuckle. "Prost Amerika! Thank you for the second amendment. You've made bearing arms to defend good Germans in Amerika quite convenient."

Günther is going down a rathole. But it's my fault for not sharing the plan. "Let me tell you something," I say. "Right now, the weapons are incidental. Tomorrow night, while Longie's gang fools around on the opposite side of town, we will be burning down their holy shrine, the YMHA."

The look on his face couldn't have been more surprised if I had popped out of a cake. "Mein Führer. You're playing with fire," Günther says. "They're not just criminals. They are run by the mob. Murder Inc. is what they call themselves."

I pluck lint off my uniform. "Fire turns gunpowder into life lessons, James," I tell him. With a vengeance, I rub my hands together and visualize myself steamrolling Longie Zwillman and his minions.

YAEL, ALIAS RIKE:
Munitions Dump. Andover, NJ

The headlights of the truck shine on two guards. They aim the barrels of their rifles through our windshield. We are parked behind the munitions dump in Andover near Camp Nordland. Freddy opens the car door and the night air grabs me. He slides out with his hands up. The guards advance with their guns, one with the double barrel eyeing me like a raccoon. The first guard starts the code. "Wonach suchen Sie?" he asks. If we don't know the answer to "what we're lookin' for," cold bullets will splinter our kneecaps.

"Wo sich fuchs und hase gute nacht sagen?" Freddy answers. Earlier, he made me memorize the answer; "Where the fox and hare say good night," an old German expression meanin' the middle of nowhere.

The guards lower their guns. "Schnell!" the brute whispers.

The guard opens the passenger door for me to exit. On the way to the back of the truck, I zip up my black jacket and pull a dark cap over my head. Hopefully, Harry got word of this heist and the Minutemen will show up soon. It's been a tough week to get intel to him. Wires are gettin' crossed.

We open the back doors. Paul, Herbert, Walter, and Hugo send up clouds of dirt as their boots hit the ground. I check my watch. "It's barely after midnight. We're early, aren't we?" I say to Freddy.

"If you recall, never really set a time with our men. And you know what they say about German efficiency, ya?" Freddy responds. He seems stiff. Not like him.

Two at a time, we load crates of ammunition from the Andover munitions dump into the truck. I jerk. There's a thud. Dangit! Herbert and Walter dropped one of the crates. Everyone freezes.

"Vorsichtig!" I warn. "Take your time." My German is becoming second nature. "Otherwise, you'll blow us to Kingdom come." I load the crate myself.

"Double time," Freddy orders. "Let's finish and get out of here." I check my watch again. It's only 1:40 a.m.

No sign of the Minutemen. Harry knew. Longie knew. They'll be here. We get in the truck. Just as we're pullin' away, Freddy checks the rearview mirror and grins. "Ha! Suckers took the bait." The bait? I'm confused.

Suddenly, there's clamoring, like the sounds of pots falling out of a kitchen cabinet. In my sideview mirror, the reflection of Minutemen runnin' out of the warehouse with steel pipes in their hands shakes me.

Freddy flashes a smile at me. "Kuhn ordered those gangsters out of the picture," Freddy remarks. "We planted a message for a 2:00 a.m. heist at the armory. The fish fell for it hook, line, and sinker."

From the back of the truck, Paul quizzes Freddy. "I don't get it."

"Times up for the Newark Minutemen," Freddy says. "Our fellow troopers are an hour away blowing up their headquarters at the YMHA right now! And there's no one around to stop us. Why?" Freddy laughs. "Because all the Minutemen fell for a trap. They showed up here at an old armory. We pulled a good old-fashioned bait and switch."

I flinch. The dark reality floods my mind. My gut clenches. I wipe my hands on my pants, streakin' the fabric with sweat. This YMHA bombing is a critical misstep. Why did I let my guard down? I assumed Freddy trusted me. Who do I think I am?

"You okay, Kamerad?" Freddy gives me two slaps on my knee. "We're gonna drive back to Newark to watch that building burn into ashes."

My saliva tastes metallic. "Of course!" I fake a smile. "We pulled the coup of the century!" I rub the sweat that's trickling down my back against the seat. "You know me. Normally, I'm first in line for a celebration. Darndest thing. I hurt my back liftin' that crate those bozos dropped." I unzip my jacket and feign pain. "Drop me at my car pal. I gotta take a rain check! You guys go ahead without me." I'll never trust anyone out of my own circle again.

YAEL:
Outside. YMHA. 652 High Street. Newark, NJ

In Newark, cars jam the road as people gawk at the pulsin' glow above the buildings. Plumes of smoke coil into the air from the roof of the blazin' YMHA. I slam on my brakes. The car in front of me is stopped dead. My throat gags from the fumes of flames archin' into the night sky above the city. "Holy moly," I whisper. "It's all my fault." I punch the steerin' wheel with the heels of my hand. "I gotta fix this!"

I turn the wheel, drive over the sidewalk, and slip the car into an alley. It'll be safe here for now. I get out and shunt around masses of people.

The carbon burns my nostrils. The firestorm booms against my eardrums.

This is getting me nowhere. Time for a new plan. I pull myself up a fire escape. It squeaks like a rusty gate. I scramble up and emerge on a neighboring roof a few buildings south of the Y. Before me is a nightmare of white plumes braided with black smoke. The vapors produce an orange monster devouring the YMHA. There is a deafening rumble as wooden roof beams gasp their last breath before crashing toward the pavement. Screams escape from below. The roof seems to melt in front of my eyes, releasing more flames and billowing smoke from the hole.

Somehow, my legs vault me to the next building. I climb and swing, maximizing my momentum to reach the inferno. From the roof, I find another fire escape, climb halfway down, and then leap toward the ground. I lose my footin'.

Longie grabs my arm. Of course he's there. "I got ya!" he exclaims. I watch the furious flames twistin' in his eyes. A moment later, we fight our way toward the blazin' building through the frantic press. Our knees drive through the watershed in the street. Hundreds help the firefighting teams battle the monstrous fire. We find Benny and Al wrestling with a ferocious nozzle, their faces smeared with soot, reekin' of scorched skin. The heat clobbers my face as I grip the hose. Abie arrives and positions behind me. Next to us, Nat, Puddy, and Maxie aim another hose at the violent fire swallowing the building.

Nat yells over the noise. "It's my fault." He gapes at me. "I bumped right into the firebug putz two nights ago. He set this whole thing ablaze."

Just then Harry rushes toward us. He holds something ragged in his arms. His face is ashen. I look into his arms. Oh, my gosh.

"It's Esther," he screams. "We got her out, but she's bad from the smoke."

I smudge the brown soot on her forehead. She doesn't move. My chest twists. My heart begs her to be okay. The firelight flickers off her brown eyes. They're open. My heart calms.

"Come on, then," Longie bellows as he beckons Harry and me. He grabs a nearby cop. "We need your car, Officer Paddy. Harry's sister was caught in the fire."

"You got it, Boss. I'll drive ya." The officer spreads the crowd and we follow.

Harry's arm supports Esther as he lays her into the car. She's raspin' for breath and her lids waver. She slumps against Harry. She'll be okay, this time. But I swear nothing like this will ever happen under my watch again.

As our siren's blazin' toward Hawthorne Avenue, the skyline smears before me like smashed, runny eggs. That's when I see Freddy and his Kamerads perched on their chaises on the sidewalk watchin' the sanctuary cook. The cretins are laughin'. I can smell their rotten satisfaction.

A furious chorus blasts payback through my brain.

CHAPTER 26

Check Hook

YAEL, ALIAS RIKE:
Atlantic Coast. NJ

Our trooper unit, outfitted in civilian clothes, scopes the Jersey Coast for military buildup and vulnerabilities. German intelligence has asked the American Bund to ramp up espionage in the States. Freddy and Paul, Herbert, Walter, Hugo, and I shoot photos of naval vessels, ports, waterworks, and munitions factories.

After the night of the fire, ties with my Kamerads feels brittle and jumpy at the same time, like drinking too much coffee. But I'll fake it as best I can until my mission ends one way or another.

The fact is, the more I bond with my Kamerads, the riskier it gets. I'm treadin' across a fragile thread. I know I'll be asked to do other things that will put my people at risk. I'll need to make sacrifices and compartmentalize my emotions. My greatest threat is makin' my own mistakes. Nat was right about Krista. I was reckless. At this point, maybe I'll never see her again anyway. Staying undercover comes down to icing my rage and cauterizing my devotions. Just turnin' feelings off.

After the reconnaissance, we visit Newark shippin' port to deliver packages to Gestapo agents from the German cruise ship Europa. While we're waitin', I shoot photos of the ship's officers. They're wearing their Death's Head skull caps. Red armbands with the black spider squeeze their biceps. Old wounds open. I lose it. With my camera against my face, I charge up the gangway and click away at everything foreign.

"Halt!" A Gestapo agent yanks my camera. How did I not see him?

I pounce on him. Two other agents twist my arms.

Freddy runs to my side. "We're part of Führer Schwartzman's special ops team!" he yells. "Take me to your commanding officer." He deals me a dirty look. I stay still.

As I wait for Freddy, the scent of the shallow marine water and the waftin' fog triggers a raft of painful memories. This is the exact port where my father was slaughtered. In my mind's eye, I see the three men in American Nazi uniforms appearin' and disappearin'. I recall the sharp exchange with my father as if it were yesterday. I close my eyes and shake my head as if this will erase the torture.

Freddy taps my shoulder and I jolt. My eyes blink open.

Jumpin' back, Freddy peers at me. "You're sweatin' Rike," he says.

"Oh, sorry, I didn't m—"

"Here's your camera." He thrusts it at me. "Now, let's get out of here." I see concern cloud his eyes.

CHAPTER 27

Roll with the Punches

YAEL, ALIAS RIKE:
Classroom. Camp Nordland. Andover, NJ

"Hugo! Unbuckle Rike's belt," Nordland's first officer and Schwartzman's right hand man, George Wilhelm Kunze orders. We were all given a new belt when we entered class. Is today some kind of torture trainin' class at Camp Nordland?

In front of a classroom of trooper trainees, Hugo and I face each other. Hugo's thick fingers struggle with my belt, but he finally removes it.

"Hold up Rike's belt so everyone can see the buckle," Officer Kunze commands. My pants sag, but the class focuses on the belt as Kunze lifts the front steel cover. It's branded with two SS runes. "Underneath, there are four concealed triggers." He squeezes two tabs and out pops a mini gun barrel. "When you want to fire, press a trigger on the left. That releases the firing pin and blasts the cartridge from the right. You got four triggers for four shots."

"Brilliant," Herbert exclaims. "A last-ditch effort for a prisoner's escape."

"If you connect your hand with a string, you could rig it to fire when you raised your arms to surrender," Paul says with a smile.

"The name is the SS-Waffenakademie Koppelschloßpistole or the 'belt castle gun,'" Kunze says. "A friend of mine designed them. You are the first Nazi soldiers in the Reich to wear these." Does this mean American-Germans are guinea pigs? What else is in store for us?

In front of the stormtrooper class, Officer Kunze begins a lecture. "If you control land, you control the world." He picks up a long stick and walks down the aisle. Kunze halts in front of the world map. "Long ago, Genghis Khan captured the heart of the Eastern hemisphere. This makes up Eastern Europe. From the heart, it's easy to control the Supercontinent." He circles his stick around Europe, Asia, and Africa. "Today, our plan is the same. Conquer Eastern Europe, dominate the heartland, control the world island, then the world." Kunze turns his attention to the troopers. His eyes gleam. "Tell me! How do we accomplish this from the outside and inside?"

Hugo stands up. "From the outside, we apply good ole fashioned brute force. Inside, we soften the victims," he says.

"We arrive as the good guys," Freddy explains. "Rescue the poor chaps, right Herbert?"

"Then, they're ripe for the picking," Paul says. "We terrorize, sabotage, and assassinate where we must."

"Gut." Kunze points to Austria on the map. "The cry for Heim ins Reich is strong. There is a cry for both German regions and all Volksdeutsche to come home to Greater Germany. Or, just as good, Germany can go to those living outside."

I finish his logic aloud. "All German blood everywhere belongs to the Reich." I realize my outburst is awkward. No one interrupts Kunze. My fellow troopers stare at me. What was I thinkin'?

But Kunze claps. "You are correct, Rike. As a show for Germans everywhere, last February, we demanded self-determination for all Germans in Austria and Czechoslovakia. Our own Austrian Nazis answered, and Hitler liberated them without a shot being fired, declaring the full annexation of Austria. Next, we will save the three million German-Czechs who live in Sudetenland. They have been imprisoned on this land since the Great War. Our brothers there are persecuted. There's no equality. There is a crisis, and we will restore order and crush the sub-humans in the rest of the Slavic nations who are interfering with our race." Kunze gestures to the map and waves his hand over Germany and Austria. "With Austria and Germany knitted together as one, our path is clear."

Walter rises with permission from Kunze. "This puts us on the southern flank of Czechoslovakia, the gateway to Poland and Russia," he says.

Kunze stomps his boot with approval. "Ya. Gut! Czechoslovakia is the key to controlling Eastern Europe." His green eyes sparkle approval, and his smile seems to swallow his face. While I despise his politics, I have to admit that Kunze's charisma mesmerizes me. I see why many follow him. People gravitate to the dynamic. Unfortunately, they also assume these types have thoughtful and humane answers to thorny problems. Far from it!

Herbert, who has listened with rapt attention jumps to his feet. "Once we reclaim territories that are rightfully Germany's, we can conquer other territories for all people of German blood who belong to us. Including our colony of America."

"Ya," Kunze agrees. "As Nazis, the goal is Germanization of the world—the cultural assimilation of land into the German Reich." He marches to the front of the classroom and pulls down a map. "Your contribution starts now," he explains, pointin' his stick in the middle of the image. "Here is the New York Water supply. Herr Schafspelz, explain how it works."

Freddy stands to attention. "A tunnel delivers water from upstate. Gravity moves it through aqueducts into local Manhattan reservoirs."

"Gut! You did your homework," Kunze replies. "Sit." He walks around the perimeter of the room. "Today you work together. Devise a plan to poison the New York State water supply." It's all I can do to not scream. We are at war!

We pull notebooks from our bags. We organize into groups and begin.

Up front, Kunze searches his briefcase. He stops and looks around. "Herr Saxon," he calls to me. "Go to the office and get my book *The Jewish Question*. It's in my office cabinet."

YAEL, ALIAS RIKE:
Office. Camp Nordland. Andover, NJ

In Kunze's office at Camp Nordland, I find *The Jewish Question* in the bottom drawer of the wooden file cabinet by the window. I shove it under my arm and kick the drawer closed. The force of my kick pops the top drawer open. It's filled with stuffed manila folders. Did I just hit the lottery? This is too temptin' to pass up. I turn my head and peek through the cracked door. There's about ten women outside the office typin' and sortin'.

I listen to their conversations. "Our German ship smuggled these uniforms past customs. They went right to the consulate," a German-accented woman brags.

Another German woman flaps yellow and blue file cards so fast I think she's gonna lift herself off the ground. "Who wrote *J* on this yellow card? Yellow isn't for Jews. Light blue cards, ladies. Light blue with a *J* is for Jews. How many times do I have to explain the system. Enemies of the state get a big red *F* for Feinde. If they're German, add a *D* for Deutsche. *F* Feinde, *D* Deutsche."

Suddenly, through the open door, I hear a familiar voice, a female's voice. "I'm here to pick up the Red-Eye files." The command is crisp. There's no question about the identity. I peek out. It's Krista's sister, Heidi. She's supposed to be at Camp Siegfried, hours away. What's she doin' here? How could I get so unlucky with my timin'? The book slips from my hands and smacks the floor. Her head flips toward me. I plaster myself against the wall. Starin' down at me is a poster that reads, "Hitler Youth is Germany's Future." Yeah, I've heard that a lot lately in my circles.

"By whose orders?" the file-system woman asks Heidi. Heidi turns toward the woman. I grab the book. What if that girl out there had been Krista instead of Heidi? Would I have smashed out of the office and grabbed her, knocking aside anyone and anything German? Would I have rescued her and taken her far from uniforms and foreign salutes?

Heidi's voice shakes me back to the dank of the Jersey German office. "This comes with direct orders from Führer Kuhn," Heidi snorts. "By the way, I'm your new boss. I'll be back next week to evaluate the entire file system." A car horn honks. "Schnell! There's a car waiting outside for me."

Heidi glances toward the office again. Are her ears perking? The woman hands her the file. Heidi wraps her arms around it. She stretches her neck toward the cracked office door. I hold my breath. A screen door creaks open. Heidi twists her neck and moves toward whoever is at the door. "Auf Wiedersehen!" she says. I hear the screendoor slap behind her.

That was close. Squeezin' the book under my arm, I move back to the file cabinet and check over my shoulder. I cock my ear to listen. None of the women seem to be payin' attention to me. I flip through the folders.

The colored tabs on the folders each have labels. First tab: *American Bund Mailing list, 25 million.* Son of a gun! That's huge! Second tab: *American airplane production forecast.* Holy cow! What's that doin' in a Nazi file cabinet? Third tab: *Munitions factory inventory.* These papers are written on official letterhead. Fourth Tab: *German American Bank accounts.*

I pluck papers from the middle of the files. My boot is big enough to hide them. I stuff them inside and smooth my pants leg.

"Hey! What are you doing?" a voice snaps.

Startled, I drop the book and fling a file into the air. I spin around.

Freddy catches the book with his foot. His dark sunglasses block his eyes.

"Christ! You almost gave me a heart attack." I bend down and collect the papers. "Darn book was crammed behind all these files." I glance up at Freddy. He wrinkles his forehead. I still can't see his eyes. What's he thinkin'? "Are ya gonna just stand there and admire my good looks or help

241

me?" I curl my lip and ready myself to pounce?

As sudden as a struck match, Freddy laughs. "You son of a gun! If I didn't know ya better, I'd think ya were lying." Freddy helps me put the scattered papers back into their files.

I roll my eyes skyward. As my father used to say in Yiddish whenever he dodged a bullet, "Dadd a koyl." The risk was worth it. Now we have proof that the Camp Nordland Bund office is a clearing-house for smuggled uniforms and spies.

KRISTA:
Office. Camp Nordland. Andover, NJ

I honk the horn. I knew I shouldn't have let Heidi go into the Nordland office alone. She's probably bossing everyone around. If she was self-important before, now she thinks she's a queen bee. She told me Führer Vandenberg appointed her as a spy for the Bunaste. She said she'll track Germans and others here. I didn't know we spied on our own people. She said it's important to know what America is up to so Germany isn't destroyed again. And I guess she's the head tattletaler.

I look at my watch and sigh. It's a two-hour drive back to Camp Siegfried. I get out of the car and walk up the steps to the Camp Nordland office. Through the screen door, just as I suspected, Heidi is bullying the staff. I open the door and flip my hand for her to hurry up. For once, she listens.

As I drive down the lane, I glance in my rearview mirror. Two soldiers walk out of the office. It can't be. I swing my head around, but they're gone. I could have sworn that it was Yael.

The car bumps as it hits the ditch.

"Krista! Watch where you're going!" Heidi yells at me.

I recover the wheel and drive on. My heart shivers. Why am I being haunted? Yael is my past. Let's keep it that way.

CHAPTER 28

Left Jab

YAEL:
Yael's Apt. Hawthorne Avenue. Newark, NJ

If I close my eyes, I might not wake up. Can I go on with my feet in two boxin' rings? I'm drained from livin' a double life.

I lay my head against the cool oak floor under my red boxin' gloves. The gloves dangle in my bedroom window like a hypnotist's coin on a string. The flappin' white curtains over me dupe me into thinkin' the warm breeze will relieve my sweaty body, but all they do is fan a fly toward my ear. I swat at the buzz. The bug dodges my hand and torments me. Anyway, it's good to be home from a brutal day at Camp Nordland. Could I have been flippin' through Kunze's files only just this mornin'? Did Freddy almost catch me? Did Heidi almost see me? What if that had been Krista? Krista. Does she think I've abandoned her?

My knuckles massage my forehead and hide the ache. I roll on my side. There's something under my bed. I stretch my arm and drag out a dusty, rat-chewed paper. When I blow on it, the dust backfires up my nose and triggers a sneeze. What do ya know? When the dust settles, I'm face to face with the familiar fightin' eyes of Benny Leonard on the cover of *Muscle Builder*. I blow air from my nose and turn over the paper. There's writing. I'd never seen Pop's message on the back in his chicken scratch—as Mama used to call it. I read, *Yael, My Malach.* He always called me his angel. The first line says, *Benny Leonard is the greatest pound-for-pound fighter ever.* My father taught me that Leonard treated boxin' like a science. Leonard studied moves and executed them like a precision machine. His strategy kept opponents off balance and made other boxers do what they didn't want to do. The next line says, *When you were born, we almost lost you. You only weighed two pounds. But you, too, were the greatest pound-for-pound fighter ever, and one day the world will learn why you survived.* In the moment, my steamy head clears. I gather strength from Leonard and accept I'd rather be killed before surrendering to my enemies.

Through the open bedroom window, Harry's voice filters up. He's talkin' to Longie. The strength to stand up and greet my *family* is sapped and would take the effort of pushin' my body's weight up with a sword. I listen.

"Boss. Look at this sign nailed to the tree," Harry reads the words. "Hitlerism in America. We stand for Liberty, Duty, Truth. Real Freedom of the Press.' Geez!" I hear him blurt. "Doesn't anyone stop these guys from littering our streets?"

Harry's right. By the time I got home after midnight, the signs were up. Earlier, there were plenty of people lettin' it happen. No matter how hard the Minutemen fight, if no one cares, we won't make a dent.

I hear crumpling. Harry's cleanin' up the street. "Hey, Boss!" he says. "Look. Those are Yael's boxing gloves, hanging in his window."

At least I can relax knowin' he sees the signal and will visit the dropbox. I didn't have the energy tonight to bring Harry the package in person. The files will be wrinkled from my boot, but they're damning. And hopefully, the troopers won't miss one roll of film I pinched from the coastal espionage mission.

"If anyone can get the goods, it's Yael," I hear Longie's muffled voice.

"I'll head over to the Big Yard and do the pick-up." The resolve in Harry's voice rings clear.

Longie's gonna be blown away with the evidence. There's also a Nazi meetup. Harry will know that *W10Redd* means, "rendezvous Wednesday, 10:00 p.m. at Redd's tavern bar."

YAEL, ALIAS RIKE:
Redd's Tavern. Market St. Newark, NJ

In the dimly lit club, I squint to read 9:45 on my watch. Redd's Tavern is filled with us uniformed Bunders and troopers. We chug beer and bellow, slap each other on the back of our uniforms, and share stories about the Fatherland.

If all goes according to plan, my Minutemen boys will get to meet my fellow stormtroopers for the first time. The waitin' gnaws me like a kid pullin' his ma into a candy store. As I operate deeper within the inner circle, the risk becomes greater. What would the Nazis do to me if they found out the truth? They keep that card file on every enemy, for goodness sake.

On a wooden table, I organize the photos from the trooper mission for Freddy and our unit to review. The boys kick sawdust from the floor as they gather around with their steins of thick German lager. Paul hands me his photos. We clack glasses and each take a swig of our foamy drinks.

My attention is drawn across the room. Near the bar, a pasty-faced man in a short-sleeved shirt, maybe ten years older than me, hangs up the wall phone. He approaches us. Uninvited, he hauls over a chair from another table and slides it in between Paul and Herbert, forcin' them to scoot apart.

"Overheard you fellas talkin' about the German American Bund," pasty-face says. He examines the photos on the table in front of me. "Nice photos of the coast."

"And. You are ...?" asks Freddy. He's a natural sentry.

"Hans Vogel." He salutes his freckled right arm at Freddy.

Freddy scans him from head to boot. Hans withdraws his hand. "I just moved here from Chicago," he says. "Got laid off. I'm joining the Bund to meet Germans."

"You don't need to join the Bund to do that. We have gatherings for everyone," Freddy says as he eyeballs the guy.

I nod toward the photos. "This is a photography club," I say. By now, it's easy to slip into my stormtrooper act. Sometimes, I even forget I'm fakin' it.

"But I want to join a Nazi group," Hans explains. "Help Hitler wake up sloths. You should know, my ancestry is pure."

"The Bund isn't Nazi, you bloody wise-guy," Herbert says.

Hans tilts his head. "I mean you've got the same Hitler ideas that I have."

"You're barkin' up the wrong tree, buddy," I say. "We aren't radical. We all have personal dislikes, that's it."

Hans continues his pitch. "Just like you, I'm against atheist communists. I don't want Negroes, Catholics, and Jews anywhere near my home. It's our duty to help defend America."

Freddy sets down his beer and grabs the table with both hands. "Get this straight. We're law-abiding Americans. We like to get together, take photos, have a good time. Wer weiß, warum die Gänse barfuß gehen."

"Who knows why geese walk barefoot?" I whisper the English translation to Walter.

Paul looks at Hans and interprets. "We're saying that's just how it is, Herr Vogel. I'm sure you understand, mein Fruend."

Vogel flings his hands up in surrender. "Look, I'm not trying to Jemandem einen Bären aufbinden."

Frownin', Walter stands up. "Yael, let's get more beer."

We clomp across the wooden floor and order beer at the bar. "What was that guy sayin' in German?" I ask Walter. "I'm guessin' he's not really tryin' to tie a bear to someone?"

"Scheisse, Rike." Walter scolds. "Ya really got to brush up on your native tongue. He says he's not takin' us for a ride."

"You trust him?" I ask Walter. "The guy seems kinda peculiar. Plus, he looks Jewish." I plant a seed with Walter.

Walter glances back over his shoulder at the intruder. "Ya. He's probably a dirty spy." He tenses and turns toward the entrance. "Scheisse! Now what's this?"

Like the calm before a storm, a low-pressure swipes the room. The vacuum is filled with a horde of Minutemen. Chairs scrape the floor. The men spread out like a pebble hittin' a pond. I read the scene. How do I move so I don't blow my cover?

Commander Nat Arno struts around the table. His movement knocks some photos to the floor. "Hey, fellas," he says. It's hard to tell whether Nat is addressing his soldiers or the German uniformed crowd. "Whatta we got here?"

Minuteman Puddy struts the other way. "Looks like these nature lovers took photos of the Jersey shore?" he says.

Square-jawed Abie picks up a photo. It tings when he shakes it.

Trooper Paul tries to grab it back. "Put it back, ya lousy twit," he says.

Abie whips the stiff paper away and hands it to Maxie.

"Sticks and stones break our bones, but names don't hurt us," Puddy says.

Commander Nat claps Paul on the shoulder hard. "Finders keepers!" he jibs.

This thing's gonna blow any second. My chest tightens. Harry hovers. My best pal defines everything a Minutemen should be, strong and nimble. "Interesting how our American battleships in these photos blend into the horizon," Harry shouts. Abie and Harry rip photos in front of Freddy's face.

Freddy's torso chocks. In one motion, he throws his whole beer, mug and all, at Abie's face. But he doesn't know about Abie's quick reflexes. Abie ducks. Behind him, Paul feels the flyin' mug right between the eyes.

Good ole' Herbert catches Paul before he hits the ground, but he gets doused with blood.

In the next beat, a frenzy flails. There's a clappin' of fists and chairs. Splinters beat me like a hailstorm. I cover my face to ward off the flying shards of dishware.

From the corner of my eye, I see Puddy and Maxie sprinkle beer across the photos on the table. They finger paint the golden liquid. I'm not the only one who sees. Freddy dashes toward them. But he's in for a surprise. Al lobs a chair to Benny, who pivots and swings it across Freddy's body. Freddy goes flyin'. He splats against the wall and slides down. My instinct kicks in and my lungs tighten. My knees slide across the sawdust to Freddy's side. He clutches his head. Sugar! It's the right move for my undercover self, but I wish my concern hadn't felt so natural. Whose side am I on, anyway?

In front of me, I have a bigger problem. Hugo and Walter each hook one of Harry's arms. I stiffen. They face him toward a swastika flag on the wall. His loud groan pains me.

"Rike! Come!" Walter calls. "Make him kiss the swastika."

My choices are limited and I step toward him. Saliva ebbs from my mouth. I grab the neck of Harry's shirt and plaster his face against the flag. Blood from his crooked nose blots a red triangle into the black swastika.

Harry's bloodshot eyes gleam. "Tell your friends, Lig in drerd," he growls.

"What the heck is that babble?" Walter snorts. "Show him who's boss!"

My right cross knocks Harry's lights out. He's gonna let me have it for stealin' the upper hand. But I had no choice.

LONGIE ZWILLMAN:
Bandbox Nightclub. Weequahic Park, NJ

My Bandbox Club in Newark's Weequahic Park rumbles with the Minutemen. The red leather seat next to me bounces when Harry slides around the booth. Benny sets down whiskeys for us and slips next to Harry. Harry rests the glass against his swollen cheek.

The lighting's low and the smoke is thick, but past the table lamp, I recognize Yael's vigorous gait advancing through the crowded room. I'm anxious to see him, but I'm gonna have to be patient. Abie stops him with a bear hug. Maxie slaps him on the back. They follow Yael on his adventure toward my table. Next stop, Yael wraps his arms around two hourglass shaped women. One of the dames takes his hat and places it on her head. The other tries to take his briefcase, but he cleaves it.

Puddy and Al appear in front of my table and skate into the empty side of the booth. The booth is gettin' tight, but no matter. We're family. Nat arrives. He looks left toward Benny and Harry, then right. He plugs his cigar stub in the ashtray and shoves Al against Puddy to claim a seat.

I wave over my cigarette girl, Lillian. She holds out a cigarette box. "You're a doll, Lillian," I coo. I hand her a roll of bills. Before I can ask her to send over drinks, a red-lipsticked gal with a tray full of bourbons flashes a smile. Ice rattles against glass as she sets each one on the table.

Here's Yael. Over the ruckus, wooden legs rasp against the carpet as he pulls a chair across from me. On either side of him, the wide shoulders of Maxie and Abie make him look like he's going to soar.

Harry winks at Yael. "I think I owe ya one?"

"The fish lady curse you babbled at the Nazi boys will be payback enough; Drop dead and bury yourself." Yael shrugs.

Harry touches his finger to his forehead and salutes. Yael returns the honor with his signature curled-lip smile.

"Boys, boys," I say. "All in a day's work."

Yael slides the lamp toward Nat and sits down. He reaches down into his leather case and lobs photos and folders onto the table. The quiet of Minutemen sifting through materials basks the noise.

Benny holds up a photo. "Are these shots of Hitler youth camps in Germany?"

"Hitler Camps, yes," answers Yael. "But they're in Long Island. New

York."

"Jumpin' Jehosaphat!" Maxie yells. "This is where we got license plates for FBI!"

"Yup," Yael says. "Turns out half of the fifteen hundred Bund license plates belong to employees of our New Jersey defense plants."

"Dagnabbit!" Al exclaims. "We gotta clear those moles out."

"There are twenty-five of these camps across America," Yael says. "They're filled with fanatical kids and their parents. They each worship fascism as democracy."

"As you know, Yael's been undercover digging up evidence of ties to Hitler's coup mounting in America," I say.

Puddy knocks his head. "Knock on wood. We're gonna put that kakameyme Fritz Kuhn in the slammer," he says.

"Führer Kuhn has divided America into three colonies," Yael says. "He calls each region Gaus. He's modeled it on the Nazi bureaucracy. Gaus are divided into ninety-three locals called ortsgruppen."

"Give 'em the details," I say. "Explain it from Hitler's Volksdeutsche to Lebensraum." I want them to feel the toxic breath of a kingdom rising far away in Europe. The details give it flesh and bones.

"Germans call themselves Volksdeutsche," Yael says. "The idea is that the German-blooded of the world shouldn't have to stuff themselves into the borders of Germany. Under the plan, Germans livin' in Austria will colonize it for Germany. The same for Russia and France and England. This gives Germans Lebensraum or livin' space." Yael sighs when he sees my lips straighten across my face. He knows I'm proud.

"America is the crown jewel," I add. "As we speak, there is a shadow Hitler-Nazi party darkening our country."

Abie points at himself with both hands. "What happens to us good ole' natives who aren't German?"

"Good question, pal," Yael says.

"Can you spell diaspora?" Maxie growls.

Nat picks up a newspaper and flips through it.

"That's their propaganda newspaper ya got there, Nat," Yael explains. "It's called *Deutscher Weckruf und Beobachter*. They call it DWB for short."

Nat's cigar dangles from his mouth. "Hold the phone!" He holds his cigar. "My German's not perfect, but Einhunderttausend means they got a hundred-thousand members?"

"Could be high, could be low," Yael says. He shuffles the files and slides one to Nat. "Get a load of this. I almost choked on my tongue when I found a mailin' list with twenty-five million German-American names."

Harry faces me. "On the undercover front, Yael has joined the German occupation in America. He maps military sites, water supply, bridges, and subways. Nazi's are loaded and locked."

"They're gonna blow us to bits while we're asleep in our pajamas," Puddy says.

"We've gone toe to toe with the stormtroopers at rallies," Yael says. "They're more than just a bunch of thugs. They're America's Gestapo. They're trained to paralyze our coasts, poison water, immobilize trains, and deaden communications. Assassinations are another tool in their box."

"With guns stolen from our armories," Maxie grumbles.

Yael shakes his head in revulsion. "And burnin' up our headquarters at the Y."

Benny hands Yael a drink. "We can rebuild bricks and steel."

"The challenge is they're usin' democracy against us to take control, like Hitler did in Germany," Yael says. "They're building an American Nazi party with the likes of Charles Lindbergh as their leader."

"Some are above board. Some not," I say. "Kuhn's friend forged FDR's signature and stole hundreds of passports from the State Department." I gulp my whiskey.

"Not only that. Germany can bomb us as easily as their neighbors," Harry says. "My aunt reports they have a thousand long range bombers."

"Those bombers can attack New York and fly home in one shot," I say.

"The Sauerkrauts got us in the corner," Puddy says.

"What's the bone Hitler picks with the American Bund all about?" Al asks. "Seems like he doesn't wanna be tied to 'em."

"It's calculated," Yael answers. "Hitler and his gang don't love Kuhn, but American Nazis follow him, so he's an asset."

"The bottom line is we're at war, boys," Nat says.

I clack my empty glass against the table. "Nat, double the Minutemen at all Nazi meetings. Benny, destroy propaganda before it hits the streets. Abie and Puddy. Break into Bund headquarters. Get proof. Maxie and Al hang out at Nazi bars."

Al salutes. "We got training for that, Boss."

"I'll plant mistrust on the inside," Yael adds. "We can set some booby traps."

CHAPTER 29

On the Ropes

YAEL, ALIAS RIKE:
Newark Subway System. NJ

"Führer Kuhn wants every detail of this Newark subway mapped," Freddy says. He shines his flashlight on doors, lights, and stairs. His beam reflects off of metal. "Map those pipes, too."

Freddy and I slosh ankle deep in water through the Newark subway tunnels. The water pumps groan. "Are our people really gonna bomb this subway?" I ask. The mere idea of it twists my heart like water wrung out of a wet towel.

Freddy squeezes the flashlight against his ribs and aims it at the notebook in his hands. "Where else can you terrorize two million people in one place?" I hear the smile in Freddy's words. He scratches diagrams and jots notes. "Two thousand trains run every day. Imagine the scope of it! If this doesn't make world headlines, nothing will." When we trained for this mission, Freddy and I were playacting, like kids playin' hide n seek. Now it's real. In this moment, I don't recognize him. He's the enemy behind the mask.

I force my brain to numb. "There's a honeycomb of tunnels along Morris Canal from Newark to NY," I say. "What's the target?" How am I gonna relay intel to Longie and FBI without raisin' suspicion?

"My bet?" Freddy says. "Underneath four corners near Bamberger's Department Store. Newark's got the busiest intersection in America." Brilliant deduction. Bamberger's sits near Four Corners, Broad, and Market. Freddy is Nazi material through and through. And sadly, the bloodthirsty side of him is showin' through, too. "That's a wrap for seventy-two hours. Let's get out of here."

I've got to get this news to Harry. Otherwise, I'm gonna be responsible for mangled bodies buried under heaps of Newark rubble. And the aftermath is gonna be more than soldiers, more than just adults. We're talkin' about innocent business people, shoppers, even mothers pushin' baby carriages. I close my eyes. What if Lena and Esther go shopping?

YAEL:
Newark Subway System. NJ

"What the heck ya doing here?" Harry asks me. He knocks me up against the wall of the Newark subway entrance. Three days ago, he saw my gloves hangin' and got my warning about the bombing plans for the Newark subway system. Tonight, the FBI and Minutemen will try and stop the terrorism.

"Nazis are attacking our homeland," I say. "I'm not standin' down!"

"Stormtroopers will be here tonight," Harry scowls at me. "Guys who think you're one of them, you idiot. You wanna blow your cover and get us killed?"

"Look, Harry. I promise to stay in the shadows." My eyes spasm. "I'll run communications. I know Morse Code better than anyone. Trooper trainin' taught me something useful."

Harry bites his lip. He knows he's beaten. "I'm only agreeing because these FBI numpties know less than my little sister Esther," he says. "You're better than these knuckle draggers."

Deep underground, Harry takes charge. He delivers the combat plan. The team is a combination of primed Newark Minutemen and green FBI recruits. On one side, we have fighters who take orders and execute with precision. On the other, we've got a bunch of pencil swingers.

As any good leader, Harry leverages folks according to their strengths. "We'll use Morse Code to communicate," he explains. "Patrols hidden along the subway will flash the number of enemies approaching. This way we will know which direction and how many we are dealing with. We'll be able to adjust our attack position. If you know nothing else, you must know the numbers." He turns to me. "Yael. Review the code with the team."

Are they all listening? I swipe the light under their chins. "The numbers one through zero all have only five flashes, some short, some long," I say. "The first five start with short, the last five start with long." The reflections in their eyes are the only glimmer in the subway. "A short flash and four long means *one*. One short, means one enemy approaching. But you must follow with four long. If *two* enemies are approaching, you signal two short flashes and three long. *Five* is five short flashes. No long ones." My light flashes five times to demonstrate. "Five is the middle. After five, you start with a long flash, followed by short."

I ask one of the FBI men to demonstrate *six*. He fumbles to turn the light on, shows one long flash, followed by six short.

"Wrong. There is always, always a total of only five flashes," I snap. "Why the heck did you flash seven. Benny, demonstrate for our G-man."

Benny flashes one long and four shorts.

"Minutemen, team up with a G-man," Harry says. He shows patient restraint, much more than me. If I were in charge, my code would be *Bravo Foxtrot*-code for pathetic soldier. "Once in formation, you send the signal for an *O*. Yael, show them the response," Harry commands.

My light seers three *longs* into the men's faces. Al mimics my signal, trying to sear it into their minds.

"If we do not receive the *O* signal, we will assume you have been caught," Harry says. "We will abort the mission. When you receive *O* from us, three longs, you advance from your assault position to our attack position back here."

Benny shakes his head at the clueless FBI men. "The idea is you come back to help us when the enemy reaches our attack position," he says. He crosses his fingers at me.

"The other code you need to know is *X* for abort. Yael, show 'em," Harry says.

My light flashes: *long, short, short, long.* This time Abie shines the code for abort into the eyes of each FBI man.

"We expect the enemy at 0000," Harry informs.

Benny doesn't take a chance with this crew. "That's midnight, guys."

"On the double!" Harry shouts. "Take your positions."

The mission begins. We receive all *O* signals back. Phase one, success. The rest of the men, including Abie, Benny, and Al, take the attack position near the spot where we expect the bombs to be deployed. Like clockwork, at 0000, we receive a signal from the south tunnel.

The sound of heavy boots ring against the rail. Then we see flashlight circles getting bigger. Indiscriminate German conversation echoes.

In an alcove off the rails, I perk up. Dangit! Paul, Herbert, and an older trooper attach straps around the pipes. Goosebumps harden on my arms. Those were the pipes I drew on a map just three days ago. Walter and another senior trooper unpack explosives. Walter's snowy hair shines under Hugo's flashlight. Where's Freddy?

Harry sees my swingin' jaw. He shoves me back into a dark nook and grabs my collar. "Look, buddy. I'm gonna tell you once and then I'll knock ya out," he says with barely a sound. "You stay in this corner like a fly in honey. Ya hear?" He pushes his finger across my lips so I can't answer if I wanted. I nod, provin' I got the picture. Harry crouches and hugs the wall.

The shadows of Newark Minutemen play like a picture-show against the wall. But it's not make believe. Tonight, my brothers Al, Abie, and

Benny aren't just in the ring. They could be blown to pieces. I hear the sickening thuds of fists on flesh. The element of surprise gives us the upper hand. Gray arms and shoulders flail. Smacks sound like bricks against cement. We clobber the troopers. The bad guys flee with the unused explosives.

But then there's trouble. Paul's arm stretches. His gun aims at our men's backs. It's all I can do to not call out. Harry dives on him, but it's too late. The bang of the gun rips my ears. I don't hear a cry. I think it missed. Like a crab pinchin' a minnow, Hugo's beefy hand shackles Harry's neck. Harry flails. His fingers find Herbert's slick hair but can't hold. Walter helps the team wrestle my pal down. I stand in the shadows helplessly as they drag him away. When they're out of sight, I shine my light in his stead. Harry's trail of blood winds through the floor of the underground.

FRITZ KUHN:
Bund Headquarters. Nye Avenue. Newark, NJ

In a small room at Bund headquarters, a bare light bulb swings from the ceiling. Paul and Herbert each hold an arm of our kneeling prisoner. Troopers guard the door.

"Who told you we were going to dynamite the Newark subway?" Führer Schwartzman asks. The skin on his face pumps like a piston.

"We hooked a prize fish," I say to Hermann over his shoulder. "Looks like we've got a Minuteman to filet. Do whatever it takes to make that Jew squeal."

The disgusting Minuteman spits in Hermann's face. My officer's face turns purple. The boys bend the prisoner's shoulders and the man squirms. Hermann wipes the phlegm off with his handkerchief. He backhands the oversized pig and makes his nose bleed.

"This is what a Newark Minuteman looks like up close?" I say. "Do you know who we are?" I step next to Hermann.

The thug's chest heaves. He stares through me like I'm a window. He will soon feel me. "Du hast wohl die Sprache verloren?" I taunt his loss for words. "After we finish marinating his body, crunch his fingers with your boots."

Hermann's knuckles spear the thug's stomach. As his fist connects, a loud noise shakes the building. I rush to the window. What? My car is burning! Three scoundrels hover over it. Through black smoke, I see a man wave my tailpipe at me. He mouths "*KAY-O*." Fury rises in me like mercury in an oven.

The office door crashes open. We swing around. It's none other than the nest of Minutemen that have been in my hair one too many times. Their muscle-mouth commander and his square-jawed minion teem in.

Paul drops the prisoner's arm and shoves Hermann and me out the window and onto the fire escape. Inside, the Minutemen yell and beat my guards with lead pipes. I hear bones cracking. Below on the sidewalk, I see the gang drag the prisoner away, blood streaking behind him. I fire my gun. It hits the commander. Curses! They escape. But evil can't hide from something bigger and better. We are coming to flush the darkness away!

YAEL:
YMHA Locker Room. 652 High St. Newark, NJ

A yellow light swabs the outstretched bodies of Harry and Nat. They lie side by side on two tables in the YMHA locker room. Benny sews the needle through Nat's skin where the bullet passed through his arm. Nat hisses. Maxie tips caramel thick whiskey into Nat's mouth. It dribbles around his ear.

Next to Nat, Al socks his handkerchief into Harry's mouth. Abie pours alcohol on Harry's raw wounds. Half-conscious, my best buddy doesn't flinch. His split-lip wets the handkerchief red.

Steps away, I shove the punchin' bag. It's heavier than usual. Puddy catches it. "What's wrong, pal?" he asks me. My face must be betraying me.

"I hope they don't put two and two together," I say. "I knew about the bombin' plans tonight. Not many people did. Will they think it's a coincidence that Minutemen showed up?"

Puddy lets the bag go. It thumps against my chest.

Harry stirs on the table. "You're too darn lucky, ya numbskull," he says. Harry's swollen eyes are purple, but his voice tells me he's gonna be alright. What would I do without him?

"What if they suspect ya?" Benny asks me.

"They suspect everyone who isn't in their white paint bucket," I mutter. "They lump everyone else into different color ones."

Harry props himself on his elbows. "These men are weak. They'll shoot themselves in the foot," Harry says.

"We should get the press to report on them shootin' at us tonight," I say. "Harry, can ya get a story run that says we fight Hitlerism against terrorism and assassination attempts."

"It'll hit tomorrow's evening news," Harry says. "We'll make Nat a hero."

I stop my fist before it hits Benny's grimace face. He flinches. "We just gotta rattle them with our stutter step shuffle," I say.

Benny fake punches me back. "Hey, I'm hungry," he says. "Anyone wanna egg in a bread hole?" Hands fly up as Benny scoots toward the kitchen.

"Don't get careless, Yael," Harry says. He hacks blood on the floor. "You're pride has landed you flat on your back more than once." It's been a brutal night for Harry, and he's takin' it out on me. He has no clue how much I've swallowed for this mission. Sometimes, I don't even remember who I am.

"Can't a guy get any sleep around here," Nat whines. He's splayed out on the table with a rolled jacket under his head for a makeshift pillow.

"Sweet dreams," I say. I couldn't imagine life without Nat either. He'll be a legend. I switch off the light.

CHAPTER 30

Toe to Toe

YAEL, ALIAS RIKE:
Lounge. Camp Nordland. Andover, NJ

My sweat-soaked shirt underneath my uniform sticks against my ribs. The suffocating heat inside the Camp Nordland lounge makes the space more claustrophobic than it already is. Sundown has brought no relief. The steamy air triggers a sleepy stupidity in me.

Seated in chairs around the empty fireplace are my fellow stormtroopers: Freddy, Paul, Herbert, Walter, and Hugo. I lick the salt from my lips and step toward them. On the couch, a high ranking officer in his forties seems to be holdin' court.

Freddy puffs his chest. "Rike! Meet my Uncle Günther," he says. "He's Führer Kuhn's guest and one of Hitler's most trusted bankers. Uncle Günther's been around the Bund before it was called the Bund. Uncle, meet mein treuester Freund, Rike Saxon." Freddy's red-cheeked uncle smiles without showin' his teeth.

I salute the officer. "Heil Hitler!"

Uncle Günther pats the couch and spreads his legs. "Here, Officer

Saxon," he says. I sit down next to him. "Your Führer is hosting me in cabin eight tonight." His stomach strains against his belt. I bet the guy never misses a meal of golden-fried wiener schnitzel. "Freddy, you need to meet your two cousins. They are young women now." He elbows me.

"We're always huntin' for nice German Fräuleins to breed," I say. "Especially those of such quality Aryans." Did that really come out of my mouth?

"Aren't we all!" Günther bellows as he takes another gulp of beer. "As I was saying, in the old days, Adolph asked us to keep the red, white, and blue weak until he was ready." He raises his glass and calls for a toast. "Now it's time. To Germandom in America!" We meet his toast.

"Uncle was just going to tell a story about the bootlegging days back in '33, right after Hitler sent him to America," Freddy says. "Uncle. You actually stole the bootlegger's booze and carved a swastika into the Jew's chest?"

A chill saws my spine. There's a flash before my eyes: *My father's naked arms dangle at his sides and slime drizzles down his spongy chest.*

Red-faced Günther guzzles his mug of beer. He slams the empty stein down on the table, causin' me to jolt. In my addled mind, the noise becomes a loud pistol slammin' on the cover of my boyhood hidin' place just under the bow of the boat. I struggle for a breath.

"Ya!" Günther's voice thunders. "I killed him right in front of his son. And used the Jew's own knife." Günther slips an old knife from his holster. He tosses it on the table. It clacks and skids. This has seen some good meat carving days, ya?" He slaps my knee and belly laughs. Nausea erupts inside me. I now recognize his profile from Nat's photo.

Freddy beams. "Brilliant! Uncle, did he squeal while you were carving him?"

"Honestly, I was more focused on my artwork than his music," Günther says. His wiry eyebrows shade his eyes like an awning.

The other soldiers raise their glasses and bellow with laughter. The blood drains out of my dizzy head.

"And then, and this was pure art …" Günther says as he puts his hand on my shoulder. "There were two of them. We hung them off the docks with ropes from their own boat." He claps my back and horselaughs. "Trust me. We did America a favor." The men laugh at the joke.

My pulse flutters. I feign a grin and check Pop's frozen watch. "Excuse me," I mutter. "I need to make a call." I stand and turn. I press my cold beer to my cheek.

Like a pyramid erected in the sand, Kunze, Schwartzman, and Kuhn block my path. The tick of Longie's watch bangs in my ears like a timebomb. Should I kill them all right now?

FRITZ KUHN:
Lounge. Camp Nordland. Andover, NJ

"Trooper Rike Saxon," I say, extending my arm at the soldier. "Führers Kunze and Schwartzman were just joining me for the gathering."

"Günther. Have you been telling tall tales and contaminating our youth?" George asks.

Far from it," Günther says. "Building bridges with our youth, George. Youth and mother country." He leans back and nurses his drink.

The face of Saxon flushes red and makes his sapphire eyes glisten. He's obviously excited to join the company of George, Hermann, and myself. The boy checks off so many of the Aryan qualities. He compliments the gathering in the Camp Nordland lounge of my own design. I have to pat myself on the back. I built this blut and boden uber summer resort close to Andover, a hangout nest for admirers of the Fatherland. Thank goodness for my foresight to add my own personal version of Hitler's private Berghof home. I've already told Adolph it's waiting for his visit.

Rike wipes his brow. "It's a hot one tonight, mein Führer," he says to me. "I was just going to get some air."

I shrug. "It's been worse." Over the empty fireplace, I admire my prized Heinrich Knirr portrait of Hitler. "You like it?" I ask Rike.

"It's impressive," he says, swiping his brow again.

All eyes follow mine. "The artist, Knirr, lived near our family in Munich until the Great War. Günther , you knew him too, ya?" I get a chin wave from him. He doesn't appreciate art like I do. "Knirr is the only artist Adolph lets paint him. He has agreed to paint mine, too." In this portrait, Hitler seems frozen, as if someone's aiming a gun at him. He wears his beige party uniform. "This is the same uniform being designed for me to wear in the American Reich."

The troopers vacate seats, and the officers and I join Günther. I invite Rike to sit next to me. "By the by," I say to Rike. "You will pick up some propaganda films for me tomorrow from a German ship. I need them delivered to Camp Siegfried."

"Of course, mein Führer," he says. At least he looks less overcome with heat, now that he's settled. Freddy waves over the server to refill our steins.

"While you are there, take photos for the paper," I tell him. "I hear you are experienced."

Rike's eyes zip in his sockets. He's most likely laying his plan of attack. He constantly impresses me.

Freddy picks up his uncle's knife from the table. "Mein Führer," he says. "Any leads to your car bombing?" He hands the knife to his uncle.

"The whole caper points to those warmongers, Newark Minutemen," I say as I bang my fist on the table.

"Don't worry, Fritz," Hermann says. "We won't let anyone jeopardize the world you've built for the Reich."

I stand and my men rise. "We've been chosen by the gods to unify our thirty million brothers here," I say. "Time to make America great again. Ein Vok. Ein Reich Ein Führer!"

"Yes!" Hermann cheers. "One people, one empire, one Führer!"

Rike raises his mug. "Free America!"

I squeeze Rike's shoulder and grin with pride. I am confident this young soldier will rise with the German Reich in America. I am glad that he will serve next to me.

"Free America!" We all cry out together.

CHAPTER 31

Uppercut

YAEL:
Officer's Cabin. Camp Nordland. Andover, NJ

A key turns the lock of the Camp Nordland cabin. The door opens and a drunken Uncle Günther trips into the dusky space. As he hums a German tune, he burps a sour belch. He closes the door, clunks his beer on the night table, and drops his briefcase on the floor. He flips the light switch. The room remains dark. He flicks the switch up and down. Nothing.

My shadow streaks through the darkness like the wind. It lands a shattering punch across Uncle Günther's cheek. Khsime! I hear his jaw pop. Günther is down for the count. I drag the knocked-out flesh into a chair, tie his hands behind his back, and bind a gag around his mouth. I pull the knife from his holster and wrap it in my palm. I exhale. When I cut the front of Günther's uniform shirt, the buttons bounce on the floor. I snatch his beer from the table and splash his face.

Günther shakes. He glimpses his white hairy skin. Frantically, he flails his legs. Without the use of his hands, he wipes his eye on his uniform shoulder.

"I considered a Star of David branding," I say. "But it's sacred, so I decided to return the swastika you carved into my father's chest." Inside me, a black fury swells. "Ring a bell?" I grin.

Günther's eyes widen with a horrified recollection. He chews the cloth.

I carve each line of the swastika deep into his bare chest. Just like the foghorn muted my father's cries, the gag stifles his. I reach into my pocket and pull out a flashlight. I shine a circle of light on the drippin' red design carved into this monster's chest.

Günther whimpers.

I throw his fat briefcase on the bed and unpack the papers. "Chase National bank accounts," I read. "Dollars exchanged for German money." There are hundreds of names listed on the report. There must be millions of dollars swapped here. I think aloud, "Why are Germans in America buying German money?" I straddle the hog-tied body and lower the gag. "Hey you! What's a Rueckwanderer Mark?"

I punish his silence by hackin' his cheek with the flashlight. Then, I place the light on the floor. I pick up the knife and nick his throat with the blade.

He laughs. "You're too late, anyway," he says. His overripe pear stench makes me gag.

My knuckles crunch his jaw. "Talk!"

"What do I have to lose? Rueckwanderer means re-migration." Günther spits out bloody phlegm. "I told you once before. You're a smart Jewish boy. Think. Why would German Americans want German money rather than dollars? And puzzle this. How do you think Germany is funding interest rates that would make your head spin?" An evil laugh ripples from between his thin, red lips.

"I don't get it. Are you sayin' that Germans are sendin' money to go back home? Why would they want to go back to Germany?" My head lifts to a noise outside.

Günther snaps the ropes around his wrists. He grabs me, sendin' the knife skatin' across the wooden floor. Papers flutter in the air. We wrestle, both scramblin' for the knife.

Günther wins and pins me. "Ich glaub' mein Schwein pfelft!" He celebrates the turn of events. "In case your German is rusty, that means my pig is whistling so it's my lucky day." He raises the knife. "I'll answer one part for you to take to the grave. The bank funds the interest rates with none other than the blood of your kin." He pauses to let this sink in. "Ha! All the Jews who flee Germany leave behind a lot of money for us to throw in the air and shower under." Günther thrusts the knife toward my chest. My fighter instinct kicks in. I roll. The knife slices my arm. I elbow the beast in the face.

"Shturkh!" he cries. He topples.

I snatch the knife and plunge it into the middle of the bleedin' swastika on his chest. Günther stiffens. His eyes pop and he lets out a death rasp. That's for my pop," I say. Bloodthirsty for revenge, I yank the knife out and plunge it through his liver and catch the stink of his bile. I remove the weapon and wipe the bloody scum on the bastard's uniform.

FRITZ KUHN:
Jazz Tavern. Near Camp Nordland. Andover, NJ

Even though I'm one of the few white people, the Scott Free jazz club near Camp Nordland is one of my favorite after-hours spots. Tonight, I tap my boot to "Flat Foot Flogee" and entertain one of my many mistresses. I slip a diamond ring, complements of the Bund Treasury, on the middle finger of Virginia Cogswell.

Virginia's hand covers her heart. "Fritzy! You treat me like an empress. How can I thank my soldier boy?" she coos in a tone that signals she will thank me later.

"Nothing's too good for you, my former Miss America," I say. I place her hand on my thigh. "I love this Negroid tune," I say to my courtesan. One hand pushes her skirt higher, and the fingers of my other hand strum her bare knee. When it comes time to whitewash this country, I will still preserve the colored music.

YAEL:
Jazz Tavern. Near Camp Nordland. Andover, NJ

I dart through the frenzied leg-kicks and aerial flips of the Negro troupe hoppin' to jazz swing. I duck behind the dark bar, lift the handset of a payphone to my ear, feed it with coin, and dial. Over the music, I whisper an urgent message to Longie. "Boss. Can ya let Nat know to pick up a body behind Andover's Bund Hall at the dead drop?"

On the other end of the line, Longie knows. "So ya settled the score after five years," Longie says. "You okay, son?"

I reach into my pocket, pull out my father's knife, and study it. "I got my father's knife right here, the one stolen all those years back." Fresh red blood is smeared over black, caked blood. The reality lines my lungs with fresh air.

Then, like a flash of lightning heatin' the air before the thunder, a familiar German accent crackles behind me. "Nothing's too good for you, my Virginia. Money's pouring in. No one will notice," the guttural voice says. "Listen! I love this Negroid tune." The next words make my neck hairs prickle. "Officer Saxon, is that you?"

I slip the knife into my pocket and pivot. "Führer Kuhn. What a pleasant surprise." I drop the phone handle and salute.

"Making late night telephone calls?" Kuhn asks me.

"Runnin' late, mein Führer. Didn't want my mother to worry." I zip up my jacket. Is there any blood on my shirt that's gonna let the cat outta the bag? Behind me the phone swings. I know Longie can still hear me.

"Hmm. Thought your mother was dead?" Kuhn says as he frowns.

Virginia pulls on Kuhn's arms. "Let's dance Fritzy."

"Officer Saxon, may I introduce Virginia."

"My pleasure, Mrs. Kuhn." My hand extends to her.

Virginia sneers at the reference to Kuhn's wife.

"That's none of your business!" barks Kuhn.

"Of course," I say. I change the subject. "By the way, as you requested, I'll bring the films to Camp Siegfried and shoot the photos for you tomorrow. I have a friend there." A lump forms in my throat. Will I see Krista? Do I trust her enough to share my story of revenge?

Kuhn is suddenly quiet. He examines my face. I've said too much.

"Fritzy. Let's go," begs Virginia. She pulls on Kuhn's sleeve.

He pats Virginia's hand. "Who do you know at Camp Siegfried?" He scans my body. Son of a gun. If he's not like a snake sensin' every move I shouldn't be makin'.

"Oh, just a friend from the neighborhood." I attempt a grin. My eyes lock with Kuhn's. "Axel Von du Croy." Crap! Why did I say that?

Kuhn squeezes his brow. "Axel Von du Croy? I know him well." Of course he does. "Give him my regards."

We exchange a salute and he leaves. I hang up the danglin' phone handle.

CHAPTER 32

Sucker Punch

KRISTA:

Food Pantry. Camp Siegfried. Long Island, NY

A strong arm from inside the dark food pantry near Camp Siegfried's mess tent yanks me inside, covers my mouth, and slams the door. I reach back, swat off a hat, drag my fingernails down a man's head until I find his ears, and pull down with all my weight. When he lets go, I twirl and seize his fingers and stretch them in opposite directions. Then I jab his throat with my fist and he gasps for air.

"Woaww," an animal noise chokes out. "It's me," the voice moans.

My eyes adjust. "Oh my stars!" Yael presents in full Nazi uniform. My hands fly up to cover my mouth. "Yael. You're a stormtrooper. How the—?"

"Nice moves," he says. He coughs and retrieves his hat. He shoves his hand into his pocket. "Yes. I'm Stormtrooper Trainee Rike Saxon, protecting the German-American cause." His mouth curls in that playful, lopsided grin that drew me in from the first moment on the Newark waterfront. His camera flashes and blinds me for a second. I didn't even see him take it out of his pocket.

"Holy cow! Yael, what are you doing?" The smell of sour milk on the shelf stings my nose. Now I know why the deer stay away from the food storage.

"Capturing your image," he says. "I'm here to shoot iconic Camp Siegfried photos for Führer Kuhn and you're the most iconic." His blue eyes bathe me. In the close quarters, he leans in closer. But he's gawking.

"Your neck. It's wounded," he says with a gasp.

I adjust my collar with my shoulder to hide the gash. "Just night-hiking scrapes. It can be a little rough." I don't owe him any explanation. Does he think he can judge me?

"I thought this was summer camp?" There's a calm about his question that forewarns a storm. By now, he knows the truth about Camp Siegfried.

I raise the stakes and say what he's thinking. "Even the pregnant girls are assuming their responsibilities without complaint." My defensiveness raises its head. When Yael's not around, the expectations of my life are so clear. But dagnabbit! Every time he shows up, his questions turn my brain inside out.

"I'm breakin' you out!" He locks eyes with mine.

My throat closes. I revere this man of principle. But his principles are different from mine. To change would be as difficult as breathing water instead of air. I inhale what I know and relinquish my struggle. "Yael. I've changed my mind." The ripping inside me that I had feared doesn't occur. In fact, an iron coolness chills my veins.

"Don't be scared, Krista," he says.

Why is he mocking me?

"Axel and I have a responsibility that's bigger than me." I harden my heart and yield to the machine that is Germany.

He takes my hands in his. "I know our lives will be challenging."

Why is Yael trying to reassure me? He's ignoring my decision. He's as bad as Axel. His steel blue eyes penetrate mine. My heart flutters, but I pull away.

"But we are strong together," he says. His voice is warm and compelling.

Many have warned me to plug my ears against this bewitching man with his gentle promises of our future. I escape his eyes. "There is a potency that is beyond us," I say. "That power has no intention of losing me to you. Who knows if you can even give me children, my highest purpose." The coldness aches, like ice held too long against a broken nose.

"Not give you children? Where do you get this?" his voice rumbles. Yael leans in and scours my eyes. "If this is what you're throwin' in my face, I'm sure you won't hesitate to throw me under the bus. They've brainwashed you!"

"Leave now or I'll yell for help!" I shout. Even as I scream, something shakes me. Dagnabbit! I still care for this enemy. While I must heed the advice of my commanders and protect my future, I offer him one warning. "Be careful, Yael. This is so much bigger than you could imagine. There are hundreds of groups across the country uniting into the German-American National Alliance."

"I'll take care of you." He clasps his hands around mine.

My warning has landed on deaf ears. "I'm not yours to take care of." I pull my hands away.

"You are sacrificing happiness for their cause," he says. His begging is pitiful.

My eyes give him nothing. "You can't understand, Yael. We're leaving for home soon. With my whole family." He must accept that I now shoulder my duty.

His eyes dull. "They've broken you," he murmurs.

"I've accepted this is my life," I say. The deadness in his face frightens me. I'm not sure whether to fight him or just run away. Maybe that's one and the same?

"You've been eaten alive out here," his voice loudens. "You've been isolated from the world. Your feet are dogged from marchin' to the Axel-future." His typically glinting eyes glower like a muddy creek after a storm. "I thought you were stronger than this, Krista?" His heft of desperation tears my heart.

I turn off my feelings for Yael. I visualize serving Axel, hosting in his honor, bearing his children for the Reich. Who knows? I may already be carrying his child. "Strength is about making decisions. I belong to Axel, now. And to our Father, in the Fatherland. My life is written. It's not a bad future." I pause. "Auf Wiedersehen."

Abruptly, the door swings open and light blinds me. My eyes focus. "Dags?"

"What's going on? I saw a flash in here?" Daggy says. She studies Yael, then me, and then Yael again. "You. You're the boxer, in the photo. You're not one of us," she says in a lifeless voice.

"Dags, I can explain," I say. My teeth nick my bottom lip.

Daggy turns to Yael. "I thought the flickering light was an electrical short. I've already alerted Axel," she says. "You better get out of here before he comes."

My heart is shackled, but I still care about Yael. While it's too late to turn back, I don't want harm to come to him. "Go, now," I say. Will he decode my clues about Hitler's big picture? It's too late. The mob and the government and their secret militias can't thwart the attack. But maybe Yael can save himself. I push him out the door.

CHAPTER 33

Shop Worn

YAEL:
En Route to Schwabben Hall. Irvington, NJ

The sweltering heat inside the back of the rickety plumbin' truck makes me wish for a glass of iced tea to roll against the back of my neck. My headache locks me in a cage fenced by barbwire. I struggle to bear the raucous of voices and coughs and grunts and bodies. The truck screeches to a halt at Hawthorne and Clinton Place. I brace myself against the corner. The back doors swing open with a whine. The streetlights flood the container and scorch my eyes. I peer at the silhouettes of armed Minutemen loadin' the cargo bed for our raid on German Schwabben Hall in nearby Irvington. Color spots flash against the jacket of the approaching Harry. I crave the darkness.

Harry wedges his shoulder between Abie and me. The stickiness from his body gums against mine. His grimace reveals that he smells the stink of bad booze radiating from me. His shakin' head warns me he's about to give me crap. But Puddy saves me when his metal pipes crash down on Harry's foot. He kicks the clubs back at Puddy. Harry's in a rare peeved mood, not tolerating much tonight.

From the driver's seat next to Nat and Longie, Benny shouts back to Harry through the cab opening. "Hey cousin, Harry Levine." Benny floors the truck and the boys grab shoulders to steady themselves. Weapons drop, clank and roll. The truck bounces as it hits each street hole.

"Hey, cousin," grumbles Harry. "Watch where ya drivin." Harry scowls as I grasp his knee for balance.

"Benny. Ya drive like your ninety-year-old bubbe," Puddy shouts. He taps fists with Maxie."

Maxie almost misses the brass knuckles that Al tosses him from the other corner. They were headin' right for my teeth! I wish Abie would stop beatin' that bat against his hand. My head feels like it's crackin' open.

Under the Minutemen chatter, I mumble to Harry. "Whooselse comin'?"

Harry growls at me. "You look like crap."

My mouth feels like I'm suckin' on marbles. "Yeah. Just tri-erd, tired livin' two lives," I slur. I rub my eyes. I've gotten maybe eight hours sleep in the past week.

"What are you even doing here?" asks Harry. "You're not fit to fight and if your Nazi brothers spot ya, we all suffer!"

I ignore him. "Yoose gots my intel, right? About German-Americans swappin' dollars for German dough," I say. "It means these folks are savin' to go back to Germany. They think there's gonna be a war. And they thinks they're gonna win."

Harry examines me with his calm doctor-like eyes. He knows I'm wasted, but he doesn't know why. For some reason, he softens. "Yeah," he says. "The FBI found out investors get huge interest if they go back by 1939."

I swallow and let this sink in. "How much are we talkin'?" I ask.

"Tens of millions," he says. He pushes his eyes into mine. "This ties the American Nazis to German Nazis," Harry says. "We have Kuhn on the ropes, buddy." He leaks a grin.

He's forgiving me, I think. Maybe I've done something right? I feel a little more sober. "By the way, remember to check Kuhn's finances, how he spends that dough," I tell Harry. "He was puttin' on the ritz for his mistress with Bund money." I curl my lip.

"Be careful," Harry says. His face stiffens and I can see he's worried.

Beyond the earshot of the others, I blurt to him. "Krista's leavin' for Berlin soon with that Nazi bonehead."

"What?" Harry gasps. "So, she's more than a puppet. She's sold herself to the devil. I didn't think she'd cave." Harry says what I've been holdin' in.

"She's a brainwashed zombie." I pound my own leg way too hard. I've screwed up. I shoulda rescued her sooner. "I'm gonna break her out of her chains!"

"You can't," Harry says. "You're not part of her world. She's not part of yours."

My head drops. How can my wingman say this? My insides knock around like a pinball.

"Let her go," he says. I feel his eyes burrow into me like jiggers under skin.

My strained eyes stare back at him. How could this person who knows me better than anyone in the world be so wrong? "I gotta save her!" The plea comes out louder than I expect.

He grabs my arm. "Ya don't even know if she wants saving."

Benny slams the brakes. We jolt forward. We must be at the Hall.

I slide down and pull Pop's old wool cap over my eyes. It smells of seawater.

Nat flings the back steel doors open, and the commotion knocks into us like a locomotive. No matter. The boys scramble out. When I lean forward to follow, Harry shoves me back so hard, the side of the truck dents. He gets in my face. "Don't you dare put us at risk! I'm not gonna catch another bullet between my teeth for ya." He clomps across the bed and jumps out. He eyeballs me and slams the back door.

I rub the back of my head. I hear Nat outside the truck. "Hey, kid!" he yacks. "Ya hold our wallets in case we get locked up. And kid, don't even think of taking off." I imagine Nat grabbin' the boys collar for good measure.

Next thing I know, muffled cheers shower from above. I creak open the back door. The young freckled-face boy holdin' the pile of wallets wrinkles his forehead. I shrug. Demonstrators swarm around the lighted building decorated in twin Nazi and American flags. No matter how many times I see our red, white, and blue side by side with the spider symbol, I question where I am. A banner reads, *Take our Country Back from the Mixed Race that Ruined It.*

I wince. Through the street noise, I hear a familiar guttural voice through the open second floor window. Dangit. It's my Führer from Camp Nordland. I hear Kunze. "Our *Junges Volk* youth magazine praises German heroes in America. Rallies are up. Publicity is better than ever." Harry was right. If Kunze had seen me, my mission, and maybe me, would've been blown to kingdom come. I'm a screw up.

"We German-Americans defend White America," Kunze shouts. I hear the bang of his fist. "We will fight foreign Jewish Bolshevism for our United States." Through the opening, I watch the shadows of Nazi-salutes against the wall.

Inside, cheers erupt. But like a penny jammin' the blades in a milkshake blender, the celebration sputters with coughin' and gaggin'. I hear glass explode and then the hiss of gas. A jar filled with liquid rolls toward me. The boy with the wallets picks it up. I know what's mixed inside the goop: blackened matches, onions, garlic, cabbage and hair.

"Stink bombs," I say to the boy. I've made them myself.

Smoke billows out the window, releasing the rotten egg smell of burnt hair and sulfur. The boy rubs his eyes and mine tears.

Suddenly, the Hall goes dark. Nat must have pulled his signature assault trick and told the men to cut the wires.

The front door explodes open. Stormtroopers huddle around Kuhn like a turtle shell protecting its skin. They disappear behind the building. As the guests stumble out, they squeeze their eyes against pepper smoke. Anti-Nazi fighters smother the exit and attack the rest of the chokin' Bund members. I hear bones crunch amid the thuds of wooden bats smackin' flesh.

The chaos grows menacing. Police unleash tear gas. The boy next to me vomits on my shoes. I scuttle to a pocket of fresh air. Across the street, a bunch of Minutemen chase soldiers into the Bund Haus. Within seconds, smoke pours out of the building. The place is on fire! The German-dressed soldiers have no choice but to escape back into the madness of the mob into the mélange of swingin' fists and bats.

I must decide whether to jump from the fryin' pan into the fire. I play it safe, swing away, and then sling away.

YAEL:
Ahavas Sholom Synagogue. 145 Broadway. Newark, NJ

Hours after the Schwabben Hall riot, Harry finds me. From my seat toward the front of the sanctuary, I hear his familiar gait when he passes through the bronze doors of Ahavas Sholom Synagogue. The light from three menorahs on the altar slap shadows against the walls. I glance over my shoulder. Harry enters the dark, hallow building. He slips a kippah over his head. I drop my head in my hands and my kippah tilts on mine.

The high ceiling ricochets the clickin' echoes of his shoes. I hear Harry stop. I feel him slide down the wooden pew next to me. He stays silent and gives me time to just be. "I'm so sorry for your loss," he whispers.

My eyes follow shadows rubbin' Harry's face. "My loss?"

"Krista. That's gotta hurt," Harry says. "She crumpled you up like a piece of paper. But, ya know. A wad of paper is strong."

"Maybe," I say. "But if you unfold it, you can't wipe away the creases. The hurt doesn't go away. And the saddest part, Harry, is she left me out of fear." I sigh.

"Fear's a powerful thing," Harry says.

"You see this?" I rap my arm with a karate chop. "I can't feel that. I'm numb. She knocked my wind with a knak, a body punch." I cross my arms over my stomach. I feel like someone's standin' on me. "I haven't felt so hollow since my parents died," I say with a crack in my voice. A sob the size of a baseball presses against my throat. I swallow it down.

"You must miss them so much," Harry says.

The chapel feels vast. There's a beat to the emptiness. It sucks me into its nothingness. "I could have saved my father," I say, my eyes blisterin' with hot tears. "Instead, I watched him hang from a rope." I swallow. "He died for me."

"He couldn't have lived with himself if anything had happened to you. He died so he could live through you."

I brush away my tears, but my throat quivers. The muted color in the room becomes murky. "I don't know what I'm supposed to do next." I can't remember why I'm doin' what I'm doin'. Krista and I have more in common than she thinks.

"Everything you need to know is already inside you," Harry says in a soft voice that makes me think of my pop. Memories wash over me: *On that horrible day five years ago, I wait on my bed in the dark, propped up against the wall. The hissin' begins, like a beast crawlin' closer. The familiar dirty smell, like cigar smoke, snags me right before a clunk and rumblin'. The steam valves let out the heat from the radiator near my bed. Longie steps into my room. His long shadow falls across me like a wool blanket. He plunks down the suitcase that my mother had handed me just a dawn ago and joins me. He explains that my mother suffered a fatal heart attack, and my brothers are at the hospital. I bicker, not a heart attack, a broken heart. Longie tells me that my mother's wish was that I keep my father's light alive. He reaches in his pocket and pulls out my father's watch. The time is frozen at 6:11 to mark his death. "When you're older, you'll wear this," he says. He takes off his watch. "And you wear this one right next to it." Retribution ticks inside me.*

"You got your revenge," Harry says, bringin' me back to the here and now. "You took down your pop's killer. Now move on."

"Yeah," I spit out. "But nothing's changed."

Harry straightens his back. "You need to step back, buddy, out of your shallowness," he says. "You've forgotten your mission."

My slumped body hardens. "Why the heck do you think you know me so well?"

"I don't. But who cares? The problem is you don't know who you are. And you're afraid of finding out."

I jump up. My fist springs. Harry catches my left hook with his bare hand and rises. He squeezes it. "You're lost. You don't know whether to move forward or backward." Harry hits me right between the eyes with his words. "You're trying to be someone who doesn't even exist."

I wrench my hand away. "I've tried everything." My insides throb, like a blisterin' burn about to rupture. "I've sacrificed, lied, even killed a man. And all I got was a kick in the heart!" My voice rumbles against the vaulting walls. I feel like I'm shatterin' into a million pieces.

"Yael," Harry says. "You have to unknow yourself. Remake yourself to who ya wanna be. Because right now, you can't see beyond your darn knuckles." This time, Harry clutches my restin' fist and holds it between his hands. "You don't have to win all the fights. Step out of the ring. Step out so you can see."

My lungs suck the air from me. My head spins. I spiral down until I feel like I smack rocks. I don't know how long I'm there, but the darkness presses up against my skin. It steals my senses. My muscles cramp. Why can't I hear my breath?

Then something strange happens. The silence is so barren. I hear a creak, like someone steppin' on a dry floorboard. My eyes blink. I see the room around me shift from the blurs of gray pencil sketches into the moving, speakin' images of a film. I feel myself happen. I step forward into the story. I become unafraid of fallin' again. Because I know there's people waitin' for me.

I lock eyes with Harry. "I'll be worthless if I fail my father or Longie or you or the men or my country." I see myself in his eyes, the way he sees me—strong, loyal, steadfast, oh yeah, and sometimes an a-hole. My sense of rejection dissolves into this reflection. I realize that havin' or losin' someone isn't about me. The revenge against Pop's killer becomes incidental. Gettin' his killer only band-aids a symptom. My ego has blinded me. "This isn't about me," I say under my breath. "I have to stop what's goin' on in the world around me. I have to stop it for us."

Harry squeezes my arm. "Your father would be proud of you. You bear witness to his history. You fight and warn others."

My guard falls. "Harry. In the battle, do I abandon Krista? She's trapped."

"What do you want?" he asks. He waits for my answer.

"I wanna be her freedom," I tell him.

"Dangit, Yael!" He shakes my shoulders. "She's part of the America you're fighting for. You'll give her freedom one way or another." Harry's response drenches me with the chill of ice water.

I put my arm around Harry's shoulders.

"Let's bring down Kuhn!" we say together.

CHAPTER 34

Rabbit Punch

KRISTA:

Training Grounds. Camp Siegfried. Long Island, NY

The rain whips my worn face. I persevere through the Camp Siegfried training grounds competing against seven other troops, all trying to outmaneuver each other. The earthy scent of petrichor unearthed by the thrashing rain warns me that underfoot, the training ground is turning into a sludgy field. As I tread forward, the mire sucks my boots into it. Flashes of my father's stories from the muddy Great War assault me—the rotting corpses swaddled in sludge, the odor of putrescent flesh, bodiless hands stuck in the muck reaching for nothing. Our officers prepare us for correcting a past they swear will repeat itself. We are the next generation.

All the heavies push us beyond our human limits, Führer Vandenberg, Führer Kuhn, Dinkelacker, and Axel. The officers, protected from the rain under the fly-tent shelter, order us to wave Nazi and American flags with verve, beat drums with ferocity, and march with brutality. I used to be afraid of stopping. Now, even if I wanted to rest, the hum keeps me moving.

Frank drills our squadron. He forces us to pull through mud channels, climb over craggy ropes, repel down glassy rocks. The monstrous commander forces precision and fortitude in an effort to impress his superiors. He inflicts barbaric castigation with each mistake, including intimidating, humiliating, and assaulting anyone who makes a misstep. As a result, we morph into a stampede, like panicked animals. Drained, I slip in the muck. Cort stumbles over me, and we struggle together in the mud. He frees himself from the ooze as I thrash in the mess. Klaus almost stops to help, but Frank wags his arm at his embattled infantry. The others skirt the fallen, sacrificing their Kamerads for their own survival. What happened to "we're all one German?" Even the pregnant Sascha is pushed forward without regard.

"Schnell!" Frank yells. The rain bangs around me. "Your Führer is disgusted. You wallow in slime, whining like a squealing Jew. Shed that cowardly skin and display your warrior blood." But the machine in me sputters. I steady myself and step out of the muddy pit. The threesome of Heidi, Führer Vandenberg, and Dinkelacker scrutinizes me with cold eyes.

Axel brays under the shelter. "Attention!" he bellows at the entire brigade. He acknowledges the apex has passed. Everyone halts, experiencing the respite of a boxer between rounds. "For Germandon to live, you must excel for the Nazi cause. Abgewiesen! Report at 5:00 a.m. tomorrow."

A changing wind slaps my cheek and the storm weakens. The shattered and grimy scouts disband. Axel beckons me. I plod toward his tent. He clasps his hands behind his back. "Krista. I spoke with my father today," he says. "He has planned a grand reception for us." He shakes away the water dripping off the end of his Nazi hat.

I can't believe his self-absorption. Did he not see what I just went through? No matter how hard I try to worship this man, his ego blocks me. "Did you say something?" I rub my sore calves.

Heidi arrives and overhears Axel repeat his announcement. "Krista, I know it's hard to hear through the rain. But Axel just delivered exciting news," she says. She turns to Axel and covers for my silent ingratitude. "Axel, our family is grateful for our future together."

The sound of splashing footsteps running through the mud distracts me. "Herren!" Penn yells. "We need you by the lake, now! Someone's drowned!"

"There's been an accident," Axel shouts to Frank. "Notify the commanders."

Minutes later, Axel, Heidi, and I arrive at the lake. Frank, Führer Kuhn, Dinkelacker, and Vandenberg stand cold-faced as a bloated body is pulled from the water. Rock-filled bags tied to the legs stretch the skin of a girl's body. The wet shirt clinging to the dead skin reveals her belly. My stomach flips. I drop to my knees. The breathless body is Daggy's. I imagine her flailing arms as she sinks, watching the cloudy water deepen overhead, sucking the lake water through her windpipe into her lungs, panicking with a silent scream as her hair rises upwards until her heart stops pounding.

Heidi tries to hoist me up, but my mud covered arms slip through her hands as my deadweight anchors me to the soil. My knees tremble. "Catgut," I mumble.

"She's delirious," Axel says. He holds my slimy, brown hand.

"Look at Dag's legs," I say. "She used the catgut from her guitar to tie the bags around her legs." Daggy was a good person. She was my friend.

"Too bad!" Führer Kuhn says. "The good news is we only have one casualty this summer. The unfortunate part is that she was fertile."

The Führer won't meet my eyes.

"We found out yesterday she was pregnant," he says. "But no one has the right to show pain. Suicide is a weakness. She's better off dead." I can't believe my ears.

I depend on these familiar people around me. That's how I survive. I have trusted them to protect me. But in front of my eyes, this trust has vanished like a sun dropping off the horizon. I slip my hand out of Axel's. Which way should I run?

Suddenly. A gray animal whines beside us. "Nnnaa!" We hear the explosion before we see the bundle on the ground. Cort, still covered in mud from the drills, lies flat on the ground, a gun near his head. A curl of smoke rises from the black bullet hole in his temple. My friend Cort has joined Daggy's rise to freedom.

I can finally hear, completely. I want to throw Führer Kuhn into the water and watch him drown. I hold out my hand. "Please ,Yael, take it," I say to myself. The coarse nothing against my skin burns.

CHAPTER 35

Parry

YAEL:

German Turn Verein. William St. Newark, NJ

The guys and I are packed tighter than sardines. We are waiting for the doors of the Bund rally at the German Turn Verein club to open. The steam of hundreds behind us pulsates against the police wall. Riddled throughout the crowd are hundreds of demonstrators and Minutemen. Their energy pumps against the enthusiasm of the fascist demonstration.

Like a torpedo, Puddy appears from nowhere and knocks me against Abie and Harry. "Yael," he screams. "Ya gotta get outta here! A little bird just told me the American Hitler himself is the surprise headliner tonight."

"Cripes, Yael! We need this like we need a hole in our heads!" Nat exclaims.

Harry snatches Maxie's hat off and pulls it over my head and past my ears to cloak me. He shoves me into the shadows, lifts the collar of my jacket, and opens his mouth to scold me.

I raise my hands in surrender. "I know, I know. I'm dead if Kuhn recognizes me. I'll be careful, pal." I look around at the hundreds of troopers and police crawlin' around, guardin' what must be thousands of fever-pitched Bundists marchin' into the German club on William Street to hear their leader. They're gonna pack 'em in the gym tonight, and I'm not gonna miss unpackin' 'em.

Harry gleams at me. "We keep a low profile, understand?" He pushes me up toward the other guys, and I give him a quick nod. He yanks my hat down lower.

At the entrance, two cops give Nat, Puddy, and Abie dirty looks when they pay our admission for the Bund meetin'. "We're just helping ya watch for unpeaceful remarks, Officers," Nat says. "We've got your backs." He shapes his fingers into pistols and points them.

One of the cops glares at Nat. "No funny business, squirt. I'm not tolerating even a little spark, ya hear." What a joke. The police protect the rally while the FBI pull our strings to stop it. It continues to surprise me how it takes punchin' out these Nazis' lights to turn everyone else's on.

"We've been assured there will be no anti-Semitic remarks tonight," Abie says to the cops. "So everything should be fine. Right, Puddy?"

Puddy pushes a roll of dough into the cop's hand. "We're peace lovin' guys, Officer. Makin' sure everyone in our country gets the right to meet and speak."

Magically, the cop steps back and lets us pass. Maxie bats his eyelashes, and Benny sticks his lit cigar between the cop's lips.

Harry holds me close. "We're staying near the door, pal," he growls into my ear.

Inside the Great Hall of the Turn Verein, Führer Kuhn calls out from the podium. "Heil America! A special message to all the youth here tonight, direct from Führer Adolph Hitler across the ocean in Berlin. He says you are the flesh of our flesh, the blood of our blood, and your young minds are driven by his spirit."

Cheers rock from the room. Everyone but Harry and I sit in the auditorium.

"Inside of us, the true patriots of America march with Germany,"

Kuhn shouts.

The audience roars in unison. "Heil Hitler!"

"As our forefathers bled and fought for our country, let us clean up America from Jews and non-Aryans." He bangs his chest with his fist.

"America for Americans!" The audience cheers.

Suddenly, Puddy stands on his chair and shouts. "How in blue blazes can you sing freedom rings in one breath and wave swastikas in the next?"

Kuhn lets silence dot the moment before he answers. He leans close to the microphone. "FDR's democracy is a poison apple that Americans have been tricked into biting!" he screeches.

A stormtrooper with brass knuckles grabs Puddy off of his chair. "Special compliments from Führer Kuhn, Freund." The trooper kicks Puddy between the legs.

Before Puddy hits the ground, Abie cracks a chair over the trooper's head. "That's what ya get for not following Queensbury Rules, ya ugly Palooka."

As if a referee just clanged the startin' bell of a boxin' match, the scene explodes. From my view by the door, hulks of men charge out of every corner of the gym. Chairs splinter across skulls and belt buckles slice thighs and shoulders. The hall echoes with crashes, thumps, and smacks. Troopers in high black boots kick shins. Fighters crack jaws. I duck under a flyin' chair. Harry and I box at the bodies thrown our way. In the distance, I see Kuhn gettin' ushered to a back exit by his elite eight troopers. I tug my hat down.

Out of the blue, someone hits me hard from behind and I drop to my knees. The khaki shirt of a stormtrooper wraps around my neck and drags me into a dark corner. I shield my face. "I'm gonna say this fast," a voice rasps. "Tomorrow night. Camp Siegfried Lake. You know the drill."

My hands guard my face.

"Yael. KA-BAM. It's me. Al Fisher. Got it." He grabs my chin and turns my head toward his face.

I move my hand away from my face. I squint at Al's mug. He's undercover, too.

"Sorry, pal," he says. "But gotta keep my cover. Al grabs my collar, clocks me, and everything goes dark."

CHAPTER 36

In Your Corner

YAEL:
Woods. Camp Siegfried. Long Island, NY

The heat of the day hangs against the stagnant night air of the Camp Siegfried woods. I lean my hand against the bark of a tree. With my foot, I push the pine needles into a triangle. I flap my cotton shirt to splash air across my hot skin. Tryin' to cool is as vain as holdin' a spoon with boxin' gloves.

Through the trees, there's a crackle of light that's either far away and big or close and small. Hard to say for sure. I camouflage myself behind the tree. Abruptly, the flicker snaps at my face. A lightning bug punctures the darkness. Reachin' out, I cup my hands around it. My fingers turn yellow from the captured glow, the same color of light that penetrates your eyes when they're closed.

There's a snappin' of twigs followed by a familiar female voice. "Hello, Yael."

I pivot. My heart pounds.

"I changed my mind," Krista says. I smell her hair. It's perfumed with the smell of campfires. Her body breathes the mixture of minerals and soil that's been soaked by the sun. Heat washes over me, sendin' blood to my cheeks. I open my hands and the lightning bug glows and flies away.

Her eyes follow the light. "I'm sorry the way I treated you, Yael. I didn't mean what I said."

I say nothing, not forgiving her, not condemning her.

"Can I convince you to free me, like that insect?" she says to my emotionless face. "I don't want this life anymore. I can't be in this place. I swear it's not a trick. Because I know you, and I know that's what you're think—"

"Sshh. Turn around." I hold her waist as she twists. "You see that moon?" I say.

Krista nods, easin' into the crook of my shoulder. The hollows of her cheeks seem familial, the raise of her eyebrows so personal. I feel like I've known her all my life.

"My mother died after my father was branded with a swastika," I say under my breath. "He was slain by American Nazis."

"Oh, no," she murmurs, tensing her shoulders into my chest.

"My greatest memory of her is a Jewish fable she told me about her name," I say.

The light of the moon plays on Krista's cheekbone as she gazes up. "Tell me," she says, relaxing her body.

"There was a queen so beautiful she was named Esther after the ancient word for the new beginnings of the moon," I say. "You see, just like the moon, the power to renew gives us freedom."

I embrace Krista and continue. "I ask myself, and I ask you, why ask for the stars, when I'm over the moon for you. I'm gonna rescue you." At this moment, my feelin's take off on their own. I no longer need to beat them down or fear they will destroy me. All of them are unforced and welcome.

"I'm ready," she tells me. Her lips part and she runs her tongue over them. My lips touch hers. They're soft as bread dough. I release her for the moment, knowin' I'll have her for the rest of my life.

"I'll find a way," I say in a hushed tone. "It's better if you don't know the details. Do you trust me?"

Krista shrugs. I don't think she doubts me. She's just afraid.

"What about your family? Especially your father?" I ask.

"My sister has already warned my father about my waning loyalties. I haven't heard from the daunting Officer Günther Brecht yet, but he will confront me."

"Günther?" I freeze, visualizing my knife carvin' a swastika into his spongy chest. "Günther Brecht is your father's name?" My memory flashes to a large man escorting his two German daughters, one in a red dress.

Krista's neck twitches. Did she feel me stiffen? No, her eyes are following the trail of a lightning bug. She ignores my question. I'm not sure I'm ready for the answer anyway. I take a deep breath.

"Yael, there's something else." I see my blue eyes inside her green ones. "There's a secret I want to tell you."

My nerves prickle. "I'm here for you, Krista, no matter what."

She blows air through her lips. So, she's nervous, too. Somehow that makes me feel better. "My father told me the truth about who I am," she says.

"You mean who your real father was?"

"I've actually known all my life, but could never admit it to myself." She turns to face me and clasps my hands. "My real father was Jewish. I'm half-Jewish. Papa buried the secret for obvious reasons."

All of my assumptions whirl as if caught in a violent wind. The new vantage point is dizzying. But before I know it, the truth is freein'. Now I know how that lightning bug feels.

"I better go," Krista says. She hands me a paper. "Here. There's a rally like the one in Nuremberg from the movie we saw. It's planned for President's Day at Madison Square Garden. Read that. The Führer is callin' it a "Mass Demonstration for True Americanism, honoring George Washington."

"Kuhn says great historic events are prepared underground until they suddenly appear," I say. "That's the day he's been plannin'."

"Führer Kuhn's calling for all American Nazis to conquer America under Hitler's plan," Krista explains. "We chant *Der Tag* meaning the day to seize control. The day Nazism triumphs in America."

Madison Square Garden is an American icon like George Washington. American symbols bank history. They cash in on the myths that galvanize our union. "To fill the Garden is a symbol of success for the American Nazi Bund, something bigger than them," I say.

Krista's face shines pale in the moonlight. "Yael, the Nazi threat is no longer about Jews or Reds or something far away in Europe."

"No, it's not. The Nazi threat is here, ready to possess all Americans."

KRISTA:
Woods. Camp Siegfried. Long Island, NY

After meeting Yael near the Camp Siegfried Lake, I hurry back to the tents along the dark path in the woods. I hear branches crack behind me. Out of the corner of my eye, a flashlight beams. The next thing I know, there's a slam-bump against my torso. The impact rattles my teeth and empties my lungs. A body straddles me and pins down my shoulders. I open one eye. Through blackish-red light, Heidi comes into focus. She barrels her eyes into mine. "What are you scheming?" she asks through clenched teeth." Through my hearing ear, I listen to busy crickets chirping instead of her rattle.

"What do you care?" I ask. "Oh, never mind. I know. You care about having someone to boss around." I wiggle to get free from her. She releases me and we both stand.

"It's my duty to guide you," she says. "I'm the one who pulls your head out of the mud. I'm the one who keeps you safe. Now spill the beans! What have you been up to?"

I brush the dirt off my clothes and count the number of cricket chirps.

Heidi once taught me how to tell the temperature through them. There are three chirps a second. In fifteen seconds, they'll be forty-five twills. Add forty and get ninety. Wow. Ninety-degrees. Even nature is itching tonight.

Heidi grabs my cheeks with one hand. Her face twists. She swings her hand at me. I duck and her hand scrapes across the tree trunk behind me. "You little brat!" Heidi yells. She shakes the tree splinters off her hand. "It's time to add you to my files as a traitor." The good news? She realizes I'm my own person.

An awkward silence falls between us. Heidi was my role model. Even more, she protected me from pain, from our father, our common enemy. All I ever wanted was to make my older sister proud. But somewhere along the line, jealousy and fear rotted her compassion. Now, with my betrothal to Axel, a new commander runs my life. She's pushed aside. In fact, my new position subsumes her. Heidi must eat her own poison. The roles are reversed. How ironic. How liberating.

"Why should I tell you anything," I hiss. "You've betrayed me once. I'm not stupid enough to ever trust you again."

"What are you talking about?" Heidi asks.

"You stabbed me in the back!" I say. "You told Frank my real father was Jewish. And now Frank threatens to tell others."

Heidi, stunned, steps back.

"This world I've been living in isn't good. My whole life has been a lie," I say. "And tell Frank to never touch me again, or I'll slit his throat." I walk away, taking normal steps. Then my knees kick higher. My step reaches farther. Now, I'm marching to my own drum.

CHAPTER 37

Anchor Punch

LONGIE ZWILLMAN:
Hotel Riviera. Clinton Avenue. Newark, NJ

"Get me the full name of the man I executed in the cabin at Camp Nordland," I hear Yael tell Harry through the open door. I enter my office at Hotel Riviera where the Minutemen are waiting for me. Nat follows behind me.

"Yael." I clutch his shoulder. "Günther Brecht is the man you executed. He's the man who killed your pop," I tell him. "Krista Brecht's his daughter."

Yael clutches the top of a chair back. "Holy moly!" he gasps. "That means that Günther was Freddy's uncle. Wait. Freddy and Krista." His face pales. "They must be related. They must be ... cousins?" He wraps his stomach with his hands. Harry helps him sit down in a chair. The others step close.

Nat raises his eyebrows at me.

I crouch down in front of Yael. "I know this is hard, son. But think." I put my hand on Yael's knee. "Is there any way Freddy knows you're friends

294

with Krista."

Yael rubs his head. "He doesn't know."

"Does Krista know about Freddy?" Nat asks with an "I told you so" tone. He lights a cigar.

Yael clenches his fists. He realizes that lives depend on an honest answer. "No, Longie. Krista knows nothing about Freddy."

I study Yael's crumpled face to find a seed of doubt. I don't see one. He's hurting, but his eyes are steady.

Benny puts his hand on his shoulder. He pulls away.

"And she won't find out anything!" Yael cries. A blue vein in his neck juts. "She won't." Yael turns to Harry. "What did we find out from Günther Brecht's files?"

"We hit the mother lode, pal." Harry rolls his eyes. "Camp Siegfrieders bought ten million dollars' worth of German Rueckwanderer marks."

"Why would Americans use their savings to buy German dough?" Benny asks.

Abie guesses. "Must think value's going up?"

"A hint," I say. "Accounts flow right to German hometowns."

"That money gives American Nazis money to go back," Benny guesses.

Harry says, "American Nazis are investing in—"

"A German war victory," Yael finishes.

"Before a war even starts," I add.

"So does the money prove ties between Kuhn and Nazi, Germany?" Abie scratches his head.

Nat rolls his fist in his palm. "Our friend at the German consulate kindly spilled the beans." Nat draws a thick puff of cigar smoke into his mouth.

"To buy RMs, Germans must swear they will return," I say.

Puddy clenches his fists. "Nazis down for the count!"

"KA-POW!" Al shouts.

"FBI gonna freeze the funds, Longie?" Abie asks.

When I shake my head no, they raise their eyebrows. "FDR took our plan instead," I tell them. "We give the names of investors to coppers in precincts across America. They'll feed them bait. Follow them."

"We hook the darn Nazis, instead," Nat says. He blows out a big puff of smoke.

"Then reel 'em in," Maxie says.

"FBI wants a paper trail, too. Invoices and receipts from Kuhn," Harry tells us.

"We have the go-ahead to wiretap," Nat adds.

Yael's face reddens. "Heck, unless I'm an iron dumbbell, we've just landed the mythical anchor punch."

"KA-POW-BAM!" shouts Al.

The austere Harry mimics a punch starting from the ground up. "The anchor punch is that perfect counterpunch. Invisible to the naked eye—"

"—that leaves your opponent flat on the mat not knowing what hit him," Yael says as he finishes Harry's thought.

YAEL:
Newark Bund Headquarters. Nye Avenue. Newark, NJ

Nervous as a cat on hot bricks, I shine a light on the door of Kuhn's empty Newark Bund office. Puddy picks open the lock and the door clicks open. Harry keeps watch as we enter the dark room.

Puddy shines his flashlight on a color edition of a magazine. "Wowie, zowie!" he exclaims. "Kuhn's got the new comic book." He riffles through the pages. "This new hero can jump over skyscrapers and fly and stuff." Puddy stuffs the comic book inside his jacket. "Isn't wiretapping illegal?"

"When did you get all moral, Puddy?" I say, scanning the room. I point to his pocket. "That Superman guy is the American super-immigrant from outer space." I chuckle at my own wit.

"Longie got a go-ahead from the top," Harry says. "Yael, take the flashlight." Harry cracks the door and keeps watch.

Puddy grips a small light in his mouth as he plants a wiretap bug in the phone. Next to him, I take pictures of Kuhn's paper strewn desk. There's a Bund invoice for a diamond ring, that German RM money, and phone receipts.

Suddenly, Harry's hand flaps like a flailin' bird. He waves everyone into the closet and closes the door behind us. From inside, we hear Kuhn and Axel enter.

When Kuhn switches on the light, I see my shoes. "Did you have a good trip from Camp Siegfried?" Kuhn asks Axel.

"Ya, the train was easy, mein Führer," Axel's voice answers.

"Let me grab my coat from the closet and we'll get dinner," Kuhn says. "I want to hear how we can help you in Berlin." Kuhn's bootsteps boom toward our hidin' place.

I tense. Puddy levels a pistol at the door.

"Führer!" Axel calls to Kuhn. "Is this your jacket on the coat rack?"

I hear the footsteps slide and stop. "Ah, yes. Danke." Kuhn's boots clomp. "Hmm. I thought I organized those papers on my desk." Papers rustle.

"With all due respect, mein Führer, I can't miss the train to Siegfried tonight."

"Yah, of course." Footsteps clatter around the office and scrape the floor. "Where is that new comic book I wanted to show you?" Papers shuffle. "Have you heard about the American superhero strong enough to spin the world backwards? The Jew writer, Jerry Siegal, is intellectually circumcised if he thinks he's going to trump our Super Aryans. Oh well. Let's go."

Two sets of boots klopp toward the office door. "By the way," Kuhn asks Axel. "Do you know a young man around your age named Rike Saxon?" The office door clicks shut and a key scratches the lock.

After a minute or two, I crack open the closet door. My hands are shakin' like a fall leaf. I wish I could've heard Axel's answer to Kuhn's question.

CHAPTER 38

Throw Your Hat in the Ring

YAEL, ALIAS RIKE:
Initiation Facility. Camp Nordland. Andover, NJ

Static shocks me when I touch my wool uniform in the candlelit darkness of the initiation room at Camp Nordland. I take it as an omen. Just don't know if it's a good or bad one. The grainy outline of an American flag is displayed six inches lower than the Nazi flag. My calf muscles ache from standin' in dark silence for three hours. They're wearin' us down. They want to bury us and have us open our coffins into some new life. My mind wanders, and I recall Harry's father, Isaac, describing his initiation into the Freemasons: "*Initiations make comrades sacrifice together so they feel they've done something important together. Secrets bond them, so much so, that if one of them were to die, the others would feel like they lost family. This way, they never leave the group.*"

A drummer's roll combined with tappin' footsteps awakens me from my muse. Candle flames demark the room as muted flag bearers and stormtroopers form the shape of a *U* with us trainees at the open end.

My eyes adjust. I see Führer Kuhn at the head of the *U*.

To Kuhn's right stands Secretary Wheeler-Hill. To his left, Führer Schwartzman stares into space at some force beyond the room. After all movement stops, Schwartzman begins. "Today, you will consecrate the secrets of our order," he says. "You will pledge your loyalty to the Nazi storm flag, the swastika, the myth of the Aryan. You will pledge to fight side by side with all German Kamerads. Your oath is identical with allegiance to Germany."

I recall more of Isaac's Freemason story. *"Everything we learn has never been a secret. Even the Big Bang theory from just a decade ago is the same story from the Bible for thousands of years. So when someone tells you they have power, especially power to predict, be wary. These people are often pasting pieces of history and myths together to create their own reality, some more sinister than others. Then once they control their own universe, they use symbolism to brand their followers to them."*

Drums roll and the silent ceremony begins. Schwartzman places the corner of a Nazi flag on top of our stars and stripes. He pushes the flag edges into the hand of each initiate. They salute, and they take their place inside the *U*.

Then it's my turn. I stretch out my left hand and salute with the right. Like a wind-up doll, Schwartzman places the corner of the Nazi flag on top of the American one. He grasps my left hand. His eyes suck mine. He's tryin' to breach me like a plumber's snake rootin' out sewage from a pipe. It's clear. He's clawin' for my heart. I break his stare and return a strong Nazi salute.

Führer Schwartzman commands us. "By accepting your consecration you are swearing this sacred oath. You will render unconditional obedience to the Führer of the German Reich, Adolf Hitler, Supreme Commander of the Wehrmacht. As a brave soldier, you will be ready at any time to stake your life for this oath."

The initiates repeat the oath. "I consecrate my life to Hitler. I will sacrifice my life for Hitler. I will die for Hitler, my savior, my Führer."

"Sig Heil! Sig Heil! Sig Heil!" we chant.

After initiation, our group swigs beer and sings Hitler stormtrooper songs. Freddy throws his arm around my shoulders. He turns to Herbert. "Hugo told us the Ambassador recruited you for a secret operation in London—Operation Willi."

"He owed my pop a favor," Herbert says. "Yes, I'm chuffed to bits. And no. Can't talk about it."

Paul smiles and turns to Hugo. "I hear you got your own coup assignment."

"Guarding the women's Camp at Siegfried will have its benefits, yes." Hugo chews the inside of his cheeks.

Secretary Wheeler-Hill approaches and congratulates us. He tilts his chin up at me. "Officer Saxon. You haven't received your orders yet, have you?" His hand juts out of his jacket. The gossip is that Kuhn will have me by his side. When he does, Longie's ready to pounce the inner circle.

"We've selected you for a great honor," he says. The ears of my closest Nazi friends perk. "You will serve Führer Kuhn. You have been chosen as one of the Elite Eight."

Freddy thumps my back with his palm. The others rustle me.

Wheeler-Hill turns to Freddy. "Herr Schafspelz, I welcome your uncle's request to host you at my Stuttgart, Germany home for your assignment. He hasn't returned my call. Is he in town?"

Dangit! They're speakin' about Günther. My heart flutters. Have I covered all my tracks? I watch the skin on their face for clues. Am I bein' cornered? My wrists itch. My lungs won't pump.

"Herr Secretary. I'd be honored. I'll let my uncle know," Freddy says. He half-smiles at me. "I'm training in Germany. Sabotage," he explains to me.

I inhale. One of my hands grabs Freddy's and the other wraps around his shoulder. It's a shug, half shake, half hug. This enemy isn't exactly my friend, but he's my Kamerad. I'm close enough to whisper a secret, but can still slit his throat if necessary. "Here's to a partnership that will last a thousand years!" I say.

300

"Officer Saxon. You're from Stuttgart, too, ya?" The Secretary raises his eyebrows. "Where precisely is your family home?"

I don't hesitate. "Sadly, taken durin' the Great War." I'm glad I practiced that answer with Longie.

The Secretary grimaces. "You've no need to be ashamed. The Versailles Treaty raped us all," he says. "How could anyone in their right mind expect us to repay the titanic bill the world sent us. The enemy rubbed Salz on die Wunde. They castrated our Germany military." His neck bulgin' over his black collar turns blotchy red. "But now, Germandon redeems itself! Our splintered country, our religion, politics, our entire culture will be whole again. And Hitler save anyone who mettles with us this time!"

YAEL, ALIAS RIKE:
Bathhouse. Camp Nordland. Andover, NJ

The lukewarm Camp Nordland shower water beats against my eyelids. No wonder I've never showered here before. My hands stroke my slick body. But the filth of the evil doctrine I've just wed turns my skin to sandpaper. My job isn't done. I have cornered the American Hitler and his German-American Nazi Bund. I've gained evidence to put Kuhn behind bars for good and dissuade American fascism. I've somehow averted the bloody path to assassinate him. I'm en route to rescue Krista. But until this country chooses a path, anything could happen to America.

The bathhouse door creaks. "Who's there?" I call over the whooshin' water.

"Rike? You're here late. It's Freddy."

"Yeah. Just cleanin' up," I shout over the runnin' water.

"You're a pal. Leaving me with freezing water," he teases but knows it's true.

"Whatya doin' until ya ship out?" I ask Freddy. I'm gonna miss him.

"I'm staying at the Camp," Freddy answers above the water pipe squeals. "Hey, come with me to Germany, Rike. Kuhn'll let you defer your assignment."

Keys and metal clank against the cement floor.

Geez. Sorry, pal, I knocked your stuff off the sink," Freddy says.

"I think the Führer has plans for me right away." I rinse the soap out of my hair.

"What's this?" Freddy asks. A silence skips across the slate. The shower curtain rips open. Freddy holds up his uncle's knife—the one that originally belonged to my father.

My heart sticks in my throat. "Oh, that," I stumble. "Lucky I found it." I turn off the shower and snatch my towel off the hook. "Ya wanna give it to your uncle?"

Freddy stares at me. "What the heck?"

"What are ya lookin' at?" I ask.

Freddy gapes at my genitals. "You're circumcised." Freddy steps back. "You double-crosser. You're Jewish."

We study each other's flarin' pupils like a matador and a bull. Freddy charges me with the knife. I bind the towel around his neck and throw him down, knee him in the head and knock him out cold. The blood from his nose smears the gray floor. I get dressed and toss Freddy over my shoulder.

LONGIE ZWILLMAN:
Curbside. Hawthorne Avenue. Newark, NJ

At curbside on Hawthorne Avenue, I watch Nat and Abie. They drag Yael's captive from his car trunk. The kid's gagged and tied up, but his eyes scorch Yael like a welding machine ready to char him.

"Give him the third degree," Yael says. He squints at the disheveled Freddy. "Cover up Uncle Günther's disappearance."

"Nat, get FBI to cover up," I say. "Kuhn needs a story or he'll get suspicious."

The long ride up from Camp Nordland gave Yael time to think. His past few months must have projected hundreds of frames per second against his windshield. He probably shivered at each scene, listened to each cough and laugh and shout, scratched each part of his skin that was touched. Now, he's trying to digest the whole thing, like a boa eating a calf. His blue eyes wave. I'm worried.

"Yael," I say. "You won't see Freddy again."

He's sickly calm.

I wrap my long coat around his shoulders and take him inside.

CHAPTER 39

The Main Event

FRITZ KUHN:
En route to Camp Siegfried. Long Island, NY

Secretary Wheeler-Hill narrates the bus tour to my VIPs en route to the Camp Siegfried Convention. "Herren! Führers! Now that we've crossed into Yaphank, we will sightsee through the German Gardens bungalow neighborhood." He wipes the perspiration off his forehead with his handkerchief. "As you know, our town operates under one deed owned by the German American Settlement League. Most poignantly, this soil can only be owned by German blut!" The tourists purr. He points out the window. "Here we are on German Boulevard which merges into Goebbels Strasse." The riders include thirty special Führers and guests.

The air streaming through the window of the bus keeps the staining of my best uniform to a minimum. But it's a struggle.

The bus chugs through the sticky air. We make a right on Berliner Strasse and another on Goering. The riders grab the top of their seats through the bumps. We turn back onto German, left onto Westfalen, and drive all the way to Adolph Hitler Strasse.

The Secretary wipes his forehead again and resumes his narrated tour. "The Linden trees that line Adolph Hitler Strasse replicate the most notable street in Berlin, Unter den Linden. The saplings were imported all the way from the Fatherland." His chest swells. "And now our own Führer Kuhn will speak to you."

I stand to a resounding Heil Hitler salute that shakes the bus. Commanding attention from these men fills my soul with verve. They worship me—something I don't get from my own wife and kids back in Chicago.

"Now onto the crown jewel of Yaphank and the flagship of our American Hitler Youth camps, Camp Siegfried," I say. "We welcome you to a day of pomp and circumstance at the Summer Convention for the German-American Nazi Bund."

Youth Director Theodore Dinkelacker interrupts me. "Camp Siegfried is the great outdoors for Germans and our youth," he says. It's amazing that he doesn't have a drop of sweat on his forehead. "The oasis is a sanctuary to escape city life and discuss the future of the world. Here we execute a superior Nazi ideology against the American Constitution and shape a community to improve the human race."

"Free America! Free America! Free America!" the busload of leaders cheer.

YAEL, ALIAS RIKE:
Convention. Camp Siegfried. Long Island, NY

I drop Harry off on high ground above Camp Siegfried before my descent to rescue Krista at the convention. I'm disguised as Rike Saxon. Harry's binoculars swing around his neck. It's good to know his eye will be on me.

At the gate, a guard wearin' a steel helmet and holdin' a lance asks for my stormtrooper ID. I show it to him and he directs me to the lot. "Heil Hitler!" he says.

I park and navigate to the main hall. Through the window of the building, I view a larger-than-life paintin' of Hitler. Souvenir statuettes cover a table. Bookshelves are filled with what is undoubtedly German propaganda.

The screen door flies open, and I just about jump out of my pants. Axel and Frank barge out and hurry toward the thousands arriving from Yaphank and beyond. Axel gives Frank orders. "Something's wrong with the audio equipment for the presentation. Fix it."

Axel turns his head and calls. "Krista. Shnell! We are going to be late." Axel notices me standin' in my innocuous stormtrooper uniform. Not seein' through my disguise, he beckons me to help.

"Seems like sound systems never work," Frank grumbles. "Darn, it's hotter than the devil today."

Another trooper approaches Axel. I seize my chance to hide. The trooper salutes and clicks his heels. "The Camp Siegfried train is due to arrive on time in Yaphank with the visitors," he says. "People should be here any minute."

The screen door bangs shut. Krista stands outside. Our eyes meet. Her mouth opens, and I watch my name teeter on the tip of her tongue. Have her loyalties shifted yet again? Will she sound the alarm? She glances at her commander, Axel, but I hold her eyes. Krista folds her arms across her uniform.

Without lettin' anyone see, I raise my arm to address her but not with the outstretched arm of a stormtrooper soldier. Instead, I bend my elbow and the unyielding air holds up my salute. Within my honorable pause radiates the blindin' light of ancient battles in my mind, the daily march around the walls, the blares of a ram's horn, and the crush of walls comin' down. I squeeze my fingers together, hold my arm horizontal to the ground, and tap my hat with the American salute. I'm not extending my servility of the Nazi salute to Krista. I'm exchanging my commitment to self-sacrifice.

"Danks!" Axel clips at the soldier. He searches for me, the lone stormtrooper, to deliver orders. But I'm gone, like a smudge on the soil. From my concealment, I see him hunt for Krista. He watches her disappear back into the building in pursuit of a ringin' phone. Or perhaps, a lightning bug.

KRISTA:
Office. Camp Siegfried. Long Island, NY

"Brecht. Hallo," I say, answering the main office phone at Camp Siegfried with the formality demanded from German protocol.

"Will you accept a collect call for Yaphank-493?" the operator asks. "The call is from Freddy Schafspelz."

Through the phone, I hear the caller brush his clothes. "Geez," he mumbles. "I tore my pants to shreds escaping that mobster prison boat."

"Spreche ich mit Schafspelz? Hallo? Am I speaking with Mr. Schafspelz?" I ask.

"It's about time!" the voice shouts in German. "It's me! And you will address me as stormtrooper Schafspelz. This is an emergency. Get me someone in charge!"

"I'm sorry, Herr Schafspelz. Everyone is busy at the Bund Convention. Can I take a message?" If I'm going to escape with Yael, I must control this call.

"I'm Officer Schafspelze!" Freddy bellows. "You need to arrest a spy, right now. He's had me locked up in a fishing boat at the Newark shipping docks. I escaped. I found a phone box to warn someone." I hear the caller scold someone. "What the heck are you looking at, you dirty old fisherman? Never seen a barefoot Nazi?" He talks to me again. "The traitor's name is Rike Saxon, and I'm sure he's there. Our Führer's life may be in danger." My head spins. Rike Saxon is Yael. There are a lot of people's lives in danger at the moment.

Axel barrels into the office. "Krista. What are you doing? We are late now. I'll meet you at the stage." I can feel his panic, like he's outrunning an avalanche.

I nod toward Axel and seize the opportunity to end the call. "I'm sorry, sir. There's no one here by the name of Saxon. You have the wrong number." I place the phone handle on its cradle and cut the call.

Axel blinks at me, as if he's trying to recall something. He pushes me out the door and toward the crowd.

KRISTA:
Convention. Camp Siegfried. Long Island, NY

At the staging area, the fervor of grand regimented Nazi discipline is titanic. Like a battleship parting the sea, fraternal American and Swastika flag troops lead hundreds of marching soldiers toward Camp Siegfried from Yaphank town. The fife, bugle, and drum corps blares a German march that rumbles my heart chamber. Hundreds of guests arrive. Men and women are dressed in their Sunday best and small children wear replica Bund uniforms. As all arrive, scouts clip to attention. They sing from their lungs. "*Today Germany hears us, tomorrow the whole world.*"

Suddenly, a breeze tugs my hair. War is in the wind. Even though a shot has not been fired, this machine is moving at full speed. Is it too late for America?

YAEL, ALIAS RIKE:
Convention. Camp Siegfried. Long Island, NY

Camouflaged as a stormtrooper, I blend into the thousands of Nazis across the sprawlin' Camp Siegfried sports field. There's not a patch of green grass to be seen. There's not a voice I can hear over the hails. I know Krista will be standin' toward the front with the other special guests. I move my eyes across the massive crowd like I'm searchin' for a typo in a newspaper. Over there. I see a hand, ashen and slender. Extended in the air, her arm shakes just enough that I would notice. I catch my breath.

Her stance is so much of the woman she is under her uniform. I realize how vulnerable she's been, how close I almost came to losin' her, how desperate I am to rescue her.

She stands next to Heidi, their right arms stiff in the air, aligned with thousands of others, like the squares on a chess board. In front of her, an assembly congregates, crushing against the stage, hypnotized in solidarity. On the stage, the American and swastika flags flank the loomin' Führer Kuhn. Kuhn's sidekicks, Kunze and Wheeler-Hill, bookend him on one side. On the other, there's Dinkelacker and Vandenberg.

I stand on my toes to better view Krista. The knife in my pocket joggles. As far as I can tell, Axel and Frank are nowhere to be seen. It's now or never. I serpentine through fanatic bodies guardin' their space. With each step of progress, I'm thrust back by the bodies of people. The sun beats against my forehead. My lips stick together. Inch by inch, I squeeze myself into gaps until I'm feet away from Krista. The clamor drowns out any chance of her sensin' my presence. I fumble forward. I get close enough to brush Krista's left hand with as little force as an insect wing. With any luck, she will not ignore the touch. She twists her neck toward me. Her eyes widen. I wag my head, hoping she will follow me. She's still. I can't tell if it's out of conflict or caution.

My eyes triangulate on Krista and the corners of the bandstand. Her head tilts to monitor the stage. Up there, Kuhn points to the swastika banner behind him and grasps the microphone. It shrieks when he adjusts it. He blows his heavy breath on it. It projects a bass blast, signaling he will speak. "This banner represents Aryans, not just in Germany, not just in America, but around the world," Kuhn says. His voice hammers the Camp.

Arms shoot up, saluting the American Hitler. "Heil Hitler!" a roar cheers.

"Where's Papa?" Krista shouts to Heidi over the raucous. "Shouldn't he be on the bandstand with the Führer?"

"I haven't talked with him for days, but he'll be here," Heidi yells over the noise.

Krista motions for Heidi to repeat. Heidi is pushed forward by the crowd.

Krista's body stiffens like a deer ready to bolt after a noise. She steps back. Her neck stretches, struggling to find me in the sea of fascism worshippers. She must feel me, because she follows my path.

Kuhn's voice vibrates through the sound system. "We will bring a common racial bond to Amerika," he cries. "One hundred percent of the best Americans will be one-hundred-percent Hitler's Americans."

I check over my shoulder for Krista. Frank's head appears in my view. He scans the audience. Maybe looking for Heidi? Or Axel? I turn my head away and take a sharp right through a cluster of gray-haired, crooked men bouncin' like they're young again. Hopefully, I'll make it to their age.

"Nazis will fight for the German Empire, for a better America," Kuhn's voice sermonizes.

I crane my neck and see the top of Krista's flaxen head movin' against the throngs of cheerin' Bunds-people. She lifts her chin and sees me. We sigh together.

"Krista! Stop!" Heidi's voice shouts. This could be trouble. Frank squeezes toward Heidi.

Then bad goes to worse. Axel stops and turns to Heidi's call. He follows her stare and realizes Krista's sneakin' away. Then, like a dot-to-dot puzzle, his eyes track to me. I crouch, weave through the crowd and dash.

After swimming through the crowd, I finally reach the car. I hover by the back door of my car for what seems like an eternity. I shake my head, fearin' it's too late. My jaw drops to my chest. I close my eyes. Should I leave without her?

"What took you so long?" Krista's voice says into my ear.

I don't want to open my eyes, fearin' I've imagined her voice. But I do. I tilt my neck back and give her a crooked smile. She pulls my hand. She's right. There's no time to waste. She opens the back door and slides into the getaway vehicle. I open the driver door and rifle through my pants pockets for my keys. I breathe a guff of relief when my sweaty hands grasp the cold steel. As my body slackens, a heavy hand grips my shoulder.

The ground rumbles as the audience across the field cheers Kuhn.

The grip tightens on my shoulder. "Stormtrooper!" a voice roars as a force wrenches me around. "You! The Jew from Newark." It's Axel. His face turns chalky."

I wallop him with a left hook.

He topples and thumps the ground. "Guards seize him!" he hisses.

Frank slams the door shut. Two guards lock their arms around me. I wrestle away and throw heavy punches. One cracks a nose. The other crushes a windpipe. Frank swings at my head. I duck. Then it's my turn—I bust Frank in the mouth. Axel stumbles to his feet and lunges toward me. I swing the car door open. Metal bellows against Axel's knee bones like cymbals. He stumbles back. I dive into the car, slam the door, smack down the door lock and fidget the key into the ignition. The key drops to the carpet floor. Dagnabbit!

I hear the car window shatter before the shards spray against my face. Krista screams. Frank thrusts his hands through the opening and grips my neck. I don't know how my knife ends up in my hand, but I stick it into Frank's wrist. The handle dangles halfway out of his flesh. I reach down and pat the floor faster than my beatin' heart. The cold metal stings me. I grab the key, insert it into the ignition, and pump the gas pedal. The car takes on a mind of its own, veerin' around obstacles.

In the rearview mirror, past Krista's stricken face, I see Axel sway to his feet. "I'll exterminate you!" Axel roars through a cloud of powder. Frank shakes the knife out of his hand. The two soldiers hurry into a nearby car.

"Geez Louise! Axel just threw an old woman out of her car. There's nothing low enough for him," cries Krista from the backseat.

In the side mirror, I see Frank and Axel bear down on us. My eyes focus forward. Looming in front of me through the yellow dust is a large figure. I slam on the brakes and fishtail onto the grass. The car skids feet away from—son of a gun, Führer Fritz Kuhn. He aims a gun toward my face. I duck and accelerate as a bullet clips my ear and splinters the windshield.

I speed toward Harry's hideout. Blood sprays everywhere. "Open the door!" I scream at Krista.

Krista swings open the backdoor. Harry dives in.

A bullet grazes Krista's shoulder. Blood soaks her white shirt. My foot lifts off the gas. The car slows. Krista slumps onto Harry.

Harry bangs on my seat. "Step on it!" he yells to me.

I slam my foot against the accelerator. Blood from my ear splatters the window. We leave Camp Siegfried behind us.

FRITZ KUHN:
Office. Camp Siegfried. Long Island, NY

"Flüche! Flüche! Flüche!" I curse to my officers in the Camp Siegfried office. My men bungled the capture of one of the most nefarious characters to walk on German American soil. No one says a word. They know better.

I channel all the superpowers of the German universe to hex every one of those bloody Newark Minutemen and their Kingpin and the entire Italian and Jewish mob and any other gangster. I condemn the corrupt U.S. government and FBI and Roosevelt and Hoover who supply money, information, and men.

I scream to the cowering soldiers in front of me. "Rike Saxon! Whatever the heck your real name is. You will pay! Longie Zwillman will pay. The Newark Minutemen will pay. I will save America from you and your kind! I will make America great again!

CHAPTER 40

Bare Knuckles

YAEL:

Harry's Apt. Hawthorne Avenue. Newark, NJ

"What the heck?" Harry flips around the magazine that Aunt Rose handed him across his kitchen table. On the cover, a velvety photo of a demure man sittin' in uniform won't even look the camera in the eye. His stringy hair flops to one side as if he'd just squeezed it between a greasy thumb and finger. His caterpillar mustache bushes like it's not glued down very tight.

"Adolph Hitler. *Time* Man of the Year?" I read the magazine cover over and over. I lean back in my chair across from Harry. After the gritty escape from Camp Siegfried, the toasted coconut smell of butter pound cake at Harry's home had comforted me. Now the crumbs curdle in my stomach.

Lena splatters broth on Nat's lap and he jumps up."Slicha! Slicha!" she apologizes and pats the dish towel on his wet pants. He pats her hands and smiles.

"This is an offense to humanity!" Isaac tousles his silver hair with his free hand. He reaches over and takes the magazine from Harry.

Two steps away in the livin' room, Aunt Rose sits on the couch next to Krista. She lifts the bandages wrapped around Krista's shoulder.

"The recognition doesn't honor greatness," Longie explains to us. "*Time* gives the award to the person with the most news coverage." The prickly outrage in the room sparks like a live wire.

Isaac reads from the article, "Adolph Hitler is the greatest threat that the democratic, freedom-loving world faces."

"Next thing you know, Stalin will win next year," Aunt Rose complains in her educated British accent. She sticks Krista's bandage back on her shoulder. I sit down on the other side of Krista.

"I'm sorry for your ordeal," Aunt Rose says to Krista.

Krista seems perkier after a cup of hot tea and some soup. "This is only a battle scar," she replies with a weak smile. "The escape is my win."

I wrap my arm around her shoulder.

She turns to me. "Now, where Yael goes, I go. I'm ready for his people to be my people."

Aunt Rose smiles. These words have been said before and show profound loyalty. "You've been through a maze of choices," she tells Krista. "The only ones that matter are the ones we make in the end. Nice to finally meet you."

Krista inhales and nods. Though she's exhausted, her face rests. "The journey has been very confusing, like stones skippin' across the water. I've had to navigate the sounds, even though I couldn't hear all of them. But I've chosen the right path."

"We'll help you understand your roots," I say, flashing Krista my crooked smile.

Her eyes return my grin. Krista reaches in her pocket. "I meant to give this to you, Yael. At camp, we recited this each day. It's written by Hitler." She hands me a pamphlet.

I read softly. "By fighting the Jew, I fight for the work of the Lord— Der Führer, Adolf Hitler, we believe in Thee. Thou hast laid upon us the duty and the responsibility. We speak Thou beloved name with reverence, we bear it with faith and loyalty. Thou canst depend upon us Adolf Hitler."

"A man who thinks this way believes it's his destiny to rule the world," I remark.

"How can German-American children have a chance in the American way when this starts off their school day?" Lena says in her Russian accent. "They aren't all bad. Many are the innocent victims in this nightmare."

Isaac shakes his head. "Hitler crowns himself God. He enslaves hungry people with weapons and poison slogans. He forces naked men to crawl in the street, forces old women to clean SS latrines. Now his claws stretch across America."

"Hitler wants all men to be his slaves," I say. I hand the paper to Aunt Rose. She puts it in her bag.

"Longie. Nat. You must stop this decay in America!" Aunt Rose says.

"We've gotten enough evidence for the FBI and IRS to jail Mr. Kuhn for fraud and extortion," Longie replies.

"We're bringing down the American Hitler Kuhn with his own plan," Krista says. Her eyes perk up and open wide.

"Now we need a united American voice for the knockout punch," I say.

"On President's Day, we hear he's forming a brand new party for the Nazis, calling for a democratic Nazi party vote," Harry says.

"He's using democracy to rule America," Krista says. "How do we fight that?"

I look at Longie and he nods. "We shine the spotlight on his event in Madison Square Garden," I explain. "We flaunt his Nuremberg Rally like a giant billboard. Inside, we disrupt their rite. Outside, we gather hundreds of thousands to protest. Let America see the evil on our doorstep just as big and black and red as that American Hitler—Fritz Kuhn—can make it. In the end, I believe in us."

CHAPTER 41

Check Hook

FRITZ KUHN:
Newark Bund Headquarters. Nye Avenue. Newark, NJ

As we prepare for the February 20th President's Day rally, the flurry of activity in my Newark Headquarters on Nye Avenue fires my adrenaline. The phones are ringing, the typewriters are clacking. To top it off, the news coming out of Germany over the radio makes my day. Across the ocean, true Germans are taking back our country, giving back jobs to rightful Aryans, sweeping undesirables under the rug.

My secretary hands George Kunze a stack of papers. He taps his finger. "What do we do with this Madison Square Garden agreement from their Major Dibbles. It says here they restrict anything anti-Semitic for President's Day?" George asks.

I snatch the document from his hand and tear it up. "On President's Day, we unveil to the world the Nazi conquest of America." An attentive young woman rushes over with a trashcan. Her smile gives me a moment of peace. I drop the papers in the bin. "We tell them what they already know. FDR brings crime and chaos into the neighborhoods. We bring order. America's future is on the ballot."

"That won't be hard with twenty thousand spectators and three thousand stormtroopers," George says.

"Add to the top of the list—eliminate that traitor Rike Saxon," I say. "Take him down once and for all! And don't let me down!"

"On it, Fritz! His real name is Yael Newman. He's a Newark Minuteman."

LONGIE ZWILLMAN:
Miami Club. Clinton Avenue. Newark, NJ

At my Miami Club, my boys and I are busy preparing for the February 20, 1939 President's Day rally. The news out of Berlin horrifies me. I hold up the front page of the *New York Times*. "There's been a mass exodus from Sudeten because England and France have agreed to give Czechoslovakia to Nazi Germany."

"It's only a matter of time," Yael says. He peers at the newspaper on the table. "First Austria, now Sudetenland. Germany's digesting the belly of Europe, and the rest of the world will collapse into his arms."

"Back to work everyone!" Harry says.

My associates and the Newark Minutemen plan the battle against the Nazi coup underfoot. I watch groups divide tasks, organize photos of un-American activities, file FBI evidence. I choke up. These men are giving voices to the voiceless. They deploy teams of Minutemen, meet with FBI, and listen to Nazi wiretap recordings of sabotage plans. I'm convinced. Injustice is outmatched.

Minutemen are here in full force: Nat Arno, Yael, Harry, Abie, Al, Maxie, Puddy, Benny, Hymie 'The Weasel' Kugel, and many others from our syndicate including Meyer Lansky and Willie Moretti.

CHAPTER 42

Below the Belt

KRISTA:
Sidewalk. Hawthorne Avenue. Newark, NJ

When I kick the leaves on the sidewalk, they glimmer under the Hawthorne Avenue streetlight. The glint sparks a childhood memory from Berlin. I remember, *the park rangers rake the fallen leaves into huge piles. A young Heidi ties our sweaters together. On the count of three, we run and jump into the red and gold leaves and pretend we are riding on a cloud.* My foot crunches a batch of brown decaying leaves and I snap back. I wonder. Where did my sister go?

I hasten my step toward home. Well, Yael's home. But it's starting to feel like mine, too. Even Dov and Linda are warming up. The other night, I almost blew it. They let me babysit. I pushed Li'l Abner around the block in his baby carriage and got lost. I sweated until I got my bearings. I plunge my chilly hands into the pockets of my burgundy and tan wool coat and tuck my chin into my collar. Tonight, it took me longer than expected to help Lena and Esther clean their house for the Friday night dinner tomorrow. No matter, because my timing is good. There's Yael getting out of his car in front of the house right now.

Odd. A moving car without its headlights creeps past me. Is that two uniformed men in the back seat? No. It can't be. But it is. Führer Kuhn. Unexpectedly, the car accelerates. The front passenger window rolls down. A gun barrel slithers out. "Look out!" I yell to Yael. He spins toward me.

The gunman sprays Yael's car with bullets. He dodges the assault. As he ducks behind another car, two waiting stormtroopers seize him. One trooper traps his arms against his sides. The other grabs his hair. They drag him into the dark alley. I hear struggling, but he's outnumbered. My body shudders. I have to act. They won't fool around. They've already tried to shoot him. I check my options. The fire escape offers a surprise attack from above. I climb it to the top of the building.

KRISTA:
Alleyway. Hawthorne Avenue. Newark, NJ

My shoes crack against the tar on the top of the building. But not too loud for anyone to hear. In the alley down below, I see two stormtroopers twist Yael's arms behind his back and force him to his knees. Another trooper presses the gun muzzle against Yael's head. My arms tremble faster than my beating heart. I creep down the other fire escape, just above them.

The leader with the gun yells at Yael. "You fed me lie after lie!" Even from where I'm perched, I catch the gunman's eyes narrow. "You made me think you were family. Family doesn't betray. But you did," he seethes. "You are a vampire, ravaging the easiest victims, worshipping the carnage you leave behind." I remember when Heidi called Yael a vampire that night on the beach. I've learned he isn't.

"Freddy. You are confused," Yael says. "If you are free, you can't be betrayed. Understand what you are. You're a prisoner of Führer Kuhn, and you don't even know it."

Freddy's laugh bounces through the stone alley. "My treacherous foe, you're the prisoner," Freddy says.

319

The troopers heave Yael to his feet. I move while they're distracted. My body shuttles down the building and my feet touch the ground.

"Führer Kuhn is holdin' your mind captive in the palm of his hand. Be strong. Break away," Yael pleads with Freddy. "Do good!"

Dag nabbit! How can I save Yael? How can I create a diversion? My eyes search in the shadows. Is there a rock? A bottle? Anything? I inch closer. I hear the gunman talking to Yael.

"Do good? *Good* has a different meaning during war, doesn't it?" Freddy asks. "One day, I'm the good guy. The next day you are. And the next? Well—" Freddy cocks his gun.

"Please don't shoot him," I say under my breath. "I've lost my family. I can't lose Yael." I bite my lower lip and muster the courage. My legs crouch for a pounce.

Then, sudden as a split decision, I hear clicking steps. Newark Minutemen emerge from the darkness. Abie and Benny dive on the two stormtroopers. They grab their shoulders. Slug them right and left. Harry steps out of the shadow and cracks a bat across Freddy's body. The gun from Freddy's hand launches and skids across the pavement right below me.

Freddy drops to his knees, clutching his arm and gasping.

Just as Yael steps toward the gun, I jump in and snatch it. I point it at Freddy.

"Krista, get back!" Yael yells to me.

"Krista? That's your name? Wait a minute. You aren't *the* Krista Brecht, are you?" Freddy's eyes jump from my shoulders to my knees. The jutted jaw on my face gives him the answer. "I've been looking for you," he says and flashes his white teeth.

Harry steps in between us. "What do you want with her?" He sways the bat.

"Tell her, Yael," Freddy's voice dares.

My brow squeezes. "What's he talking about?"

Harry grabs Freddy by the collar and lifts him in the air. "I don't know what your game is, pal, but I'm gonna knock you from here to—"

"Harry. Wait." Yael steps forward.

Harry hesitates, then drops Freddy.

"Cousin Krista," Freddy says. He points with the pinky of his unbroken hand. "Aren't you wondering why your father hasn't reached out? It's not that he's angry with you. The truth. Your loyal Newark Minuteman killed your own papa."

I stare at Yael. How many shocks am I going to get tonight? Is it true? "Where do you come off with this?" I growl at Freddy.

"Your two-faced friend Yael also killed my uncle." Freddy stumbles to his feet. "Funny thing. They're the same person. Officer Günther Brecht."

Ice jets through me. My weapon aims at Yael. Is he an assassin? Am I next?

"Krista. Let me explain." Yael holds up his hands.

I clench the gun. "Go on," I say.

"Your father was the Nazi that murdered my father. The one I've been chasin' my whole life. I caught him. I didn't know he was your father." Yael steps toward me.

"Stay back!" she shouts. My soul trembles. "Why didn't you tell me?"

"I have no excuse. I'm so, so sorry."

Suddenly, Freddy dives against me and wrestles away the gun. He points it at Yael. "This is for all American Nazis. German blut above all."

"Thank you," I say. "You've freed me."

Freddy smiles, relishing the moment. "You're making the right choice, Krista." He sneers at his own toxic power. As Freddy rubs his finger against the trigger, I thrust his arm up and spin away. My arm cocks. I leverage my full body weight and turn my left foot and hip at the same time. My shoulder and upper back muscles drive the punch across Freddy's right cheek. His face whips left, he staggers sideways, hitting his head against the wall of the building. The gun flies from Freddy's hand, spirals through the air, and clatters on the ground.

With blood streaking down the side of his face, Freddy steps in my direction. He narrows his eyes at me. "You will burn," Freddy says, gritting his teeth. "You might be German, but you are also another half-animal muddying our country's landscape." He sneers. "Frank told me you're not so pure."

The next seconds blur. Freddy clicks open the front of his belt. I hear a tick. Yael tackles me and scoops up the gun. Bullets from Freddy's spybelt whizz past my deaf ear. A gunshot shouts. Freddy crumbles to the chewed pavement. A curl of smoke rises from the muzzle of the gun Yael is holding.

The human shell housing Freddy's soul deadens. He mumbles with his last breaths. "Der Tag is here."

The hero I almost walked away from smiles at me. He massages my knuckles. "Thank you, Yael."

CHAPTER 43

The Take Down

LONGIE ZWILLMAN:
Downtown. Newark, NJ

"In order to stop Kuhn's rally at Madison Square Garden, we must keep fear alive," I tell Nat, Yael, and Harry as we pound the pavement of Newark with Meyer Lansky. "The fear keeps hope alive," I say. The wind tries to blow the fedora off my head. I clap it down. Not even the invisible is going to take me down.

With FDR and Hoover's covert support, our first stop is the New York State Capitol to meet with Mayor Fiorello LaGuardia. We pressure the Mayor, as well as Attorney Thomas Dewey, to cancel the event.

"There's no one who wants to collect against those slandering Nazis more than I do," LaGuardia says. "They called me a dirty Talmud Jew when I proposed the Chamber of Nazi Horrors exhibit for the World's Fair. But Civil Rights won't let me stop Kuhn's event at the Garden."

"Fiorello. You're the poster boy for America's melting pot, for God's sake, you're half-Italian, half-Jew." I cup my palms in front of me. "How can you let this slide?"

"My hands are tied, Boss. Free speech is free speech, including Nazis."

"It's some nerve using George Washington's birthday to launch the Nazi party in America," Yael says.

"The Bund is a disgusting spectacle who is turning our founding father into a fascist dictator." Attorney Thomas Dewey says as he paces. "We gotta stop this libel, Fiorello!"

"Can we talk to the cops to at least give us leeway at the event?" Harry asks.

"Here's what I can do," LaGuardia says. "Let me put in a call to Brooklyn Police Captain Max Finkelstein. I'll have him put in his toughest Jews, Catholics, and blacks on the outside of The Garden. We'll mix War Vets inside."

It's a start. We take to the streets to rally our friends and foes alike. We think the Communist Party will be our strongest advocate. They're diametrically opposed to the Nazis. We approach their leader, Earl Browder. In his office, I look at him across his desk and pitch a united front. "Earl. I know we haven't always seen eye to eye, but if our minorities splinter, the Nazis hold a majority in America. That's a problem for both of us."

Browder's bright blue eyes smile. "Eye to eye? We're pretty much toe to tongue given I want to save the unions and you want to control their purse strings."

Nat lights a cigar and hands it to Earl. "Earl, this is survival," the commander of the Minutemen says. "Let's put our differences aside."

Earl watches smoke snake from Nat's mouth. "I'd like to say yes, Arno. Always nice to rack up debts from you. But we're in opposite corners." He won't take Nat's olive branch.

"Mr. Browder," Yael says. "Aren't you for America and Russia teamin' up against Germany?" Yael tees up a good angle.

Browder's ruddy cheeks draw on the cigar. "Yeah. We can't let Nazis pull us down here in America or abroad."

"Germany's Nazis are already dug into American soil. Help your Russian party join us against Fritz Kuhn and his Bund," I say.

"The enemy of my enemy is my friend?" Browder flashes his whites. "Longie. All bull aside, you know I like you guys," he says. "After all, you and I almost single-handedly put the president in office. But marching against fascist-free speech is a different story. That's a conflict of interest that will cramp the Communist voice."

"With all due respect, Mr. Browder, we're taking the biggest risk," Harry says. "We're gonna be disrupting the rally inside the Garden. Whether we win or not, we lose if we don't have support on the outside."

"Harry's right," Yael says. "Americans gotta stand against a Hitlerite world."

Browder puts his elbows on his desk. "Here's what I can do," he says. "I'll talk to my buddies in the Socialist Workers Party. They're a propaganda machine and will print up *Stop the Fascists* flyers." We wind up our talk and head for the sidewalks. It's an uphill battle, but we're facing the right direction.

At the newsstand outside of Browder's building, Nat grabs *The Forward Daily*.

"Hey, ya gotta pay for that!" the newsboy says. Longie flips the kid a nickel.

"Listen to this crap!" Nat reads the paper. "There can be no more shameful thing for the Jews and opponents of the Nazis than such demonstrations, which will lead to bloody fights and riots." He wads the paper up and tosses it back to the kid. "I'm not built for walking fine lines."

"We'll figure it out," Longie says as he puts his arm around a war-torn Nat.

For weeks, Minutemen canvas the neighborhoods. It's a house of cards, but we have no other choice but to build a united front.

The Spanish and Latin American neighborhoods ache to strike the blow at fascism against Franco. But they don't want to be singled out. They'll show up if others do. Either way, they promise to spread the word.

Negroes will show up, no question. They vow to stand against the racial myths.

The working-class Knights of Columbus and Catholics will stand up against religious intolerance. They promise to march with anti-Nazi signs. We work the angles to get them to come to the demonstration.

German-American workers want to avenge their brothers. We think they'll come with their anti-Nazi signs. But sometimes they resent getting lumped in with Nazis.

When we meet with the Italian anti-fascists they sing "Bandera Rossa" and say they will take it to the streets. Irish Republicans struggling for freedom feel the same way and will picket in their neighborhoods.

Older Jewish men and women argue they need to keep a low profile but commit to marching through neighborhoods. After all, they don't forget that a few years ago, Germans were killing their fathers and brothers in the Great War. The contingent who strike against the pogroms swear to be at the Garden.

The American Legions and Veterans of the World War just fought for democracy. They're a machine against un-American activities and chomp at the bit.

News reporters Walter Winchell and Dorothy Thompson and others use their networks and mediums to fight with words. Walter Winchell promises to tell Mr. and Mrs. America that "the *Ratzis* are going to celebrate George Washington's Birthday at Madison Square Garden—claiming G.W. was the nation's first Fritz Kuhn. There must be some mistake. Don't they mean Benedict Arnold?"

Behind the scenes politicians and lawyers fight the legal battle. District Attorney Thomas Dewey keeps the heat on the FBI, Rep. Sam Dickstein and Rep. John McCormack, and the ruthless Rep. Martin Dies keep the heat under the Nazis.

YAEL:
YMHA Boxing Gym. 652 High St. Newark, NJ

I zigzag through the Y wedging between a hundred or so boxers who are pumpin' and hittin'. Every time I come in here, there's more men workin'. The hum is invigorating and sobering at the same time. My gym bag knocks Al's spiked shoe out of his hand and onto the floor. "Sorry, pal," I say. I scoop it up and rub my finger against his metal spike. "You missed a spot." I dodge the rag he snaps at me. I deftly sidestep Maxie's billy clubs flippin' in front of three laughin' young boxers. I stop in front of Benny.

Benny cracks open a wooden crate filled with lead pipes. He shoves one of the pipes under my arm. He hands a fistful to Harry and Puddy. They distribute them around the gym to the Minutemen. Benny leaves to get another crate from his truck.

Abie listens to the baseball highlights on the radio as he's countin' brass knuckles. "Eight, nine, ten ..." he counts.

I toss my bag onto the table next to him and sit down. The bag distracts him when it plunks. His chin drops, and he shakes his head like a dog waggin' off a fly. "Dagnammit! I lost count." He starts over.

As I tie my shoelaces, I hear heavy thumps against the gym floor. I raise my eyes and see Nat. His body walks with heightened senses. He doesn't have to say a word. The men form an unmistakable force around him, like yellow jackets swarmin' a hive. Above, Longie peers over the rail of the hangout. Harry turns down the radio. The room quiets. The strong faces around the Y face Nat. These are men who never ask why or utter maybe. These men think about the win every day and never turn back.

"What's the news, Nat?" Puddy asks. He hands Nat an iron bar.

Nat catches his breath. He slaps the bar against his palm. "Things are heatin' up. There are some bad rumors over in Germany, and they're gonna fuel the Nazis here. We're working hard, but we gotta work harder. We won't rise to the level of our expectations, we will only fall to the level of our training."

The air charges with men's voices. The walls shake against hand-punchin' fists. The space heats with pumping lungs. Chaos crackles, like wild horses banging against fences. The air feels fragile, like it could break.

"We won't win because we believe we are some Supermen," Longie shouts from above. Everyone tilts their heads toward his voice. "We will win because we've practiced so much, day in and day out, that we will throw the right punch or duck at the right time. And I'm not just talking about the physical moves."

Suddenly, I hear the radio announcer interrupt the regular broadcast. "Kristallnacht, a wave of destruction in every town is unparalleled in Germany since The Thirty Years War."

"Hey. Someone turn that up," Harry says as everyone stares at the talking box.

The radio announcer says, "Today, November 20, 1938, in Berlin, Germany, the broken glass of thousands of Jewish homes and buildings, now symbolize the shattered Jewish lives."

Benny rushes back into the gym. "Germans have just terrorized its citizens. The British call it the worst pogrom since the Middle Ages. The French compare it to the Turkish genocide," Benny calls.

We listen to the announcer. "Jews had been forced to place their heads on the ground. Guards removed their vomit by wiping it away with their hair. Women were undressed and raped in the streets. Victims were taken to the Buchenwald concentration camp where they were tortured and beaten to death. The prisoners were even forced to urinate into each other's mouths."

On the floor of the gym, Longie appears next to me. "Aunt Rose said the underground intercepted a telegram from the Gestapo Chief Heydrich. It went out last night. The orders instructed that healthy male Jews be sent to concentration camps. They say a hundred thousand people in Germany have been killed, tens of thousands of businesses destroyed." His stony face is anything but empty. As the news chills me, his face fills me with fiery divinity.

"Back to work, boys!" I say. "We've got a war to fight right here on American soil. Then we'll stop the Germans."

CHAPTER 44

Knock Out

KRISTA:
Outside Yael's Apt. Hawthorne Avenue. Newark, NJ

To veil my panic from Yael, I button his overcoat. "Be careful," I say under the open doorway of his apartment building. Today is President's Day, February 20, 1939. I scan the daybreak movements on the street. In front of us, two young boys splash their boots through slush. Along the curb, a man struggles to open his car door with his glove-covered hands.

Yael raises his elbow to block the morning sunrise from his eyes. When he licks his chapped lips, I wish I could bring him back inside and make him finish his oatmeal. But I know he's down a road of no return and would have nothing of it.

My brain buzzes, solving nightmare possibilities of this day. A high-pitch grind rouses us both. Dugan's bread truck slides across the ice. It stops just short of the coal truck unloading black rocks down the metal chute into the basement coal bin. I tremble. That was a close one.

Yael grasps my shoulders. "If we've done our job, a hundred thousand people will demonstrate outside Madison Square Garden tonight."

"Will you get inside?" I ask. My teeth chatter. Yael puts his arm around me.

"We got a bunch of forty-cent tickets for a couple dozen Minutemen. The rest of the gang will sneak in or be outside."

I tilt back and scrutinize Yael. I straighten his hat so it touches the top of his red ears and rest the back of my warm hand against his frosty cheek. He won't smile.

"Go inside," he says. He's with himself right now. His task has begun and nothing will pillage his energy until it's complete. "I need to go."

As he jaunts down Hawthorne Avenue to meet Harry at the trolley for their voyage into New York City, my arms clap my wool coat to fight the cold. When he's out of sight, I reach for the door to go inside. Something stops me. Did I hear my name?

"Krista! Krista." I recognize the calling voice. Heidi yells to me as she shuffles her feet across the icy sidewalk.

I turn a deaf ear to her.

"I know you hate me," Heidi calls. She turns up our walkway. "And I know what Frank did to you. Papa confused me. I understand that now. He told me it was honorable to use women for making more Aryans."

My hand squeezes the door latch.

Heidi's face wrinkles. She pleads. "I'm so sorry." I feel her cold breath lick my neck.

I can't look at her. "You betrayed me, Heidi. You were my sister, and you abandoned me." She was more than my sister.

Heidi opens her mouth, but no words come out. I turn to leave.

"Krista," she begs, but I refuse her. "Please trust me one last time. Yael is in danger!"

"What?" I spin and grab her arm. "Tell me!"

"They've been watching him. He's an enemy of The Bund. They're ruthless, Krista. They will attack him and the Newark Minutemen at Madison Square Garden, or worse."

"I must warn him."

"I'll go with you, Krista!"

EPILOGUE 1

February 20, 1939

YAEL:

President's Day. Inside Madison Square Garden. New York, USA

Eight of us muscle through the fanaticism shakin' the overpacked Madison Square Garden. We wedge between Hitler disciples and chafe against Nazi regalia. The evil glares tell me we're not makin' friends. We clamber over seats, step on black boots, and duck under Hitler salutes. We're searchin' for the other members of our militia to gain a foothold that will help disrupt this ominous occasion. The Nazi American Bund has twisted our iconic coliseum into a Nuremberg-like rally on the American day that celebrates democracy—George Washington's birthday.

Hundreds of Newark Minutemen infiltrate Madison Square Garden to stop Der Tag, the Day. It's the Nazi plan to take over America. I'm countin' on our troops to slide their hidden iron bars down their sleeves into their fists and rip it up. We've trained and the battle is simple. But it won't matter unless the American people are outside, demonstrating as one, beheading the rattlesnake temptin' our country to bite the apple.

Madison Square Garden is turned into a Nazi Party coliseum. American flags and Nazi Bund banners with swastikas swallow the stage. Around the balcony, Nazi propaganda banners read, "Wake Up Americans," "Smash Jewish Communism," and "1,000,000 Bund Members by 1940."

The amplified voice of American Nazi Bund Secretary Wheeler-Hill vibrates the hat on top of my head. "My fellow white Americans and non-parasitic guests! It is my privilege to welcome you to this patriotic demonstration sponsored by the German-American Nazi Bund. George Washington, whose birthday we are celebrating today said, 'BE UNITED AMERICANS!' Today, as Americans, we are failing to honor Washington and our Constitution. But we have a savior. It is my pleasure to introduce the man we love for the enemies he has made, our American BundesFührer, Führer Fritz Kuhn."

The introduction sets the Nazi assembly afire with cheers and stomps.

The American Hitler enters the stage to wild Nazi pomp and circumstance. Twenty thousand American Nazis cheer, "Free America, Free America, Free America," as they salute the Nazi parade marchin' through the aisles.

To think, if I were still undercover, I'd be one of those stormtroopers guardin' Kuhn on the stage. Deep within the inner circle, my mission would've rid us of Kuhn once and for all.

Around me, the Sam Brown belt-wearin' audience raises Nazi salutes to the six-foot, two hundred plus pound bully. An amplified voice booms. "Fellow Americans: I do not come before you tonight as a stranger. You will have heard of me through the Jewish-controlled press as a creature with horns, a cloven hoof, and a long tail."

The crowd guffaws.

I gaze at the stage. Below the towering portrait of George Washington, the Hitler-uniformed Bund leader, Führer Kuhn leans into the microphone at the podium. "If you ask what we are actively fighting for in our charter … First, a socially just, white Gentile-ruled United States."

Cheers erupt and vibrate the roof beams.

"Two. Gentile controlled labor unions free from Jewish, Moscow-directed domination."

The audience clatters their boots against the floor.

"Gentiles in all positions of importance in government, national defense, and education. Cleansing of the Hollywood film industries. Cessation of abuse of the freedom of the pulpit, press, radio, and stage. Cessation of dumping political refugees on U.S. shores. There's only one first. America First!"

The audience cheers.

"We, the German-American Nazi Bund, put the state before the individual, true American Nationalism—Patriotism. This comes with your unswerving obedience to those of us who lead. We are determined to annihilate any inimical enemies of the Aryan Volk. We will make America Great!"

Führer Kuhn paralyzes me. My distraction is costly. Axel Von du Croy and his stormtroopers have crept up behind me. They grab me and drag me toward the exit to the tune of a female voice singin' the American anthem. *"For the land of the free and the home of the brave—"*

KRISTA:
President's Day. Outside Madison Square Garden. New York, USA

My elbow cracks against the sidewalk and shoots a pain to my neck when I slip on the ice. From the ground, my eyes focus on the black letters mounted on the Madison Square Garden marquis above the Rangers versus Detroit signage. I read, "To Night. Pro American Rally."

Under the street lit avenue, the noise robs me of all senses. It's the rumble of hundreds of thousands of people. Not just any people. American people defending their home. Irish-Republicans. Italian anti-fascists. I hear their voices. Yes, communists and socialists. Negroes and Catholics and Jews. I read their signs. Vets. Anti-Franco Spaniards. Poles and Russians. German-Americans. I watch their differences move across their faces. But they're shouting the same message. In the end, Americans don't disappoint. We are battling, united, and loud. I rise.

The street quakes. Seventeen-hundred police in combat gear with thick jackets, hard hats, and leaden-rolled newspapers turn the Garden into a fortress. Many are on horseback, creating an impregnable wall.

But the wall can't hold back two hundred thousand shouting, mobbing, fighting people, demonstrating against fascism outside the iconic coliseum. The mob presses against the police. Unified voices condemn Nazism with shouts that drown out police sirens. Big American flags bob, prodding the march forward. "Down with Hitler" chants boom through the streets. Demonstrators carry signs that read, "Drive the Nazis out of New York! Smash anti-Semitism!"

The front doors of the Garden crash open and a tangle of bodies burst onto the sidewalk. Nazi soldiers rail on Yael and Harry. Moments later, additional Minutemen smash open the doors and descend onto the rumbling scene between swastikas and Minutemen.

Heidi and I push toward the front of the Garden, through the throngs of people. I grow hopeless. Suddenly, as if a curtain pushes away from a window, I see Axel pounding on Yael.

As I thrash to reach Yael, my winter coat flaps open to the raping cold wind. "Yael!" I call his name, but it drowns under the noise as if my words are swimming through water.

The fists of Nazis and Newark Minutemen puncture through the crowd like eyes of bucks flashing through thickets. Minuteman Harry punches Nazi Frank across the jaw. Four Nazis retaliate and beat Harry with iron bars. He falls to the ground. Frank rebounds and pounces on Harry, splattering slick red blood across the sidewalk. I feel my own blood run from my face. My respite is the terror that pumps my lungs. It rescues me from fainting.

As I move forward, aggressive police push me back, their commands sharp and uncompromising. They're in automatic mode, not caring about the souls trapped in the bodies they grapple. I shift my head right and then left searching for Heidi. My heart can't keep up with its beats. She's nowhere to be found.

Ahead, Al wings a lead pipe against an American Nazi. He slips on the blood underfoot. Benny scoops him up. Maxie appears out of nowhere and rabbit-punches the charging soldiers.

The clack of horse hooves bears down on me. I slip between two police riders. My eyes blur. The animals whinny. Then I realize, I'm caught in the firing line of none other than Nat Arno. He tackles a mob of Nazis who are stomping on Abie and Puddy. The impact knocks over demonstrators who somersault toward me. I dart to avoid being trampled and crouch down to ready myself.

That's when I see Yael. He topples toward the sidewalk. I watch Axel attack him with what Yael once called a nerve-rifling liver punch. I'm overrun with dread that I might never touch his warm hand again.

Yael curls and rolls. He gazes at the trodden Harry, lifeless on the street. Yael's throat rises then falls. He stiffens, like he's forgotten how to breathe, his eyes large, like a cat with rigor mortis.

Through tangled bodies, I gain a view of what Yael's frozen eyes see. Poised over his life-long pal, Harry, Frank hovers like a vulture over a carcass.

Like a slit of light shining through a ripped canvas, I find hope. Yael seems to breathe again. His chest rises just as Axel thrusts a fist toward his face. He sways, and boom, Axel's hand cracks the pavement. Yael rolls back toward Axel and head-butts his face so hard I hear a blunt crack through the uproar. He shoves Axel's body away like he's shedding a morning blanket.

Yael rises. He seizes a flagpole lying on the street. He swings it and cracks it across Frank's knees. Frank crumbles away from Harry.

Yael touches Harry's neck, checking for a pulse. I read Harry's lifelessness on Yael's face. His head falls onto Harry's chest. He turns to me. The wispy fog floats between us. His body appears and disappears through the haze.

Suddenly, a cold darkness blankets me. I feel a presence looming. I tilt my neck up. The flailing hooves of a police horse pedal above me.

Yael lunges toward me as the horse's mighty mass falls down toward both of us. Blackness devours us before we know our destiny.

EPILOGUE 2

1945

HARRY:
New York Harbor. New York, USA

Soon after President's Day at Madison Square Garden, Fritz Kuhn was indicted for anti-American activities. The pressure and evidence had piled against him. Within six months, he was jailed for tax fraud and embezzlement.

The months following the night at The Garden, the tension in Europe built. The writing was on the wall. In September 1939, Hitler invaded Poland.

America still resisted entering the war, but on December 7, 1941, Japan bombed our own Pearl Harbor in Hawaii. We had no choice. The Axis woke up a sleeping giant. America finally engaged the enemy.

There were many heartaches during the war. After my death at the Garden, I watched Ma cry every time the phone rang. She knew Yael, his brothers, and so many others were out there fighting. Pop prayed. Esther wrote Yael every week.

Now, the end of the war is here. At New York Harbor, 1945, hundreds of thousands of soldiers are returning under Operation Magic Carpet.

Families and friends rush to search and find their loved ones.

I watch. A woman anxiously pushes through the mob with two small boys in her arms. From where I'm looking down, I see her blonde coiffed hair and the back of her jacket but not her face. She's just as elegant as when I knew her down on earth.

Finally, Yael, my brother-in-arms, appears in his American uniform. He wraps his arms around the woman and her two children. When they turn to make their way out of the port, I behold the whole family together. It's them. Yael and Krista and their four-year-old twins, Joseph named for Yael's father and my own namesake, Li'l Harry.

Yael reaches in his bag and brings out two wrapped gifts. The boys rip them open and shiver with excitement. Knowing Yael, I could've guessed. They hug their brand new red boxing gloves. In front of them, the car door of a Pierce Arrow opens.

ACKNOWLEDGMENTS

I am grateful for my mom, Esther Levine Kaplan, for trusting me with this story, helping to bring it to life, indulging me with the answers to every question, and reading every draft. I am also grateful to my cousin and partner on this story, Bruce Levine, who recommended book deals and constantly fed me sources. Also, his son-in-law Joe Miale helped me negotiate book partner deals and educated me about working with managers. Cousin Linda Zlatkiss, who grew up with my mom, earned her invitation to the academy awards with her selfless efforts helping me to understand the life of the times and Yiddish expressions, reading the story, and not hesitating to make connections. Cousin Pauline Levine, may she rest in peace, added much color to the scenes growing up with my mom on Hawthorne Avenue.

I am blessed to be married to Doug Barry whose acknowledgment of the story gave me validation to delve into a story that would impact the world. He was a force in making sure I was treated fairly and protected throughout and convinced key people to be involved. And he should know that he is my role model in believing that ideas can become realities, even though the journey is scary. It was my seventeen-year-old son, Jackson, who I asked to read the first storyboards. His reaction was the most honest endorsement I could have received and truly gave me hope that someone would like the story. When my nineteen-year-old daughter, Shaya, wrote in a scene in the screenplay for herself to play, I knew the story had the millennial appeal to make it a blockbuster. When my twenty-one year old, Brittany, directed the way-too-long multi-media presentation, I knew I had created an exciting three-part story. She literally designed the cover of the book. When oldest son, Zachary, analyzed the sizzle reel for the movie, I knew I had something that was worthwhile. Also, my dad, Stanley Kaplan, has always been an inspiration in making me feel I had the gifts to do anything. And thanks to my Auntie Sandra who always asked and listened.

Thanks to Sue Turley who became my first partner for selling the screenplay. She believed in the story and helped me get to the very top through back doors in record time. Additional thanks to her partner, Annie Rocco, for her incredible introductions to the Redfords and Spielbergs. Equal thanks goes to Dan Adler who understood the story and its "why now" appeal, pitched it, and planted seeds with some of the best talent in the industry. He wins for indulging every irritating call I made to him at all times of night, everywhere in the world.

Enormous thanks to award-winning author, Catherine Stine, for editing the book with such poignancy and insight. She taught me how to translate a screenplay into a novel. Thanks to Thescriptjoint who helped shape a novice screenplay into a salable work and Richie's advice on the sales process. I also value the ever presence of my friend, Steve Katz, who always makes me think. It was he who suggested I approach the director of "American stories that have never been told." I did and we got very close to working with Robert Redford and his team.

I am indebted to Sheri Joseph for teaching me about storytelling and character motivations and forcing me to go places in the story I wouldn't have otherwise. She gave me the nudge I needed to create the website. Along the way, I learned there were not a lot of people who truly read a story and take the time to give feedback. Sheri was one of the rare ones. The debt goes even further when she "encouraged" her son Kevin, who works for an entertainment company, to help me with a presentation. Long story short, Kevin gained immediate interest and ended up leading the purchase of the story by his company, Fulwell73, and created our partnership with the impressive Leo Pearlman, who is dedicated to making a quality film.

Thanks to draft readers who included my sister, Iris Tuttle, and her eighteen-year-old son, Ethan Tuttle, who read both the screenplay and book and gave some of the best comments of anyone, my sister Donna Lewis who rightly encouraged me to go through the story with a fine tooth comb, and her husband Mark for his advice. Thanks for further support from my nephew and nieces Justin, Marissa, and Jillian. Thanks to my cousins, NJ Freeholder and Mayor Brian Levine and his daughter, Ariella, for their early feedback, as well as stories through the years from their father, my Uncle Joe. Thanks to Uncle Harry's son, Rudy, for confirming details.

Thanks to Coral and Mike Kisseberth who commented on the sizzle reel, Jill Kinney and Sam Walravens who each read one of the first screenplay drafts, Terry Castle who gave early feedback and made me use Firstdraft, Tom Newell, for his business advice and leadership and then legal support, Don Enright for reading the screenplay and encouraging me to make it more dangerous, Teri Jacks for her emotional support, Andi Thompson for her connects and bent ear, Nicole Klionsky for identifying the perfect cast, Julie Soja, Wendy McCarthy, Lisa Matthews, Suzanne Carswell, Gretchen Graham for their support, John Baldecchi and Jessica Flaum for their feedback and advice, Denise Bauer for getting it onto one of our former president's desks, former newspaper editor, Rob Rosenthal, for his interest and accompanying me to the Hoover Institute for research, Jane Howard for testing characters against the enneagram, Inka Von Sternensfels for checking my German, David Hawk for his enthusiasm and recommending *Save the Cat*, David Hall for offering to drive me on my book tour, Robin Abrams for her connections, including author Stacia Deutsch and LA Jewish film organizer, Hilary Helstein, Talent Manager Roger Strull for his interest and connections to agents and writers, and my dog Kona for keeping me company during those late writing nights. NewarkMemories.com also gets a special thanks for their timeless resources.

Thanks to Marin City's Ed Boon, who taught me to box so I could flavor the boxing scenes. Thanks to Howard Metcalfe, the son of undercover writer John Metcalfe, who helped me understand the life of working undercover in the American Nazi Bund, shared his personal files and family book and granted permission to use his father's diaries from the Hoover Institute. The FBI archives and reams of documents from the *Investigation of un-American propaganda activities in the United States: Hearings before a Special Committee on Un-American Activities, House of Representatives* provided voices and testimonies and contained priceless Bund documents, initiation rites, home-movies, names, financials, photographs, songs, and more. The *March of Times: Inside Nazi Germany* directed by Jack Glenn in 1938, video images from the 1939 President's day Nazi rally at Madison Square Garden, as well as reprinted speeches in the "Free America Pamphlet" distributed that day helped to bring authenticity to the story. The Oviatt Library at CSUN provided unique resources and speakers. Warren Grover in his book *Nazis in Newark* reinforces stories about the Newark Minutemen and the Jewish mob. Chilling resources such as *Ice Creatures: The Nazi Educational System* by Dr. Tamar Ketko, and the expertly researched book *Wunderlich's Salute* by Marvin D. Miller leave no doubt to the ties between Nazi Germany and the German-American Nazi Bund.

Finally, thanks to Mike Zeller for introducing me to my publisher, Morgan James Publishing, and David Hancock, Karen Anderson, Jim Howard, editor Cortney Donelson, as well as Margo Toulouse and Taylor Chaffer at Morgan James for embracing the book with so much enthusiasm.

BETWEEN THE WARS

	GERMANY	AMERICA
1918	The Great War or World War 1 ends	
	Versailles Treaty is signed	Prohibition begins
1923	Nazi revolt tries to overthrow government. Hitler jailed.	German Nazi party members form The Free Society of Teutonia
1929		Stock Market crashes. Depression begins.
1930	Horst Wessel achieves martydom	
1933	Hitler becomes Chancellor of Germany Nuremberg rally Dachau concentration camp opens Jews excluded from civil service Book burnings Hitler eliminates Catholic Party	Franklin D. Roosevelt becomes President Prohibition ends Friends of New Germany Nazi-party forms by authority from Nazi Germany FBI approaches Jewish mafia to help stop Nazis in America Newark Minutemen forms
1934	President Hindenburg dies Hitler becomes Fuhrer Nuremberg rally	Congressman Dickstein investigates Friends of New Germany *Friends* object, Riot at Schwabenhalle Hall against Minutemen and demonstrators Irvington Riot with Minutemen *Friends* challenge Freedom of Speech, Courts rule against them. Assembly Bill 272 passes to prevent anti-Nazi activities
1935	Nuremberg race laws passed Ban on Jehovah's witnesses Parag. 175 persecutes homosexuals Lebensborn forms to breed Nazi babies	Nazi Youth Camp Siegfried opens in Yaphank, NY Friends of New Germany establishes thousands of cells nationally
1936	Berlin Olympic Games Nazis charge priests with homosexuality	German American-Nazi Bund forms with six subsidiaries Fritz Kuhn is elected Führer 25 Nazi Youth Camps form across the country Bund publishes *Deutscher Weckruf und Beobachter* newspaper

Between the Wars (continued)

1937	Buchenwald Concentration Camp opens Himmler condemns Christianity	John and Jim Metcalfe go undercover in the Bund for Chicago Times 12-day series published in Chicago Daily Times Congressional Committee to investigate un- American activities forms Nazi Youth Camp Nordland opens in Andover, NJ
1938	Gypsies classified as alien race *March*. Germany annexes Austria *October*. Germany annexes Sudetenland *November*. Kristallnacht pogroms erupt	*January*. March of Times newsreel about Nazis airs Chicago Times publishes Metcalfe Brothers undercover story FBI discovers Nazi spies, agent sells story to Warner Brothers Congressional investigation on Un-American Activities begins Nazi spies caught on American soil German American bank leaders sell German money to fund German military Camp Siegfried engages in Lebensborn-type activities
1939		*February*. Pro-Nazi rally at Madison Square Garden *April*. Confessions of a Nazi Spy movie releases *April:* Fritz Kuhn is indicted and jailed in December
	World War II begins when Hitler invades Poland	
1941		Japan bombs Pearl Harbor. America enters War US government shuts down Camp Siegfried FBI raids American-Nazi youth camp in New Jersey. Tapes seized
1942		Government seizes films and documents from Bund national headquarters FBI proves German American financial connection to Nazi Germany
1945	European War ends Kuhn deported to Germany and jailed	European War ends Japanese War ends
1951	Kuhn dies	

ABOUT THE AUTHOR

Leslie K. Barry is most recently a screenwriter, author, and executive producer. Her previous professional work includes executive positions with major entertainment companies including Turner Broadcasting, Hasbro/Parker Brothers, Mattel, and Mindscape Video Games. Other areas of business include executive for the first e-shopping platform called eShop and marketing for Lotus Development, the US Post Office, and AOL. She was an Alpha Sigma Tau at JMU (James Madison University) in the heart of the Shenandoah Valley and attended a grad program at Harvard.

She has spent the last twenty-five years with her husband, Doug Barry, in Tiburon, CA raising their four kids, Zachary, Brittany, Shaya, and Jackson, and their dog, Kona. On the side, she's devoted to genealogy where she has uncovered many ideas for developing untold stories that help us appreciate the context of history, preserve lessons of the past, and honor memories through family storybooks. For fun, she likes to travel, ski in Sun Valley, Idaho, play tennis, and visit her family in Maryland, Virginia, and South Carolina, where she most enjoys Maryland hard crabs and hush puppies, Lido's pizza, and chocolate horns.

You can visit her website at NewarkMinutemen.com.

CPSIA information can be obtained
at www.ICGtesting.com
Printed in the USA
BVHW030730290320
576268BV00001B/1

9 781631 950728